HEMISPHERES

HEMISPHERES

THE FURTHER LIFE OF ALEXANDER MACLEAN

A Novel

By
ROBERT DEWAR

Copyright © 2022 Robert Dewar

The moral right of the author has been asserted.

Apart from any fair dealing for the purposes of research or private study, or criticism or review, as permitted under the Copyright, Designs and Patents Act 1988, this publication may only be reproduced, stored or transmitted, in any form or by any means, with the prior permission in writing of the publishers, or in the case of reprographic reproduction in accordance with the terms of licences issued by the Copyright Licensing Agency. Enquiries concerning reproduction outside those terms should be sent to the publishers.

This is a work of fiction. Names, characters, businesses, places, events and incidents are either the products of the author's imagination or used in a fictitious manner. Any resemblance to actual persons, living or dead, or actual events is purely coincidental.

Matador
Unit E2 Airfield Business Park,
Harrison Road, Market Harborough,
Leicestershire. LE16 7UL
Tel: 0116 2792299
Email: books@troubador.co.uk
Web: www.troubador.co.uk/matador
Twitter: @matadorbooks

ISBN 978 1803135 144

British Library Cataloguing in Publication Data.
A catalogue record for this book is available from the British Library.

Printed and bound in Great Britain by CMP UK
Typeset in 11.5pt Adobe Garamond Pro by Troubador Publishing Ltd, Leicester, UK

Matador is an imprint of Troubador Publishing Ltd

In recollection of the kindness of strangers.

For an account of Alexander Maclean's early years,
read *Mallaig Road*.

Chapter One

The Boy Who Walked Alone

During his years at high school, Alexander Maclean learned to value the solitary walks he took, and to escape often to the world of his free ranging imagination.

Alexander's family lived where the city's northern suburbs merged with countryside. However, this countryside did not comprise a landscape of pretty woodlands and rolling fields. This peri-urban South African countryside incorporated for the most part uncultivated scrubland, and *veld* grassland with few trees, and those few were mostly wattle, Scots pine and blue gum, with only an occasional indigenous acacia still standing.

But to feed his need for solitude, Alexander sometimes walked home alone from school in the afternoons. He crossed a tiny stream, whose clean flowing water was channeled between steep banks of red earth, then walked across a wide tract of open *veld*, and finally (skirting one of the last remaining commercial market gardens in the district still in operation), he reached the fringes of their suburb. White cumulus clouds ambled slowly across the inverted bowl of the azure Highveld sky, and the sun (so much warmer than any sun ever known over the British Isles, which is where Alexander's forebears came from) shone down on him, and the red dirt and rocky quartzite ground were intensely familiar. He felt a sense of wellbeing, of belonging.

There was almost no animal wildlife left in that region fringing the suburbs, but once, Alexander came across a scattering of porcupine quills on the ground. The birds were plentiful, and sometimes Alexander saw a small creature belonging to the rodent family. Once in a while he would see a snake (only very rarely was it of a venomous species, such as a *rinkhals*, mamba or puff adder; usually the creatures fell in the category of what Alexander knew as "mole snakes" or "grass snakes"), but such sightings were rare, although Alexander was very light footed and quiet when he walked. He would see many colourfully marked insects, all larger by far than are seen in northern Europe. They looked as if they had been brightly painted, or equipped with antlers or horns, by their fanciful Maker.

Alexander enjoyed the solitude. It was during these early walks when he was still a school boy that he learned how much he needed sometimes to be alone, far from the sight or sound of his own kind, if he was to sustain happiness.

Alexander's family returned to the Mother City after he had graduated from high school. He was far, far happier now, living on the Cape Peninsula with its dramatic, mountainous topography, the mountain slopes clad in dark pine forests, and never far away was the boundless shining sea with its infinite horizons. There was more wildlife to be seen. Troops of baboons were common; less so were the small, timid antelopes that Alexander sometimes saw. The sunbirds flitted and hovered in small flocks. They were brightly decorated, tiny shining creatures full of iridescent colour as they sipped nectar from the proteas and other wild flowers on the slopes of the mountains.

During this nineteen-seventies era, when he went walking during the week, Alexander only very rarely saw any other people in the mountains. He learned to feel close to God in these mountains. The mountains taught Alexander his first theology.

Alexander knew where the perennial springs were to be found in the mountains, where sundews, small carnivorous plants that grew amidst the mossy surrounds of these springs, lured tiny insects to their sticky haired leaves and trapped and digested them. When he spent a day in the mountains, Alexander rarely took water with him, not even during the baking summertime. He took only a collapsible tin mug, with which he drank at these springs; water so pure and refreshing it was a blessing.

Sometimes Alexander would walk the length of Long Beach, a distance of more than four miles, beginning his walk at Kommetjie, the small village far down the Peninsula on the cold Atlantic Ocean shore. There were then no housing developments nearby; the village was tiny, with a ramshackle hotel where Alexander's uncle sometimes took him for a beer. Walking that wild strand, with its white sand gleaming in the sunshine, and the incoming Atlantic breakers crashing in the surf, Alexander felt a sublime peace envelope him, for he only rarely saw another human being once he had left Kommetjie behind him.

Alexander had learned that he felt most at peace in surroundings where Man was incidental, not central, to creation. He was to seek out such regions throughout his life. In later years, Alexander was to walk – most often alone and without a rifle – in one of southern Africa's most unspoiled wilderness regions, far from towns or people. There were then still great herds of elephants and buffalo in that part of Africa. There were herds of antelope and zebra also; groups of giraffes, and a wealth of bird life. There were many small mammals too, and snakes were not uncommon. Alexander used to walk in open leather sandals, and one day as his right foot was about to come down, he heard a *"hsshhh…"* from the ground before him and he leapt backwards off his left foot, and there lay a puff adder, fat and lazy and with a diamond patterned back, sunning itself on the sandy path. A puff adder's venom is cytotoxic. The wound its bite leaves will suffer necrosis, and leave you disfigured for life.

When Alexander got up early enough (and most mornings he got up very early, before the dawn), he would find hippos grazing ashore, before they retreated to the river for the day to seek both safety and the cool of the waters. At night Alexander would often hear the long sawing roar of a leopard not far away. Once, on his way back to the lodge in the late afternoon, having been out walking alone all day, Alexander had to crouch beneath a stand of jackal berry trees atop a vast termite mound, as he watched a column of elephants containing mature adults, adolescents and babies, walking by no more than fifty yards from him. Some of the outlier bulls were much nearer. The dust raised by the passing elephants hung pale gold in the still air, illuminated seemingly from within by the westering sun. Alexander felt a frisson of excitement, allied with a suffusing joy. He lost count of the elephants' numbers after he had tallied over three hundred of the great beasts. He had very rarely felt so intensely alive. The scents and aromas of the bush were powerful in his nostrils; the sound of the birds calling was a cacophony of noise; the warm air caressed his bare forearms and bare legs; he could taste the aromatic air as he drew it into his lungs.

When Alexander walked alone in the wilderness, all his senses alert, his shadow on the sandy ground a mere pool of shade at his feet, lengthening suddenly towards the day's end, he would experience his life as an epiphany, for at such times he was wholly identified with all creation. He could justly claim (looking back in later life) to have known something of what that first Eden must have felt like for the first man.

Chapter Two

The Community

Alexander, who was known to family and friends as Sandy, had been sickly as a child (he had suffered from asthma, and he had been prone to colds and flu), and he had a sensitive, artistic, introspective nature. He learned early in life to escape a reality that seemed at times far from satisfactory, such as incapacitating illness, or misery at school, through reading. This gave him a love of language, and a love of books for their own sake: the heft and weight of a well bound book pleased him; the scent of the ink on the pages of a new book gratified him. The possession and ownership of books was his earliest collector's hobby.

During his later adolescence, Alexander learned that he could also escape the weight of too much consciousness, of too much burdensome awareness, by walking far; by testing his endurance. Alexander sometimes felt that he had much to escape. At high school, he became fearful that he was monstrous, an abomination.

Many years later, Alexander could no longer remember what sort of religious instruction he had received at school, but given that South Africa's educational programme was officially termed a Christian National Education, and that the mores of the nineteen-fifties prevailed in South African society well into the early nineteen-seventies, the religious instruction classes at school would have been entirely Christian in content – and a stiff-necked, Calvinist Christianity at that. Decades later, Alexander could however remember one lesson during what was termed "Guidance class." The male teacher informed the sixteen year old boys that if they had not yet kissed a girl (and Alexander had not), then there was something wrong with them; that their sexuality was askew.

So Alexander approached his later adolescence fearful of who – of what – he might be; fearful of being scorned, rejected, and outcast if he was found out. So he walked, and read books, and walked harder and further – and read more books. He learned that self-sought solitude is far from being always a lonely condition.

Aged twenty-one, Alexander found himself living in a Christian community. By now he was keeping a diary, a habit he was to follow with more or less diligence for most of his life. These diaries, although their bindings were to differ over the decades, were almost always of at least a half page a day, and in them Alexander recorded the day's events, and his feelings, thoughts and observations. His diaries were the means whereby he maintained a lifelong dialogue with his inner self.

He lived then with four other young men in one of the wings of a very old Cape Dutch house set in twelve acres of oak and pine woods. There was a stream running through the estate, the water so clear you could safely drink from it, for the stream arose only a few hundred yards higher up the mountainside. There were trout in the stream.

Aside from his studies, Alexander had practical duties to undertake on the estate. He would fell the dead timber and cut back the encroaching saplings in the woods; he used a petrol-driven chainsaw for these tasks. But he did not have to work himself too hard. There was no one overseeing his work; he did each day only what he felt needed doing. There were several Cape Coloured gardeners tending to the carefully manicured lawns and the trim hedges, and the flowerbeds full of cannas and gladioli, hydrangeas and rose bushes. Alexander enjoyed the work. It meant that he was often alone, and when the sound of the chainsaw was stilled, and he sat quietly for a while, the woods would return to their own tranquility, and many years later the sound of doves cooing could take him back in a flash to the memory of those days.

Sometimes Alexander would sit beneath a tree where the stream widened into a shallow pool, and the sun shone on the water and made the stones and pebbles beneath the surface dance and coruscate with gold and rich umber. The languid movements of the trout beneath the water, and their sudden fleetness when startled – catching the light like quicksilver – delighted him. He sketched the scene often, and rendered it in watercolours with his friend Patrick, a boy his own age who lived not far away in a grand house set on the hillside, with a garden made up of terraces, in one of which was a swimming pool.

The young men lived as a fraternity in the wing they occupied. They cooked for each other, and kept house together. They were a decent bunch of youngsters, but as with any group, there were one or two for whom Alexander felt a special liking. One of these was a cheerful, rangy, energetic chap who, like Alexander, had been to school in Johannesburg. The other was a Cape Coloured boy, sweet natured and angelic featured, called Nathan.

These young men were not sworn to celibacy (for they were members of the Anglican communion), and most of them were fond of young women. Some of them – Alexander included – would bring a girlfriend to tea (or in the case of the young fellow educated in Johannesburg, two Cape Coloured girlfriends one day, twin sisters both, whose beauty had something of the Mediterranean in it), where they joined the community's hierarchy and their families and guests on the lawns in front of the big house on a Saturday afternoon. Sometimes they would take their girlfriends with them on group hikes up the Mountain. One such well known ascent commenced only a few hundred yards further up the side of the mountain, through the gates of the Kirstenbosch Botanical Gardens. Alexander had met his girlfriend, Catherine, on the Union Castle liner. He had been returning to Cape Town by sea after spending nine months in Britain earlier that year.

Alexander was in charge of the liturgical vestments for the small private chapel in the big house. He had to ensure that the correct colours for the day were laid out across the wide countertop in the vestry, ready for the celebrant (who was usually the head of the community himself) to don for Holy Communion. There was green for ordinary; white for Sundays; red for martyrs; and heavily embroidered gold for certain feast days, such as major saints' days, or Easter Sunday and Christmas Day. There was a deep, rich, Tyrian purple for requiems.

Alexander had to dress the altar each morning with the correct colours for the day, and the tabernacle also, in which the consecrated elements of the Holy Communion were kept. He enjoyed handling the rich cloth. The heavy embroidery – employing real bullion where gold thread was required – gave him much pleasure.

Alexander drove the head of the community to official functions. Most often these were in Cape Town itself. This churchman would sometimes have to meet with government ministers and officials. 1976 was a dramatic year, a watershed in South Africa's history, and the Church was at the forefront of the struggle for racial justice. Sometimes Alexander would be called upon to drive a considerable distance, to a church in the Winelands or the Boland. Occasionally, Alexander had to drive the head of the community to the airport, and collect him on his return. Alexander enjoyed these chauffeuring duties. Cape Town was still a beautiful old city. There were then few high-rise buildings located on the Foreshore, where today there is an entire city in itself reaching for the sky, which has shifted Cape Town's centre of gravity much nearer to the docks and the harbour.

Early the following year Alexander was appointed a lay minister. The head of the community sent him to his own seamstress, a Cape Coloured woman, to have a cassock tailor-made for him, with thirty-nine tiny cloth covered buttons down the front, and a wide, generously tasselled sash to wear around the waist. In days gone by, Alexander would then have been considered to have been in minor orders.

Alexander loved the friend he had made, who lived higher up the hillside. This young man, Patrick, had a head of thick, curly blonde hair and gentle, expressive features, which were redeemed from outright girlishness by an obstinate jaw line and a wide, generous mouth. Patrick was a gentle, deeply thoughtful young man, his search for God having taken him for the moment down the road of eastern mysticism. Alexander was lost in admiration for him from the moment he first saw him, in the company of one of the young men, standing in his bathing trunks by the side of the swimming pool at the big house, beads of water running down his torso.

Alexander was afraid of the intensity of his feelings for Patrick. He kept undeclared the depth of his affections for his friend. At times he felt something like despair at what he felt for him.

Chapter Three

The RMS Windsor Castle

During the latter part of the British summer of 1976, Alexander, aged twenty-one, had lived and worked in Oban, a port town on Scotland's south-west Highland coast. He had been happy there, but towards the end of August he had left Oban for London by train one morning, on his first leg of the long journey home for Cape Town. On the evening before his departure, Alexander had been sitting reading in the room under the eaves that he shared with three other young waiters at the hotel, when he was sent for, and told to put on a clean shirt and a tie. Wondering, he did so, and he went downstairs to the hotel lounge, where he found that a farewell *cèilidh* had been organised to wish him *bon voyage*. There were a couple of young fiddlers and an accordion player, the latter a middle aged man wearing a kilt. The music was cheerful, and encouraged you to dance, and Alexander did so. The party lasted until around midnight, and Alexander found then that he had drunk rather too much whiskey.

'The thing about you Islanders, Màiri,' he was telling a girl from the Islands with whom he worked and for whom he felt much tenderness (her eyes were the colour of the deep ocean, her hair was the same shining black as polished jet, and her very fair complexion glowed with an inner light), 'is that you are poets and wanderers, like me. That's why I get on so well with you.'

Then he kissed the girl, who laughed, and said, 'I think it's time you went upstairs and lay down, Sandy *mo ghràidh*.'

Since mid June the ten o' clock evening news on the television had been full of bloody images of riot and death in South Africa; of *toyi-toying* black demonstrators performing that deeply disturbing, spontaneous crowd dance of Africa, before surging forward and receiving blasts of buckshot from pump action shot guns in the hands of the Police. There had been scenes of buildings set afire, and cars overturned and burning. And so the good folk at the hotel in Oban thought that Alexander was the great Hero to be returning to such a war zone.

Alexander had a savage hangover when the train for London pulled out of Oban the next morning. But he was young, and he recovered quickly during the journey south. He spent a few days with his aunt and cousins in Berkshire, before taking the train to London from Slough early on the morning of the 3rd September. In London he caught the boat train from Victoria Station. At about eleven in the morning the train came to a halt alongside the passenger terminal on the quayside where the liners docked at Southampton. Alexander had already checked his shipboard baggage in at Victoria Station.

The heat wave had broken, but the day was dry. Mounting the gangway, Alexander felt tremendously excited. His childhood voyages by ocean liner were still bright in his memory.

At dinner that first night, among the people whom Alexander met for the first time at their table, was a very attractive, well spoken, patrician featured English girl about his own age, with honey blonde hair with a natural wave in it. Catherine was travelling to Cape Town to take up an English teacher's post at a private girls' school.

'What part of England is home?' Alexander asked her.

'Devon,' she replied. 'My father is a Royal Navy officer based in Plymouth. But you don't sound South African, Sandy.'

Alexander smiled. 'I'm not, originally. We're from Kenya. We left when I was a boy. Where will you be staying in Cape Town?'

'I'm staying with an aunt in Rondebosch,' Catherine replied.

'We lived in Rondebosch when I was young. It's a comfortable, very respectable suburb.'

Catherine laughed. 'I'm glad to hear it!'

Alexander also laughed. 'Are you by any chance fond of hiking?'

'I have n't done any real hikes, but I enjoy long country walks.'

'That's good, because I'd like to take you on a hike in the mountains, Catherine. I know the mountains of the Peninsula very well; all the hikes, and the routes to the top.'

Catherine smiled at Alexander. 'I look forward to that.'

As the days grew steadily warmer the further south they steamed, the youngsters began to gather on deck at the swimming pool in the evenings, rather than in the lounge. Pool parties would last well into the early hours, and they would have stocked up with cans of beer at the duty free bar. Alexander had never before been quite so drunk, so often. On the way to becoming drunk, he was liberated from all his fears and anxieties about himself, and he felt attractive, witty, amusing, and above all, likeable. What a wonderful discovery to make, he thought, that this is what drink can give me.

The ship arrived off Table Bay at dawn. They had departed Southampton eleven days earlier. Alexander was up on deck very early, and he was intensely moved as he gazed at the silhouette of Table Mountain, and at the sky bursting into flame over the African continent. As the ship drew closer, Table Mountain loomed ever larger above the old city, and the sun had begun to climb from behind Devils Peak. By the time the ship passed the breakwater, it was already broad daylight, and as they entered the Duncan Dock, Alexander could hear the sound of steam shunting engines at work, clang-bash, woof-woof-woof-woof-woof!

Alexander was home, having been away for nine months. The following month he joined the other young men at the Christian community.

Alexander left the community in May 1977. He thought to himself, 'I cannot live here anymore.' The intensity of his affections for Patrick had become a burden heavier than he could bear. And one day, Nathan had approached him for advice, troubled because he and a friend from his school days felt a powerful erotic attraction towards one another.

'Will I go to Hell, do you think?' Nathan asked Alexander. 'The Bible says it is a sin, love like that between two men.'

'Nathan, it is not love between two men that the Bible condemns – think of David and Jonathan – but, as the Bible puts it, lying with a man as with a woman. Love is surely never a sin.'

Alexander looked at Nathan's face, unmarked as yet by life's cruelties and harshness. It was an open, but right now, troubled young face. Alexander felt a huge tenderness for the lad in that moment. And (he knew) more than simple tenderness. It was then that Alexander made up his mind to leave the community.

But in leaving, Alexander felt as if the world had turned its face against him. His dreams of eventual ordination in the Church had been, he felt, destroyed by the emotional burden of his feelings. He wished he could have believed there was someone he could have turned to for guidance, or simply for comfort and reassurance. But at school, Alexander had learned to be a very private person, hugging his hurts close to him. He did not now know how to share them with someone else.

On the morning that Alexander commenced the long, one and a half day drive to Johannesburg, he drove up the road to Patrick's home, and Patrick met him in the driveway. Alexander did not get out of his car. Perhaps he said, 'I will miss you very much,' and perhaps Patrick said, 'Take care,' but as Alexander let the clutch out and began to pull forward, Patrick reached through the open window and his fingers brushed Alexander's bare forearm.

Alexander felt an electric shock, a jolt of contact, such as he had never experienced before, and he drew a sudden sharp breath, and this, this memory of an intense physical communication with his friend was to trouble him for many years.

Chapter Four

Hillbrow, Johannesburg

During the following one and a half years, Alexander felt adrift, lost and lonely. He spent much of that time in England, but he found neither happiness nor direction there. By January 1979 Alexander was living with his family, who had moved to Johannesburg. He applied for a job he saw advertised in the classified section of the Johannesburg daily, the *Star*, and he began working for a tiny private investigation agency with a two room office suite in a high-rise near the Carlton Centre complex. Alexander quickly showed an aptitude for the work. The agency specialised in uncovering commercial frauds and in gathering business intelligence. Alexander's boss was a likeable rogue in his thirties named Luciano, who had lived in Johannesburg since his childhood, the son of Italian immigrants.

Soon after starting work in the city centre, Alexander moved into a bachelor flat in Twist Street, opposite Joubert Park, down the hill from Hillbrow. This flat was a neat, furnished place a few floors above the street, with a balcony overlooking the park, which was laid out in colourful flowerbeds and had well kept lawns and large, mature trees. There was an open air giant chessboard with supersized chess pieces. Middle aged and elderly men from Europe played in front of a scattered audience. Joubert Park was still a safe place for white people to visit in the late nineteen-seventies.

Alexander would often walk to work in the city centre. Some evenings after work he drank beers and smoked Gauloise cigarettes – heavy, harsh Gallic cigarettes – with his boss in the piano bar on the top floor of the Carlton Hotel. Inside, there was a baby grand and a piano man, and later in the evenings, a *chanteuse*. Outside on the rooftop there was a swimming pool, and many big leafy shrubs and small trees growing in large tubs. It was like a garden in the sky, and you could sit and drink beers and look down at the street thirty floors below you.

Other evenings, Alexander would trek up the hill to Hillbrow, to sit in the Café Wien, or the Café de Paris, and drink *cappucinos* served by smart black waiters in long white aprons. Eastern European *emigrés* and old men who had fled the Communists after the War, would gather at these cafés to gossip and play chess and backgammon, and read the foreign newspapers. During the weekends, Alexander favoured the Café de Paris, with its wide first floor balcony, and (shaded from the sun by a large, colourful umbrella) he would eat *Sachertorte*, that most delicious of central European *gateaux*, and drink coffee, watching the parade of street life below.

One evening at the Café Wien Alexander met a group of youngsters. One of their number, a tall, slim young woman with blonde hair and a wide, smiling mouth, caught Alexander's eye as he looked her way, and leaning across, she said to him, 'You're a new face. Do you live in the Brow?'

'Yeah – down the hill in Twist Street.'

'I'm Alice. Why don't you come join us?'

Alexander shifted his coffee across to their table and sat down. Alice introduced him to the others. There was one other girl, with a Jewish look about her, who had dark, shining hair and heavy lidded, sleepy eyes. Her name was Robyn. These young people all lived in or near Hillbrow, that cosmopolitan district of high-rise apartment blocks, and tiny little houses dating back to the 1920s, full of character, overlooked by tall neighbouring buildings. One of the youngsters was a boy aged eighteen, who had matriculated the year before. He was six years younger than Alexander. Terrance, as Alexander was to learn, was extremely creative. He had a slight build and dark good looks. He was in his first year of fine art studies at the University, and he lived with a much older sister in her flat in Berea. A rapport quickly developed between Alexander and this artistic boy. Terrance would visit Alexander at his flat in Twist Street, bringing his guitar with him, which he played rather well. Sometimes he showed Alexander extraordinarily detailed and imaginative pencil or ink sketches he was working on.

'Sandy,' Terrance asked him one day, 'would you give me some driving lessons, please?'

'Have you got your learner's?' Alexander responded.

'Yeah. You drive well – you can coach me, cant you?'

'OK then. We'll give it a go.'

But after their first very stressful outing in Alexander's big Rambler, with Terrance at the wheel, Alexander had to decline further sessions. The Rambler's steering wheel was heavily geared, in that era before universal power steering, and it took getting used to, if you were not to wildly over correct when steering the big heavy car. Coupled with the car's power, and the willingness with which it surged forward at the merest touch of the accelerator, this made for a potentially disastrous combination. After several near collisions, Alexander's nerve cracked, and he said, 'I think you need to learn on a smaller car, Terry.'

Visiting Terrance's family home in the well heeled suburb of Rivonia, Alexander met Terrance's younger sister, Una, a kid aged eleven years. The first time Alexander met her, the weather was very warm, and the girl was dressed only in shorts and a tee-shirt. She was barefoot, with a deep tan. She had very bright green eyes. Una had a rich artistic imagination. She showed Alexander a project she was working on. It was a fantasy, arboreal world, set in a dry, peeled bark multi branched hardwood tree limb which the kid had seen potential in, and which she had dragged home from some nearby *veld*. This tree top world hosted a complex of tree houses in miniature, connected by walks and ladders, and peopled with tiny carved wooden figurines. It captivated Alexander.

'This is wonderful, Una!'

'You see, I had this idea of a forest tribe who live in the tree tops.'

Later that year Alice moved to Yeoville, an old suburb a couple of miles from Hillbrow, and Alexander, the only member of the group with a car, helped shift her things, including her cat. Alexander was to spend many happy evenings gathered with friends at Alice's Yeoville flat, puffing on a joint as it was passed around the circle, chatting, and listening to rock music on her sound system.

'What's up, Sandro,' Alice would greet him, for Sandro became his nickname among these friends. Evenings with Alice and the others, listening to music tapes, gave Alexander the education in rock music that he had failed to acquire while at school. Unlike most of the kids at school, he had rarely listened to the radio as a teenager.

Once in a while Alice threw a party at her flat (it was always somebody's birthday), and the small apartment would be pulsating with young people, dancing to loud music, drinking, and passing a joint – a marijuana cigarette – around. There would be literally barely room to move. The cat would be closed in the bedroom, to which people came and went when they required somewhere a little more private. The first floor apartment had a small balcony, and sometimes, on a hot summer's night, there would be so many

Chapter Four

people gathered on the balcony that Alexander would not have been surprised had it parted company from its parent structure and landed in the street below, among the black street kids who congregated below such parties, and who danced and capered in exchange for coins of small denominations thrown from the balcony.

There was a bohemian air of heightened sexuality at such parties (and at similar parties Alexander would attend at other flats in Hillbrow, Berea and Yeoville, and occasionally, at houses in the suburbs), and he would sometimes find himself dancing with another boy. Once, at a party in Alice's flat in 1979, Alexander's dance partner of the moment happened to be a good looking young man whose short platinum blonde hair, wide set eyes and high, sharp cheek bones suggested a Baltic ancestry, but when this young man suggested to Alexander that they remove to his flat (he lived in the same apartment block as Alice), Alexander declined. This element of low key homo eroticism was very much a feature of those times in the set in which Alexander then moved.

Hillbrow in the nineteen-seventies and the nineteen-eighties was a compound of all the sin and vice and hopes and energy of that wicked gold mining city, Johannesburg. It was riches and terrible poverty; it was every ethnicity and tongue and creed under the sky, gathered in one crowded district consisting largely of high-rise apartment blocks, some of which were twenty stories high. However, families were raised in Hillbrow. Children grew up there, went to schools nearby, and many Hillbrow residents attended church services on Sunday. Rents were low, even by Alexander's ill-paid standards. It was very easy to rent a flat. There were shops, cinemas, bars and restaurants in the Brow; everything needed to service a vast and varied community. At Highpoint Centre there was a twenty-four hour supermarket, Fontanas (upon which Alice's gang would descend, overtaken by urgent appetite, after an evening smoking marijuana). There was a public indoors swimming bath in Hillbrow, and of course there were the big European cafés. If you were merely a timid bourgeois boy up from the suburbs with your girlfriend on a Saturday night, and you wanted a safe thrill, and to be able to tell your mates you had been to the movies in Hillbrow, you could park your car below Highpoint, and watch a movie in the nearby cinema complex, and you need hardly set foot in the scary night time streets of Hillbrow at all.

Among Alice's group, going clubbing on a Friday or Saturday night was an important way of blowing off steam. Alexander had a good sense of natural rhythm, and boundless energy, and – an exhibitionist by inclination – he was not shy on the dance floor. He found club dancing addictive. He lost himself completely in the driving, hypnotic beat of the dance music pounding in his ears, with only occasional breaks for visits to one of the bars, or to the roof garden to smoke a joint. Alexander and his friends visited one club in particular many times: this was Mandy's, in End Street. He was usually accompanied by Alice, Terrance, Robyn, and others from the group. Mandy's had a reputation for sexual ambiguity and frantic dancing on its two dance floors – accompanied by often heavy drinking and the smoking of marijuana in the jasmine-embowered booths of the roof garden. Having danced right through the night, Alexander and a group of friends, feeling utterly drained but still buzzing on the amphetamines (which they knew as "speed") that they had taken the evening before, would make their way across the jaded city at dawn, shivering in the sudden chill, to the towering Carlton Hotel in the city centre for a full breakfast in the hotel restaurant, washed down with flute glasses of Bucks Fizz. It would be mid morning before Alexander crashed – quite often at Alice's flat, sometimes at his own place in Twist Street – with the suddenness and totality of a tree being felled.

It was at Mandy's one night that Robyn first made her interest in Alexander very clear, and nothing loathe to further his experience of living life to the full, Alexander responded in kind. It was with Robyn one night that Alexander was to lose his virginity.

It seemed to Alexander, a young man himself, that Hillbrow was a young man's Mecca. Young men from the suburbs and from further afield – from the *dorps* of the *Platteland* – would find their way to Hillbrow in their quest to alleviate the stifling boredom and dullness of their suburban lives, or to escape the narrow confines of their country towns, or to make their fortunes – or just to let off steam on a Friday or Saturday night. For Hillbrow – and Yeoville, one or two miles further east – were full of bars and nightclubs. Some of the sturdy Afrikaner country lads, stranded in Hillbrow, penniless, landed up hiring themselves from Johannesburg Station (competing with the heroin addicts) to middle aged homosexuals in the evenings, who cruised the station parking lot in their cars. Some of these young men hung around the illicit gay bars (for homosexual sex was outlawed until 1994 in South Africa), and hoped to be taken home for the night, and given a bath and supper, and in return for the comfort they offered their protectors, they would perhaps be given twenty or thirty Rand also, and then, in the morning, returned to Hillbrow. Alexander learned early on that Hillbrow had a dark underbelly. There was a lurking spirit of true wickedness that was particularly apparent late at night, if you were n't too drunk or too high to notice.

And there were black beggars located up and down the two main streets, Pretoria and Kotze. There was one black beggar who seemed to be seated directly on his legless trunk, on a small wooden platform with castor wheels at each corner, and he propelled himself around with hugely calloused fists. Others occupied disused doorways, set back from the pavement, and they would sit there, their stick-thin limbs stuck out in front of them, covered with hideous carbuncles and growths and sores weeping fluids and horror. One or two turned sightless eyes up to a blind

Heaven, and held out quavering hands. One of these latter had a small apprentice squatting by his side, to be his eyes. If Alexander gave these unfortunates some loose change as he passed by, it was less from pity than from an atavistic compulsion to avert ill fortune.

There were black street children also, scores of them, dressed in cast-offs and rags, often barefoot, who swarmed all around you when you parked your car at night, on your way to the movies or a restaurant, and you gave these kids small denominations of silver, and told them there would be more when you returned, if your car was still safe.

And at the far end of Pretoria Street, only a hundred yards from Brief Encounters, Johannesburg's best known gay bar, was the Hillbrow Police Station, a large fortress-like building of red brick and raw concrete, with its communal police cells for drunks and petty thieves and muggers and drug dealers, and every other worker of night time vice.

By the late eighties Alexander had become much more conscious of Hillbrow's dark side. By then, Hillbrow seemed to him to be like an aging stage *artiste*, the paint and powder cracking on her ravaged features, this wicked old woman who still whored herself to youngsters foolish enough to fall for her dubious charms. The district was steeped in a corruption of the spirit, and Alexander was experienced enough by then to recognise this, yet still – still! – he could not keep away from this ogling old has-been.

It was at this point in time that Alexander was introduced by a friend, who managed a bar he frequented, to the Balkan Football Club, which was located behind an innocent, narrow entrance in Pretoria Street. If you did not know it was there, you would have passed it by. You turned off the pavement into this entrance, and you walked along a narrow, covered-in, dimly lighted, dog-legged alley, deep in the bowels of the buildings above it. This alley terminated in a heavy steel grill protecting a metal door. You stood so the closed circuit monitor could see you, and you pressed a bell: the buzzer sounded, the locks disengaged, and you were inside.

The Balkan Football Club was essentially a cavernous, windowless, dimly lighted, dingy bar, open twenty-four hours a day, every single day of the year. There was a side room that opened off the main area, where you could drink in a little more privacy if you wished. The bar was frequented by gangsters, off duty policemen, prostitutes and their pimps. It was a sleazy, corrupt environment, and if you still found this sort of thing appealing, you were close to sinking forever, beyond trace.

Alexander (whose stay in the district had been broken by long periods spent living elsewhere) was the last white tenant left in his block of flats in Yeoville in 1996. By then, he visited Hillbrow only to drink in the early hours at the Balkan Football Club, or to visit Brief Encounters, which was one of the very last of the old bars in Hillbrow still open for business. The great European cafés, so elegant, so cosmopolitan, so very civilised, had become black shebeens; the streets of Hillbrow, Berea, Bellevue and Yeoville, as Alexander was to find out, were no longer safe for a white man to walk alone, particularly at night.

Chapter Five

An Encounter in Leicester Square

When, in 1976, Alexander had made his first unaccompanied visit to Britain (during his early childhood in Kenya, the family had twice visited England by sea on long leave), he had arrived in southern England in the depths of a cold January wintertime which he found shocking in its severity. But he delighted in the bright, burgeoning spring days of April and May, and he sweltered in the exceptionally hot summer that followed. He was already in love with England and with the English, long before he had ever left Cape Town, for his mother had read him stories from English children's books as a little boy, and he had learned to read because he wished to read these stories for himself. He knew all the Beatrix Potter children's stories almost by heart, and the animal characters were old and much loved friends. Aged four, he had run outside one morning to the edge of the forest that bordered the family's back garden in Nairobi, to try to find a red squirrel like Squirrel Nutkin, but instead he found only a troop of little black faced monkeys in the trees, and one of the naughty little imps peed from a tree twenty feet above him and made Alexander laugh so much he almost wet himself. But he did not find Squirrel Nutkin there.

Chapter Five

Alexander was able to quote from A. A. Milne's stories about Christopher Robin and his bear, Winnie the Pooh, and from the poems in *Now We are Six*. He had a clear image in his mind's eye of the Hundred Acre Wood where Owl and Eeyore lived, just as he had a clear image of rolling English countryside from any number of English children's tales written before the War, such as the stories of *Milly Molly Mandy* and her English country cottager's life, by Joyce Lankester Brisley. Before he reached his teens he had read the magical and moving classic, *The Wind in the Willows*, by Kenneth Grahame. As a teenager he had very much enjoyed reading the adventure novels of the English nineteenth century writer G. A. Henty, in which Englishness of a certain class was presented as vastly admirable, and through which the Empire was glorified. Alexander read many less dated novels set in England. Of course, a Scot via his paternal bloodline, as a teenager Alexander also began reading the historical novels written by Nigel Tranter, which were set in Scotland and which taught him so much about the history of the ancestral land he had never known.

As a prepubescent he read English comics such as the *Beano* and the *Dandy*, and a little later he was reading *Lion* and *Victor* and *Hotspur*, and he also read the more serious comic publication, *Look and Learn*, which (together with these other comics) arrived by airmail from England every week. But it was the southern England of the inter-war years with which Alexander was most familiar from his reading. He was reading the *Just William* stories by Richmal Crompton into his early adolescence. These stories delighted Alexander and made him laugh. He could relate to William, who prowled the English countryside around his home, seeking adventures and falling into mishaps and mischief, for Alexander too was a great neighbourhood wanderer as a young adolescent, his air rifle in his hand. And in his early teens he galloped through the *Billy Bunter* stories, that Fat Owl of the Remove, and he found sufficient similarities between Greyfriars,

Billy Bunter's minor public school, and his own high school in South Africa, to relate to the background in the series of novels.

As a very young man living in Cape Town he bought the English country magazine, *Country Life*, each week, with its page after page of beautiful country houses for sale, and he also read *Punch*, and these publications held a promise that Alexander had no doubts would be redeemed, if ever he was to visit England. And he was not to be disappointed.

By the time Alexander left home in Cape Town aged twenty, he had become familiar with an England that, in his mind's eye, consisted only of the glories and wonders of London, that great imperial capital, or of the long settled countryside: the latter an idealised landscape of lovely rolling hills and cool green woodlands; of quiet, slow moving rivers whose banks were hung with drooping willows, or fast flowing, clear streams rising high in the hills; of quaint thatched half-timbered cottages, and noble country houses. And he was to find all these things during his visit to England in 1976.

In early 1980, seized by the restlessness which periodically overcame him, Alexander resigned his job as a private detective and left South Africa for London once again. Alexander squandered Time. He had then no sense of the brevity of life, and he felt no great drive to use his time productively.

Alexander was to remember London and the south of England in the seventies and eighties with some affection in later years. London had not yet been spoiled for him. The cold, mercenary hand of Thatcherism had barely begun to alter the character of the people of England's south-east, and was yet to make them callous, grasping, greedy and uncaring.

Although this was Alexander's third visit to England (not counting his childhood visits), he was still very much aware at times of some striking cultural difference between South Africa and England. Prominent among these was the treatment of blacks

Chapter Five

in England. The black and mixed race people he saw may have looked similar to those with whom he was familiar in South Africa, but they spoke very differently, and they were far more assertive and confident. The blacks in England did not cringe and bob their heads at Alexander.

With the coming of his first English springtime in 1976 Alexander came to know the wayside plants that members of his family would identify for him as they went walking along country lanes. He delighted in the apple scented white hawthorn blossom, the mayflower, that grew in all the hedgerows. Alexander learned why people in the cold North yearn for and love the springtime. Decades later, a blackbird's song in Alexander's garden in springtime would trigger happy memories from long ago; memories of a time when he was young, and when everyone he loved was still alive.

Alexander learned how to name some of the trees of the Old World: the horse chestnuts with their fantastic floral displays in late spring; the ancient oak trees, guardians of his North European ancestral soul; the wild cherries in the woodlands with their mass of small white blossoms; the noble beech trees, which mantled so much of southern England with a woodland that was cool and green and welcoming in the summertime. To Alexander the yew trees in the English country churchyards seemed ancient as Time; twisted, gnarled, glowering; the most ancient of all the trees he might see about him, redolent of a period when they were associated with dark magic, before the light of Christ reached the British Isles. Alexander came to recognise hazel, ash and rowan, and some of the less considered trees also.

Alexander breathed an air of adventure and promise in London. During his stay in London from early1980 through to late 1981, he drank at the Salisbury pub in Saint Martin's Lane, with its yellowed, nicotine stained, pressed metal ceiling; its decorative etched and frosted glass divisions along the length of the banquette in the saloon bar; its gingerbread carved woodwork; its massive, polished bar counters; its red plush chairs, and its pretty gas lights and *torchères*. Arriving at the pub during the late morning, or at lunchtime, Alexander would drink a pint of Guinness; visiting in the evenings, he would order a single (or sometimes, a double) Irish whiskey with his Guinness. He enjoyed the atmosphere of camaraderie and good humour at the Salisbury; the scent of yeasty ales and pipe tobacco and cigarette smoke; the warm, cosy fug when it was cold and wet outside. In the back room, which was completely lined with mirrors (Alexander thought of it as the Narcissus Room), he was befriended by a group of men somewhat older than himself: educated, professional types, or theatre workers, musicians and artists. He enjoyed their conversation. He hardly appreciated that many of these men found him attractive and engaging; someone they looked forward to seeing.

During the weekends, if Alexander was not away visiting family in the countryside, he explored London on foot, walking many miles. He climbed the narrow stairs inside Saint Paul's dome, between the brick built weight-bearing inner cone and the skin of the outer dome, to the golden gallery just beneath the ball and lantern, with its panoramic views of London stretching away to the horizon, and a great reach of the River visible, busy with pleasure boats, barges, scows and tug boats. He visited Westminster Abbey and the Tower of London. He explored the Science Museum in Kensington, with its wonderful collection of transport themed displays, which (like the National Gallery, another of his favorite destinations) he was to revisit many times over many years. He took a riverboat to Greenwich and the Maritime Museum, and a boat upriver to Richmond.

He grew to love London (but he knew nothing of London's East End), and to appreciate the subtle differences in character between the series of villages which made up its boroughs. He came to know his way around parts of Camden (where the canal and lock and the houseboats lining the canal became a favorite destination), and much of Westminster also (with its monuments to *imperium* and might, and its magnificent Byzantine-style Catholic cathedral, with its towering campanile). He explored Kensington and Chelsea. There were no skyscrapers yet in inner London; there was no docklands development; there was no Canary Wharf. Saint Paul's Cathedral still towered above all other structures in the City.

In London (and this process began with his first visit in 1976, and continued with the time he spent on Scotland's west coast), Alexander learned at last what he had failed properly to learn at school: he learned how to become a social creature; how to chum up with other young people; how to make use of such kindnesses as came his way. He learned that people were often kind to the personable young; he came to appreciate how the young themselves will so often approach their fellows with hearts wide open and spirits filled with amity; how the old will forgive the young trespasses that would go unforgiven, and fester, when committed in later years. Alexander learned above all that many people found him likeable. He even began to suspect that he too was personable and charming. He had never guessed at this before.

In 1979, aged twenty-four, Alexander was to lose his virginity to Robyn, the girl he had first met with Alice's group at the Café Wien. Robyn was visiting him at his flat in Twist Street one evening, when she began kissing him as they sat side by side on the sofa. Alexander responded in kind, initially out of courtesy, but he was curious and inventive, and it seemed quite natural when, after ten minutes of increasingly heavy petting, Robyn should take his hand and lead him towards his bed. Despite his lurking fears that he was an aberration, Alexander had found the experience enjoyable, and he and Robyn were to make love a second time later that night – for Robyn had indeed stayed the night. It was not until 1981, however, that Alexander had his first (and last) same-sex encounter.

Alexander was browsing in a bookshop off Leicester Square, when he noticed a pleasant featured, auburn haired young man his own age observing him discreetly. As Alexander left the shop, he lighted a cigarette, and this young man, a cigarette in his own fingers, approached him.

'Can you give me a light?' he asked Alexander, his accent Scottish. Close up, Alexander could see that he had not shaved for a day or two, but his beard was very fair.

Alexander, who had been smoking since early 1979, flicked his Zippo and held it to the young man's cigarette. The young man cupped Alexander's hand between his own to form a windbreak. Alexander experienced a stirring, a frisson of excitement, at this artfully casual physical contact. How did a very young man with no experience of such an encounter know immediately that this was a sexual proposition? For of this Alexander was certain.

The young Scot drew at his cigarette. 'Thanks. Do you live in London?' he asked Alexander.

'I live just south of the River. What about you?'

'I was looking for work in London, but I'm going home again soon,' the young man replied. 'I need somewhere to spend the night. Would you maybe know of somewhere?'

'You can come home with me,' Alexander replied. 'I live with a Church of England minister, but he wont mind if you stay overnight.'

'Thanks, I'll do that,' the young man responded.

The two of them went back to the flat in Kennington that Alexander then shared with a Church of England curate about four or five years his senior in age. There, the young man he brought home with him, who had lively, flashing brown eyes, wolfed down a plate of ham sandwiches, and then asked if he could take a bath and borrow a razor.

The worldly young curate recognised Alexander's guest immediately for what he was, and, laughing, said, 'I did n't know you went for a bit of rough, Sandy.' Alexander was not familiar with that gay cant term.

The next morning, Alexander felt unclean. He was suffused with regret and remorse. His imagination had thus far barely encompassed the physical reality of such intimacies with another man. The young Scot asked whether Alexander could "lend" him fifteen Pounds, and Alexander, despite having very little spare cash, gave it to him, upon which, the young wanderer went on his way.

Chapter Six

The Church in London

God would not let Alexander go.

Alexander's paternal ancestry had been Catholic for centuries, but his grandfather had lapsed from the Catholic faith, and until his final year at school, when Alexander began attending Sunday Mass at a nearby Catholic church, Alexander had had no exposure to Catholicism. Over time, Alexander came to favour Anglican High Church services: he was drawn to the Anglo-Catholic tradition, and to the splendid celebrations of Holy Communion within this tradition, far outshining as they did most celebrations of the Catholic Mass.

With the family's return to Cape Town in early 1974, shortly before Alexander's nineteenth birthday, he had joined an Anglican congregation in Constantia, in which suburb Alexander's family had bought a house. It was a lovely little church built of stone, with a sparely decorated, simple interior, relying on its use of honest materials for its beauty; dressed stone, plastered and whitewashed interior walls, and a roof supported by timbers darkened with age. Alexander had been christened in an Anglican cathedral in East Africa; Anglicanism was not alien to him, for it had come to him through his mother's side of the family. He was confirmed by the Archbishop in Constantia later in 1974.

The Rector in Constantia was Canon Michael, and it was he who had called Alexander back from his visit to Britain in 1976, having arranged for him to join the community in Cape Town as a means of assessing whether or not he had a calling to the ministry. It was not in fact the serial horror story being screened on British television every evening – the scenes of riot and murder in South Africa – which had initiated Alexander's departure from Oban. That departure had been planned for some time.

God bothered Alexander mightily. God had bothered Alexander since his late adolescence. God did not bother Roy, his younger brother. Perhaps Alexander did indeed have a calling to the Christian ministry: not the one he had always imagined, as an ordained minister, but a wider, secular calling, and many years later, Alexander would strive to practice that calling, in much of what he wrote for the public to read, and in the manner in which he tried to live his life. But Alexander, coming to manhood, was a poor witness for Christ, for he was far too immature, and he was untested as yet. He was an even worse witness through his thirties and forties, for at times during those years his life was a mockery of traditional Christian values.

During Alexander's first visit to England, in 1976, he had been a member of an Anglo-Catholic congregation in South Kensington. Saint Thomas' had been designed by a well known Victorian ecclesiastical architect, William Butterfield, and was built of pale yellow brick, darkened by the filth, until quite recently, from London's coal fires, and banded and patterned with red brick and stone. The interior was decorated throughout with polychromatic images, composed of painted tiles, illustrating the Stations of the Cross and Biblical scenes, in a high Victorian neo-romantic style, and there was a Lady Chapel with a carved wooden statue, two thirds life size, of Our Lady, covered in gold leaf. Saint Thomas' was more gloriously Catholic than many Catholic churches.

Alexander came to belong to Saint Thomas' congregation because he shared two floors of a house in a mid nineteenth century terrace in West Kensington with a Church of England curate attached to the church; this was the first of two Church of England curates he was to share a home with in London. Alexander thought the man was effeminate and camp, and he had an occasionally sharp and cutting tongue in him. But Alexander tolerated him (and the curate, in his favor, put up with a young man who had no sense of shared domestic obligations at all). It was a comfortable and convenient house share in a good part of London, with a small park directly in front of the house.

Saint Thomas' was a very smart parish. The curate, whose family was well connected, sometimes had guests from the top ranks of London society come to dinner. Some of these guests were intrigued by Alexander. One, Lady Kingsleigh, said to him, 'You're not at all as I've always imagined South Africans to be. You have hardly any accent at all.'

'I'm not a genuine South African, Lady Kingsleigh. I was born in Kenya.'

'Ah! That explains it. We know Lord Newtonmore well. He had a farm in Kenya. Perhaps you knew him?'

'My parents may have known him,' Alexander answered her.

There was another young housemate, a boy Alexander's own age, with a bright, outgoing personality, whose family lived in Cumbria. He had been educated at one of the great public schools in the south. The two young men, the ex-public school boy and the young man from the colonies, got on well together, and some evenings they would go to the pub or the movies together.

At supper one evening, Ranulph, the young Cumbrian lad, said to Alexander, 'I've been offered two tickets at half price to see

Chapter Six

Rudolf Nureyev dance in the *Sleeping Beauty* at the Coliseum next Monday night. Would you be interested, Sandy?'

'How much do the tickets cost?'

'Twenty Pounds each.'

This represented a huge sum to Alexander at the time.

'It's a once in a lifetime chance, Sandy.'

'Yes, OK, let's do that,' Alexander said.

Alexander was not a ballet fan, although he had been to a few ballet performances at the Nico Malan Theatre in Cape Town, but after the show the following Monday night, he felt that the magnificent production, starring the world's greatest male ballet dancer, was something to have experienced.

It was during his third stay in London, between early 1980 to late 1981, that Alexander went to live with the second of the Church of England curates he was to house share with. This young priest was attached to a church near Vauxhall. At night, Alexander would wake sometimes to hear the reassuring chimes of Big Ben across the River, which was not far away.

Alexander had two spinster great aunts living in London. These ladies were his maternal grandmother's sisters. One, who still contributed articles for magazines, was a gregarious old lady who lived in a tiny cottage near the River in Richmond. Despite Alexander only having visited her three or four times in total between early 1976 (during his first visit to England) and late 1981, she had acquired a great fondness for him. The other, older sister, who was more withdrawn and artistic, lived a retiring, private life in a pleasant flat with a tiny balcony in Saint John's Wood. Alexander visited her a little more frequently, if only because he found it easier to reach Saint John's Wood than to reach Richmond. Like his grandmother, the old lady had grown up in France. She was a painter, like her father, Alexander's great-grandfather, and she had managed to acquire many more of her father's works than had his grandmother or his mother. Her flat was filled with family oil paintings.

Alexander's maternal grandmother was now living at an old age home in Wimbledon, opposite the Common. During 1980 through to late 1981, and again in 1988 (when Alexander was once more living in England), he paid his grandmother an occasional visit. She had managed to hang onto a few of her fine old pieces of furniture and a collection of *bric-à-brac*, and some of her father's oil paintings, so her room was full of character. It had a large, south facing window, and was flooded with sunshine on sunny days during the summer. Alexander's grandmother was by 1988 suffering from mild dementia (she was over ninety by then), so when they played chess together in her room, over cups of tea and some cake or biscuits the old lady had laid in, Alexander allowed her occasional cheating to go unchallenged.

'How many servants did you have when you were a girl in France, Granny?' Alexander asked her. He knew that his grandmother enjoyed reminiscing about her childhood in France before the First World War. Her family had been well to do.

'Oh gosh, I don't remember. Quite a few.'

'Was there a boy who polished the boots?'

'Oh yes, there was a boots boy. And a footman. There may have been two footmen. I remember a man who polished the silver. My governess was not exactly a servant. She came from Alsace you know'

Once in a while Alexander would hire a car and fetch his grandmother at the home and take her for a long drive, with some particular destination in mind. September 1988 was the last time Alexander took his grandmother on such an outing. They visited Hampton Court Palace, a vast, imposing Tudor residence beside the Thames, built around a number of courtyards in the early sixteenth century by the mighty Cardinal Wolsey, Henry VIII's Chancellor. Alexander's grandmother was by now very frail, a tiny, shrunken figure not even five feet tall. She clung to her eldest grandchild's arm as they walked beside the River. The sky was grey

Chapter Six

and overcast, and a cold wind was blowing across the waters of the Thames. They had not walked far before Alexander felt that his grandmother needed to sit down, so he led her to the Tilting Yard, where there was a café where they could sit indoors and drink tea. Alexander was always hungry, so he ordered each of them a slice of Victoria sponge cake. By late October of that year, Alexander had returned to South Africa, and his grandmother died the following January. She had been alive when Wilbur and Orville Wright made the world's first powered, heavier than air flight in their fragile machine; she had travelled in a Jumbo jet on her last visit to her daughter's family in Africa.

Chapter Seven

University and Growing Up

The young man of the early nineteen-eighties was still many years away from growing angry and despairing. Too few promises had yet been broken – either by Man, or by God; too few treacheries had yet been experienced; too little heartache had yet been suffered; too few battles had yet been terribly lost; too few hopes had yet been betrayed; too few friends had been lost forever; too few people had rejected the love he had offered them. Oh, that young man was still such an innocent!

No wonder that his skin remained, for now, smooth and unlined; that his hair remained, for now, thick and shining; no wonder that each morning he could still awake to find his energies renewed and his hopes rekindled. The God of broken promises and hopes foresworn whom he would one day come to know, had so far revealed Himself only briefly. He was yet to permit the young man to know the exhaustion of striving to cling to hope, when the pursuit of that elusive and fickle blessing has been too many times proven to be a fool's endeavour. A full accession of wisdom was years away yet from Alexander, and so he lived those years in hope.

Chapter Seven

But if his inner eye had been as wide open as it was eventually to become, then, even as early as the first three months of 1977, Alexander might have been able to apprehend that which his spirit already knew: namely, that he had a doom upon him. Within just a few months of the beginning of his friendship with Patrick, who lived in the big house up on the hill, Alexander began to bring an occasional half jack of whiskey back to his room in the wing in which he and the other young men lived. He would sip at it secretly, privately, alone in his room in the evenings. A wise observer, had there been one, would have recognised that Alexander's spirit was sick already with the foretaste of despair. But the young man of 1977 lacked the experience to know what his secret drinking signified; he could not recognise the spiritual sickness that lay behind it.

So Alexander sipped and he sipped, in his self imposed solitary state in his room in the evenings, and he felt himself to be guilty of some terrible secret sin (no – the drinking was not in itself that sin: even then, he knew that much), and he withdrew by degrees from engagement with the community, and it became inevitable that he would have to go away.

In February 1982, Alexander returned to university in Johannesburg, to continue studying for his undergraduate's degree. Peter, a civil servant, one of Alexander's acquaintances at the Salisbury pub in London, had said to him sometime in 1981, 'You have a good brain, but it seems to me that you're wasting it. Go back to university.'

Others of Alexander's acquaintances as he sat and drank with them in the evenings, in that room of many mirrors at the back of the pub, agreed with Peter. The curate with whom he shared the comfortable flat within sound of Big Ben had said much the same thing, worried by Alexander's lack of direction. And so, Alexander had written first to his university, and then to his parents, and plans for his return were made.

The university credited Alexander with his first year passes from 1973, the year following his matriculation from high school, and gave him permission to enter his second year. In South Africa the academic year followed the calendar year, so in February 1982 Alexander began his second year at university. He was just short of his twenty-seventh birthday.

During his first year studies, nine years earlier, Alexander had been a very immature seventeen and eighteen year old, and he had remained as near solitary an individual as he had been for much of his time at high school. He had not yet learned how to make friends. By the end of that year Alexander understood, if only subconsciously, that he still needed to do a lot of growing up, and so it was that the years 1974 and 1975 saw him working full time, first as a retail management trainee, then (still aged only nineteen) as a department manager and buyer for a big retail concern in Cape Town. He was saving up for his trip to Britain.

The nine months he spent abroad in 1976 were the catalyst he needed to escape his shy, solitary ways, and allow another, far more self confident, far more sociable side of his personality to develop.

In December 1981, leaving behind a wintry England, Alexander flew back to Johannesburg, where he began his second year at university early the following year. Before the first term was over, he had acquired a circle of acquaintances, along with two or three genuine friends. One of these, a Jewish lad his own age, who intended studying law after he graduated, lived not far from Alexander's family home, in an adjacent suburb known as the "gilded ghetto." Filled with wealthy Jewish families living in large houses, there was also a King David high school in the suburb, where the sons and daughters of well to do Jewish parents went to school.

Like about ninety percent of the Jewish population in South Africa, Warren's family was originally of Lithuanian extraction. He was not physically prepossessing, but he had a daunting intellectual capacity that Alexander admired. The two had first become aware of each other during Politics tutorials, and over coffee and a shared meal in the Students' Union one lunchtime, they found that they shared many of the same intellectual interests. But Alexander felt, despite his time abroad, that Warren was altogether more worldly wise than himself. Warren was, he thought, better equipped for making a success of his life than he was.

A far more emotionally charged friendship was that which Alexander formed with a fellow student ten years his junior. He had noticed him one day as the young man was working at a table in the main library, his head bent in study, books strewn around him. Alexander had stared, and then the owner of that head of shining, coppery hair had looked up, and the two had held each other's eye for a long moment. Alexander had immediately recognised that this beautiful young man had a part to play in his life.

A few days later, Alexander came across a friend on campus who was chatting with the owner of those coppery locks. Alexander stopped and greeted his friend. The young man with the shining hair had smiled at Alexander, and said, 'I see we have another Bowie fan in our midst.'

Alexander was wearing his Air Force surplus greatcoat that day (it was a Highveld winter's day) and on the left lapel of the greatcoat he had pinned a small enamel David Bowie badge. He held a pipe in one hand. He had been smoking since 1979, and during his second term back at university, he had switched to a pipe. He took to it immediately. The fussy ritual – the reaming out of the bowl, filling the bowl with fresh tobacco and tamping it down – gave him pleasure. In 1982 there were no restrictions on smokers on campus. Alexander smoked his pipe at the back of lecture halls; he even smoked his pipe in his favourite library, the Jan Smuts Library. Within a short while, several young men on campus had acquired pipes and were battling to become pipe smokers, but Alexander remained the only dedicated pipe smoker among the undergraduates, for these young men had not the patience for a pipe, or they could not acquire the knack of it. Among the academic staff, only some of the older men smoked pipes.

With his military greatcoat worn during the winter, his baggy, pleated trousers with wide turn ups, his highly polished Oxford brogues, his jackets worn even in summertime, his hats (during the summer an inexpensive Marks and Spencer Panama he had bought in England, and in the wintertime a fedora, bought in Rocky Street in Yeoville, or a genuine Harris Tweed flat cap he had bought in England in 1976), and of course his pipe, Alexander stood out among the student body. His accent, rare in Johannesburg (being an amalgam of the public school English of the people with whom he had lived and socialised in London, superimposed on his natal colonial Kenya accent), emphasised his air of eccentricity. As for his lecturers and professors, it was his handwriting, as much as his intelligent mind and his readiness to speak out during tutorials, which made an impression on them. Alexander had been taught cursive script at school using an old fashioned steel nib dipping pen, and he had used only fountain pens ever since. At university his essays and course work were beautifully written in black ink in an almost eighteenth century copperplate style, for he wrote with a wide calligraphic nib.

Alexander's friend, then, with the beautiful young man standing at his side, had made the introductions. 'Gregory, meet Sandy. Sandy – Gregory.'

Aged just seventeen, Gregory was a prodigy both of physical beauty and intellectual prowess. A product of an expensive boys' private school in Johannesburg, with a comfortable access of family wealth behind him, he was another of those floppy haired boys with money, brains, beauty, and flawless complexions who were to feature in Alexander's life. Through them, Alexander was able

Chapter Seven

to experience a vicarious joy. Through them, Alexander inevitably came to know an increase of despair.

For one and a half years, Gregory and Alexander were often together, on and off campus. Many mornings, Alexander would give Gregory (who was still too young at first to have applied for his driving licence) a lift to university. They would listen to music tape cassettes on the car's cassette player as they drove. One of the compositions to which Gregory introduced Alexander one morning was Allegri's *Miserere Mei, Domine* (a setting of Psalm 51, "Have mercy upon me, Oh God, according to thy loving kindness… " probably composed during the 1630s for Pope Urban VIII). Alexander had never before heard such sublimely beautiful choral music. He was intensely moved. This remained throughout his life one of Alexander's favourite compositions, which he was to listen to often, first on tape, then in later years on CD.

Round one o'clock, Gregory and Alexander would join the group of friends (which often included Warren) which met for lunch in the Students' Union. The two went to the movies together; some afternoons they hung out together at a record bar and coffee shop which Alice and her boyfriend managed in Yeoville, a part of town that was popular and trendy among the young. Alexander introduced Gregory to his usual running course, a distance of about three miles through a big park and nature conservation area in the northern suburbs, not far from Alexander's family home. Alexander took Gregory hiking in the rugged, wild Magaliesberg, one and a half hours' drive from the city.

In return, Gregory introduced Alexander to the gym on campus, and taught him a regime of exercises designed to build up his body. (Like not a few excessively beautiful boys, Gregory sought to compensate for his prettiness by building up his physique. He had a fine body, many years away yet from that descent to muscle bound seediness that is the destination of so many bodybuilders). Alexander worked out twice a week at the gym for the remainder of his years at university. He continued to run also, and he joined the university fencing club.

In 1979, while he had been working as a private investigator, Alexander had fenced foil (and occasionally épée), at a sporting and country club, the Wanderers, of which he had become a member, in Johannesburg's northern suburbs. But he had not kept up the sport during his time in London. The subtlety and cunning, speed and grace of this one-on-one sport appealed to him, as participation in team sports at school never had. So too did the special gear: the long, flexible foil blades themselves, into which Alexander carefully introduced a slight curve to the tip of the blade, by drawing it repeatedly under and up from the sole of his shoe every time he bought a new blade; the white knee breeches; the long white stockings; the padded plastron fastened over the right side of the chest below the jacket; the tailor-made, padded protective jacket itself, which reached down beneath his crotch; the protective mask – and the thick, heavy leather gauntlet for his right hand. Alexander learned sabre at university. Sabre, with its cutting edge, called for a rather different skill set to foil, a purely thrusting weapon. Alexander enjoyed fencing sabre, with its huge guard and its association with cavalry regiments. The rules for sabre were very different to those for foil. Alexander became a competent upper-mid ranking fighter, and he took part in competitions with other clubs. Membership of the university fencing club brought him new friends.

During these years at university, Alexander, who (other than a small reputation in cross country) had achieved no sporting renown at school, and whose only exercise then had been tennis, occasional cross country, and the long walks he took to satisfy his own desire for solitude, became very fit indeed. He was growing into his looks, too: instead of looking like a tall, skinny, awkward boy, he had become a rather striking young man. His physique filled out a little more; his shoulders broadened with the muscle he had

Chapter Seven

built on them; his features lost some of their childish smoothness and acquired something of a man's angularity. During those years Alexander was very conscious that his appearance worked for him, and this, along with his sense of physical wellbeing, further enhanced his self confidence. Intellectually more than competent, deriving much pleasure from his course studies, fit and healthy, very much aware of his good looks, rather charming when he set his mind to it, and with an active social life, Alexander was inclined at times to arrogance.

A girl Alexander knew at university said to him, 'I love the way you walk, Sandy – like a tomcat strut.'

Alexander laughed. 'I like that! Tomcat strut. It sounds like the title of a jazz number.'

'But it's true! You lope along, like a big cat.'

For a number of girls were now drawn to Alexander. Although he had no regular girlfriend for long during his university years, he enjoyed friendships with several girls in his classes, with one of whom he was physically intimate on a number of occasions. The girl's name was Amanda; Amanda who thought that Alexander walked like a big cat.

Alexander was developing what verged on being a dangerously overcharged relationship with Gregory; there could be no happy outcome to such a relationship if sustained for too long. Then Gregory found a girlfriend, and he and Alexander saw much less of one another.

During 1984, his honours year, Alexander took to visiting the sports bar at the bottom of campus during the lunch period, where (remembering the Salisbury pub in London, and the Guinness beers he used to drink there) he would drink one or two bottles of Castle milk stout, the nearest equivalent in South Africa to Guinness. In this solitary drinking (for the sports bar was hardly frequented at all during the lunch hour), Alexander was continuing the secretive habit he had fallen into at the community in Cape

Town, where he had sipped at whiskey alone in his room in the evenings. This was secretive drinking too. He mentioned it to no one; he invited none of his acquaintances to join him. There were warning signs here that a hardened toper of many years' standing would have recognised. In growing older, Alexander found it more and more difficult to shake off a periodic depression, something akin to despair, that had first whispered of its presence as long ago as early 1977 in Cape Town.

Chapter Eight

Going Sailing

God had not ceased to bother Alexander during his years at university. But gratitude, and sometimes joy, although present, were not then the foundations of Alexander's relationship with Him. (Sincere gratitude was to come in later years, but Alexander was to have become much older before he truly understood what Christians meant when they spoke about the joy in Christ). It was a deep yearning for deliverance from these periods of depression and despair – a despair in which there was a strong element of self loathing – which bound Alexander to God. Alexander sometimes felt that there was a mismatch between the man his Christian faith expected him to be, and the man God had seemingly made him to be. This conviction that there was something central to his being which needed healing, became ever more strongly defined as Alexander grew older. He was storing up an enormous legacy of tension and self loathing, which would eventually explode into catastrophically self destructive behaviour.

During his first term back at university, Alexander read a short piece in the Johannesburg daily, the *Star*, about the need for volunteer "big brothers" at Saint Michael's Boys' Home in

Johannesburg. He went to see the headmaster, and thereafter, through the course of the next two years at university, Alexander gave up an afternoon twice a week at the boys' home. During his third year back at university, his honours year, Alexander reduced these visits to once weekly, as he had too much reading to do. He did not involve himself with the boys' sports (there was another young volunteer who enjoyed organising the boys' games), but instead he spent these afternoons helping them with their homework. Alexander was good at this. He was patient, a good teacher, and he did not talk down to the boys. He was "Sir" to them, and for the most part, the boys liked him and respected him. Sometimes Alexander would gather four or five boys on a Saturday and pile them into his Rambler and take them on outings to the Zoo, or to the War Museum, and other popular venues. Or he would bring them back to his parents' home, and they would spend the afternoon at the poolside, and stay for an early supper which his mother gave them.

Other than his family, only Gregory and Warren knew of this voluntary activity on Alexander's part. Otherwise, he kept the knowledge of it to himself, for the pleasure and sense of self worth it brought him were too intensely personal to share with any but his closest friends at university.

Throughout his time at university, Alexander had been attending Mass most Sundays at Saint Charles in Victory Park, known locally, due to its singular design, as the Lemon Squeezer. This was the Catholic church he had first come to know as a seventeen year old while still at school. However, he was unable to go forward to the altar rail during communion, for he had not yet been received into the Catholic faith. As it happened, the Roman Catholic university chaplain, a suave and worldly Jesuit priest, was a distant cousin, perhaps fifteen to twenty years Alexander's senior. As a teenager, Alexander had met him once or twice at family gatherings, and now he made his acquaintance once again.

Chapter Eight

'What a charming and elegant young cousin you have become, Alexander,' Father Robert declared on meeting him again. 'I must ask you to the next dinner I give for CathSoc. How are your mother and father?'

In late April 1984, during his honours year, after three months' preparation, Alexander was received by the Roman Catholic Church. His sense of history informed him that he was merely returning to the church that every one of his ancestors had, before the mid sixteenth century, been a member of – and his paternal ancestors much more recently than that.

Alexander had a plan. He intended seeking ordination as a priest in a religious order in the Catholic Church. He had in mind joining the Franciscans. However, he needed to build some credibility as a Catholic first; he needed a record of parish membership behind him.

At about this time, one of Alexander's spinster great aunts in England died. Alexander had only visited her a few times at her home in Richmond, but the old lady had taken a liking to him. She had found his interest in her pre-Great War childhood in France, and in her flapper's life in London, gratifying. She could talk and talk, and Alexander never appeared to grow bored. She had once been a regular contributor to *The Lady*, that doyenne of magazines for butlers and children's nannies seeking a position, and for ladies of a somewhat conservative outlook seeking advice on domestic economy, on dealing with servants, and on matronly fashion. This old lady left Alexander four thousand five hundred Pounds in her will, a sum which translated at that time as about thirteen thousand five hundred Rand. Alexander had a good idea of what he hoped to do with this windfall: he wished to buy a small sailboat.

Having obtained his honours degree, Alexander returned to Cape Town in early 1985, where he arranged to board with his aunt's family on his grandfather's farm. Alexander's grandfather had bought the farm (positioned midway between Fish Hoek and Kommetjie, half way down the Cape Peninsula) in 1974, after the death of Alexander's grandmother. Alexander regarded the farm as his real home. No matter where his own family was located, the farm, with his grandfather (until his death in January 1987), his aunt and uncle, and his two young cousins – along with various young visiting family friends staying for indefinite periods – was a fixed and beloved star in Alexander's universe.

His grandfather had bought just under one hundred acres of land, most of it overgrown by scrub, wattle and Port Jackson willow, with some patches of *fynbos*, but there were several acres cultivated with maize, and there was a large kitchen garden. The farm was worked by a couple of Cape Coloured labourers (who, with their families, lived in shacks behind the farmhouse). Another two acres comprised paddocks bounded by creosoted split rail fencing, with stabling for four horses, a feed and tack room, and a cow byre. There was also a big chicken run, protected by a chicken wire fence and roof against jackals and mongooses, with an enclosed chicken coop, and there was a smaller covered run with a shed for the half dozen geese at night. During the day the chickens and geese had free run of the farmyard. A dairy cow was always kept at the farm, and there was a large collection of dogs and cats.

The farmhouse, which was set back from the Fish Hoek – Kommetjie road by a distance of about three hundred yards, and was approached via a sandy drive edged with pines, eucalyptus trees, and ten year old podocarpus trees, was marked on the government survey maps of the district. The house dated back to the 1850s. It had a wide, roofed, full length *stoep* along the front of the house, one end of which had been glassed in above the solid waist-high balustrade, creating a small fourth bedroom, which is where Alexander slept. There were also two large wooden cabins in the grounds, where young friends of the family lodged during their sometimes extensive stays.

Chapter Eight

On the eastern side of the farmhouse, acting as a windbreak against the prevailing south-easterly winds, was a double row of very tall, ancient Scots pines. At night, Alexander could hear the wind soughing in the pine trees, and sometimes he could hear the muted roar of the Atlantic breakers on Long Beach near Kommetjie.

Alexander had always been happy here. It was impossible to feel lonely at the farm. He was swept up by the family's love, and he was on amiable terms with the young family friends who stayed in the wooden cabins and ate with the family in the evenings. One of these was a lad named Michael – Mike to most – who rode Alexander's aunt's horses like a Red Indian. He rode the way Alexander wished he could ride. His skin was very brown, and he had fine dark eyebrows, and chestnut hair reaching to his shoulders, and he often rode bareback and barefoot, his long legs dangling straight either side. When he rode, he seemed to become one creature – centaur-like – with the horse. He was in a relationship of a year's standing with Mary, one of Alexander's young cousins. He and Alexander got along very well.

Mike, like Alexander, had a streak of melancholy in him, and like Alexander, he sometimes felt an urgent need to seek solitude. However, these two young men, the one dark, the other fair, and so similar in many ways, would sometimes go out riding together during the morning, when the cousins were away at university in Cape Town, crossing the Fish Hoek – Kommetjie road, then riding through the scrubland beyond, skirting the marshes and quicksands (the location of which they both knew well), until they reached Long Beach, a four mile long strand of glistening pure white shell sand, on which the great Atlantic rollers crashed after a storm, and which stretched in a long shallow curve from near the tiny village of Kommetjie, all the way to Noordhoek mountain. There was no urban development then anyway near the beach. The two of them would canter, with occasional gallops, the entire distance along the damp sand at the edge of the waterline, the horses' hooves flinging up sprays of water, sparkling and iridescent. They would make a more leisurely return ride, and sometimes, if the sun was hot, they would unsaddle their horses and watch with delight as the animals flung themselves into the shallows and rolled on their backs, kicking their hooves in the air. Afterwards Mike would smoke a cigarette with Alexander, lying back against the dunes, the saddle blankets spread in the sun and the horses' reins held loosely in their hands. Back at the farm they would take care to curry comb the horses thoroughly, to get the salt and sweat out of their coats and skin. There was an affinity between the two young men which needed no great amount of conversation to sustain. Alexander was happy then.

Alexander had introduced himself to the priest at Saint John the Evangelist, the Catholic church in Fish Hoek. He began going to the nine-thirty morning Mass on Sundays. Later, once he had bought a small sailboat and had become a member of the False Bay Yacht Club, he would most usually attend the Saturday-for-Sunday Mass at five-thirty p.m. on a Saturday afternoon.

His aunt, who knew so many people up and down the Peninsula, introduced Alexander to an acquaintance of hers, Charles, who was a yachtsman and a member of the False Bay Yacht Club. Alexander met him one early evening at the club bar. The False Bay Yacht Club is located on Simon's Town harbour. There is a lawn in front of the club house with tables where members and their guests can sit in the sun and bring their own food if they wish. Charles (who was in his forties and lived above Simon's Town) and Alexander brought their lager beers out to a table on the lawn.

'I know of a Hunter Europa for sale,' Charles told Alexander, after the latter had explained to him that he hoped to buy a small sail boat priced at no more than eleven thousand Rand. 'If you were to buy it, I would be happy to put you forward for club membership; they're a popular class.'

Alexander had been looking at the sailing and yachting magazines during the last few months. He recognised the name. 'She's a nineteen-footer, is n't she?' he asked.

'*Ja* – fin keel, six foot beam, one and a half thousand pounds displacement. They're a development of a daysailer, but with the cabin, the Europa has two bunks below, and a fair whack of stowage space.'

'Where is she moored?' Alexander asked.

'Up against the jetty,' Charles replied. 'I think if you bought her, you would be able to keep the mooring.'

The two of them walked across to the wooden mooring jetties and Charles pointed the boat out to Alexander. It was a pretty little vessel. They returned to the club house and bought another beer each and sat drinking on the covered deck upstairs and talked about the boat some more. By the time they parted, it was dark, the sky full of stars. Charles had told Alexander he would talk to his fellow member (who was selling the Hunter Europa because he was moving to Johannesburg), and give the man Alexander's aunt's telephone number.

Before the end of the week, Alexander had met the Hunter's owner, been for a short sail with him in the tiny yacht, and had bought the boat for eleven thousand five hundred Rand. It came outfitted with a marine VHF radio transceiver, an inflatable tender, a four-stroke five horsepower outboard, a full suit of sails (including two genoas, a spinnaker and a spinnaker pole), a good cockpit bulkhead mounted compass, and charts of False Bay and the west coast of the Peninsula as far north as Table Bay and Cape Town. The bunks were equipped with foam mattresses, and there was a chemical lavatory below. In addition, Alexander found himself the owner of various nautical *bric-à-brac*. Alexander knew he was getting a bargain, especially with the marine VHF radio and the charts thrown in. Charles had spoken to the club secretary, whom Alexander met that weekend, and by the end of February 1985, Alexander had become a member of the False Bay Yacht Club. His bank account had only a couple of thousand Rand left in it by the time he had paid his membership and mooring fees. He would have to find at least a part time job.

Alexander went for his first proper sail in the Hunter (which was named "Synchronicity") that Sunday, and, although it was his own boat, he crewed for Charles. They met at the club at about ten in the morning, but it was almost eleven before they cast off. They sailed up the east coast of the Peninsula, half a mile or so offshore, on a broad reach, looking into Fish Hoek Bay, then continued the short distance towards Kalk Bay. A moderate breeze was blowing. Whitecaps crested the surface of the sea, and periodically, cold spray flew back from the bows and slapped Alexander in the face. His sleeveless padded top and his shorts were soon wet. But the sun burned bright and hot, and he did not become soaked through. Offshore from the commercial fishing harbor of Kalk Bay, they set a new course, this time on a close haul, as far as Seal Island, which they circled (although keeping a very wary distance), to give Alexander a feel of tacking a few times in succession. Then a long, broad reach back to Simon's Town, making their mooring around tea time.

During the sail, Alexander could hardly imagine when it might be safe to employ the genoa, let alone the spinnaker. He mentioned his concerns to Charles, who replied, 'During autumn and winter you'll find we have occasional days of perfect weather – sunny, with light winds: that's when we tend to use the jenny most.'

Charles had advised Alexander to bring, despite the hot sun, a sleeveless padded jacket (which he borrowed from Hannes, one of the young live-in guests at the farm) and a beanie with him, against the wind chill. Alexander was glad of Charles' advice, as he was also glad of a litre bottle of water he had brought with him. The combination of burning sun (for it was it was high summer in those latitudes), wind, and ocean glare, had dehydrated him. He felt somewhat burned out, but deeply content, by the time they reached the mooring jetty, and he hugely appreciated the first of two ice cold lagers on the club house deck, with a stacked plate of ham and cheese sandwiches to fill the emptiness in his middle.

'You'll probably want a sailing partner,' Charles advised. 'If you introduce yourself to a few of the lads in the bar some evening, I expect you'll find someone who would crew for you.'

'OK . . .' Alexander replied, but he was not at all sure he wanted a sailing partner. Nonetheless, Alexander soon fell into the habit of drinking a few beers at the club bar twice a week, and so he came to meet some of the younger members. Some of the young men sailed only Hobie Cats. Others crewed for other yacht owners. But one of the youngsters, a cheerful, dark haired young fellow named Roger, told Alexander he could crew for him sometimes.

Alexander had already been for a couple of long solo sails before meeting Roger. He found that sailing – like hiking, or riding – was an activity that you could pursue alone, without feeling lonely. Alexander felt supremely content out on the water alone in his small boat. Time ceased to have any meaning; there was no sense of its passing. He lived in an extended present that was at times almost sublime, his mind empty of troubling thoughts, the boat requiring subtle handling and coaxing, a living thing, needful of the empathetic bond he felt for her. Sailing a small boat and riding a horse, Alexander thought, called for much the same attributes and condition of mind.

He had copied an idea he had seen on several other small yachts: a length of shock cord doubled around the tiller, and led to either side of the cockpit and back again via cleats. This would hold the tiller where Alexander set it, and he could go below, to use the chemical loo, or he could handle the sails, without needing to be anxious about not having a hand on the tiller at all times.

Alexander's new friend from the yacht club, Roger, worked three evenings a week at the Golden Bell, a popular pub and restaurant squeezed between the railway and the rocky shoreline at Kalk Bay, not far along the coast from Fish Hoek. He told Alexander that there was a barman's position coming vacant in a week or two. In the early afternoon a day or two later, Alexander visited the Golden Bell, where he spoke with the manager. Aged twenty-one, Alexander had worked behind the bar at the hotel in Oban some evenings, in addition to his usual duties waiting at tables. The manager, not much older than Alexander, was taken by his charm and plausibility, and offered him the job.

Alexander began work Tuesday week, at five p.m. He would work four evening shifts a week, and on this, he calculated, he would be able to pay his aunt something towards his board and lodging, and cover his few outgoings, of which keeping a yacht and running his car were to be the major ones.

Chapter Nine

Frances and The Golden Bell

The Golden Bell – or simply, the Bell, as it was popularly known – attracted a young crowd at the bar. Alexander's interactions with most of the young clientele (the majority of whom saw him merely as the amiable barman, and, having paid for their drinks, walked away to join their friends at their tables), were fairly superficial, but with two or three regulars, he formed slightly deeper relationships, for they wanted to chat with him. Alexander was good at this: the customers liked him well enough, and some of the older customers would tip him, or offer to buy him a drink, but he kept his drinking for the two or three evenings a week he would visit the FBYC bar at Simon's Town.

Alexander formed somewhat closer friendships with some of the staff. He did not see much of his sailing friend, Roger, at work, for their shifts did not often coincide, but two nights a week a student at Cape Town University would work a shift with Alexander at the bar. Alexander got on well with this youngster, who was eight or nine years younger than himself, and was majoring in Romance languages. The kid laughed at Alexander's halting French, but it was not mocking laughter, and Alexander grinned back ruefully. '*Parbleu!*' he declared. '*Nom d'une plume!*'

This youngster, Andrew, lived with his parents in Fish Hoek. Alexander invited him to come sailing and riding with him, and during the next few months, Andrew crewed for Alexander in Synchronicity three or four times, and joined him on a ride twice. Alexander grew to be fond of this personable young man.

There was a waitress at the Bell who was very clearly drawn to Alexander. She was older than most of the waiting staff, possibly around Alexander's own age of thirty. She was attractive, fairly slim, with short brown hair and a pleasant smile, and she appeared to have no relationship entanglements. There was, Alexander could see, a shadow of some deep hurt in her eyes.

'Where do you live, Sandy?' she asked him one evening as she fetched a bar order.

'On my grandfather's farm, between Fish Hoek and Kommetjie,' he replied. 'With my aunt's family. What about you, Frances?'

'I've got a cottage at Saint James,' she answered. 'Do you keep horses on your farm?'

'Yeah – my aunt has four horses. Do you ride?'

'When I can,' she replied. 'I better get these drinks to my table – see ya later.'

Alexander had already sailed solo across the wide False Bay to Gordon's Bay and back, but it was only when Andrew was crewing for him one weekend in late March that he tied his boat up at the Gordon's Bay Yacht Club jetty, and (with reciprocal club membership applying) the two of them visited the club's restaurant for lunch. From Simon's Town to Gordon's Bay on the far side of False Bay was a close reach sail all the way, the Hunter's best point of sailing, with barely a correction of the sails or the tiller until Gordon's Bay was gained. The return sail was just as easy: a broad reach all the way home again on the opposite tack.

Chapter Nine

Alexander took pleasure and pride in using the outboard engine as rarely as possible. When docking, he would strive to judge the amount of way the Hunter had left to her as precisely as possible, letting go the sheet of the mainsail, and approaching the jetty under headsail alone, which he would let fly shortly before Synchronicity reached the jetty, so that he could cast on as the boat lost the last of her way. The pleasure that sailing brought Alexander meant that he felt complete of himself, rarely feeling the need for company when he was on the water, although he did enjoy Andrew's cheerful, easy going companionship.

Alexander had asked Mike at the farm if he would like to come sailing with him, but Mike declined.

'Horses and firm dry land are my thing, Sandy,' he said with a laugh, 'not the horrors of going to sea in a very small boat.'

At work, Alexander was drawn to Frances. In May, he took Frances riding a couple of times, and some evenings, when neither of them had a shift to work at the Bell, he would take her for a drink at the yacht club. Alexander persuaded himself that friendship was all that Frances wanted of him. In this, he was before long to find himself mistaken.

After a while, Frances would sometimes invite Alexander back to her cottage for a coffee at the end of their shifts together. One night she snuggled up to him on the couch. As it seemed to be expected of him, Alexander drew her closer to him. This was to happen again on subsequent visits, but it would have been kinder had he rejected her overtures from the start. One night in late June Alexander gave Frances a lift back to her cottage in Saint James at the end of their shift. Frances' car was not running just then. Snuggling up to him on the couch, she said, 'Why don't you stay the night, Sandy?'

Alexander was momentarily at a loss. Perhaps on another night he might have been more eager to respond to this invitation, although he doubted that – his Catholic faith was something he was then taking quite seriously, and he had plans in that regard. As it was, he felt tired, and wished only to get home and go to bed. After a short, awkward silence, he replied, 'Frances, I can't. I don't think it would be a good idea.'

Their next few shifts together at the Bell were awkward. Frances could not avoid Alexander. She had to bring him her drinks orders to prepare. But by early the following week, Frances had quit her job at the Bell.

With the onset of the winter rains from early June, and gales in July and August, Alexander stripped Synchronicity's sails and stored them in the bow and stern compartments below. He lifted the outboard engine from the transom and stored it on the cabin sole. He doubled up the mooring cables. He knew that there would be occasional days of magical weather through the winter, days of light winds and sunshine. He intended sailing the Hunter on such days if he could. Between June and September he went for a sail four times in such conditions, once alone, twice with Andrew, and once with Roger, the young club member who had first befriended him. On each occasion the sun was shining and a light breeze was blowing. Apart from small wavelets, the sea was calm.

The short, wet, cold Cape winter was over by late September. The oak trees turned green again. The club again asked Alexander whether he would consider racing in the Hunter Europa class in the coming season. Again, Alexander declined. He had no wish to race. That was not why he went sailing.

While Alexander was always happy on the water, sometimes on dry land he felt a profound sense of separation from the rest of humanity, particularly when he was in a crowd. The farm was the exception; there, he was gathered up by his family's love, and gratified by Mike's friendship. Away from the farm, the only times he never felt lonely were when he went riding, or hiking in the mountains, and of course, when he went sailing. But at other times, even amidst a friendly group, such as that at the club bar, where he knew many people by now, he felt in some essential way removed from the company, as if there was a glass wall between them and him. Alexander was certain that he had a calling to the religious life, and he thought perhaps this sense of separation from his fellows would disappear once he had joined a religious order.

In October 1985 Alexander wrote to the Order of Friars Minor (better known as the Franciscans) in South Africa, asking whether they would accept him as a postulant next year. The Novice Master contacted Alexander's parish priest in Fish Hoek, and the latter must have supported Alexander's application, for in December, Alexander received a letter from the Franciscans, intimating that they would accept him as a postulant in February the following year. Aged thirty-one, Alexander would be five, even ten years older than most of the other novices.

In January, Alexander paid his annual membership and mooring fees at the FBYC. In February he said goodbye to the priest at Saint John the Evangelist in Fish Hoek . He said goodbye to Andrew too.

'Sandy, I can't pretend to understand what you're doing,' Andrew told him. 'But I hope you'll be happy. I'll miss you, my china.'

Alexander was touched to see that Andrew's eyes were moist and gleaming. On an impulse, he embraced his friend, who hugged him back.

Then, very early one morning, having said goodbye to his grandfather, to Mike, and to his cousins the evening before, and with his aunt standing watching, in her dressing gown, on the *stoep*, Alexander set off in his big car, long before the first lightening of the sky in the east, on what was going to be a very long drive to Ladysmith, in Natal, a few miles outside of which, near a tiny hamlet named Besters, the Order of Friars Minor had their novitiate located at that time.

Chapter Ten

The Novitiate

Saint Anthony's was a mission church due north of Ladysmith. The original buildings, about one hundred years old, were of beautifully cut and trimmed stone, with high ceilings and tall windows, and a row of ventilation windows just beneath the ceilings, to allow the trapped heat of the baking summers to escape. The church was an oddity. It had been built by Italian prisoners of war, and its façade was Italian baroque, with a scrolled central gable, pilasters either side, and symmetrical square towers at either corner, the whole plastered and painted white. You had to leave the Johannesburg – Durban highway to reach the mission. Not far beyond the mission was the Sand River, fringed with willow trees.

Alexander arrived at Saint Anthony's at about eleven o' clock that night. As he turned the engine off and got out of the car, his ears were ringing from the long journey. Otherwise, there was complete silence. Father Boniface, the Novice Master, who (with the other priests) would be waking again just before three a.m. to recite Matins, the first office of the day, awoke when Alexander knocked quietly at the door to his room, which opened off the veranda of the main house. He took Alexander to the kitchen,

Chapter Ten

and offered him some sandwiches and a mug of coffee. There was no one else around. Then Alexander was shown to his bare room in a red brick block. The room had plastered walls painted pale blue, a simple iron framed bed with a cotton counterpane on it, a rickety chest of drawers with an old wooden framed mirror sitting atop it, and a metal curtain rod spanning one corner of the room at shoulder height, with steel and plastic coat hangers hanging on it. There was a plain wooden desk, a grudgingly padded chair, and above the desk was a crucifix, our Lord gazing down with pity at this bleak environment. The window had a pair of thin, unlined, cotton print curtains either side. There was a single light bulb suspended from the ceiling, with a metal soup plate shaped shade above it. Below the crucifix was a wooden bookshelf, empty at present but for a Jerusalem Bible, a thick, heavy breviary, and a missal. Ablution and lavatory facilities were at the end of the corridor.

Alexander met the members of the community over breakfast at eight-thirty that morning, having had about six and a half hours' sleep. He had had to wake at six-thirty, for the office of Lauds, recited just after seven a.m., which was followed immediately by Prime, then the Mass, after which breakfast was served. There were four priests: the Father Guardian, who was in his fifties; a very ancient retired priest who had spent most of his life in Goa, whom Alexander took to – he was sweet and gentle, and as Alexander came to know him better, he often went for short walks with him, and listened to him talk about his life in India; then there was the Novice Master, Father Boniface, who was in his forties; and lastly, there was Father Joseph, a very fluent Zulu speaker, who (driving a Land Rover) undertook the bulk of the mission's pastoral work.

Alexander was one of four novices, one of whom was black. David, a Zulu from Eshowe in his mid twenties, was closest to Alexander in age, and would be going to the Seminary in Pretoria the following year. Alexander did not take to him. There was something sly in his smooth, clever features, in his sidelong glances. The youngest novice was a boy of eighteen, Timothy, who was also a postulant, having arrived to commence his novitiate just a week earlier, whilst Jeremy, who was a local lad (he had grown up in Ladysmith), was twenty years old, and had completed his postulancy the year before.

Alexander was aware that in joining the order he wished to escape the uncertainties, loneliness, and insecurities of life. But he believed that he acted in good faith, for he thought that he would make a good friar. Alexander was zealous by nature, wholehearted, and possessed of a powerful will. His determination to prove his vocation was to sustain him for nine months.

Father Boniface soon discovered that Alexander had a fine tenor voice, so he was appointed Precentor. He led the three sung offices of the day. There were eight daily offices making up the Liturgy of the Hours, or Divine Office, of which the young men attended seven. The first of the daily offices, Matins, was said only by the priests. Lauds and Prime, which were spoken, not sung, preceded the eight o' clock Mass. The three sung offices were Terce, at nine in the morning, then Sext, at noon (which was followed by lunch, then a while later by Nones at three o' clock), and Vespers, sung at six p.m. The Angelus was recited immediately after Nones, and the Angelus bell was rung. This was followed by tea and coffee, with sandwiches. After Vespers there was supper, then an hour's "recreation," when the whole community met in the priests' sitting room. There was general conversation, and Jeremy usually played some classical guitar. He played very well, and had a true but reedy voice. Alexander played chess with the old retired priest and with Jeremy. Compline, which was spoken, followed recreation, soon after eight p.m., and after Compline, silence was observed. The novices attended to their ablutions, then retired each to his own room, to read (and in theory, also to pray).

Chapter Ten

After Nones and the Angelus, Alexander would often take a walk with one or more of the other novices, following a sandy path alongside a field of *mielies*, until they reached the Sand River, there to sit on its banks beneath the willow trees for a while. One baking hot afternoon, Alexander and Jeremy walked to the river, and sat in the shade of a willow. They watched in silence the slow movement of the brown waters. Then, still staring at the river, Alexander began to declaim:

'*By the rivers of Babylon, there we sat down, yea, we wept, when we remembered Zion.*
We hanged our harps upon the willows in the midst thereof.'

'What Psalm number is that, Sandy?' asked Jeremy.
'Psalm one hundred and thirty-seven, I think. I don't remember who turned it into a popular song. Do you?'
'It was Boney-M,' Jeremy replied.
Only on Sundays was the routine broken, for at half past nine the main Sunday Mass was celebrated, which many of the local Zulu folk attended. This was celebrated in the Zulu language. Father Joseph was usually the main celebrant. Each week, one of the novices took it in turn to read the lessons in Zulu. When it was Alexander's turn to do so, he would spend part of the preceding Saturday afternoon reading the lessons aloud, the first few times in the company of a native Zulu speaker – the Zulu cook if she was available, or any one of the local people he had managed to waylay. Alexander did not ask David to hear him. After a while, it became established that Alexander would meet a Zulu lad aged about sixteen in the novices' recreation room every Saturday afternoon, because Alexander was keen to further the lessons in Zulu that he and the other two white novices were being taught once a week by Father Joseph. After three weeks had passed, the two began to meet in the open air, where it was cooler. They sat in the shade of

an acacia tree. The Zulu boy would tutor Alexander and correct his pronunciation, until he was satisfied that Alexander had it right. In return, Alexander would help the lad with his school work.

This youngster was being educated at the school run by the friars' sister community of Poor Clares, which was located not far from the novitiate. The lad's name was Dumisani, which means "Give praise (to God)." At this, the height of a roasting Natal summertime, Dumisani often wore just a pair of shorts, and he always went barefoot. He had a fine, spare physique, the colour of old, polished mahogany, and features of remarkable regularity. They were not the typical moon faced features of the majority of Zulus. In this heat, with temperatures reaching the lower thirties centigrade, Alexander wore only a hoodless brown Franciscan habit of thin cotton, belted at the waist. He wore open leather sandals on his bare feet. At his neck, beneath his habit, he wore a small silver crucifix on a chain which his distant cousin, the university chaplain, had given him. Alexander found himself looking forward to these Saturday afternoons.

'*Sawubona, Dumisani,*' he would greet the lad. '*Unjane?*'

'*Ngiyaphila ngiyabonga, Sandy. Unjane?*' and Dumisani's features would light up in a grin showing very white teeth.

But as time passed, Alexander began to miss the camaraderie of the Bell, and of the FBYC bar. He missed the joy of a close reach across False Bay in Synchronicity. He missed being a part of the many facetted lives of the people he had known. By comparison, the priests and novices at Saint Anthony's were almost childlike in their simplicity and limited experience of life. Alexander missed his friendship with Mike on the farm, and he missed Andrew, with whom he had worked at the Bell and who had so often crewed for him. And he missed his freedom. He thought about this, and he concluded that his vocation was not a genuine one. Sincere it was, but true, it was not. Had it been a genuine vocation, this life at Saint Anthony's should have satisfied him. It did not.

Chapter Ten

It was by now July, midwinter. The grass was sere and brown, and there was a heavy frost some mornings. The offices of Lauds and Prime in the unheated church in the very early mornings, followed by the Mass, were a mild torment to Alexander. He prayed, 'What shall I do?'

Alexander decided, if only for his pride's sake, not to quit yet. But by November, the air warm once again, the green things growing, he could no longer sustain the fiction of belief in his vocation. He went to see Father Boniface.

'I do not believe I have a vocation, Father,' he said. 'I made a mistake in coming here. I want to leave the novitiate.'

Father Boniface looked surprised. 'How long have you felt this way, Alexander?'

'Since at least the midwinter, Father,' Alexander replied. 'Perhaps I had a vocation once. But it's faded now.'

'Wont you stay longer, Alexander?' the Novice Master responded. 'We believe you may have a true vocation. You have not given yourself much time to test it.' Father Boniface, a heavy smoker, lighted a cigarette. 'Why do you think your vocation is not genuine?' he asked.

'I miss the world too much. I miss my old life. I shouldn't feel this way!'

'Stay at least until the end of the year, Alexander.'

'I really do wish to leave, Father.'

'Very well. We shall pray for you. When do you wish to go?'

'Tomorrow.'

Father Boniface looked pained. 'OK – if you come to see me in my office just after recreation this evening, I'll return the six hundred Rand you brought with you, and give you your car keys.'

Alexander had been keeping his car's battery charged, and checking the engine periodically, taking the car for a drive every ten days or so, but Father Boniface kept the car keys. That afternoon Alexander told Jeremy he was leaving the next morning.

'Oh Sandy!' Jeremy burst out. 'But why? Why are you leaving?'

'I don't think I have a true vocation, Jeremy. I'm pining after my old life too much. I should n't be missing it so much. I think the sooner I leave, the better.'

'I'll miss you, Sandy. We must stay in touch.'

'I'll miss you too, Jeremy, and we will stay in touch. I'll make sure of that.'

That evening in Father Boniface's office, Alexander insisted the mission keep back one hundred Rand. *'Pro amore Dei,'* he said.

At six o'clock the next morning, Alexander drank a coffee he had made in the kitchen. He had very little in his bag. He had arrived with very little nine months earlier, and he had acquired nothing since. He had already said goodbye to the other young men immediately following Compline the evening before. The Father Guardian had not spoken to him yesterday, nor had the Father Guardian been present in Father Boniface's office after recreation. A compound of shame and pride prevented Alexander from saying goodbye to the other priests.

Alexander drove all day, bypassing Durban, then on down the Natal South Coast and into Transkei, and by sundown he had still not crossed into the Western Cape. It was almost dawn before he pulled up at the farm. The return trip had taken him longer to complete than the journey north nine months earlier; he had stopped more frequently along the way, and for longer periods. His ears were ringing, and he was feeling dehydrated and lightheaded, but along with several barking dogs, his aunt had come out in her dressing gown to greet him. She hugged him, then took him through the silent house, and he felt tears prickle in his eyes as he saw the familiar furniture, paintings and ornaments; he was home again. He scratched the dogs behind their ears, and picked his way through the cats. His aunt went back to bed, and he had a large drink of water in the kitchen. Then he made himself a coffee and a sandwich, and took them out onto the *stoep*, where he smoked

Chapter Ten

a cigarette. The sun was just rising behind the windbreak of old pine trees. The sky through the tops of the trees was a fiery yellow, fading through diminishing tones into a pearlescent silver-grey which shaded into gunmetal, and between the bases of the pines, their trunks and branches dark silhouettes, he could see furnace-red. The cigarette felt dry and tasteless in his mouth. When he had drunk his coffee and eaten his sandwich, Alexander made his way back inside and used the lavatory, the glass of water having at last rehydrated him, then he went to bed in his tiny *stoep* extension room.

Chapter Eleven

A Death in the Family

A strong breeze was blowing when Alexander went out in Synchronicity two days later. He had reefed the mainsail and the roller reefing jib. He reveled in the sense of liveliness and motion. This was what he had been missing, a long way from the sea, during those baking hot, dry days in Natal. Alexander grinned at Andrew, who grinned back. They exchanged few words when they were sailing together. But later, over a couple of lagers in the club bar, Alexander caught up with Andrew's life, and chatted with one or two other members also. He was interested to see that Andrew had acquired a pretty brunette girlfriend during his absence, who arrived soon after they sat down at a table in the club bar. Andrew introduced her as Theresa.

'So you're Alexander?' the girl said. 'I'm pleased to meet you. You are some sort of a monk, aren't you?'

'I was a friar. Not anymore,' Alexander replied.

'It's the celibacy that would get me down,' she said, and smiled at Andrew. Andrew caught Alexander's eye, and his cheeks reddened slightly.

Chapter Eleven

On New Year's Day, 1st of January 1987, Alexander's grandfather died. He had been hospitalized for just over a week. It had been a subdued Christmas season at the farm. Alexander's father was at the bedside. He had driven down from Johannesburg, where Alexander's family had been living since early 1977. He had taken Alexander's room on the *stoep*. Alexander was sharing one of the wooden cabins with an Afrikaner lad named Hannes, a lieutenant in the South African Navy. He was an on-off boyfriend of Alexander's cousin, Jenny.

Alexander was not present when his grandfather died. Alexander had not been feeling very well on New Year's Day; he had been celebrating New Year's Eve at the FBYC bar the evening before. But when the telephone call from his aunt at the hospital came in the early afternoon, and his cousin, Mary, brought him the news, he felt suddenly very sober. Alexander was Rory's eldest grandchild, and the eldest son of Rory's only son. His grandfather (unlike his grandmother) had been a somewhat distant figure during much of Alexander's childhood, but Rory had mellowed as he had grown older, becoming gentle and thoughtful, and he and his grandson had often chatted together during 1985, and those periods of 1986 that Alexander had been at the farm. About a year earlier, sitting together on the *stoep*, Rory had suddenly, without preamble, said, 'Sandy, if there's ever anything wrong, something you want to talk about, you can tell me.'

There was so much that Alexander wished he could have shared with his grandfather, but he said nothing at all.

At the graveside at Muizenberg Cemetery (where Rory's remains were laid to rest alongside those of his wife, Alexander's grandmother, who had died thirteen years earlier), Alexander wished he had known his grandfather as well as his cousins had. He saw his father, always a man whose feelings were close to the surface, with tears running down his cheeks as the coffin was lowered into the ground, and he wished he were a better son to his father. But his feelings for his father were too overlaid with shame and guilt for him to show his father the sympathy and love he felt for him in that moment. Since his early twenties, Alexander had felt that he had let his father down badly, and this had made for a growing distance between the two of them. So he looked away, but his own eyes were moist.

Alexander had resumed his old job at the Golden Bell in Kalk Bay. Andrew no longer worked there, but they saw one another frequently at the yacht club, and Andrew often went sailing with Alexander. Alexander had made it clear that Andrew was to treat Synchronicity as if the boat were his own. But Andrew always asked him before going out for a sail – usually with his girlfriend. Seeing Andrew with this girl, Alexander felt loneliness, a condition that was rarely very far away, draw near to him. He resumed riding with Mike, whose quiet companionship he valued.

Towards the end of that year, Alexander began to feel a familiar restlessness. There was no reason to feel restless, unless it was that his present circumstances were too comfortable, and that his life felt aimless. He had some money saved. And there was the yacht, a potentially useful asset – but he felt he could not sell Synchronicity, unless it was to Andrew, for morally, she belonged as much to his friend as to himself.

In mid December, Alexander asked Charles, the family friend who had helped find him the yacht, to keep an eye on Synchronicity, and to let him know via his aunt if any expenses came up that Andrew could not meet. A week before Christmas 1987, Alexander said goodbye again to his aunt and uncle, to his cousins, to Mike, and to Andrew. He packed his belongings into the Rambler, and set off for Johannesburg, where his parents and brother lived. He covered close to one thousand miles in fifteen hours in the big car. As he drove through the Great Karoo, that stark, burning landscape, where the road ran arrow straight, forever disappearing into a constant heat shimmer on the horizon, he knew that he did not wish to leave Africa. Why then was he set on doing so? Why was he determined to do something that he feared would cause him much hurt? He had no answers to those questions.

Alexander stayed three weeks at his parents' home. His imminent departure for England cast a shadow over his time there. He was unaware of the unhappiness his restless spirit was causing his parents. His father asked his mother, one night as they were going to bed, 'Why is Sandy so restless, Livia? What is it that he's looking for?'

'He's searching for happiness, I think.'

'I don't understand! Why is he so unhappy?' his father exclaimed.

'I think he feels adrift in the world. I don't think he feels he belongs anywhere.'

'Does n't he know how much we love him?'

'I think he knows, but that's not enough.'

Alexander landed at Heathrow on the morning of 11th January 1988, at the height of the British winter. Did he yet recognise that he was endlessly perpetuating a pattern? Alexander wondered sometimes why he was never satisfied, never able to settle down and be content. He did not yet understand that he was constantly in flight, forever trying to flee not from circumstances – but from himself.

At times Alexander came close to understanding what kept him in constant motion. He believed that his periodic doubts over his sexuality were akin to the thorn in the flesh with which Saint Paul had been afflicted.* There were times when he feared he was forever to be denied lasting happiness; that he was laboring under a divine curse. He would be seized by anguish and despair, and he did not know how to bear it, except in flight.

It would be many years before Alexander understood that, no matter how far you flee, you cannot outdistance yourself.

---

* 2 Corinthians 12:7-8

Chapter Twelve

The Friary Arms

During 1980 Alexander had befriended a man about ten years his senior, whom he had met quite by chance one afternoon in a pub near Victoria station, and with whom he had fallen into conversation. Over time, Paul, who was short, dark and stocky, had taken him home to his flat near the Catholic cathedral in Westminster, to meet his wife. They had a young son, then aged about four or five years. The friendship had blossomed. Alexander liked Paul's wife, a plump, pretty, cheerful South African woman named Anneliese, a great provider of tasty meals and tempting snacks. He grew to be fond of the little boy, Peter, also. Alexander had always got on well with children. He was genuinely fond of them, unless they were horribly spoiled and badly misbehaved. Small children (and dogs) generally liked Alexander in return.

Paul too was from South Africa. He and Alexander would play several games of chess together during the course of an evening at Paul's flat, while talking and sipping at their glasses of whiskey. They shared an interest in metaphysics and theology. Paul was particularly influenced by the early twentieth century Austrian mystic and philosopher, Rudolf Steiner.

Chapter Twelve

'You should have gone to university, and studied philosophy,' Alexander told his friend.

'I've left it too late now. When I was younger, my family could n't afford it, and my matric results were n't good enough to get a bursary.'

During the mid 1980s, Paul and his family had left London for a small town named Berkhamsted in Hertfordshire, about an hour's drive from London, on the A4251 which ran north-west from the Watford Junction. Alexander had continued to maintain a correspondence with Paul.

Now, in January 1988, Paul had found Alexander a rent-free apartment at Kings Langley, a large village on the A4251, a few miles nearer London, but still surrounded by pretty countryside. Paul met Alexander at Heathrow. The bitter cold on Alexander's face as he stepped through the doors into the open at Heathrow and walked the short distance with Paul to his car in the parking garage, shocked him. He spent a night with Paul and Anneliese. The next day, he moved into a spacious first floor furnished bedsit, in one of the wings of an Edwardian mansion built in the Arts and Crafts style around a medieval core which housed the original hall and solar. The Friary, Kings Langley, sat atop the valley through which the Grand Union Canal ran; it had once been a religious house, then a crown property after the dissolution of religious foundations during the Reformation, then the possession of Henry VIII's final (and surviving) wife, Catherine Parr. Several families of school teachers now lived in the old house, which belonged to a private school adjacent to the property. The grounds comprised several meadows, some woodland, and an apple orchard (in which were rows of wooden beehives), and were home to a donkey and a nanny goat. Farm lands adjoined on two sides, the private school on the third side, and the village and Langley Hill road on the fourth. Diagonally opposite the gates to the house was a pub, the Friary Arms, which Alexander was to get to know rather too well.

The bedsit comprised a very large single room, with a kitchen alcove at one end. It was lighted by a continuous range of windows which ran across the front of the room. It shared a front door downstairs with a similar bedsit below (which was currently unoccupied), and was reached via a wide flight of stairs alongside the ground floor parlor-hall, a staircase which gave access not only to Alexander's bedsit, but to a guest bedroom and to the first floor solar, a beautiful space within the original medieval core, poorly lighted by a number of narrow lancet windows set deep within the thick stone walls. This room had a vast open fireplace, the twin of the walk-in fireplace in the parlor-hall below, and a wonderful oaken hammer beam roof. Alexander's bathroom and lavatory were on the ground floor, down the wide staircase and along a short corridor. It was an odd arrangement, because the lavatory and bathroom were shared by the guest bedroom and by the ground floor bedsit, and the lavatory itself was also used by the members of the nonconformist congregation which met in the upstairs solar for church services on Sunday mornings. Alexander's walk to the lavatory on a winter's night was a long and a cold one. The medieval core and the adjacent Edwardian additions alongside it, including Alexander's bedsit, had no heating but for the two big open fireplaces.

During his first few months at the Friary, with snow drifts piled high in the narrow lanes surrounding the property well into March, Alexander, who had only a small electric fan heater to warm his bedsit, would often sleep in front of the fire in the parlor-hall downstairs, an old duvet laid on the wooden floorboards like a futon, two more duvets on top of him. The winter of '87 – '88 was an unusually severe one, and, like a rural black peasant in South Africa, Alexander often smelled of woodsmoke.

Downstairs, a door gave onto a small, overgrown lawn and a wild wooded area behind the house, the woods comprising old established beech, oak and ash trees, and along its fringes there grew younger trees and saplings and a riot of brambles and nettles. There was much fallen timber, and Alexander foraged this timber, building up a large woodpile in an outhouse a little way along. That winter he kept the fire glowing all night, and he built it up again during the day. The fire was welcomed by the church congregation on Sunday mornings, for they met for tea and coffee and gossip in the parlor-hall after their church service upstairs.

Alexander's bedsit was rent-free, but in return he was expected to keep the solar-come-church and the guest bedroom upstairs clean, as well as the parlor-hall downstairs, and the public spaces, comprising the entrance hall, the wide staircase, the lavatory, and a tiny cubicle off the hall in which were a tea urn, a kettle, a countertop, a sink, and some crockery and cutlery in the cupboards and drawers. He began by spending two or three hours every Saturday attending to these duties. He was, as time went by, and drinking became an important element of his life, to prove not always very reliable in this obligation.

In March Alexander began working at Reiters, an international news agency in Fleet Street, London, commuting by train. He called in at the Friary Arms on his way home from work in the evenings, usually ordering a meal, his main meal of the day, and, from the late morning onwards, he spent a lot of time there on Saturdays and Sundays, eating his lunch there. The publican, a man in his thirties, and his wife, soon came to value Alexander's custom: one way or another, he spent a lot of money at the pub each week.

It was soon after moving into the Friary, one Saturday afternoon, that Alexander had visited the Friary Arms for the first time. The public bar was busy, and smelled of beer, tobacco, damp clothes and smoke from the coal fire. He went through to the saloon bar, which, like the public bar, had a fire burning in the grate. Here he found only half a dozen customers, all of whom were men.

'Good afternoon,' he sang out. Two or three of the men in the saloon bar responded in public school accents not dissimilar to Alexander's own. (In Britain, confusingly, private schools are known as public schools). One of these men, who had a short, stocky build and a smooth, clever face, and who was wearing a tweed jacket and a cravat, was quick to introduce himself to Alexander as Rupert, and shook his hand. He was quick also, in fairly short order, to interrogate Alexander, clearly trying to place him within the village social structure.

'Do you live locally, Sandy?'

'I live across the road, at the Friary.'

'Oh – you're on the staff at the school?'

'No,' Alexander smiled. 'What about you? Are you local?'

'I live just around the corner,' Rupert replied. 'May I ask – are you working locally?'

'I'm starting work in March,' Alexander replied, 'at Reiters in Fleet Street. What about you, Rupert? What sort of work do you do?'

'I'm an importer of gourmet foods from France,' Rupert replied. 'What sort of job do you have at Reiters?'

'I'm a business researcher. I specialise in sub-Saharan Africa,' Alexander replied.

'What qualifications do you need in that field, Sandy?' Rupert asked him.

'None, in my case. They offered me the job because I have an honours degree from a South African university, and because my boss believes – so he told me – that humanities graduates have the right skills and temperament to undertake research, analysis and evaluation.'

Alexander was drinking a Guinness. He took a draught from it, then asked 'Where did you go to school, Rupert?'

'Harrow. What about you?'

'I went to school in South Africa.'

Rupert smiled. 'You don't sound South African.'

Alexander laughed. 'That's true. Not everyone in South Africa does.'

Chapter Twelve

Over time, Alexander came to realise that Rupert did very little importing of gourmet foods, but lived largely off his wife's earnings. She was a chartered accountant in Hemel Hempstead, the big town not very far away. Rupert was almost always to be found at the Friary Arms when Alexander called in there. Alexander felt a measure of reserve in sharing too much about himself with Rupert. There was something slightly off kilter about friend Rupert. However, he made an amusing drinking companion.

Alexander met other local people at the Friary Arms. One of these became a good friend. Max, who was tall with craggy features, thick black eyebrows and iron grey hair which he swept back from a high forehead, dropped in most early evenings, and on weekend afternoons, with his two Irish wolfhounds. He was in his early fifties. He had been born in Germany a few years before the War. He had a nice house a couple of hundred yards away, and he was married to a staff nurse working at the hospital in Hemel Hemsptead. They had a son in his very early twenties, a regular drinker at the Friary Arms, through whom Alexander came to know a young crowd; local lads and some girls, and with one exception they were friendly and open, accepting him at face value. The exception was a young man with saturnine, scornful good looks, who made it clear he did not like Alexander. Sometimes he greeted Alexander in a mock posh accent. Too bad, Alexander thought: his accent was not an affectation, even if the assumptions it gave rise to (that he was English, and public school educated) were not in his case true.

Throughout the remaining months of winter, Alexander drank every day. He drank not just a couple of glasses of Guinness, either: early on he took to drinking rum and blackcurrant cordial, three or four tots of rum an evening at the Friary Arms. He soon discovered that he could consume very large quantities of spirits without becoming noticeably drunk. Instead he felt happier in his own skin; less conscious of a semi opaque wall between himself and the rest of mankind. Alcohol seemed to deliver Alexander for a while from the curse of intense self awareness. Working in London, he had fallen happily into the remnants of Fleet Street's hard drinking culture, left over from a time when all the big dailies were published in Fleet Street, and the street had been full of hard-drinking journalists and hacks. At lunchtime he would have one or two beers at the White Swan, or at Cogers, both located within the actual Reiters building, on the ground floor. The entrance to the White Swan faced Saint Bride's, while Cogers was accessed via Salisbury Square around the back of the building. After work, he would walk to Covent Garden at least twice a week, to drink in the small upstairs bar in a pub in Maiden Lane. This first floor bar was very theatre, with a personable young barman serving behind the counter. There were several big comfortable leather upholstered chairs in the upstairs bar, and a wide sofa covered in plum coloured velvet, and stacks of newspapers and periodicals on a table, and framed theatre posters on the wall. There was a small gas fired, artificial coal fire in the grate in the Victorian fireplace. The room, which was lighted by two big sash windows, rarely held more than a dozen customers. The atmosphere was more that of a club than a pub. All the regulars knew each other.

 Here, Alexander would down a couple of pints of Guinness and as many whiskey chasers, before even making his way to Euston Station by Underground, where he caught the train to Kings Langley. Before reaching home he would stop in at the Friary Arms, switching to rum and blackcurrant cordial. His alcohol intake every day those last few months of winter was considerable. He rapidly became first psychologically, then over time, physically addicted to liquor. He preferred never to have to be fully sober, if he could avoid it, for when he began to sober up, he felt the stirrings of mild discomfort, and if he waited too many hours before having a stiff drink, his unease and agitation of mind became acutely uncomfortable.

Chapter Twelve

This then is what happened to Alexander during those first few months of 1988. He became a practicing, rather than merely latent, alcoholic. His destiny had caught up with him at last. It was a cruel destiny, which would cause him great suffering, and would eventually come very close to killing him.

Edwin Lutyens, the acclaimed architect who, along with Herbert Baker, left his mark on so much of the British Empire, had designed the Reiters building in Fleet Street in 1935. Reiters had moved into it in 1939, just before the outbreak of the Second World War. Above the main entrance was a large recessed roundel set in the stonework, in which was a bronze figure of "Fame," a winged figure seated astride a globe, blowing a trumpet. The *Daily Telegraph*, one of Britain's leading national dailies, was located just down the street, in a fine building named Peterborough Court. It had not yet made the move to Canary Warf (and the much later move to Victoria, near Buckingham Palace). The *Daily Mail*, the *Express* titles, and some other publications, were still located in Fleet Street. But Fleet Street had been in decline ever since Rupert Murdoch had vacated his papers' premises in Fleet Street and moved the *Times* and the *Sunday Times* to Wapping in 1986 (and in so doing, broken the printers' unions). None the less, Fleet Street retained its tawdry, dynamic and boozy mystique, and it still meant something to say you worked in Fleet Street.

Each weekday morning, Alexander caught the train for Euston, London, at Kings Langley. At Euston he got on the south-bound Northern Line, and six stops later, he changed at Embankment onto the District or Circle lines east-bound, one stop to Temple, or two stops to Blackfriars, from either of which he would walk for about ten minutes to the Reiters offices in Fleet Street. He spent three hours a day in total on his commuting to and from work. He had, as a consequence, little time to cook in his kitchenette, generally eating instead at the Friary Arms. He struggled to find time to do his laundry, usually leaving it for the weekend. But aged only thirty-three, he was at the peak of his physical fitness, and it would be many years before his drinking affected either his stamina or his surprisingly good health. He did not even catch a cold that winter.

Alexander, with Max advising him, bought himself a *mobilette,* a two-stroke, 49cc pedal-scooter with automatic transmission. To start the motor, you pedaled the machine a short distance before the engine fired and took over. Alexander's machine did not have the tiny, wobbly wheels of many mopeds, but the relatively large wheels of the true Continental *mobilette,* which made for a safer, more stable, more comfortable ride. Behind the single saddle was a lidded box for carrying your shopping and whatever. The scooter's top speed was about twenty-eight miles an hour with the wind behind it. It was painted scarlet. Alexander loved this machine and kept it protected when not in use by a plasticized canvas tailor-made cover. On weekends, with the arrival of spring, he would ride for many miles down the narrow country lanes and into the Chiltern Hills, exploring the countryside. He was now able to ride to Paul and Anneliese at their Berkhamsted home. He also used the scooter to visit a German family a few miles away who had befriended him. Alexander had met them via Paul and Anneliese. This family lived in a large, sprawling, contemporary ranch-style house up a narrow country lane. There were two little boys, aged ten and twelve, their boxer dog, their cat, and various rabbits and hamsters. Their father, a tall, lean, good looking man with fair hair, who was in his early forties, was the managing director of the British subsidiary of a German engineering firm. Their mother, also fair haired, had an elegant, long narrow face. Her two sons attended the private school next door to which Alexander lived. Paul and Anneliese sent their son, Peter, to this same school.

The ten year old German boy was named Friederich, and was known as Freddy, and his older brother was Wilhelm, or Bill. They spoke English with a native middle class English accent, for they had lived in England since they were toddlers. Both had hair the colour of flax, and both were already tanned by the sunshine of late spring. They were skinny, very active little boys. Freddy was county squash champion for his age group. He was the more open of the two boys, and with his bright smile and flashing eyes he quickly became Alexander's favourite. Bill was more reserved; Alexander sometimes felt that Bill did not altogether approve of him. Freddy and Alexander played chess together sometimes. Freddy almost always beat Alexander. The brothers enjoyed riding Alexander's scooter up and down their long driveway. Sometimes Alexander was invited to dinner with the family, and after dinner he would read to Freddy (Bill felt he was too old to be read to), who sat on the sofa alongside Alexander, his legs folded beneath him, his slim body shoved up hard against Alexander, completely engrossed in the story.

Thrice that summer, Alexander rode his *mobilette* into Hemel Hempstead and padlocked it to the cycle rack at the bus station, where he caught a bus into Oxford. He enjoyed exploring the old university town, with its medieval, narrow lanes and ancient buildings; its many churches and church steeples; its dozens of belfries which, on the hour and the half and the quarter hours, would set up a great and varied chiming across the city. He enjoyed walking down Christ Church Meadow Walk alongside the River Cherwell, then along the left bank of the Thames (which in Oxford was known as the Isis), past the moored houseboats of the college rowing clubs, then up Poplar Walk, and back along Broad Walk towards the Botanic Gardens. And Alexander, who had read so much about student life at Oxford when he lived thousands of miles away in South Africa, hired a punt on each of these three visits and taught himself to handle a punt very capably on the river. Alexander was to return many times to Oxford in years to come, although no longer alone on those later occasions.

Alexander was far from discontented then, that summer of 1988. Yet, despite his contentment, his drinking increased. At work, Alexander would arrive with a double whiskey already under his belt. While he worked through the course of the morning, he forgot about the need for a drink until about midday, but he waited until lunchtime at one o'clock before leaving the building, then entering the White Swan (his favourite of the two pubs located within the ground floor of the Reiters building), where he drank one or two halves of Guinness and a whiskey chaser. He found the later afternoons in the office would begin to drag, and his focus would begin to waver by four o'clock, when he felt a growing need for a drink. He held out until five o'clock, when he had a quick double whiskey in the White Swan downstairs, before making his way either to Euston Station, or to the first floor bar in Maiden Lane. If he chose to go straight on home after work, he would always stop at the Friary Arms and drink a Guinness with his supper, and then a double rum and cordial, often another double after that. Only if he was very late returning from London would he go straight up to his bedsit, and later he would have a generous whisky or two. He kept a bottle of whiskey in his bedsit.

It became difficult by the end of summer for Alexander to keep secret his dependence on alcohol, for there was always a hint of the sweet stench of liquor about him. His faculties were not generally impaired: he did not behave as if he were intoxicated, but the tube of toothpaste he had taken to keeping in his pocket, from which he would periodically squeeze a hefty dollop into his mouth and work it around his palate, only partially disguised the stink of liquor. Inevitably, people around the top village became aware that he was a heavy drinker, and as the old house and the private school dominated the top village, this awareness was gossiped about and took wings and flew. Neither Paul and Anneliese, nor his German friends, proved as welcoming as before.

In mid September, Alexander's line manager, Nick, asked him to step into his office one day.

Chapter Twelve

'I do not want to stick my nose into your personal life, Sandy,' Nick began (and Alexander knew immediately what the topic of this talk was going to be), 'But I suspect you may be struggling a little with your drinking.'

'Are you dissatisfied with my work?' Alexander asked.

'No . . .' Nick replied, 'Your work is good. But there is talk . . .'

'Nick, I assure you, I do not have a problem I'm not on top of,' Alexander responded. But he knew that he was no longer in control of his drinking. Recently, he had taken to keeping a half-jack of whiskey in his brief case, and he had resorted to having a quick slug at his desk mid-morning and mid-afternoon.

Alexander was very bright, and drink had not dulled his intuition. By October that year he knew his time was fast running out – both at the Friary, and at Reiters. He went to see his line manager.

'Nick, if I offer you my resignation, would you give me a decent reference? My work is good – you've said so yourself.'

The manager looked thoughtful, then nodded. 'I'll do that, if you hand in your resignation by the end of the day, effective immediately.'

So Alexander walked away from the Reiters building that late afternoon of Tuesday 11th October, unemployed. His final paycheck would be posted to him within a few days, as would his reference. Alexander needed a drink. He began walking to Maiden Lane.

It was shortly after midnight before Alexander got back to his bedsit in Kings Langley. He was rather drunk. He had met almost no traffic as he rode up from the station on his *mobilette*, which he forgot to cover against the elements. He sat in that cold room, the fan heater blowing, and felt emptied of emotion. He fell asleep beneath the duvet, his clothes still on. But he had drunk a big glass of water first, and he had removed his shoes.

Chapter Thirteen

Paris

Alexander entered into that state of mind that distress, and a sense that his options had run out, always induced in him: an acute state of unreality, and he chose this moment to visit an acquaintance of his who lived in Paris. The October days were still sunny and warm. He hoped the weather was much the same in Paris. He had met Raimond at the Salisbury pub during summer. They had continued to bump into each other over a period of several weeks. Raimond, a little younger than Alexander, had been working in London during June and July, a member of the stage crew of a French theatrical production. He had invited Alexander to spend a weekend with him at his flat in *l'onzième Arrondissement*, near the *Père Lachaise* cemetery. Alexander telephoned him, using the public telephone outside the Friary Arms. Having told Raimond that he hoped to arrive in Paris before midnight of Friday 14th, Alexander arranged to hire a car from the National Car Hire branch on the A4251. He would be using the first credit card he had ever possessed.

Max dropped Alexander off at the car hire branch on his way to work on Friday morning. The Ford Mondeo's headlamps had been fitted with yellow Perspex covers which redirected the main beams slightly to the right. French cars then had yellow headlights. Alexander reached Dover in the early afternoon, and, although he had been sipping from a half-jack of whiskey during the long drive down, he navigated the complex lanes system without mishap, and was waved through immigration control. He rolled onto the ferry at about three o' clock. It was only many years later, when he was growing old, and a journey like that would have frightened him, that he came to realise how bold he must have been, undertaking such an epic journey alone, and for the first time – and far from sober at the time. Alexander's only Channel crossing so far had been in an old Mercedes bus with a friend of his from Cape Town in early July 1976, aboard a giant hovercraft. On that occasion they had been making for Pamplona, in northern Spain, for the *Fiesta de San Fermín*. This was the running of the bulls festival (popularised by Ernest Hemingway in his book, *The Sun Also Rises*), that attracted young backpackers and campers from across Europe and beyond.

At Calais, driving on the right hand side of the road, Alexander set off for Paris. It took him almost four hours, with one motorway halt for coffee and a visit to the lavatory, to reach Paris. It was now growing dark. Alexander was approaching Paris from the north. At the junction with the *Boulevard Périphérique* he turned left, and followed the *Périphérique* around Paris to the east, until he reached the turn off to the *Cours de Vincennes*, which led into Paris. At the huge traffic roundabout of the *Place de la Nation*, where Alexander wished to turn north into the *avenue Philippe-Auguste*, his somewhat addled and exhausted wits deserted him momentarily, and instead of turning right into the roundabout, following the traffic flow anti-clockwise, he turned left, and proceeded half way round the circle against the oncoming traffic. Cars swerved, the finger was given, epithets were hurled at him (*"Espèce d'un cochon!"* and *"Sale Anglais!"* were just two of these), and it was with great relief that he swung left into the *avenue Philippe-Auguste*, making sure to get into the right hand lane. Raimond's flat was near the *Père Lachaise* cemetery. It was not far now.

'*Sandy – Bienvenue!*' Raimond declared. '*Comment allez-vous? Le voyage à-t-il été bon? Voulez-vous peut-être un café et un sandwich?*' Raimond, who was in his socks, and was wearing narrow black jeans and a canary yellow sweatshirt, embraced his British friend, kissing him on both cheeks. Alexander returned the embrace, but refrained from kissing Raimond. He would have felt much more comfortable with a firm handshake.

After a very welcome coffee, which the Frenchman made in a Lavazza stove top pot, and a sandwich, Raimond and Alexander sat on the sofa, with background music playing softly, and drank some of the wine that Alexander had bought at the ferry's duty free shop. There was only a large double bed in Raimond's tiny flat, which the two men had to share. Alexander, exhausted by the day's stressful journey and the large amount of liquor he had been drinking through the day, fell asleep almost as soon as he lay down. In the morning, over coffee and warm croissants with *confiture*, Raimond, who was an easy-going, rather thin young man, asked Alexander what he would like to see in Paris.

'I don't know Paris at all,' Alexander replied. 'I would like to visit *Notre-Dame*. Oh – and the Jim Morrison tomb in *Père Lachaise*. But I'm in your hands.'

'You are in my hands?' Raimond responded with a naughty grin. '*Quel merveilleux*! OK – this morning we will visit *le Père Lachaise* for Jim Morrison, and then *Notre-Dame*, and perhaps a walk in *Le Marais*. *Le Marais* is a preserved *quartier*, with old merchant houses of the sixteenth, seventeenth and eighteenth centuries, and many *cafés* and bars of atmosphere.'

'I shall enjoy that, I'm sure.'

The sun was not shining. It was in fact rather cool, with a light drizzle. However, Alexander had brought with him his long Aquascutum tweed overcoat – very stylish, without padded shoulders – which had cost him three hundred Pounds at the Aquascutum shop in Regent Street earlier that year. He wore dark woolen trousers with a pleated waist, and turn ups. His shoes were almost new, bespoke brown leather brogues by Lobbs, which he had been given by a paternal great-uncle in the Cotswolds, whose narrow Maclean feet were identical in shape and size to those of his great-nephew. He wore a dark brown fedora hat which, like his trousers, he had bought at a shop in Sloane Street. Beneath his overcoat he wore a dark brown woolen jacket. He had acquired several cravats, and he wore one now, and around his neck was a lightweight woolen Rupert Bear scarf. He felt he was adequately dressed for the weather, and during the weekend he came to feel at least as elegant as the stylish young Frenchmen like Raimond whom he was to see so often in Paris. Young *Parisiens*, Alexander was quick to notice, dressed rather more elegantly than did their counterparts in London.

Alexander (so bereft was his adolescence of the cultural interests of his peers) had never heard of Jim Morrison until Alice began to educate him in rock music. When he had first heard *Riders on the Storm*, he had been enthused. Later, he had watched Francis Ford Coppola's movie, *Apocalypse Now*, with Jim Morrison's atmospheric and doom laden track *The End* as a visual-oral image he did not think he would ever forget. Alexander had of course read Joseph Conrad's *Heart of Darkness* (the novel which inspired the movie *Apocalypse Now*), while he was still at school. That Jim Morrison was both a beautiful and a tragic figure, only twenty-eight years old when he died in 1971, added to his music's appeal for Alexander.

But Jim Morrison's tomb came as a terrible shock to Alexander. It was rather small and insignificant, to be sure, although the bust of Jim Morrison's head was well done, but it was thoroughly defaced with graffiti and a garish amateur paint job. With the candles stuck in their own wax, and the empty wine bottles with flowers in them, arranged at its base, Alexander thought the tomb looked like a Voodoo shrine. Although he said a prayer for the repose of Jim Morrison's soul, he was glad not to linger.

'Let us hope *Notre-Dame* is not also spoiled,' he remarked.

On later visits to Paris, Alexander was to visit *Notre-Dame de Paris* again, which had not disappointed him on this, his first visit. They had coffees, salads and a *croque-monsieur* each at a *café* in *Le Marais*. By then, the drizzle was coming down quite heavily, and it was mid afternoon, so they returned to Raimond's flat. In the evening they walked less than a hundred yards to a *brasserie* where Alexander ate a simple and very good supper of green beans fried in oil with buttered potatoes, accompanying a couple of grilled trout, followed by a cheese platter. (Because Alexander tried to avoid eating cow's cheese, which disagreed with him, and he had already had more than he should at lunchtime, he had asked the waiter to point out the *fromage de chèvre*). They shared a carafe of house white during the meal, followed by an excellent coffee.

On Sunday morning Alexander and Raimond visited *Les Halles*, a vast modern retail development located where the old fresh produce market of Paris had once stood. Here, Raimond wished them to enter a shop selling pornography, but Alexander said, *'Non, merci – Je ne l'aimerais pas,'* and so they passed the shop by. They walked to the *Centre Pompidou*, and Alexander, now feeling ready to find fault with the rest of the day, was struck by how ugly the building looked, with its angular exoskeleton on display. The sun came out, and they had an unmemorable light lunch sitting outside a café, opposite the *Centre Pompidou*. During the afternoon, Raimond and Alexander walked through the streets of *Montmartre*, a quarter far removed in character from the grand boulevards of central Paris. *Montmartre* retained its small town atmosphere. The two men had taken the

Funiculaire to the top of the hill. There they entered *le Sacré-Coeur*, and walked around the impressive, soaring basilica, built in a dramatic Romano-Byzantine style. Alexander was struck by the huge mosaic work of Christ in Majesty above the apse, full of scintillating colours. Standing on the terrace outside (for the rain had stopped, and a weak sun now illuminated the city), Alexander gazed across Paris laid out below, with the distant landmarks of *Notre-Dame*, *la Tour Eiffel*, and the gleaming gilded dome of *l'Église du Dôme* clearly visible.

'*C'est magnifique, oui?*' Raimond commented.

'*Oui, c'est une très belle ville,*' Alexander replied. His mood had improved. That afternoon's exploration of *Montmartre*, and yesterday morning's visit to *Notre-Dame* had certainly been the highlights of Alexander's weekend in Paris. But he was to enjoy far happier visits to Paris in years to come.

Alexander drank, sipping from a newly opened half-jack of whiskey, on the long drive back to Calais, the effects of the liquor only partially ameliorated by the two strong coffees he had on the ferry. Alexander was still sipping from the whiskey bottle as he drove from Dover to Kings Langley that Monday evening. He passed out on his bed at about ten-thirty that night. He was awake again by the cold early hours; he needed a pee. After the trek to the downstairs lavatory, and back to his room afterwards, he lighted a cigarette, drank some more whiskey, then slept again.

Alexander awoke at eight the next morning. He felt dreadful, and his head was hurting. The room felt very cold. He turned the fan heater on, went downstairs to the lavatory, then drank two glasses of water, accompanied by 500 milligrams of paracetamol, followed by two cups of black coffee with plenty of sugar, in which were stirred a generous tot of whiskey each (for Alexander knew from experience that hair of the dog was essential, if he was not to suffer a severe hangover. What, after all, was a hangover, except a need for more liquor?)

As he sipped at his coffee, strengthened with a hefty tot of whiskey, Alexander felt an overwhelming sense of failure crash like a breaker over him, and threaten to drag him out into the deep waters. It was time to face up to reality.

But what he said aloud was, 'I want to go home.'

Chapter Fourteen

Fame and Fortune

Alexander took an evening flight for Johannesburg on Thursday 20th October. He had sold his *mobilette* to his friend Max, who wanted it for his son. Max drove him to Heathrow. Alexander felt a tremendous sense of deliverance, the shedding of what had recently become a heavy burden of loneliness, exile and defeat, as he landed at Jan Smuts Airport in Johannesburg on Friday morning. He had drunk no alcohol during the twelve hour flight, nor during the couple of hours of check-in and waiting at Heathrow. This was the longest period he had gone without a drink since springtime that year. His father and mother were waiting at Jan Smuts Airport to meet him. It was early summer in South Africa. At home, Alexander was delighted to see the old family cat, Lulu, still alive, although very frail. She was aged twenty-one now. Alexander's mother was clearly happy he was back. Of his father's views, Alexander was less certain. It had been a long time since Alexander had felt entirely easy with his father. This saddened him, and he knew by now that the fault was his, more than it was his father's. He remembered how he had loved his father when he was a little boy.

'I don't want to live in England again, Dad,' he told his father. 'I don't seem to be very lucky in England. Perhaps that's because it's not my home.'

'You were always set on living in England, ever since you were a teenager,' Alexander's father responded. 'But you're right. It is n't our home.'

Alexander's brother, Roy, was living not far from their parents' home. 'I missed you, Sandy,' Roy told his older brother. 'I'm glad you're back.'

'Thanks Roy. I don't seem to make the right choices anymore. I hope I can make this one work.'

Alexander, at the age of thirty-three, was now living with his parents again. This shamed him. But he vowed to himself that he would change this as soon as he could. It was his mother who, about a week after his return, suggested that he approach a TV casting agency for roles in television commercials. Alexander looked through the Yellow Pages, and telephoned an agency not too far away. The agency was impressed with him, assuring him that the cameras would love him. Within less than half an hour after his arrival at the casting agency, they had lined up an audition for him for the following morning. By noon the next day, he had landed a role featuring in a TV commercial which was to be shot the following week. By the end of January the following year, Alexander was to have featured in three more TV commercials, one of them for the original client.

Alexander earned two thousand Rand for his first shoot. Roy was impressed.

'You earned as much in a day as I earn in two weeks!' Roy exclaimed.

'Yeah, but you have a steady income. Who knows when I'll next earn anything?'

With his fee, Alexander bought a second hand Audi, the latest but one luxury model with the two litre, five cylinder, electronic ignition and fuel injection engine, with automatic transmission and an air conditioner. He bought the car at a substantial discount below the list price, via the good offices of a cousin who worked for BP in Johannesburg, who was able to pass on one of the BP time-expired company fleet Audis to him for only one thousand eight hundred Rand. Alexander was delighted with this car. The big old AMC Rambler, which had always been registered in Alexander's father's name, had at last been sold by his parents during his absence in England. A car was essential in South Africa, far more so than in England.

By the end of that year, Alexander was able to put down six months' rent for a very comfortable, partially furnished flat in Bellevue, with a wonderfully ancient cast iron white enameled mains gas cooker in the kitchen and a rather more contemporary washing machine. Bellevue is an old suburb located between Hillbrow and Yeoville, consisting of single story houses dating back to the late 1920s, and low-rise, often art deco, apartment blocks of the 1930s. The lease was to commence on January 8th, 1989.

By late January 1989, Alexander had acquired a limited and passing fame. He was sometimes recognised and stared at in shopping malls, and once a group of giggling teenage girls approached him, and one of the girls asked him for his autograph.

'OK,' Alexander said to the pretty, dark haired girl. 'What's your name?'

'Charmaine.'

He wrote in the small note book she handed to him, with the ballpoint pen she provided, *"To Charmaine, with love from Sandy, the Château Liberté Wine Man."* He added a couple of Xs after these words.

Alexander hardly registered his maternal grandmother's death in London on the 7th January, although he had loved her very much. It was the old cat, Lulu's death, only two days earlier, at the age of twenty-one, that knocked Alexander off his feet. She had become very frail and thin and unsteady on her legs, and she had clearly been suffering from pain through December of 1988, and on the 5th January, with Alexander and his mother the only family members at home, he could not bear to think of the darling old puss suffering any longer.

'Mum, we've got to call the vet to have her put to sleep. It's not fair on her. She's helpless: she relies on us to do the right thing for her.'

His mother began to cry. Alexander put his arm around her and hugged her, then made for the telephone. Lulu was put to sleep at home in Alexander's arms. Afterwards, weeping silently, he wrapped the pathetic old body in her favourite blanket, and went into the garden and dug a hole of about three feet in depth, and as his mother stood watching, also weeping, he laid the cat's body in the grave and covered her up. As he did so, he experienced a painful flashback: a recollection of burying the family cat, Simba, in the garden in Cape Town when he was a boy; poor Simba, who had been stoned to death. Alexander felt profoundly distressed.

'Let's go for a walk,' his mother said. 'I cant stay in the house right now.'

'That's a good idea.'

Alexander drove the two of them to the Botanic Gardens above Emmarentia Dam, a few miles from the house, and here they walked for over an hour, plump white cumulus clouds progressing slowly across a vast Highveld sky above them. The birds were calling and the wind blew gently in the trees. They spoke very little to one another.

Alexander, his brother, and his mother (and in fact, Alexander's father also, despite his being essentially a dogs person) were grieving for Lulu when, two days later, the family received news that Alexander's maternal grandmother had died in her sleep at the old age home in Wimbledon.

'Oh, Mum!' declared Alexander. He embraced his mother. 'I loved Granny very much. I used to enjoy visiting her in Wimbledon.'

'I know you did. You were good to her. Mum had a very full life, and she was very old. You mustn't worry for me, Sandy. I know how Lulu's death is causing you so much unhappiness.'

Alexander was supposed to be moving into his flat in Bellevue, but he put off doing so. His grief for Lulu was excessive, he knew. It overshadowed the grief he might have been feeling for the last of his grandparents. Perhaps it was that with both Lulu and his grandmother gone, he felt the last of his childhood slipping away. He found that his left chest hurt painfully. He had begun to drink again after his first few weeks back in South Africa, keeping a bottle of whiskey in the servant's room across the back courtyard, which he had kitted out as a study. He kept some of his books there, and he had an oscillating fan, a typewriter, a radio, a desk and a chair. His mother no longer wanted a resident black domestic servant, so the room was Alexander's to use. His drinking had not become out of hand, but the day he and his mother had Lulu put to sleep, he ceased to drink. This, he felt, was to honour the old cat's memory. About a week after Lulu's death, he told his parents he was going to drive down to the farm.

'I need a complete change of scene. I'm doing myself no good here right now.'

Alexander left the next day at one in the morning. He had had only three hours' sleep, but he felt strangely alert. He had already passed Bloemfontein by breakfast time, but he did not stop. Soon after crossing the Orange River into the Cape Province, he reached Colesberg, which marked the start of the semi-arid Karoo, where the widely spaced sheep ranches each incorporated thousands of hectares in extent. It was now late morning. In Colesberg he stopped for petrol and he used the lavatory. He also bought a late breakfast at the service stop. He drove through the Karoo in the heat of the day, using the air conditioner periodically. The road ran dead straight for mile after mile, never quite reaching the far horizon which shimmered under the burning sun. If the road altered direction, the alteration was fractional, and another lengthy straight stretch commenced. In the early afternoon Alexander passed Beaufort West, and later, Touws River, having at last traversed the stark Karoo, after which the road began to run between ranges of jagged hills. His spirits rose as he ate up the distance at a steady one hundred and twenty kilometers an hour (seventy-four miles an hour). He drove through the lovely Hex River Valley, with its vineyards and sharp mountain peaks, and at the top of Du Toit's Kloof Pass he stopped again, relieved himself behind some scrub growth, and gazed across to the tiny, distant profile of Table Mountain. A troop of baboons barked at him, and kept an eye on him from a distance, the babies cavorting and leaping and mock-fighting with each other.

Alexander did not drive through Cape Town, but swung around to the south of the city proper, and turned left into Rhodes Drive below the University, and after a while he joined the Simon Van Der Stel Freeway, which ended just before Muizenberg, from where he began the strikingly scenic ascent of the Ou Kaapse Weg across the mountains. From the top of Silvermine Nature Reserve, and all the way down the far side of the mountain, the Atlantic Ocean kept coming into view, sparkling and glinting under the sun, with a heavy bank of low dark cloud on the far distant horizon. At the bottom of the pass he turned right onto the old Kommetjie Road, and shortly thereafter, he turned left off the road and made his way along the tarred suburban road that had replaced the sandy driveway to the farm.

He had known to expect changes. Following his grandfather's death, the land was being sold off by his aunt as individual suburban plots (although two or three of those plots belonged to his father), and where once there had been a long dirt driveway

Chapter Fourteen

between pines and blue gums and yellowwood trees, there were now houses being built. The old farmhouse was unchanged, and the stables were still standing, but there was only one paddock left, and the opportunities to ride out across the *veld* were fast being gobbled up by the suburban development on what had once been his grandfather's land, and over which he and Mike had so often rode in the past. None the less, there was still a feel of home about the place, and it seemed to Alexander that all the old familiar furniture and paintings and *bric-á-brac* that had belonged to his grandparents, gave him a greeting. Alexander's Aunt Margaret too made him feel very welcome.

The next day, he and Mike (who was still living on what remained of the property, in one of the wooden cabins) rode out, making their way initially between houses in varying stages of completion, before they crossed the Kommetjie road and were then able to urge their mounts to a canter. At Long Beach the tide was in, and the two of them set their mounts to a noisy splashing canter and were soon thoroughly soaked. Mike whooped with joy and Alexander grinned at him.

During the ten days that followed, Alexander went sailing in Synchronicity with Andrew. Andrew had graduated at the end of 1988, and had started work with an academic publishing house in Cape Town.

'If you ever decide to sell Synchronicity,' he said, as they reached across the Bay, 'would you give me first refusal?'

'*Ja* – I'd do that, Andy,' Alexander replied, 'But I don't know what my plans are yet.'

The visit had been a good idea. In this environment, associated only with happiness and warmth and love, the grief Alexander had been experiencing at his parents' home following Lulu's death, loosened its grip, and he determined that when he returned to Johannesburg he would find a proper job. Then he would sell his yacht to Andrew. He felt that that era was past now. He had achieved one of his modest dreams, owning and sailing a small yacht on the ocean, and he had lived again as a Capetonian. He felt intuitively that a new door was about to open for him. When it did, he must be ready to step through it.

When Alexander returned to Johannesburg, there was something providential about the way he saw an eighth-page advertisement in the Johannesburg daily, the *Star*, for a business researcher wanted for a company in Orange Grove. The company's offices were not at all far from Alexander's flat in Bellevue. Alexander knew that the job was his: there would be no applicants, he thought, who could match his recent experience working for Reiters in London. He was right; the interviews went very well indeed. The starting salary was modest, whilst not being poor. He was told that after three months, his salary would be reviewed. He began work in February. By then he had moved into his flat and found some items of good second hand furniture to complement the furniture with which the flat was already provided.

The apartment block was three stories high. It had been built in the Johannesburg Art Deco style which predominated in the district. There was an entrance hall, in which Alexander kept a desk, a telephone and his typewriter. There was a big sitting room, and an equally large bedroom, and at the end of a short corridor there was a kitchen, and a bathroom with a lavatory. A back door opened off the kitchen, giving access to a service stairway. On the flat roof of the apartment block were located servants' quarters, which were occupied by black domestic staff. Alexander arranged with one of these people to clean his flat once a week, and to do his laundry and ironing.

Running the length of the front of the flat was a veranda. The flat was on the ground floor, but it was raised almost six feet up from the street level outside. Beneath the apartment block was a basement parking garage with spaces for about ten cars. Alexander's rent, which was far from burdensome, included one

Chapter Fourteen

of these parking bays. Tens of thousands of people of all ages lived similarly in Hillbrow, Berea, Bellevue, and Yeoville at the time. It was a civilised, rent-friendly era which was to seem but a dream in future years. By 1989 the infamous Group Areas Act, the bedrock of Apartheid, was already being openly flouted in the district. It was to be repealed the following year. One of Alexander's neighbours was a young Asian man.

Alexander telephoned Andrew in Cape Town, and asked if he still wished to buy Synchronicity.

'Yes, I do. What would you ask for her?'

'I paid eleven thousand five hundred. You can have her for ten thousand five hundred, Andy. Have you got that sort of cash?'

'No – but I can get hold of it.'

'OK – she's yours then. I'll ask Charles to handle the sale, shall I?'

'Thanks, Sandy. I love that boat.'

'I know you do, and that you'll take good care of her.'

One of Alexander's old friends from Alice's gang, Terrance, was now in his late twenties. He had graduated from University, before undergoing his military service in the army. As a university graduate, he had been commissioned a second lieutenant. He and Alexander had kept up a correspondence during that period, and Terrance had illustrated his letters with often amusing, sometimes poignant, pencil or ink sketches of army life during the bloody and savage war in Angola. But Alexander had not seen Terrance since 1984.

After he had moved into his flat in Bellevue, Alexander had quickly rebuilt a social life centering on Alice's group (the core of which still contained many of the same members Alexander had first come to know ten years earlier). Now Alexander met Terrance again at a party thrown by Alice's boyfriend, and Alexander had been both moved and surprised at the warmth and affection of Terrance's greeting.

'Sandro! You've been living such an exciting life!' Terrance embraced Alexander.

'It's good to see you again, Terrance,' Alexander responded, returning Terrance's embrace. 'I enjoyed your letters so much, and the sketches you included in them. I've kept them all. You ought to write an illustrated book one day, about your army experiences. Would you like the letters back – for the sketches?'

'That's an idea – maybe sometime in the future. You hang onto them for now, Sandy.'

Terrance and his long term girlfriend were living in a big house in Bezuidenhout Valley, one of Johannesburg's old-established eastern suburbs, along with Una, his twenty-one year old sister – whose artwork as a little girl had made such an impression on Alexander ten years earlier.

In April, invited to Terrance's birthday party in Bezuidenhout Valley, Alexander met Una again for the first time since 1979. Alexander was astonished as he stared at the young woman before him, and he had to speedily gather his wits. Una, aged twenty-one, with dark chestnut hair reaching to her shoulders, and bright, deep green eyes, was not classically beautiful, but she was strikingly good looking. Her bold features, in a long, oval face, were full of energy and creativity. Alexander recovered his wits and set himself to making a positive impression on Una, employing all his not inconsiderable charm to do so, for Alexander had been felled by a complete *coup de foudre*.

After a while Una took Alexander upstairs to her studio, a large, brightly lighted room on the top floor of the house. There was no false modesty as she showed Alexander her work, which she knew was good. She spoke with a laconic brevity and directness. Her movements were graceful, and she seemed utterly unconscious of the impact she was having on Alexander. Somebody with less belief in himself than Alexander might have been overawed by her. Her latest creation was a huge bird of prey; a bird from a ghastly night vision. It was an assemblage of peeled wood painted black, and real feathers, with carved wood talons and a pair of carved warthog tusks to mimic a cruel beak, all these items foraged from the wilderness around Terrance's and Una's family game lodge in the Lowveld. The bird was swooping on its prey, wings outstretched, legs forward, talons flexed, beak wide. It was a wonderfully dynamic, somewhat sinister art piece, and Alexander was profuse in his praise for it; praise so sincere that he made an immediate offer to buy it, an offer that Una accepted. She sold it to Alexander for four hundred Rand. Alexander was happy to pay the price. But he would pay much more than that in emotional currency within a few years time.

Alexander arranged to meet Una, who was thirteen years his junior, the following Saturday afternoon in the garden of a popular and trendy bar in Yeoville. They met again one evening soon thereafter. In later years, Alexander could not remember what they talked about when the two of them were together; what, apart from a shared interest in art, and of love for Una, they might have found in common, yet they had no difficulty in spending hours at a time in each other's company.

One evening in late May, once again sitting in the garden of the popular bar in Rocky Street, Alexander (who, whatever his other failings, was not a coward) said to Una, 'Una, I've fallen in love with you.'

Was it love? More certainly, Alexander was in the grip of a powerful infatuation. He found himself wishing that he was Una; Una with her beauty, and her self-possession, and her creativity. The beautiful young woman was neither shocked nor dismayed at Alexander's declaration, and at their next meeting, less than a week later, in the garden of the same trendy bar (the evenings were growing cool now, but indoors, the bar was packed), with the night air scented by jasmine, marijuana and tobacco, Una said, 'Those feelings for me you told me about, Sandy. I think I feel the same for you.'

In the light cast by an electric light bulb nearby, Alexander could see that a lock of Una's dark hair hung across her cheek, and her downcast eyes were hidden by her thick lashes.

At about ten o' clock that night, Alexander drove Una back to Bezuidenhout Valley. Alexander leaned across in the front seat of his car and kissed her as he pulled up outside Terrance's home. He was surprised at the passion with which Una returned his kiss. She was, Alexander thought, the most stunning girl he had ever met. Back home again, he made himself two slices of toast with toasted cheese. After he had eaten them, Alexander sat sipping at a mug of sweet black coffee, into which he had poured a shot of whiskey. He could hardly believe his good fortune. Alexander felt that he had been waiting half his life to find Una. He was now thirty-four years old, and at last, someone with whom he believed he was in love, loved him (so she had wondrously told him!) in return.

Chapter Fifteen

The End of a Love Affair

Throughout that southern hemisphere winter of 1989, and into the following spring, Alexander and Una spent a great deal of their time together. They went to movies together; they ate at the curry house in Hillbrow, and drank together at venues in Rocky Street. They went picnicking in The Wilds, those rocky, ridge-top public gardens planted up with indigenous shrubs, trees and flowers, which were not very far from Bellevue. Often, Una (who had a small car of her own) would telephone ahead to say she was on her way to Alexander's flat, and so they would spend the evening at Alexander's home, content in each other's company. After a month or two had passed, Una spent her first full night at Alexander's flat, and the relationship became one of shared physical intimacies. Thereafter, Alexander became greedy for the girl's perfect body and beautiful face. Watching Una, Alexander felt lighter, less earthbound: he felt his spirit soaring as he gazed at Una's long limbs, at her beautiful features, at the grace of her movements.

In the deepest recesses of his heart, Alexander did not believe he was worthy of being loved, and so he could not truly believe that Una loved him. Nor did he believe that Una's feelings for him would endure. Alexander knew too that the love he felt for Una far outweighed that which she felt for him: where his own love was passionate and unrestrained, Una's approach to love making was almost detached, as if she were conducting an experiment, and Alexander was the subject of that experiment. And yet Alexander held some degree of power over Una for quite some time, for she was fascinated by the unashamed and nakedly voracious lust she read in Alexander's eyes.

Alexander began drinking again. He drank in terror of his inevitable eviction from this fearful Paradise. At first, he drank only in Una's company, when they visited pubs and clubs together, or he had a couple of drinks at his flat of an evening when Una was visiting. But by the arrival of spring in September, Alexander was on his way to heavy drinking again.

Alexander was doing well at his work, which he enjoyed. He had been awarded a salary increase after his first three months on the job, and a further increase, after six months had passed, came his way. He was earning quite a lot of money now. Alexander had always declined the offer of a whiskey or a lager when, at the finish of work on a Friday afternoon, many of the staff (including the managing director) met together downstairs for a couple of drinks. He would drink only a Coke or a coffee on these occasions. But from September onwards he began to join his colleagues in a beer or two, and after a while, he was putting back a couple of whiskeys after work on a Friday.

There were periods, sometimes up to a week's duration, when Alexander's fears lessened, and his drinking diminished accordingly. Such times often coincided with the two of them driving down to Una's family game lodge in the Transvaal Lowveld. It was situated in a private game reserve contiguous with the Kruger National Park. Alexander rediscovered what would be an abiding love for the bushveld (a love that had perhaps been engendered during childhood family safaris to Masai Mara in East Africa), and he delighted in driving through the mixed mopani and bush willow woodland with Una in the family's battered old Mark I open-top Land Rover, or heading out on foot into the bush with Una, both of them wearing tee shirts and sarongs (wrap around knee length cotton print material that Alexander thought of as "*kikoys,*" from the Swahili for a wrap around piece of "*mericani*" cotton cloth). They both wore leather sandals on their bare feet. Alexander wore a wide brimmed bush hat also, and he had bought himself a good bush knife which he wore in a sheath attached to the leather belt that held up his *kikoy*. Una too wore a bush knife. She regarded such outings as scavenging trips, to see what she could find for incorporating into future art works. They both felt confident in the bushveld, and neither ever gave any thought to the absence of a rifle between them, although they were often not far from rhinos or elephants, and sometimes quite close to a herd of buffalos. Once, from a distance of about two hundred yards, they chanced upon a pride of lions resting up in the shade of an acacia from the heat of the day. The two of them glanced at one another, and by mutual accord they began walking slowly backwards until they merged into the mopani and bush willow once again. Una was thoroughly at home in the bushveld, and she had a very young person's belief in her immortality. Alexander was by now the supreme existentialist and fatalist. He did not believe it was his destiny to be killed by a wild animal.

These visits to the game lodge never lasted longer than Friday night through Saturday and most of Sunday: Alexander had work to go to on Monday morning; Una had university to attend, where, like her older brother before her, she was studying fine arts. Alexander would *braai* (barbeque) over a wood fire outdoors each evening: *boerewors* with potato salad; mutton chops with *stywepap* and a tomato sauce; or cleaned and trimmed chicken breasts in a dressing of chopped fresh tomatoes, tomato puree, onions, salt and garlic, the whole tightly sealed in tinfoil and secured between the two sides of a double wire grill rack and placed over the coals. For desert there was ice cream they had brought with them, kept cold (along with the beers and the milk) in the fridge which ran off a cylinder of gas.

In later years, Alexander was to remember these visits as simple, happy times. In the bushveld he felt none of the anxiety which was so often present in his life in the city. Away from the urban crowds and the noise, the traffic and the pollution, Alexander was able to live happily in the moment. What is more, the almost unassuageable physical passion he felt for Una in the city lost its voracious edge in the bushveld, and, eschewing the narrow single beds indoors, they slept – for the most part, chastely – at night in their separate sleeping bags, side by side on the insect screen protected *stoep*.

Una tolerated Alexander's drinking, even, up to a point, finding his drink-fuelled antics amusing. For Alexander could be extremely articulate and entertaining when he drank. But once, after an evening of very heavy drinking on Alexander's part, Una, looking at him with her emerald green eyes, asked him, 'Why do you have to drink so much?'

'Because I'm afraid.'

'Afraid of what?'

'Of losing you one day.'

'You shouldn't have to need me that much,' Una responded.

They drove down to the game farm again the next weekend, and Alexander forgot to be afraid, and he drank far less than he did in Johannesburg, and both of them were happy and content. On the Saturday and Sunday mornings, Alexander taught a yellow billed hornbill to come eat chunks of whole wheat bread from his hand, whilst Una slept in.

By November, with summer having set in, and Una's affections seemingly undiminished, Alexander's fears for the future of their relationship had lessened somewhat. He drank less; he had more energy. Sometimes he organised a hike to one of the kloofs in the Magaliesberg, away beyond the northwest of the city, with Alice, her boyfriend, and perhaps one other person – and Una would be there also. They would travel in Alexander's car. Although most of the others had cars of their own now, the Audi was bigger and more comfortable than the other cars. These Magaliesberg kloofs, on the northern slopes of the range, were wondrous places where their own microclimates and ecosystems prevailed. They bore no relation to the generally rather treeless and sparse Highveld plateau. In the kloofs, in which flowed rapid streams of clear water broken by tumbling, mini waterfalls, were deep, rock-girt plunge pools in which you could bathe. These deep kloofs hosted an almost subtropical ecology. Their sides were heavily overgrown with lianas and hanging ferns; the dense forest cover was home to troops of vervet monkeys, little black faced imps who would creep up behind you as you sat and ate, and steal your food. There were leopards also in these kloofs – that was well attested, for periodically, one of these big cats would slink down from the hills where they ran into Pretoria's western suburbs, and stalk the suburban streets at night, where it would be caught on a security camera. Alice would bring some marijuana with her. It did not seem to have done her harm, all the years she had been smoking marijuana. To Alexander, she seemed unchanged from the person he had first grown to know ten years earlier. She was at that time Alexander's oldest close friend.

When Alexander was happy, liquor hardly affected him, except to raise his spirits to almost manic levels of good humour and playfulness. He could then be genuinely entertaining and very good company. No doubt this was why Una put up with his drinking for one and a half years. Alcohol did not make Alexander angry, or dour, or mean tempered, or violent. When Alexander was drunk, he hardly showed any physical signs of his inebriation, and he became amiable and affectionate and high-spirited. So he continued through 1990, and his work did not suffer. He was given another salary raise in February 1990. He was putting money away in a savings account, and he also had a sizable sum left of the ten thousand five hundred Rand which Andrew had paid him for the yacht. That he felt financially secure, that he was enjoying work for which he was properly rewarded, and that Una continued (in her fashion) to love him, helped keep his drinking under control. Only occasionally did he go on a two day binge, although he routinely drank every day, topping up at lunch time, then drinking a fair quantity in the evenings, and always starting the day with hair of the dog. He tried not to allow the alcohol level in his bloodstream to reach zero; he began to experience acute discomfort, unease and anxiety if he did so.

One afternoon in March, Alexander had arranged to meet Una at the Johannesburg Art Gallery at Joubert Park. Alexander was early. He parked his car in the underground parking garage near the gallery, then he entered the park. Killing time, he walked across the park, which was crowded with black people, many headed for the Wanderers taxi rank in Klein Street, when he was suddenly confronted by two black men directly in front of him, blocking his way. One of them held a knife low, inches away from Alexander's abdomen. Alexander backed away, only to come up against a third black man directly behind him, and when Alexander looked over his shoulder, he saw that he also had a knife in his hand.

'You want my money? You can have it,' Alexander said.

'Give me your wallet!' ordered one of the men. Alexander did so. Inside it were his credit and cash cards, and about fifty Rand in cash.

'Now your coat,' one of the men told him. 'Take it off!'

Alexander shrugged off his off-white cotton summer jacket, which one of the men grabbed. The three men then disappeared.

Chapter Fifteen

They did not run; they simply melted into the throng of black people, some of whom had stood watching the show.

Alexander turned and walked towards the art gallery. There on the steps, Una was waiting.

'Una – we've got to go home. I've just been mugged.'

Una looked shocked. 'Are you OK, Sandy?'

'*Ja* – I'm OK. But they got my jacket – and my wallet and cards. I've got to ring my bank and cancel them.'

'Where's your car, Sandy?'

'In the parking garage. Luckily, my keys were in my trouser pocket. And my silver cigarette case.'

'Are you OK to drive?'

'I'm OK, Una.'

Alexander felt strangely unmoved by the entire episode, as if it had happened to someone else. He had felt rather the same way when he had witnessed the *Guardia Civil* opening fire on the crowd of Basque separatist protestors in northern Spain in 1976; and afterwards, when he had seen and heard one of the *Civiles* lean down and fire a bullet each into the heads of two of the injured, as they lay on the cobblestones of the plaza, Alexander had continued to feel as if the scene was being witnessed by someone else, someone he in turn was observing.

When Alexander got back to his flat in Bellevue with Una, he was neither shocked nor trembling. He poured himself a scotch, then went to telephone his bank. He took a deep gulp of the scotch, and suddenly spewed it up again. His hands began to shake. He had to replace the handset.

'I'm going to make you some tea with plenty of sugar, Sandy. I think you're in shock.'

Alexander and Una sat drinking their tea, then Alexander tried telephoning the bank again. A recorded message gave him an out of hours number to telephone. The branch had closed for the day.

'Shit!' Alexander exclaimed.

He telephoned the next number, and after some waiting, he was explaining the situation to somebody the other end.

Later, Una had commented, 'Sandy, you are... I don't know... you are amazing. I don't think I could be as calm as you.'

Alexander blinked and looked out the window. 'Things happen. That's all.'

During the long Easter weekend in 1990, Alexander, his brother, Una, Alice and her boyfriend piled into the Audi and drove across the Free State to Qua Qua homeland. They followed the dirt road for many miles, climbing gradually, until they had reached Witsieshoek, over eight thousand feet above sea level, at that time a small, unassuming mountain camp in the northern Drakensberg, where they parked the car. They shouldered their backpacks and set off up the slope, heading for the chain ladder which would allow them to ascend the precipitous cliff face, until they had attained an altitude of ten thousand feet, only one thousand feet below the peak of *Mont-Aux-Sources*. They continued hiking along the lip of the Amphitheatre, their views of the world far below, and its infinite bounds, godlike.

They reached the nascent Tugela River, at this point just a shy, shallow stream, but it fell from the edge of the escarpment in a spectacular drop of more than three thousand feet. Here they made camp, pitching two two-man tents, and a pup tent for Alexander's brother. Roy, along with Alice's tough boyfriend, Roman, disappeared on day long hikes the next two days, returning in the late afternoons, but Alexander, Una and Alice were happy to sit near the edge of the drop, with only occasional chat between them, as they gazed across the limitless miles of Africa far below, to a horizon which faded into infinity, merging at last with the sky. They saw *lammergeiers*, bearded vultures, far below them, the huge birds riding the updrafts in great wheeling circles.

Some evenings, Una was busy working on art projects in her studio, or sometimes on an installation one of the TV advertising agencies had commissioned her to build for a TV shoot. Then, rather than drinking alone at home, Alexander would drive to Hillbrow and spend some hours drinking and socialising at Brief Encounters, where a friendship had grown between himself and the manager. Alexander favoured Hillbrow's gay bars over the straight bars, for in the latter there was often an undercurrent of aggression, the hint of potential violence. Hillbrow's gay bars were microcosms of society, but Alexander tended to associate with an educated, professional clientele, whose members could pass for heterosexual. They were often, as Alexander himself was, witty, articulate and entertaining. Alexander did not feel threatened by their homosexuality. On weekends they invited Alexander to garden parties and barbeques at their comfortable homes, and occasionally to dinners. Sometimes Una would accompany him. She had no particular animus against gay people. Once in a while Alexander would throw a supper party at his flat, to which he invited some of these men in turn. He would also invite a couple of Una's friends, straight women with their boyfriends or partners. He would serve a curry which he had begun preparing the day before, or a rich chicken casserole made with whole cream. He enjoyed showing Una off on such occasions, for, although she did not conform with a classic image of female beauty (her features had too much character for that), she was strikingly attractive; astonishingly so. Afterwards, Una would usually spend the night with Alexander.

In late October of 1990, Alexander and Una were invited to a party. There, Alexander saw Una dancing with a very good looking young man, and although Una had already danced with a couple of people other than Alexander that night, Alexander felt a sudden, overwhelming prescience of disaster. He felt his stomach turn sickeningly. There was an obvious mutual fascination between the two young people, and Alexander thought, 'This is it. This is what I've been living in dread of.'

In November, Una began to find reasons to reject Alexander's attempts at intimacy, and in mid December one Saturday morning she declared, without any attempt to soften the blow, 'I'm not in love with you anymore, Sandy.'

Alexander felt the blood drain from his face. 'It's Milo, is n't it?'

'Yes.'

Alexander, his voice very faint, said, 'I don't think I can bear to lose you, Una.'

Una stared at him from green eyes from which all expression had been wiped clean.

Within a few days, Una had moved into Milo's flat. He was, of course, the young man Alexander had seen Una dancing with at the party in October. Alexander now hit the bottle savagely, determined to numb his pain. He did not turn up for work for three days, nor did he phone in to the office. Neither did he answer his telephone when it rang. He drank until he passed out. When he came to, he began to drink some more. He did not eat. He did not wash. For three days he lived and slept in the same clothes. For two consecutive nights, he knocked on Alice's door late at night, late enough to wake her from sleep each time. He embarrassed her by weeping at her doorstep when she opened the door to him. Each time, she let him inside her flat. It was obvious to her that he was very drunk.

On the fourth day, Alexander turned up at work. It was only a few days short of Christmas. He was sick and trembling. Although he had made some effort at cleaning himself up, he stank of liquor and sweat. He had cut himself badly while shaving, and he had bled profusely into his shirt collar afterwards.

'You had better go home,' his boss said to him. 'I'll ask Patty to follow in her car, to make sure you get there safely.'

Patty, a young woman who undertook basic research, followed Alexander back to his flat, which was not far, in her car. She was concerned for Alexander, and she asked him when he had last had something to eat.

'I don't know,' he replied. 'I cant remember.'

'I think I should ring someone. What's your parents' number?' Patty asked him.

Alexander's father arrived the next morning. 'I've booked you into a clinic in Boksburg,' he told him. 'Surely you must see that you need help.'

Alexander was beyond arguing. He grabbed a few haphazard items of clothing and toiletries, stuffing them into a sports bag (hiding a bottle of whiskey amongst them), and got into his father's car.

The bottle of whiskey was found and confiscated immediately upon his arrival at the clinic. Alexander was technically sober within five days. He endured what he felt was Hell to get there, but as he was to find in years to come, on that occasion he had barely stepped over Hell's threshold. Sober he may then have been, but he was a long way from being well. He stayed a full fortnight at the clinic, through a bleak Christmas and a New Year that seemed to offer him little in the way of hope. His employment linked medical insurance footed the bill. He returned to work in the second week of January 1991, but within a few days he was drinking heavily again. After four days of this he was fired with immediate effect. He would be paid an extra month's salary in lieu of notice. Alexander wished he could commit suicide, but he lacked the courage, or sufficient will. Instead, after several days had passed, during which he had made a great nuisance of himself late at night to friends and acquaintances in Yeoville, Alexander re-entered the clinic. This time, he would have to pay the clinic's fees out of his own pocket.

Alexander remained sober after leaving the clinic a second time, but it was a desperate, anguished sobriety, sustained by willpower alone. He felt a burden of grief and loss so overwhelming that he did not wish to live. He wept silently at odd moments. He neglected his personal hygiene and his appearance. His parents had not allowed him to return to his flat, but had made him move into a spare bedroom at their home. After a week of this, Alexander pulled himself together sufficiently to take stock of his financial position. He still had quite a lot of money put away, despite the clinic's fees. His parents did not put up much of an argument when he told them that he was returning to England.

Chapter Sixteen

A Move to Malta

In London in February 1991, Alexander put up in a shabby rooming house, one of dozens upon dozens of so-called "hotels" near Paddington Station. It was midwinter. London was very cold, with a lowering, grey sky and incessant icy rain. Before even the onset of that first early nightfall, the day choked into submission by the gathering night, Alexander knew he had made a terrible mistake in returning to England. He would have turned tail and caught the next flight back to Johannesburg, except that his pride prevented him from doing so. Alone in that cold, bleak and ugly room his first evening in London, it appeared to Alexander that his life so far had been nothing but a terrible failure. He could not rid himself of the fear that he had at last achieved the destiny that had always been awaiting him: that of a defeated, solitary exile in a cold, dark, foreign city, without even the means to end his life when the burden of it became more than he could endure. Those first few evenings, he dared not go out. He knew that if he did, he would find a pub, and if he began to drink again, he would not stop drinking – and this, this squalid place, was not the environment to descend into alcoholic helplessness. So he stayed in his dingy room those first few evenings, the noise of the traffic outside, and the comings and goings in the building, his only companions, his yearning for Una so intense, it felt as if a giant fist were squeezing his chest. He could remember the touch of her skin against his body, the sound of her voice – and even, her scent. When at last he fell asleep, she was there in his dreams, but these were no comfort to him, for in them, Una was always walking away, not even looking back, and the sense of loss he experienced was overpowering.

Checking the "Bedsits for Rent" columns in the *Evening Standard*, within a few days Alexander found himself a bedsit in Queen's Park, north London. As bedsits went, it was not a bad place, and it looked onto the park, but compared with the lovely old flat he had rented in Bellevue, Johannesburg, it was squalor incarnate. He shared a lavatory and a coin operated shower on the landing with adjacent bedsits. Some of his neighbours were of indeterminate ethnic origin. Of the European fellow residents he came to know well enough to greet on the stairs that late winter (and even, one or two of them, to know their first names), none was British. They were Italian, Irish, and eastern European: fellow exiles all of them.

Alexander rarely thought about God anymore. He had almost lost his faith. If God was still trying to reach him, he could not hear Him. But as the winter days gradually lengthened, and there appeared the occasional weak ray of sunshine, his faith in himself, in his ability to make something of his life right now, came slowly back to life, even if its flame was weak and flickering.

'I have to go somewhere warm and bright, somewhere the sun is shining,' he told himself.

Perhaps the spirit of his maternal grandfather spoke to Alexander from the hereafter, for he thought suddenly of Malta, that tiny island archipelago in the Mediterranean where, according to his grandfather's memoirs, his grandfather (as a very young

Chapter Sixteen

Royal Navy officer with the Mediterranean fleet before the Great War) had had such a happy, jolly time. There were daffodils in London's Royal Parks, and every day the sun was stronger, and Alexander felt himself begin to live again, and he was motivated sufficiently to buy a one way air ticket to Malta in late March of 1991.

Coming in to land at Malta International Airport, as the aircraft banked and slowly descended in a wide circle over the gleaming sea, Alexander could see through the window much of the main island, which is only seventeen miles long by nine miles wide. Alexander passed through immigration and customs very quickly. He noted that his passport had been stamped with a three months visa only, for Malta was not a member of the EEC.

Leaving the airport, it appeared that within minutes the taxi was driving through heavily built-up streets; a commercial district interspersed with small industrial concerns. Many of the buildings were run down and somewhat neglected, which, in that bright sunshine, was not as depressing as it would have been in Britain. The sun shone strongly, although it was only late March. Alexander felt too warm in his pullover and coat: it had been about ten degrees centigrade at Heathrow; it felt like about seventeen – or more – in Malta. Alexander had booked accommodation in a travellers' hostel in one of the back streets of Sliema, a district found across Marsamxett Harbour from Valletta, the walled capital city. He checked in at the hostel, in *Triq San Piju V*, at about four o'clock. He had a large and a small suitcase with him, as well as a large shoulder bag.

Alexander accepted the coffee the young man on duty at the front desk offered him, then he went for a walk, following the street down the hill towards the Sliema waterfront. From the waterfront the view across Marsamxett Harbour, an extensive natural inlet, was stupendous; surely, one of the world's great urban panoramas. Valletta, the colour of pale honey – with its immensely high fortified city walls, its domes, steeples, turrets, and jagged skyline – was dazzled by the bright sun. The light scintillated on the water. Alexander was wearing a pair of sunglasses he had not worn since leaving South Africa. Almost all the buildings he had seen so far in Malta were built of pale yellow limestone. He had observed a new structure being erected: the stone was so pale when newly cut, it was almost white. He noticed a large sign calling his attention to the ferry for Valletta, running every half hour. In the middle of Marsamxett Harbour he could see further extensive ancient fortifications, on what appeared to be an island: he was to learn that this was Manoel Island.

There was a row of archaic buses straight out of the 1950s lining the promenade, in the dominant island bus company colours of yellow and orange. There were also a couple of tiny, one-horse open carriages with frilled canopies for hire, which Alexander was to learn were called *"karozzini"*. The pavement was lined with tourist shops, bars, cafés and hotels. Even this early in the season Alexander heard English, French and Italian spoken. There were a few big sailing yachts and some large luxury motor cruisers moored just offshore. The light had an intensity to it which brought joy to Alexander's heart. For the first time in many months he felt something akin to happiness.

'I'm going to find a way of staying here,' he told himself.

The next morning, exploring the neighbourhood, Alexander found the Bolthole pub at the corner of High Street and *Ghar il-Lembi*, not very far from the hostel. Inside he ordered his first drink – a beer – since leaving the Johannesburg clinic a second time, in January. The ceiling was very high, lost in shadow; the walls were covered in rock and music posters, and there was a tiny gallery above the room at one end, with a drums set arranged in it. Alexander was to listen to a variety of musical ensembles performing from that gallery as time went by. The barman on duty was young, with long blonde hair gathered in a pony tail. His accent was northern English. Alexander would treat the Bolthole as his local during the course of the one and a half years he was to remain in Malta.

There were several restaurants scattered among these narrow streets of Sliema. Alexander had meals in two or three, soon learning that *fenek* (rabbit) was a Maltese national dish. It was prepared in a number of ways, and all of them were delicious. It was only some years later, on one of his return visits to Malta, that Alexander suddenly awoke to the fact that these were not happy wild rabbits he was eating, but sad rabbits reared in cages, and he ceased eating *fenek* thereafter. The selection of seafoods on offer was, naturally (with the furthest you could get from the sea in Malta being only four and a half miles), very good. Alexander often ordered a swordfish steak with a substantial salad, and a half carafe of house white. Alexander was now drinking again, but because he was no longer desperately unhappy (his grief and sense of loss moderated by the exotic surroundings, the bright sunshine, and the sparkling ocean), he did not return to the shockingly high levels he had sustained in Johannesburg. He totally avoided spirits.

It was inside the Bolthole that Alexander saw a card pinned on the community notice board, advertising a room to let just down the street in *Ghar il-Lembi*. He went to look at it. It was a reasonably large first floor room, with a tiny kitchenette, and a shower and lavatory cubicle. The full length windows opened onto a minute balcony with wrought iron railings. There were wooden shutters which could be closed across the windows against the sun and the summer heat. Malta grew very warm indeed during the long summertime. There was a double bed, a wardrobe, a table, an armchair, and two upright chairs. There was also a small coffee table and a bedside unit. A television set stood in one corner. The curtains, of patterned cotton print, were lined. The walls were plain plaster painted a pale yellow. The room was accessed via a narrow stairway which opened directly onto the street below.

Alexander liked the room. The rent was far less than he had been paying for his miserable bedsit in Queen's Park. He took the room there and then, putting down two months' rent in advance.

An acquaintance Alexander made early on at the Bolthole, an Edinburgh Scotswoman in her early thirties named Robbie (short for Roberta), taught English at a language school. When Alexander mentioned his background as a business researcher for Reiters, and then for the Johannesburg company, Robbie said, 'The school needs someone to teach business English. I imagine you have a university degree?'

'Yes – an honours degree.'

'Why don't you come talk to the school's owner? We're in Saint Julian's. The Global School of English.'

'I would n't have thought the Maltese people needed tuition in English,' Alexander remarked.

'They don't. We teach English to visiting foreign students.' Robbie turned to the barman. 'Heh, Phil, can you lend me a pen and a wee scrap of paper please.'

Robbie wrote down the owner's name – Anton Baldacchino – and the school's address. Saint Julian's was the next district along the coast from Sliema.

The next morning, Alexander caught a bus for Saint Julian's on Tower Road (*Triq It-Torri*, which Alexander thought of as the "Promenade", for it ran beside the sea, and a wide paved promenade ran alongside it between the road and the shoreline). The road the school was situated on, *Triq Il-Kbira*, ran parallel with the *Triq Gorg Borg Olivier*, which is what the *Triq It-Torri* became. Alexander got off the bus at Balluta Bay, far too soon he was to realise, and he had to walk some distance before reaching his destination. Anton Baldacchino was a middle aged Maltese man, with thinning, dark red hair combed backwards from a high forehead. Alexander had noticed that quite a few Maltese people had hair that rufous colour, perhaps some genetic legacy from the Norman adventurers who

Chapter Sixteen

had seized Malta in the twelfth century. Alexander took to him: he had an easy manner and a pleasant smile.

'Robbie tells me you have a university degree and some business experience, eh?'

'That's right, Mr. Baldacchino. I have an honours degree from the University of the Witwatersrand. I worked as a business researcher and writer for Reiters in London, and later, for another company in Johannesburg.'

'But you do not sound South African, I think?'

Alexander grinned. 'I know. I was born in Kenya. I'm a British citizen. I've spent a lot of my time in London. I never picked up a South African accent.'

'There is a standard teaching textbook we use in our business English tuition. You will need to buy a copy at Meli Book Shop in Valletta. Here – I'll write the textbook's name down.'

Alexander realised the job was being offered to him. 'I've not asked about the salary,' he thought to himself.

'Mr. Baldacchino, what would my hours be, and how much would I be earning?'

'Please call me Anton,' the man smiled at him. 'I will pay you nine Maltese Lira an hour. You would work six hours a day. The school is closed during November, December and January. You may find you only work mornings, or perhaps three or four days a week, for a month either side of that.'

Alexander struggled with the mental arithmetic. 'May I have a piece of paper, please, Anton?' he asked.

His would-be boss pushed a piece of paper towards him. Alexander took out a pen and did the arithmetic. Nine Maltese Lira was the equivalent of about eleven and a half Pounds. That was not a bad hourly rate. He thought he should be able to cover his rent, with an adequate amount left over each month. As for the winter months, he would manage, if he was careful to put something by during the rest of the year.

'I have a three months visa,' he told Anton Baldacchino. 'How do I obtain permission for a longer stay, and the right to work?'

'That should not be a problem for a British citizen. I can help you with that.'

'OK,' Alexander smiled at Anton. 'I'd like to work for you.'

Anton held out his hand. 'The job is yours. There's some paperwork we must complete.'

Alexander shook Anton's hand.

Alexander was impressed by Meli Book Shop, in Old Bakery Street, Valletta. It had a very wide range of books, both fiction and non-fiction. Alexander had always enjoyed bookshops. He found the business English teaching textbook he was after. He studied it over the next few evenings. He was to start work at the language school the following Monday. He had already learned that his self confidence had not taken as severe a beating as he had thought; he was sure he would be good at his work. During his first week at work, he quickly became familiar with the teaching method, and he found that he enjoyed teaching the largely Chinese and other Asian students business English. At quarter past four every afternoon, he caught the bus back to Sliema with Robbie, his work colleague, and invariably they would meet again later that evening at the Bolthole pub, just up the road from Alexander's room.

Robbie had a fine boned build, and a spare, elegant figure. She had dark hair and a narrow face. She spoke with an educated Edinburgh accent, rather pleasing to Alexander's ear. She was single. Sometime in May, Robbie came home with Alexander after they had spent a couple of hours drinking at the Bolthole, and later that evening, physical intimacies developed between the two of them. Thereafter these were periodically repeated, either at Alexander's room, or at Robbie's two-room flat in *Triq Il-Karmnu*, not far from the pub. Robbie had (Alexander thought) a beautiful body, which brought Alexander much pleasure. She possessed the sort of sensitive, narrow, long nosed, intelligent features which Alexander had always found appealing.

Very occasionally, Alexander was stricken by a sense of sinfulness in his relationship with Robbie. Then he visited the *Stella Maris* parish church near his room, and spent a long time on his knees in front of the shrine to Our Lady. But even as he prayed for her intercession with her Son, he knew he could not claim forgiveness, for (like Saint Augustine, who had prayed "Lord, make me chaste – but not yet,") he had no intention – yet – of foregoing the pleasure he derived from his physical relationship with Robbie.

At such times, Alexander sometimes felt a yearning for spirits, but he knew that he dared not drink anything but beer – and sometimes, a glass or two of wine. Alexander's alcoholism was not in abeyance; it was merely under a somewhat fragile control.

Neither Robbie nor Alexander was exactly in love with the other. Over time Alexander's fondness for Robbie grew into genuine affection, but theirs was a relationship bereft of any great depth of emotional input. Alexander did not mind this. He was very afraid now of allowing his emotions to become entangled in any relationship. Occasionally, Alexander became aware that his life itself had little real depth to it, but these moments did not last. He had his work; the sun almost always shone; the proximity of the ocean soothed his spirits; the honey coloured stone buildings gave him pleasure, as did the old city of Valletta, with its high baroque architecture, its magnificent *palazzos*, churches and cathedral, and the plazas in which to sit in the open air beneath a large colourful umbrella and drink *Kinnie*, coffee, or a lager.

Just above the Sliema – Valletta ferry landing was a Maltese owned and run bar and restaurant, the Cockney Bar – or Cockney's, as it was more familiarly known. This rapidly became one of Alexander's favourite venues, as he sat at a table on the terrace across the narrow road from the bar with a coffee, or a cold lager in front of him, the glass bedewed with moisture, or a *Kinnie* (a deliciously refreshing, bittersweet Maltese-made carbonated soft drink with a bitter orange and wormwood and herbs base, served very cold), and sometimes he would order an excellent seafood lunch accompanied by a massive and substantial salad. From the terrace Alexander could gaze across Marsamxett Harbour towards Manoel Island with its massive fortifications, the fort as perfect as an architectural model. He could watch small craft entering and leaving the harbour: yachts, cabin cruisers and working boats. On the further shore Sliema's hotels, apartment blocks and houses formed a pleasing backdrop, every surface and angle thrown into high definition by the bright Mediterranean sunshine.

The Cockney's interior consisted of two adjacent rooms, extended out at the base of Valletta's sixteenth century defensive walls. Over time, Alexander came to be fairly well known here, and some of the regulars – late middle aged local men for the most part – would exchange greetings with him. Many of them had at some time lived in London. Some had been in the British merchant marine, while a few had served in the Royal Navy.

'*Hello. Kif int?*' Alexander would greet one or two of them, smiling as he entered the room.

'*Jien tajjeb grazzi,*' they would reply. '*U int?*'

From the Cockney Bar it was rather a steep climb, via a number of narrow streets with high nineteenth century tenements on either side, to *Triq Republika*, Valletta's main thoroughfare. The tenements were furnished with broad but shallow boxed in balconies overhanging the street. These balconies, with their shutters, were a sensible answer to the extreme heat of summer. Alexander was making his way up the slope once when he saw a delivery boy on a moped stop beneath one such box balcony located on the second floor. The boy whistled piercingly a few times, and a shutter was thrown back and a woman's head and shoulders appeared, and she began to lower a basket down to the street on the end of a cord. Inside the basket was a small fluffy white dog. When the basket reached the ground, the dog jumped out and began to sniff about, then do its business, and the grocer's boy placed a package in the basket, which was hauled up to the balcony. As Alexander continued to watch, he saw the now empty basket being lowered once again, and as it reached the bottom, the small dog jumped into it, and was hauled up again to the balcony. Alexander laughed with delight, then continued up the slope to Republic Street, *Triq Republika*, the central thoroughfare which runs through Valletta, and along which many noteworthy baroque buildings are located, including the Grand Master's Palace (which is today Malta's parliament house), the National Library, and set a little back, Saint John's Co-Cathedral.

Alexander explored Valletta during his weekend walks, much as he had once, years earlier, explored London on foot. Occasionally Robbie would join him, but often Alexander preferred to explore alone. He felt very much more at home in this down at heel but still elegant Mediterranean city than he had ever felt in London, which (despite several lengthy stays) he could never truly regard as home. But he felt at home in Valletta, under the hot sun, no matter that the people looked, for the most part, foreign, and that many of them spoke a foreign tongue. They did not make him feel as alien as he had often felt in England. Of particular appeal to Alexander was the extraordinary mix of shabby, somewhat neglected buildings, interspersed with grand seventeenth and eighteenth century *palazzos* in a high baroque or Palladian style. This was a lived in city, so much more authentic, he felt, than England's twee villages and market towns, primped, pruned and painted to within an inch of their lives. These exploratory walks were leisurely affairs. Alexander spent as much time each weekend just sitting outside cafés, a drink in front of him, as walking.

'The expression on your face – you look like the cat that's got the cream,' Robbie remarked, as they sat drinking coffee together outside Café Cordina one Sunday afternoon. 'What do you enjoy most about street life in Valletta?'

'The sunshine!' Alexander replied. 'And watching people, and admiring the architecture. I don't think I possess the soul of a Briton.'

Robbie laughed. 'I think you and I are throwbacks to that breed of Briton who only felt happy in some far, sunny corner of the world,' she responded.

The Café Cordina, in *Triq Republika*, was one of Alexander's favourite coffee shops. The interior had a magnificent barrel vaulted, painted ceiling, in the classical baroque style. In the invariably fine weather that prevailed from early April onwards, Alexander sat outside in Republic Square, at one of the tables beneath a large brightly coloured umbrella, in front of the elegantly housed National Library.

Alexander's greatest indulgence during his time in Malta was the acquisition of books. He was in and out of Meli Book Shop, where he bought both fiction and non-fiction. Almost always, no matter where he was living, or what he was doing, he had had a book to read in the evenings. Sometimes, this need was satisfied by membership of a public library; at other times, by purchases from second hand bookshops. In Malta, he bought new books. These were to pose Alexander a problem when he left Malta in late 1992: he had to pack them in a couple of large cardboard boxes, reinforcing the boxes with adhesive tape, and at some considerable cost, posting them to South Africa. They were sent by sea, and arrived some months after he had landed at Jan Smuts Airport.

As time went by, and Alexander struck up a friendship with a local man, Filippu Dingli, he was to be shown much more of Valletta (and also of the islands, for Filippu had a car). Alexander, who was drinking a lager and eating English style fish and chips one Saturday lunchtime at the Bolthole, looked up to see a late middle aged man with short dark hair shot through with grey, dark bushy eyebrows, and lively features, smiling down at him. The pub was very busy; there were no free tables.

'Do you mind if I sit down?' the man asked.

'Not at all.' Alexander closed the book he had open alongside his meal: a history of the Order of Saint John of Jerusalem – or the Knights of Malta, as they are better known.

'Are you interested in Malta's history?' the newcomer asked.

'Yes. Actually, I'm interested in the history of the Mediterranean and the Levant in general,' Alexander replied.

'That's my field,' the man responded. 'I'm Professor of Mediterranean History at the University of Malta.'

'I read History at university – modern European history, and the history of European colonial expansion.'

'I have of course a working knowledge of modern European history,' the man continued. 'I saw your book there. The story of the Knights is a fascinating one. Their influence on western European history was profound – in light of the part they played in keeping the western Mediterranean open to European shipping. In fact, Malta's influence on European history was out of all proportion to her size.'

The man leant across, smiling, his right hand extended. 'I'm Filippu Dingli,' he introduced himself.

'I'm Sandy Maclean,' Alexander replied, shaking hands.

The two men chatted for a while, until it was time for Filippu Dingli to leave. A week or so later, they met again, by chance, at the same bar. Filippu offered to drive Alexander the coming weekend to the *San Anton* Presidential Gardens at Attard. Filippu was at least twenty years older than Alexander. He lived in Sliema. His manner was easy going and moderate, although he could enthuse about History, in particular the history of the Mediterranean. The friendship between the university professor and the exile who did not feel like an exile at all, continued to grow, and it was to last beyond Alexander's return to South

Africa in September 1992, for Alexander stayed in touch with Filippu, and met up with him twice on holidays spent in Malta during the early 2000s.

With Filippu driving his small car, Alexander visited the picturesque fishing village of Marsaxlokk in the south of the island, intrigued to see that they were passing vineyards on their way there. He was delighted by the many colourfully painted, high-prowed *dgħajsas,* with their Osiris eyes painted at the bows, and there were a few of the bigger *luzzijiet* also moored in the harbour. Under the Mediterranean sun, colours were brighter, more intense, and the surface of the sea sparkled and danced in the sunshine.

One Friday evening at the Bolthole, Filippu asked Alexander whether he had a bathing costume. 'Bring it – and a towel – if you do,' he said. 'We're going to the beach tomorrow morning.'

The next day they took Route 1 north, following the somewhat heavily built-up north-east coast, and then headed across the island to Ramla beach in the west. As they crossed the island, Alexander was struck by the many tiny, irregularly shaped, patchwork fields irrigated by artesian wells, and separated by dry stone walls. In them, root crops rather than cereals grew.

Situated in Golden Bay, the good sized beach was made of fine golden sand. It was by now early June, and the temperature stood at twenty-nine degrees centigrade (84F). The water, a pale green in colour close to shore, looked very inviting. There were no waves at all, only the gentlest lapping of water against the beach. Alexander was wearing his bathing trunks beneath his khaki short trousers which reached almost to his knees, and he stripped off there and then, on the beach. He then understood that what he had thought was a rather colourful pair of shorts Filippu was wearing, was his bathing costume. Alexander had not gone swimming in the sea for many years. The deep tan he had acquired on repeated visits to the Lowveld with Una, was now rather faded. As he waded

Chapter Sixteen

into the sea he flung himself full length into the water. It was barely cool. When he rose from the water, tossing his head, he saw that Filippu, who was standing in the water up to his waist, was watching him with a smile.

Filippu had brought a wicker basket covered with a cloth, with sandwiches and some gateaux and a thermos of black coffee, some sachets of sugar, a couple of teaspoons, and two china mugs. There were also two bottles of the refreshing *Kinnie* drink that Alexander had acquired such a taste for, kept cold in a cold bag.

'This is super, Filippu,' Alexander told his friend. 'It's very thoughtful of you.'

Alexander lighted a cigarette. For years, he had carried his cigarettes in a very old, monogrammed silver cigarette case that had belonged to his great-grandfather, who had had the same initials as Alexander. Alexander had been using a brass Zippo lighter since 1979: one of Alice's gang had given it to him. He lay back on his towel, and gazed at the cloudless blue sky through his sun-glasses.

'I used to bring my children here when they were young,' Filippu said.

'I did n't know you had kids.'

'They are grown up now.'

Alexander wondered where Filippu's wife was. His friend had never before spoken about having any family.

'Are they boys, girls – ?'

'A boy, the eldest, and a girl. I don't see them very often. When my wife and I separated, well – the children see more of her than they do of me.'

Alexander was silent. He did not know what to say, so he said nothing.

'Would you prefer a coffee, or a *Kinnie*?' asked Filippu.

'I'll have a coffee for now, maybe a *Kinnie* later, Filippu. Thanks.'

Filippu stirred sugar into the mug of black coffee, and passed it to Alexander. Filippu, like Alexander, took his coffee black, with sugar.

Alexander drew on his cigarette and sipped at his coffee. He knew that right this moment, relaxing in the hot sun by the seaside, he was happy.

Chapter Seventeen

Maltese Excursions

The melancholia which had stalked Alexander as a teenager and a young man was apt to return with little warning, but experience had taught him that living as full a life as possible, whilst also seeking some time to be alone with himself, helped keep it at bay.

Alexander had little time now to pander to this melancholic streak. He worked five days a week till four o'clock in the afternoon. He spent at least four evenings a week at the Bolthole (without, so far, returning to the savage drinking of the past, perhaps because he was, for the present, reasonably content with his life). Alexander knew a number of regulars at this pub, including Robbie. Filippu dropped in quite often. Some evenings, if Alexander was feeling troubled, or he needed to walk off a black dog mood, he might head down the street from his room to the nearby Tower Road – *Triq It-Torri* – the busy road fronting the broad shoreside promenade, which had, in places, narrow gardens between the promenade and the sea. The promenade was a popular venue among Sliema residents for strolling in the evenings (and walking the dog, and jogging, also), with the small trees bordering it lit up by hundreds of silver fairy lights, and the sea just alongside, and the soft evening air a relief after the heat of the day. Sometimes Alexander would walk to Saint Julian's Tower, and on round the headland alongside the gardens into Saint Julian's Bay.

At other times, particularly at night, Alexander would walk down the hill to Sliema waterfront, which was lined with shops, bars, cafés, small hotels and apartment blocks. From here the nighttime view of Valletta across Marsamxett Harbour was splendid; the massive, fortified city walls glowing pale gold in the floodlights; the floodlighted steeples and domes behind the city walls stark against the night sky; truly, this was one of the great urban vistas of the world.

On the Sliema promenade, Alexander could hear the soothing sound of the water lapping below him, and just offshore he could see a few scattered lights from the yachts at their moorings, or from the night-fishers headed out to sea in their small boats. It was almost impossible for someone without a car to find a location on the island where he could be truly alone; the island was too small and too crowded for that, but Alexander had learned at school how to be alone in a crowd.

Sometimes, during the day, Alexander would make his way along the *Triq Ix-Xatt* which followed the shore of Marsamxett Harbour, walking as far as the bridge to Manoel Island, which he would then cross, and he would keep walking until he had reached the Manoel Island Yacht Marina, where he could gaze at the rows of yachts tied up at the jetties. It was, by the time he had returned to the Sliema waterfront, a long walk, so he often stopped at a bar for a lager, or at a café for a coffee, before heading up the hill for home again. By then Alexander had walked off the unquiet restlessness which sometimes overcame him if he was alone over the weekend.

One Saturday afternoon Filippu drove Alexander to Mdina, the ancient inland capital of Malta, perched on the edge of a rocky outcrop, with wide views across small green fields to the east, and

Chapter Seventeen

beyond the urban sprawl in the distance, the Mediterranean was visible. Mdina too had been heavily refortified by the Knights after the Great Siege of 1565. You approached the city from the south, to find that it was protected by a wide, deep, dry moat. You entered the city across a narrow road bridge, and went through a magnificent neo-classical gateway. Mdina's streets were a maze of narrow, dog-legging, twisting ways and alleys, but in front of the superb baroque cathedral, with its symmetrical façade and twin belfries, was a plaza. Across this tiny city, if you made your way to the northeastern walls where the ground dropped steeply to the fields far below, was the *Palazzo de Piro* restaurant, built against the city walls. The view from the terrace as Alexander sat and drank his coffee, was magnificent.

'This is a wonderful location, Filippu,' said Alexander.

'I thought you would enjoy it.' Filippu took a deep draught of his lager. 'Tell me, do you have any political views?'

Alexander put down his coffee cup, and placed the cake fork on the side of the plate. 'I don't think I have any strong political views to speak of. I'm broadly conservative, I suppose. Why do you ask?'

'I have some friends in a political movement that I wondered might interest you,' Filippu replied. 'A Maltese nationalist movement.'

'That's anti-immigration, yeah?'

'We're opposed to Islamic immigration, yes. For centuries we suffered raids by Moorish slavers, and the Knights with their galleys fought to keep the western Mediterranean free from Islamic domination. You have heard of the Great Siege – of the attempt by the Ottomans and their North African dependencies to conquer Malta. We do not wish to see an Islamic presence in Malta.'

'Filippu, I don't think I have thought about it much.'

Which was not entirely true: Alexander was very much aware of the almost overwhelming presence of Islam in parts of England.

His concern was a consequence of an historical awareness of the centuries old struggle between Islam and Christianity, and was not racially motivated. But he did not feel strongly about it. Filippu did not raise the subject again on that occasion; instead, he asked Alexander whether he would like some more coffee and cake.

Alexander smiled. 'This gateau is very good. I'll have a second slice with some more coffee, thanks.'

In November, Filippu and Alexander visited the megalithic *Ħaġar Qim* temple complex high above the cliffside on Malta's south-western coast. This collection of structures, now open to the sky, was built of massive blocks of limestone, and dated back to the fourth millennium BC. The sky was overcast. It was, for Malta, cold, and Filippu wore a padded, quilted coat. Alexander wore corduroy trousers and his old tweed jacket and a tweed cap. The location was very much a rural one, reached via very narrow lanes passing between dry stone walls demarcating the tiny, irregularly shaped fields. As Alexander considered the temple's vast age – it was more than five thousand years old – and the labour that must have gone into cutting, shaping and transporting the huge stone blocks, the work directed perhaps by a single mind, he was awestruck. How, in the 3 000s BC, had there been a large enough labour force on this tiny island, expendable in terms of being withdrawn from food production and animal husbandry, to embark on such a vast, long term project? And who were the kings, or priest kings, what was the priestly hierarchy, what was the culture, what the religious organisation, that had levied so much control over that population as to be able to gather, organise and motivate it for a construction process that lasted generations, if you included the other temple sites across Malta and Gozo islands?

There was a cold wind blowing, and Alexander now saw that Filippu's lips were turning blue. They were both rather relieved once they were sitting in the car again, and the heater could be turned on. Once Filippu was able to talk again, he said, as he drove, 'Those are the oldest standing man-made structures in the World; older than the pyramids.'

'I am awestruck, Filippu. Viewing that site raises so many questions in my mind, questions to which we will never know the answers. I cannot begin to visualize the society that prevailed when they were built.'

'You do know that at that time, Malta was very well wooded?'

Alexander reached for his cigarette case. 'What an ancient species we are,' he remarked.

'That is true – yet we are the youngest of all the animal species,' Filippu replied.

Neither of the men wished very much to do any more walking or sightseeing that cold day. Filippu drove back to Sliema, and by mutual accord, they repaired to the Bolthole for a snack and a drink.

By December there were sudden, violent storms sweeping in across the islands from the sea. Alexander was astonished at the height of the waves breaking on the promenade alongside *Triq It-Torri*; some of the waves broke thirty feet high and swept across the promenade and into the road. The winter weather brought persistent rain and cold, too; nothing like the sort of cold Alexander was used to in Britain, but it had the Maltese people wrapping themselves up as if they were traveling to the Arctic. During January and February 1992, the coldest months, the temperature fell as low as nine degrees centigrade, and it never rose higher than sixteen degrees centigrade. Alexander had no work to get up for from early November through to the end of January. He stayed in bed later than usual in the mornings, but he always got outside later in the day. He enjoyed the walk along *Triq It-Torri* promenade. There was an elemental appeal for Alexander in the stormy sea. Sometimes, the Sliema – Valletta ferry service was cancelled, because of high winds across Marsamxett Harbour. Then, if Alexander wished to reach Valletta, he would have to take the long bus ride around the head of the inlet, in one of Malta's 1950s buses, with its driver's station kitted out in religious iconography, tassels and gewgaws. He was not fond of traveling by bus in Malta. He was too tall for the tiny seats, which were too close together.

Alexander and Robbie overnighted at each other's flats often. During those winter months, Alexander felt his attachment to the Scotswoman growing. There were times when he wondered whether he was in love with her – then he remembered what he had felt for Una in Johannesburg, and he knew that if he was in love, it was in a lower key. Alexander saw little of Filippu during those winter months.

Spring comes early and sweet in the Mediterranean. In a sky of lupin blue, fleecy clouds paraded one after the other. The sunrises seen from the Tower Road promenade were magnificent. Sometimes, when Alexander awoke very early, he would pull on a pair of tracksuit pants and put on his trainers and grab a coat, then walk down the street to Tower Road and stand on the promenade and gaze at the sunrise across the sea. There were strata of fiery colours lavishly heaped one upon the other: crimson and molten gold; bands of saffron and *Sèvres* pink. This incandescent display was sometimes topped by a heavy range of lowering cloud the colour of bruised plums, hanging beneath a sky still showing the lingering night.

The days warmed rapidly. By late March, there were days when the temperature reached twenty-one centigrade. The trees edging the promenade were suddenly covered in a lacework of fresh new green. Alexander began going to work in a light woolen jacket, bare-headed, rather than in his heavier tweed jacket and flat cap, but he carried his London umbrella with him, for there were sudden heavy showers still. Occasionally there were two or three days of consecutive rainfall, but then the sun would burst through and drive away the dark clouds, and in April the warm, dry weather began to dominate. By mid April, Alexander was wearing light chinos and a linen jacket (although many of the locals were still wearing heavy coats). The air was scented with beguiling snatches of perfume, as a zephyr would waft the scent of some flowering tree or shrub to Alexander, and he would stop and inhale. In springtime you forgot that come the summer, it would be the diesel and petrol exhaust fumes from the heavy traffic that you would smell, the metallic odours trapped beneath the high pressure system that prevailed in July, August and September.

Alexander wrote to his mother once every seven to ten days. Her letters were regular weekly communications. His father, who was essentially an open, affectionate man, always sent his love, but Alexander knew that his own love in return was constrained, although once in a while, usually late at night, he sat and remembered how much he had loved his father when he had been a small boy; what a loving Dad his father had been; and Alexander felt remorse and deep unhappiness. In his dissatisfaction with himself, he had condemned to imprisonment the uncomplicated love he had once felt for his father. On the rare occasions he wrote to his father, it was almost always late at night, when his defences were down, and his heart felt tender, and he wished with all his soul that he had never had to grow up; that he could have remained a child for ever. Those late nights, when he was made vulnerable by remorse, and by nostalgia for a far distant past, were dangerous times for Alexander: then, he sometimes experienced a powerful longing for a large whiskey. But he stuck doggedly to drinking nothing more than beers and the occasional glass or two of wine.

His mother sent Alexander photographs of the tiny black cat, Sooty, whom he had acquired from friends, and given to his parents in mid 1989, to try to fill a little of the gap that Lulu's death had left. Loved, cherished and cosseted, like all the Maclean family cats, Sooty developed a great deal of character. One day, Alexander would say to himself, I shall have cats of my own.

But would such a day ever come? Alexander was making little provision for his future. He had acquired no property. In his moments of honesty with himself, he knew that his insecure and peripatetic lifestyle, while perhaps appropriate to someone still in their twenties, was unsuited to a man aged thirty-seven. However, Alexander's bank balance was growing, and this provided him with some sense of achievement and financial security.

Chapter Eighteen

A Summertime Liason

In May, Filippu invited Alexander to a reception at the old University buildings in Valletta. It was something to do with a visiting academic of some international repute.

'I thought you might like to meet some more Maltese people,' Filippu said to Alexander.

'I'd like to come. Thanks for the invitation.'

Alexander, wearing one of the two suits he had bought in London, crossed Marsamxett Harbour with the sun quite low in the western sky. The cityscape across the water was particularly lovely, the pale limestone fortifications and walls glowing with soft golden light. The reception was held in a large, elegant room in the old University buildings. The floor was of glossy, polished, patterned parquet. The walls were lined with mirrors that reached almost from the floor to the ceiling, set in heavy gilded frames between the shuttered windows. The plasterwork moulding of the cornice and frieze was picked out in gold leaf. There was a string quartet from the university's music department at one end of the room, and a bar at the other. Waiters with glasses of wine on trays also circulated.

Filippu was talking with colleagues when Alexander entered the room. Alexander took a glass of wine from a passing waiter. Filippu greeted him, and said, 'Let me introduce you to some people.' One of these, whom Filippu introduced as the Professor of Classical Languages, was an extremely elegant, beautifully dressed woman of about thirty-five. Her patrician features were skillfully made up; so skillfully, that you were not sure whether she was wearing any makeup up at all. She had very dark, shining hair, gathered up from the nape of the neck in a chignon, in a manner which achieved an air of skilled artlessness. Her flawless olive complexion would not have looked out of place on an eighteen year old girl. She spoke an excellent, educated English, and after talking together for a while, Alexander learned that she had been to Wycombe Abbey, a top private girls' school in Buckinghamshire in England. He also learned, on further enquiry, that she had been to university at Oxford.

Alexander had always felt very relaxed around evidence of wealth, and the woman's style – her hair, her understated, expensive jewelry, her costly outfit – bespoke greater wealth than was customary in an academic. Both took pleasure in the other's clearly enunciated, somewhat upper class English accent. It transpired that they had loved many of the same books as children, and this topic provided them with conversation for a while.

Alexander found himself strongly drawn to this woman. It was an attraction with powerful erotic overtones. It was true that Alexander had always been attracted by intelligent women with a restrained femininity. Catherine, whom he had met on board the ship bound for Cape Town, had possessed just such qualities. Indeed, Marija (that was her name) reminded Alexander of Catherine, despite their physical dissimilarities. For a moment, Alexander found himself thinking about Catherine. Where was she now? Did she have children? Why had he not kept in touch with her? He had not seen her since 1981, when she had been passing through London, and they had met up for drinks. She had been visiting family in England at the time, and was then living in Sidney, where she had married an Australian musician.

'A penny for your thoughts,' Marija said with a smile.

'What? Oh – yes, I was far away for a moment. My apologies. You remind me of someone I once knew. It was a happy recollection.'

Alexander was introduced to a further two or three academics as they came up to talk with Marija, but after a while, Marija and Alexander found themselves alone together again. Alexander noticed Filippu watching him, and when he met Filippu's eye, his friend smiled at him. Alexander had been at the reception for a little less than an hour when Marija told him she had to leave now.

'My son will be waiting for me.'

'You have a son? How old is he?'

'He's fourteen. He's my family now. I separated from my husband some years ago.'

'Would you like me to walk you to your car, Marija?'

'Thank you, yes please. I must just say goodnight to Filippu.'

Alexander too wished Filippu a good night, shaking his hand. Then he and Marija made their way into the open air. Alexander felt the evening air as a welcome, refreshing tonic after the crowded warmth of the reception.

As they walked through the soft velvety Valletta evening, through streets still busy with people enjoying themselves, Marija asked Alexander where he lived. When he answered 'Sliema,' she responded, 'I live in Saint Julian's. I can give you a lift home, if you like.'

'That would be nice. The ferry wont be running now. I struggle to fit in the seats in the buses.'

Marija laughed, and stopped and turned, and looked him up and down, as if assessing his height. 'I can imagine!'

When Marija dropped Alexander off at his flat in *Ghar il-Lembi*, she reached into her tiny handbag and withdrew a card.

'Here are my telephone numbers. Please give me a call sometime.'

Alexander felt a wave of happiness. 'I shall do that, Marija. I've enjoyed meeting you. Thanks for the lift. Good night.'

'Good night Sandy,' Marija said, offering him her hand, which he shook.

Alexander made himself a coffee, and took it out onto the tiny balcony, where he sat on one of the two little round bottomed wrought iron chairs he had there, and he listened to the night time traffic from Tower Road, which was still fairly busy. He could see a wide track of moonlight reflected on the surface of the sea beyond the promenade.

'Perhaps,' he considered, 'this is something I should do… after all, how often does this sort of thing happen to me?'

He lighted a cigarette and sipped his coffee.

One week later, Alexander telephoned Marija's home number on the Saturday. A teenage boy's voice answered the call. Alexander asked to speak with his mother.

'Hullo Marija. It's Sandy here.'

'Sandy! How nice to hear from you. How are you?'

'I'm fine, Marija. Are you well?'

After talking for a minute or two, Alexander said, 'I would like to invite you to a show at the Manoel Theatre. They're staging Ravel's *Daphnis et Chloé*. I thought we could have supper afterwards.'

'That would be lovely.'

'I don't know Valletta's restaurants, Marija. You can choose.'

'We'll go to *Rubino's*, then. It is just around the corner from the Manoel, Sandy. It is one of Valletta's oldest restaurants, serving Maltese dishes.'

'I would enjoy that, Marija. They have tickets for *Daphnis et Chloé* available still for this Friday and the following Monday nights. What evening would suit you?'

Chapter Eighteen

'Friday would be perfect, Sandy.'

'Good. I shall get the tickets, and I'll reserve a table at *Rubino's*. I have your address here on your card. Shall I call for you at seven?'

Later, Alexander rang Filippu, and asked him if he knew of a reputable taxi company. 'I'm taking Marija to the Manoel, and supper afterwards.'

'That's good!' Filippu declared. 'I hoped you would get to know someone at the reception.'

The following Friday evening, the taxi Alexander had booked collected him at his flat, then proceeded to Saint Julian's, where Marija lived. Alexander was wearing a dark grey single breasted suit, one of two good suits he had bought in London when he was working at Reiters. The apartment block, which was only three stories high, but which had a fine view across Saint Julian's Bay, looked expensive, with a doorman on duty and a marbled foyer. Alexander kissed Marija on the cheek in her hallway, which had a pink and blue patterned Chinese silk rug on the polished parquet floor, and some original framed oils hanging on the veneered wood walls, and he offered her the tiny corsage he had bought after work: a single yellow orchid with a small spray of leaves.

'This is beautiful, Sandy,' Marija told him. 'Bernard!' she called. 'Bring me a pin, will you.'

Her son, who was tall for his age, appeared, and Marija introduced him to Alexander. His manner towards Alexander was not warm. Marija pinned the corsage to her bosom. She was wearing a knee length dress. The material was raw silk the colour of old ivory, which suited her dark hair and dark eyes. Marija shouted goodbye to her son, who had disappeared again, grabbed a tiny gold lamé purse, and a fine black Maltese lace wrap which she wore off her shoulders and gathered in her arms, and they took the lift down together.

It was almost quarter to eight by the time they reached the Manoel Theatre. Alexander realised that the foyer had been extended into a grand neighbouring building. Marija told him this was the *Palazzo Bonici*. Alexander had not been to the Manoel before, and when they had been shown to their box in the third tier, he looked around him with some curiosity. He had always had a keen interest in architecture and interiors. Although not very large – the theatre seated about three hundred and fifty people – it was finely proportioned and superbly decorated. The three tiers of boxes were arranged in an oval all the way around the auditorium, broken only by the stage and the proscenium, and their wooden structure was entirely covered in gold leaf. The oval ceiling was painted in a pale blue *trompe-l'oeil* effect, resembling a cupola. A massive chandelier hung from the centre of it.

Maurice Ravel's *Daphnis et Chlo*é, first performed in 1912, was a one act ballet in three parts, or scenes. There was no interval. At just less than an hour long, the lack of an interval was no great hardship. Alexander thought the music was passionate and lush. He was no great fan of dance, but he often appreciated the music to which ballets were set. Marija appeared to be enjoying it.

They reached *Rubino's* restaurant some time before nine-thirty. *Rubino's* had opened in 1906, and Alexander wondered whether his grandfather, as a junior officer in the Royal Navy's Mediterranean fleet, based in Malta before the First World War, had known it. The restaurant was in Old Bakery Street, only a short walk from the Manoel theatre. It had a modest façade. The restaurant was busy, but Alexander had booked a table five days earlier. Marija clearly knew some of the other diners, for she greeted several couples with a wave and a smile, and stopped to chat briefly with a couple who had been talking together in Italian.

'I think a red wine might be a good idea,' Alexander remarked, when, shortly after they were seated, a waiter asked him what they would like to drink. 'We can order a half of white with the desserts. Unless you would prefer something else, Marija – a soft drink, perhaps?'

Chapter Eighteen

'A red wine would be good. Have you tried one of our local Maltese wines?'

'Perhaps as a house wine served in a carafe. But I would n't have known what I was drinking. Why don't you choose a local wine for us, Marija?'

When the bottle of red wine arrived, and Alexander sipped at the taster the waiter poured into his glass, he thought it was more than passable. He nodded. 'That'll be OK,' he told the man.

Marija advised Alexander to begin with the *Aljotta* – the fish soup – as did she. She ordered *Gambli homor* – red Mediterranean prawns – for her fish course. Alexander played safe and ordered the sea bass *Involtini*, with pine nuts and mint. Their conversation during the fish course revolved largely around their childhoods. Alexander recounted tales of growing up in Kenya and South Africa. Marija seemed genuinely interested. Alexander learned that her father owned a small fleet of Mediterranean freighters, the sort of small cargo ships that Alexander often saw offshore. Her father could afford to have sent her to the élite Wycombe Abbey girls' school in England.

Alexander had always enjoyed slow cooked lamb shank, so he ordered the *Haruf brazzato* for his main course; Marija ordered pork fillets marinated in honey and thyme. Their conversation moved on to travel; places they had visited, sights they had seen. Alexander was able to make Marija laugh as he recounted some of his more amusing African experiences. Like his father, Alexander could always tell a good story.

Neither had drunk more than two glasses of the red wine by the time they came to placing their orders for dessert.

'Shall I get a half bottle of white with this?' Alexander asked Marija.

'Yes, let's do that,' she responded.

Alexander, loathe to make choosing the wine Marija's responsibility once again, asked the wine steward, whom their waiter called, to advise him as to a good Maltese dessert wine. Marija ordered her dessert – a gelato of layered ice cream. Alexander asked for the *Imqaret* – dates wrapped in pastry, deep fried, and served with honey and vanilla ice cream.

'How do you stay so slim?' Marija asked, smiling at Alexander.

Alexander smiled back at her. 'I've always been like that, Marija. I can eat as much as I want; I never gain any weight. But nor,' Alexander said judiciously, 'it seems, do you.'

They were still drinking their coffees, Alexander with a cigarette between his fingers, when he signaled to the waiter to bring the bill. He had a horror of waiting at the end of a meal for the bill to be brought to him. He took the bill from the waiter, and glanced at it. The total was as steep as he had anticipated.

'Sandy, we must go halves on this,' Marija said.

'Oh no! Thank you Marija – but no: this is my treat.'

'Next time then, it will be mine,' Marija responded.

Alexander was inwardly jubilant. So there would be a next time!

The still night air was balmy as they left the restaurant. At a quarter to eleven, Republic Street was still fairly busy with people strolling. They made their way towards the Triton Fountains, where there was a taxi rank. Alexander, who could never entirely divorce himself from a sense of life's theatre, was struck by the cliché of this evening: here a tall, slim, well dressed and rather good-looking man, together with an expensively dressed, elegant and very attractive thirty-something brunette, were strolling through the night time streets of an exotic city after an evening at the ballet. He smiled to himself. Emboldened by the wine he had drunk and by the staginess of the evening, he took Marija's hand.

'I am very glad I'm here with you in Valletta, Marija,' he declared, 'rather than slouching along a wet pavement, alone, in London.'

Chapter Eighteen

'Oh – Sandy!' Marija laughed, and smiled at him. 'I'm in perfect agreement with you.'

'I may be British, but I wasn't really made for Britain. My temperament is not right for a Briton. If I had n't been born in Africa, I would hope to have been born in Malta. I envy you, Marija.'

'I love these islands,' Marija replied. 'It's where I wish to be – most of the time.'

By July, Alexander and Marija were meeting for lunch every week on Saturdays. They usually had lunch at the Cockney Bar. Marija would park her car near Alexander's room in *Ghar il-Lembi*, and together they would walk down the hill to the Sliema promenade and take the ferry across Marsamxett Harbor to Valletta. Conservative by temperament, Alexander almost always ordered either the *fenek* (rabbit), or the swordfish steaks at Cockney's. The swordfish steaks came with a vast mixed salad, which was a meal in itself. Alexander still had a very healthy, young man's appetite, and he could afford to indulge it, for he gained no weight. Since early adolescence Alexander had always enjoyed his food tremendously. Because Marija liked a glass or two of wine with her meal, Alexander shared the carafe of house wine with her, rather than ordering a *Kinnie* or a lager, as he would have done had he been alone.

Sitting at the terrace in front of Cockney's under a large colourful umbrella, looking across Marsamxett Harbour towards Sliema, Alexander felt a sense of wellbeing and ease. He was conscious that he and Marija made a handsome couple. Sometimes they sat for five minutes at a time without feeling a need to exchange a word. Marija did not seem to mind Alexander's staring at her, his lips curved in an admiring half smile. Once, Marija turned her head and their eyes met, and they both laughed, but easily, without embarrassment.

Alexander did not visit Marija at her apartment in Saint Julian's. After supper together at *Ta'Kolina* restaurant, which specialised in Maltese cuisine and which was located on Tower Road in Sliema, a destination they could easily reach on foot from Alexander's flat, Marija sometimes came upstairs for coffee afterwards at Alexander's room, and they would sit together on his tiny balcony, where the air was a little cooler than it was indoors.

One night during the third week of July, after a supper together at *Ta'Kolina's*, Alexander, moved by the cool beauty of Marija's profile, and by the romance of the Mediterranean summer night, took her hand across the tiny table on his balcony and leant towards her. Marija turned her head towards him. Other than chaste kisses on the cheek, he had not kissed her before. Now, with the fairy lights visible in the gap at the bottom of the street as they twinkled on the trees along the promenade, and the dark sea beyond that, and the yellow or white riding lights of ships that had anchored for the night shining some distance offshore, Alexander was overwhelmed by a compulsion to kiss this woman. He drew her towards him and kissed her on the mouth. Then they both stood, Alexander holding Marija's hand, but it was she who led the way to his bed.

There was a complexity of emotions at play in Alexander, of which narcissism was not the least significant. The idea of his making love to such a very desirable woman sustained its own appeal. They helped one another undress, a far from hasty exercise, for Alexander kept stopping to brush his lips across Marija's satiny skin, his touch light as gossamer. When at last both were naked, Marija trembled and sighed, and said in a soft voice, 'Now.'

Marija, a mother with a teenage son waiting for her at home, did not spend the night with Alexander. Nor would she ever do so. After they had made love together – hungrily the first time, then with less haste not long thereafter – she spent some time in the bathroom, then Alexander walked her down the street to her car, and she drove home to her son. Later that first night, Alexander worried that he might have killed the friendship. He wondered whether he would see Marija again. He need not have worried. Within less than a week, their love making in Alexander's room after a supper together, was repeated. And again after that. Alexander found himself betraying Robbie with little heart searching or internal moral debate.

And then, with the August sun blazing down, and the temperature during the still, windless days rising above thirty degrees centigrade, Marija went away on holiday with Bernard, her son. Alexander was unable to get an answer when he rang Filippu's number, so he presumed that Filippu too was away. However, the summer being the language school's busiest period, Robbie was to hand. Perhaps this betrayal of his relationship with Robbie did not come as easily to Alexander as he had at first thought, for his conscience troubled him when he was with her, and he experienced a strong urge to tell her about his liason with Marija. He did not of course tell her; it was easier to let his conscience fight its own battles.

'You don't seem quite yourself these days,' Robbie said to Alexander one evening at the Bolthole.

'It's the weather, I think. I find the heat a bit of a burden, Robbie.'

But it was not the heat.

Alexander and Robbie saw less of each other that August than was usual between them, and Alexander was intimate with Robbie on only two occasions that month. When the question of whether he was being unfaithful to Marija in turn on these two occasions entered Alexander's mind, he reasoned that he had a relationship with Robbie, but was merely enjoying a liason with Marija. Having had few friends at school to learn from about loyalty, and never having been a team player, Alexander had not come to understand the concept of loyalty to others very well. But many years later, Alexander was to find himself horrified and ashamed at his betrayal of Robbie.

Chapter Nineteen

Gozo

Towards the end of August, Filippu rang the language school and left a message for Alexander: he was back from Italy, where he had spent his holidays, and would Sandy be at the Bolthole tomorrow evening? Alexander met him there. Filippu seemed pleased to see him.

'Sandy! *Llni ma narak! Kif int?*'

Alexander grinned. '*Jien tajjeb grazzi, Filippu. U int?*'

Filippu was full of his travels in Italy, visiting sites associated with the classical writers and poets. Over the beers he enlarged at some length on the Italian contribution to Maltese culture and to the Maltese language. Then he began to talk about the ancient history of the archipelago itself. 'Have you been to Gozo?' he asked.

Alexander had not. He had wondered about joining a guided coach tour, but he had never got around to it.

'Then let's go this Sunday. We'll take the car across on the ferry.'

'OK Filippu. That sounds like fun.'

'We should leave early. I'll fetch you at your flat at eight-thirty, OK?'

Alexander had taken to wearing a pair of old shorts on the weekend, during this the hottest time of the year. They were baggy khaki cotton, reaching to his knees. He wore his old pair of leather sandals also, and a plain white tee shirt. He was fast re-acquiring his tan. When Filippu collected him the following Sunday morning, the sky was, as usual, a cloudless blue. The temperature was already in the mid twenties centigrade. Alexander wore a Panama hat he had bought years earlier in London, and a pair of sunglasses. Filippu was dressed in crumpled chinos, open sandals, a short sleeved shirt, and a floppy cotton hat. He had a camera with him.

They followed Route 1 up the north-east coast, the countryside becoming less densely urbanised after they had left Saint Julian's behind them, although many freestanding villas, the most attractive of which were built of the local limestone, were evident in various stages of completion and occupation throughout their journey. The countryside was very dry, and Alexander was glad of the sunglasses he wore. The rocky landscape glared almost white under the strong light. Prickly pear plants grew alongside the road, and occasional bright green, tiny fields, not one of them the same size or shape as the next, could be seen behind dry stone walls For much of their journey, they could see the sea not very far away to their right. Along the coast, spaced every few miles, were seventeenth century square watchtowers built of honeyed limestone. They were usually of three stories, and the entrance was one floor up, originally reached via a ladder which could be drawn up. They had been built as part of Malta's defence against Barbary pirates and slave raiders. Equipped with balefire beacons on the flat roofs, they could signal – smoke by day, flame by night – to the larger, more widely spaced towers, mini-fortresses, which had housed the cavalry garrisons which could ride out against raiders.

Buġibba, on Saint Paul's Bay, was heavily urbanised, with, further along the coast, another concentrated settlement at

Mellieha Bay, where there was a long, narrow, sandy beach. Not much further along, Alexander saw a great square castle-like fortress, the colour of old, dried blood, situated on a high eminence.

'What is that place, Filippu?' he asked.

'*It-Torri L-Ahmar* – the Red Tower. It was built in the mid seventeenth century. It is empty now. Perhaps we can look at it on the way back.'

It was about ten-fifteen by the time they reached the ferry terminus at Ċirkewwa, at the extreme northernmost tip of the island. There was a ferry, bows first, at the quay, with a ramp leading to its gaping bow entrance which stood open. Filippu did not stop to pay their fare – this could only be done on Gozo at Mġarr – but drove straight onto the ferry. Once he had parked the car within the bowels of the vessel, they went above, to an open deck where many of the passengers had gathered. They remained there as the ferry pulled out. Then Filippu said, 'I would like a coffee. How about you?'

Filippu showed Alexander the way to the lounge, which had a cafeteria at one end. They bought a coffee each, and took them to a table up against the full-length windows at the forward end of the lounge. Through the equally large side windows, Alexander noticed that they were passing the small, apparently barren island of Comino, with its watchtower at the near end, which Filippu told him was the *Santa Marija* tower.

'The island has a permanent population of only three people,' Filippu said.

As Alexander gazed at the scene, the ferry's twin on the return crossing passed them. Alexander was intrigued to realise for the first time that the ferries were like the Pushmi-Pullyu, that is, they were identical at either end, with twin bridges forward and aft. They could go either forward or astern without turning around. He smiled at a sudden recollection: an Italian armoured car from the Second World War which had duplicate driving stations at either end, which had been one of his favorite displays at the Johannesburg War Museum near the Zoo. Filippu had his camera pointed through the glass at the passing sister vessel. Then he turned and took a photo of the grinning Alexander. Alexander's smile had become a grin through an access of happiness. He was always happy aboard a boat or a ship. They were drawing closer to Gozo.

'We had better get back to the car,' Filippu said. They went below.

They docked at the port of Mġarr, drove the car into the bright light of day, and Filippu pulled over, and went and paid their return fare. They then began to ascend the fairly steep roadway running diagonally up the hillside. Once on the island's central plateau, Alexander observed that Gozo was far more rural than the main island. There were many more of the small, irregularly shaped fields hedged around with dry stone walls, dominating the landscape, and there was much less evidence of urbanisation. They drove slowly through the island's small centrally located capital, Victoria, also known as Rabat, with its medieval Citadel rising above the town itself, in which seventeenth, eighteenth and nineteenth century architecture dominated.

'Sometimes I have lunch at one of the restaurants here,' Filippu remarked, 'but usually I prefer to have lunch at Xlendi Bay – that's what we'll do today.'

As they drove leisurely through the countryside, passing the occasional tourist bus, or one of the island's 1950s-bodied buses (which here on Gozo were painted grey, with a white roof, and a narrow maroon stripe running just below the windows), Alexander could see a vast church in the distance, built of pale honey coloured limestone: it dominated the entire landscape. 'What is that church?' he asked.

'It's the National Sanctuary of the Virgin of *Ta'Pinu*, built in the 1920s with funds collected on the island. It is actually a basilica. There has been a sanctuary to the Virgin here for many centuries.'

Alexander wondered whether the contemporary Maltese people were indeed as pious today as he had always imagined they were. He turned his head. 'Filippu – how religious are Maltese people today? I mean, are they all practicing Catholics?'

'Most of us would term ourselves Catholic,' Filippu replied, 'though many of the younger people are not regular Mass-goers. The Catholic faith and the Maltese national identity are so interlinked, that it is hard to be a good Maltese without being at least officially a Catholic also.'

Alexander tried to remember when he had last attended Mass. It would probably have been about four years ago, when he had sometimes attended the late morning Catholic Sunday Mass celebrated in the Church of England church at Kings Langley. Alexander considered himself a Catholic still; he said his prayers on an irregular basis, particularly when he was hurting inside. He would sometimes recite the *Ave Maria*. But he felt no need at present to attend Mass.

Filippu drove right across the island, towards Dwejra Bay, on the island's north-west coast. The car park was full of small tour buses, one or two larger coaches, and a number of the 1950s-styled Gozo buses. They left the car and began walking across bare rock.

'Do you see them?' asked Filippu.

'The... what are they called... trilobites?'

'No – they're ammonites,' Filippu corrected him.

In the rock at their feet, in great numbers, were large spiral-shelled fossils. But as the famed limestone arch drew into view, Alexander forgot about them. The archway, a natural limestone phenomenon, was huge. It reached out across the blue water: a reasonably large boat could have been driven beneath it. Alexander could see some people, tiny from this distance, on top of the archway. Filippu allowed Alexander to draw ahead of him. 'Would you please turn around, Sandy?' he called.

Alexander turned, smiling, and Filippu clicked the camera's shutter, capturing Alexander framed by the archway beyond him.

'We'll go for lunch now,' Filippu told Alexander, when they had got back to the car.

The drive took them through Victoria a second time, and lasted almost an hour. There was no direct route between Dwejra Bay and Xlendi Bay. The island roads were narrow and winding. But as they descended a rocky defile, Alexander could see the blue sea sparkling ahead of them, and suddenly there was a small village with a short row of tall buildings ahead. There was a big car park in front of these buildings, which Alexander could now see were hotels, and they left the car there and walked around the side and so to a terrace which ran the length of the pebbly beach fronting the hotels. On the terrace there were tables and chairs beneath large colourful umbrellas against the sun, most of the tables occupied with holiday makers and visitors. In front of them was a low stone balustrade, and below that the narrow beach. The scene opened out in front of Alexander: a lovely, almost landlocked, azure bay lay between rocky headlands reaching far out on either side, with one of the ubiquitous seventeenth century watchtowers high above the sea at the furthest extent of the left-hand headland, which was heavily built up for some considerable distance. There were small motor boats and yachts anchored or moored in the bay. It was a wonderfully peaceful scene. They found a table in front of the largest of the multi-story hotel buildings – the Saint Patrick's Hotel. After he had sat down, Alexander removed his Panama and mopped his face with a handkerchief, then lighted a cigarette. Filippu did not smoke. A waiter approached them, and Filippu ordered a half carafe of house white. Alexander asked for a *Kinnie*. He felt a touch dehydrated, and it was very warm.

Filippu ordered a sea bass; Alexander a pasta dish with a salad, much as he often ate at the Cockney Bar above the ferry quay at Valletta.

'I would like to holiday here some day,' Alexander remarked.

'My wife and I spent our honeymoon here,' Filippu responded. 'Back when we were still in love.'

'But you return here?' Alexander commented.

'Oh yes – it holds happy memories. That we are now separated does not spoil those happy memories.'

The two friends lingered so long over their lunch (during which Alexander helped Filippu drink the half carafe of house white), and over their coffees afterwards, that it was almost three o' clock before they were ready to leave. They had to drive through Victoria a third time to reach Mġarr. They caught the four-thirty ferry crossing back to Ċirkewwa, and they both felt rather tired after the long day and the travelling, so they drove on by without taking the side road that led up to the Red Fort. At Sliema, Filippu dropped Alexander off, and drove straight on to his own flat. From the end of his tiny balcony, Alexander could see a pale moon rising above the ocean as he drank a coffee. Alexander did not yet know it, but his stay in Malta was fast drawing to a close, and he would not be sitting on his balcony as the evening drew in many more times.

Marija returned from holiday in early September. Alexander met her one evening at *Ta'Kolina* in Tower Road. It quickly became apparent to him that Marija had decided to treat the three occasions she had slept with him as a summer fling. She was speaking of an old family friend she had met up with again, a man now living in Italy whom she had known well during school holidays as a teenager, when their fathers were business partners and friends. When she took a photograph from her shoulder bag and showed it to Alexander, he saw a photo of a good looking, rich looking man somewhere in his late thirties or early forties. Alexander easily understood the message Marija was sending him: their affair was over. After dinner, they went their separate ways.

Thoughtful and introspective, Alexander was prone to self analysis. He recognised that he had felt slightly soiled by the nature of his narcissistic relationship with Marija, and he was honest enough with himself to view his own exploitation of Marija's passing interest in him as morally demeaning. Now that the affair was over, Alexander felt relief more than any other emotion. There had always been an element of theatrics in his relationship with Marija, and he had found it tiring at times. And now (he felt) he need deceive and betray Robbie no longer.

Alexander was never to see Marija again. But his relationship with Robbie was, anyway, about to end.

Early the following week, Alexander found one of his mother's familiar blue airmail letters downstairs when he returned from work. He read the letter on his balcony, while he drank a coffee. It took him a minute or two to apprehend that there was something wrong, some unhappy news. Alexander's mother wrote that his father had been diagnosed with an advanced brain tumor. He read that his father had perhaps no more than two months left to live – less than that now; the letter had taken a week to reach him.

Alexander took his coffee inside, found the airmail writing pad and his fountain pen, and began to write a letter to his parents. He told them that he would be returning to South Africa just as soon as he could arrange it. (He thought it quite possible that he would be there before this letter arrived). He addressed an airmail envelope and fixed the stamps to it, then he posted the letter on his way to the Bolthole. Alexander lingered in the pub for two hours, having drunk three lagers. There was a guitar and mandolin duo performing traditional Maltese folk tunes in the pub that night. Alexander allowed his mind to wander as he listened to the music.

He was conscious that he had been homesick for Africa for some time; homesick for a wider land, where you could escape from the crush of people. But he feared that old self destructive compulsion that had often harried him into actions he would later regret. Yes, I need to see my father while I still can, he thought – but I do not have to quit Malta, or Robbie, or my job.

'I love this island! I don't want to leave Malta!' he exclaimed aloud, as he walked the short distance back to his room later that evening. Yet, before the evening was out, he had decided that he would not be coming back.

Chapter Twenty

A Funeral and a Bush Camp

Alexander landed at Jan Smuts, Johannesburg, early in the morning of Thursday the 1st October 1992. As the plane began its long, gradual descent, Alexander felt his spirit expand with joy. He knew that there was not much waiting for him; he knew that he was arriving amidst an unfolding tragedy – but his soul was suffused with happiness. He had left South Africa twenty months earlier. It was now early summer in South Africa. Roy met him at the airport. They drove to Roy's house in Honeydew. Despite his weariness – he had merely cat-napped during the long night flight from Heathrow, unable to find a position in which his long frame could be comfortable – Alexander experienced that gladness of heart he always felt when returning to South Africa after a long period abroad; that sense of homecoming. The grasslands surrounding Johannesburg were greening up, the rains having arrived in late September. But after Malta, it did not feel overly warm.

'How is Dad?' Alexander asked.

'He's become a very old man,' his brother replied. He turned his head, and there was a stricken look on his face. 'He's very gaunt. You must prepare yourself, Sandy.'

They continued driving in silence for a while. Then Roy said, 'He has extreme mood swings. Sometimes he's very angry, and vocal with it. It's the tumor, what it does to his brain. Sometimes he wont speak at all.'

Alexander had designed Roy's house in Honeydew. He had yearned to be an architect since his early adolescence, but his matric Maths pass had not been good enough to get into the university's architectural school. The house was in the Cape Dutch style, with a symmetrical façade. Alexander had taken care to get the proportions exactly right. The details were also correct: there were simple, partially stepped gables at either end of the house – the house was too small to carry off curlicues on the gables – and a smaller gable above the kitchen wing at the back, matched by a gable in the centre of the front façade. One of the end gables incorporated a centrally located chimney for the fireplace in the sitting room; the others each had a louvred vent set in the gable, to let the hot summer air escape from the roof. There were four tall windows in the front façade, two either side of the centrally positioned front door. Above the front door, and extending several feet to either side of it, was a wooden trellis on four vertical, squared, varnished timber posts, with jasmine already creeping half way up the posts. Beneath the trellis there was red brick paving. It was a small house, incorporating just a combined lounge and dining room, a kitchen, a narrow entrance hall, two bedrooms, and a bathroom and lavatory, all arranged on a classic T plan, with the kitchen forming the footing of the T. There was a fireplace in the lounge, with an old, weathered teak railway sleeper for a mantelpiece. There was a serving hatch between the kitchen and the dining area. The kitchen was large enough to contain a table with four chairs, where Roy (and now, for a time, Alexander) ate.

Roy's house was the first house to be built in this new development, near the crest of a rocky slope. It had views of the

Chapter Twenty

distant Magaliesberg to the north-west. It contained a cat called Smokie, whom Alexander sometimes referred to as "The Bandit." Smokie was a very beautiful long haired grey Persian cat with a white bib and white paws. Roy was as fond of cats as Alexander was. Alexander picked the cat up and gave her a cuddle when he went inside. During the next four weeks, Smokie was to be Alexander's steady companion. Alexander had sold his car prior to departing South Africa for England (and ultimately, for Malta). The house was several miles from the nearest shops or liquor store. Almost no one called. Roy was away at work during the day. Alexander quickly became rather bored and lonely during the day. He was surprised, however, at how easily and how completely he had abandoned drinking. There were times though when he missed Malta very much. It had not been easy for him, saying goodbye to Robbie. Alexander had known that he was going to miss her.

'We had a good time together,' Robbie had said, holding Alexander's hand, 'but nothing's for ever, Sandy. Life moves on.'

Alexander realised then that Robbie's emotions had been even less engaged in their relationship than had been his own. He felt upset by this. Was he always to matter less to those he was fond of than they did to him?

However, the sun shone down every day at Roy's house in Honeydew, and Alexander would lie stretched out on a towel on the lawn, wearing only a pair of shorts, and work on his tan. His mother drove over one morning, to fetch him. The family home was only five miles away.

On Alexander's first evening back in South Africa, Roy returned from work at about a quarter to six, and they ate a supper of grilled chicken breasts which Roy had cooked, then they went to see their parents together. It was as well that Roy had warned his older brother about their father's appearance: he was gaunt to the point of emaciation, and his features were parchment white.

His hair, which had been a thick faded red, was now very sparse. Alexander's father moved slowly, painfully. He rarely raised his eyes to look directly at whoever was talking to him, as if to do so took him too much effort. What he appeared to want was to sit and doze in his armchair. He did not get up when Alexander greeted him. He did however smile, and return his eldest son's handshake. His father's hand in Alexander's own felt like a collection of loosely packaged small bones.

'I'm glad you're home, Sandy.'

'I'm glad too, Dad. I'm so sorry you're not well.'

'Yes. There's nothing to be done about that.'

Alexander's mother managed to look younger than her sixty-two years, but her features were a touch drawn, and during the course of that evening, she disappeared several times, and Alexander thought she had probably been crying.

'Oh my God,' he thought. 'This is all so horrible.'

It was to get worse. Later that evening, Alexander's mother said to her husband, 'I think you should get ready for bed, Darling, don't you?'

Alexander's father snarled. 'I'm sick of being told what to do, God dammit! I've got both my sons together for the first time in a long time, and I don't want to go to bed yet. Leave me alone, will you!'

Then his face sagged, and he said, 'I'm sorry, Sweetheart. I didn't mean to be like that.'

Roy caught his brother's eye and gave a single tiny shake of his head.

On their way back to Roy's home later that evening, Alexander said, 'I don't think I can bear this for very long. It's as if all our lives are on hold.'

Less than a week later, their father was taken to hospital. Both brothers visited him there every evening for the duration of his ten day stay, collecting their mother on their way to the hospital. Towards the

Chapter Twenty

end of his stay, Alexander's father was heavily sedated with morphine against the pain. When he was awake, he had moments of mental clarity. During one such moment, Alexander said, 'I'm sorry I was n't a better son, Dad. I'm sorry I was n't grateful enough. I do love you.'

His father looked at him, his eyes a little unfocused. Then he said, 'Sandy. You just make sure that Mum is going to be OK.'

'I'll look after her, Dad,' Alexander replied. 'Both of us – Roy and I – we'll make sure Mum is alright.'

'That's good,' his father said, and closed his eyes.

Roy received a telephone call at work from their mother during the afternoon of the 16th October. Their father was fading fast, the hospital had told her. Would they fetch her as soon as possible, and take her there?

Roy left work immediately, collected Alexander at home, then the two brothers fetched their mother and drove to the hospital. Alexander could see that Roy was on the verge of tears. They went upstairs to their father's private room. They had spoken to the doctor first. Alexander senior died soon after eleven o'clock that night. His wife and his two sons were by his bedside. Their father was only sixty-four.

It was almost one in the morning before the three of them left the hospital. Alexander drove Roy's car. Roy was in no state to do so. Alexander was dealing with the situation in the same way he had dealt with sickness, pain and hurt since his earliest childhood: he walled it off, and functioned around it, beyond its perimeter.

Alexander, by default, assumed responsibility for arranging the funeral and commencing to settle his father's affairs. The hospital would keep his father's body in their morgue until he knew what funeral arrangements he would be making. He first telephoned his aunt in Cape Town, his father's sister Margaret, then his paternal relations in Britain.

Margaret suggested that her brother's remains be interred at Muizenberg Cemetery, on the Cape Peninsula, where his own father, mother, and sister, Mary, had been buried. Alexander spoke to his mother and brother, and they agreed that Margaret's suggestion was a good one. The two brothers, with their mother, flew to Cape Town on Wednesday 21st October, which happened to be Roy's birthday. It was quite overlooked this year. Alexander had made arrangements with the funeral directors for his father's remains to be flown to Cape Town, where the funeral would be handled by a local associated concern. His aunt shed few tears when Alexander embraced her. She had always been a strong, self controlled woman, little given to emotional outbursts. Her sister in law was accommodated in Alexander's grandfather's old bedroom; Roy had Alexander's old glassed-in room at the end of the *stoep*, and Alexander shared with Hannes, who was still boarding with the family, staying in one of the two wooden chalets. The new double story house that Margaret was having built would not be completed for some months yet. Mike too was still living with the family, now cohabiting with Alexander's youngest cousin, Mary (named after her aunt), in the larger of the two wooden chalets.

The minister from the Fish Hoek Presbyterian congregation of which Alexander's grandfather had been an elder, conducted the funeral service two days later, on Friday the 23rd. Alexander, who, like his brother, was wearing a dark suit, delivered one of the eulogies. He invoked a good and a kind man, a loving father and a devoted husband. He spoke of a father loved and admired by his three sons, and respected in the community. He spoke of his regret that he had not been closer to his father in later years. He told the congregation how much he would miss his father. His eyes grew moist, and there was a catch in his voice, but he did not weep. At the graveside, Alexander recalled the previous two occasions he had stood in this cemetery, burying family members: in February 1974, his grandmother had been buried here; then, in January 1987, they had buried his grandfather next to her. He did not remember being present at the funeral of his aunt Mary when he was twelve years old. He was stricken by a sudden desperate sadness and he felt his eyes grow moist. He saw tears on his aunt's face also. She had lost both her siblings now: her sister, Mary, and now her brother also. Three of Alexander's father's business colleagues, including Graham Fellbridge, whom Alexander's father had known since Kenya days, and with whom he had set up their company in 1968, had flown down from Johannesburg to attend the funeral. But it was otherwise attended only by the immediate family, and by a few old Cape Town family friends (along with the two lodgers, Mike and Hannes, who had both been fond of Alexander's father). The funeral goers gathered at the farm after the funeral, where a cold buffet lunch was set up. Alexander and Roy found themselves having to shake hands frequently, for the most part with people they knew quite well, accepting their condolences. On Sunday, the two brothers and their mother flew back to Johannesburg. Alexander had barely wept since his father had died, although he felt as if a terribly important part of himself was now missing. He had no idea what he was to do next with his life.

November arrived. It was growing very warm, and the mosquitoes were out at night, but with several short, heavy afternoon rain showers a week, the humidity was often relieved, and the heat was manageable. Alexander wore shorts and a tee shirt during the day, and went barefoot at Roy's house. He was now very tanned. One evening he was paging through a recent copy of *Getaway* magazine in Roy's lounge, when he noticed an advertisement for a course which offered to train field guides. It promised SATOUR accreditation for those who passed the course, which was conducted on a private game reserve adjacent to the Kruger National Park.

Getaway was a South African outdoors publication. Many of the adverts in the back pages of the magazine were for stays in luxury private game lodges in the Transvaal Lowveld, and for outdoor adventure holidays. Alexander remembered the visits he and Una had made to Una's family game lodge, and how compelling he had found the bushveld. Reading the field guide advertisement a second time, an idea began to take hold of him. With his savings, he could easily afford to pay for the course. He was certain that, with his love of the bushveld, he would enjoy it very much. It would lead to his being able to earn a living, much of it in the bushveld, showing off the fauna and flora to visitors from abroad. He thought he would be good at that sort of work. He was, in time, to be proven correct. The next morning he telephoned the Hoedspruit number provided, and spoke to the course director, a chap named Will Armstrong, who was an ex-Selous Scout from the Rhodesian bush war. Alexander booked himself a place on the January 1993 course.

Alexander thought it was time he bought himself a good second hand car. He would need it to reach the private game reserve bordering the Kruger National Park, for a start. But he would need some financial help from his family. He spoke to his mother, explaining what it was he wished to do.

'But what is a field guide?' Alexander's mother asked him.

'He's essentially a guide to the *bundu*. Una and I drove down to her family's game lodge in the Lowveld three or four times, Mum. The only lasting good to have come from my friendship with Una was the discovery that I loved the bushveld. We used to go walking together in the bush. I loved it. And you know how good I can be with people. I think I could make a go of this. But I need a car. Would you help me with the cost of buying a second hand car, Mum?'

'What does Roy think?'

'Roy thinks it's a good idea.'

'Very well Sandy. How much are you intending spending?'

Alexander told his mother. She wrote him a cheque.

'Thanks Mum! You wont regret it.'

Alexander's mother smiled. 'Dad never really grew to love the *bundu*. But I know it made a strong impression on you. You have always loved the wild places, and wild animals. I remember how happy you were as a little boy when we went on safari to

Chapter Twenty

Masai Mara, and how fearless you were as a child when we went walking at Hluhluwe with a Zulu ranger, and he led us up close to a group of rhinos. And in Cape Town you were always up in the mountains. You were thrilled when you saw a cougar on Table Mountain.'

Alexander laughed. 'Oh Mum! You know it was n't a cougar! I saw a caracal cat. But it was wonderful.'

Alexander had a fairly good idea of what sort of car he wanted: a six cylinder car, perhaps five years old at the most. He studied the used car ads in the classified section of the *Star*, the Johannesburg daily, for several days, and as it happened, he bought the first car he and his brother Roy went to look at. Roy was a gifted mechanic, and he knew a lot about cars. After taking the car for a long test drive, and looking for a long time under the bonnet and beneath the car, Roy was surprisingly decisive. He said, 'I think it's a safe buy, Sandy. The price is good, and the mileage is fairly low for its year. It might save us a lot of trouble if you were to buy it.'

'I like it,' Alexander replied. 'We'll buy it.'

The car was a four year old Ford Granada, with a 3-litre six cylinder engine and an automatic transmission. The sale was a private one. The owner showed the two brothers a complete service history in the log book that came with the car. It had about 20 000 kilometres on the clock. It was the sort of big, powerful, comfortable car that Alexander and his brother understood and related to.

Alexander had given up drinking altogether since his return to South Africa. His father's death had distressed him, but he had not felt the least wish to drink over it. That Christmas and New Year were very subdued affairs in the Maclean family. The two brothers spent Christmas day at their mother's home. Small gifts were exchanged. No one celebrated New Year's Eve. The brothers stayed in at Roy's house, and they were in bed before midnight.

At odd moments during the day Alexander found himself stricken with grief over his father's death. He would never be able to make good the hurt he had caused him now. And at the same time, in a lower key, Alexander found himself grieving for the life he had left behind in Malta. He wondered whether he would ever again know the sort of contentment that he had experienced on the island. He was almost thirty-eight years old now; he feared that perhaps Robbie would prove to have been the last lover he was ever to know. He tortured himself sometimes with vivid recollections of physical intimacies with her – and before that, with Una. Then he would make a conscious effort to look forward, and to anticipate his forthcoming adventures as a field guide. Sometimes, however, he struggled not to feel overwhelmed by a sense of failure and loss on many fronts.

But he did not drink.

Alexander knew the way to Hoedspruit very well, of course, from visits with Una to the game lodge. Una's family lodge and the tented training camp that the course instructor, Will, had established, were both to be found along the same long dirt road, reaching many miles into the Klaserie bloc, which bordered the Kruger National Park. Will's camp was situated about as deep into the game country as you could get, short of crossing into the Kruger Park itself. To reach Hoedspruit, Alexander set off in his big Ford along the N4 to the east of Johannesburg, leaving the motorway at the Belfast turn off, then making for Lydenburg. This was a region that had been settled by the earliest Boer trekkers. Alexander cut through the living rock of the Transvaal Drakensberg escarpment via the J.G. Strydom tunnel. Here, as he exited the tunnel, he pulled over at the side of the road where the curio stalls stood, and he gazed at the hills, covered in bush and acacia woodland, receding into a distant blue haze. Then he resumed his journey. The road continued descending, and at last Alexander had his first clear view of the Lowveld proper, lying far below: bushveld reaching away to a horizon so distant and so obscured by heat-haze, it barely existed. As the road began to level

Chapter Twenty

out, the humid air was very much warmer, and it had a quality about it that Alexander associated with happiness and adventure, and the association probably originated as far back as his earliest childhood years in Kenya.

At Hoedspruit Alexander bought a carton of cigarettes, three six-packs of Coca-Cola cans, and a jar of good instant coffee. He did not buy any beers. He turned right out of Hoedspruit, and after about five miles, he turned left off the tarred road onto the dirt road that led into the Klaserie bloc. He passed the Hoedspruit Air Force base on the left. The first time he had driven down this road, he had been with Una. It had been night time, with a full moon, and on the way to the game lodge they had come across a pride of lions resting on the road, their hides silver in the moonlight, soaking up the day's heat trapped in the sandy surface. Alexander had had to drive very slowly towards them, and they had moved off the road only with reluctance. Later, they had seen three elephants, silvery-grey, alongside the road. But now it was noon, and the light was so strong that Alexander needed the sunglasses he wore. He felt as replete as a cat in the warmth, and he drove slowly with the window down.

After many miles of dirt road, the tall grass either side interspersed with open, sandy patches, and stands of dense bush, and scattered acacia trees, he passed the turnoff he remembered to Una's family lodge – oh, how bittersweet were the memories that arose. Some way further along he came across a hand painted signboard directing him off the road along a narrow sandy track which twisted and bumped through the mopani and bush willow which now predominated. There were many scattered big trees also: leadwood, camel thorn, umbrella thorn and jackalberry were the most common. The track dipped as it crossed a sandy dry watercourse. Alexander drove very slowly, so as not to touch down. The camp was situated in a cleared area beyond the watercourse. There was a large khaki canvas tent to one side, and through the mopani and bush willow, Alexander could see a scattering of smaller tents. The centre of the clearing was left free, except for a huge cast iron tripod pot, beneath which were the makings of a fire. There was also a place for a camp fire, demarcated by a circle of round stones from the watercourse, with a number of folding canvas chairs half circling it. There were some young men already seated on the chairs, holding beers in their hands. They all wore varieties of bush outfits, similar in the main to Alexander's old dun coloured shorts and short sleeved khaki cotton shirt. Some wore cotton bush hats on their heads. Most wore hiking boots; Alexander wore only his old leather sandals. The most vocal of these young men had a fine English public school accent. He was noticeably good looking: tall, slim, with broad shoulders and a narrow, expressive, rather arrogant face. He had floppy dark hair and an excellent tan. He came forward almost immediately to introduce himself to Alexander as Ralph Nuffield-Hawke. He pronounced his Christian name as "Rafe."

Alexander dumped his backpack on the sandy ground, and declined the beer that one of the youngsters offered him. A tough looking man with a sun cured, leathery face, somewhat older than Alexander, welcomed him to a week in the bush. This was Will, the course instructor and organiser. He was the only other man there who was wearing a pair of sandals on his feet.

'You'll bunk with Ralph,' he told Alexander. 'That tent over there,' and he pointed at one of the small tents partly hidden by *wag-n-bietjie* thorn and mopani scrub. Alexander, who took delight in having beautiful people around him, was pleased at this fortuitous pairing.

After a cold lunch, which was set out by the black camp servant on a table in front of the big khaki tent, Will, a heavy calibre rifle slung over one shoulder, led the young men into the bush. Instruction began immediately, with animal tracks being pointed out and explained, and their attention being drawn to

Chapter Twenty

useful plants. It was almost sundown by the time they returned to camp, and they had seen a variety of game. Back in camp, instruction continued, this time in the preparation and cooking of the meal at the open fire. Alexander began to realise that Will was possessed of boundless energy, and that there was to be little downtime during this week in the bushveld.

Will was a rough diamond. He was physically tough, with little polish, hard on slackers, and quick to use the sharp edge of his tongue against anyone who challenged his authority, or anyone who seemed to him to be willfully stupid. He was tremendously knowledgeable about the bush, about wildlife and natural history in general. The schedule he set was exhausting. Instruction was constant. If one of the young men angered Will, he yelled, 'Give me ten!' and the offender had to fling himself to the ground and do ten press ups, fast. Ralph was a frequent offender for talking out of turn. He appeared unable to learn that his clever off-the-cuff comments, delivered in a lazy public school drawl, irritated Will hugely – or, aware of this, he was nonetheless unable to resist indulging in them. Alexander was targeted once or twice for what Will perceived to be a lack of enthusiasm during lessons in setting animal traps. Trapping small animals for food fell under the broad category of lessons in bush survival tactics.

Several hours were set aside on a rudimentary shooting range in a clearing in the bush, where rocks brushed with whitewash had been set up at measured distances in a line approaching the shooter, to represent the surging bounds of a charging lion. Will carried a Brno 458, a genuine "elephant gun," which took only five fat rounds (plus one ready chambered). Alexander had fired a rifle before, on his grandfather's farm, but nothing as big at this one. He knew enough to hug the stock in firmly against his shoulder, but one of the youngsters failed to do so, and was thrown flat on his back by the kick when he fired the weapon the first time. Will laughed.

'Man!' he exclaimed, 'You'll have a colourful bruise there tomorrow!' He turned to the others. 'Let that be a lesson to you all,' he said. 'Steve is lion bait now.'

Alexander, unlike most of his peers, had not had to undergo military service on leaving school (this because he had informed the authorities that he did not intend relinquishing his British citizenship, and the South African military did not then want *uitlanders* serving in the SADF). He enjoyed this rough, vital, masculine environment. They were a good bunch of blokes. Alexander was still fairly fit, and although very lean, he had good muscle tone. He had a deep tan. He felt thoroughly at home in the bush, and the heat did not get him down, dressed as he was in baggy cotton shorts, a loose shirt, a bush hat, and open sandals.

There were twin showers set up behind a reed screen on the fringes of the camp. Above each shower was a large galvanized bucket on a pulley, with a shower-rose set in its base, and if you wanted a hot shower at the end of the day, you filled a bucket or two from the Mandela microwave (as the big cast iron cooking pot over the open fire was named), carried them back to the showers, lowered one of the galvanized buckets on its pulley, and emptied your buckets of hot water into it. You showered in company with the second occupant of the showers, who, one evening, happened to be Ralph, whose body, Alexander had already noted, was perfectly sculpted, and it was clear that when he tanned, he wore only the briefest of briefs. (Advancing age, illness, and the belated acquisition of maturity would one day deliver Alexander from an overly conscious awareness of other people's physical appearances, and the judgments he made of others would no longer be influenced largely by their looks).

There were also twin long drops located on the edge of the camp, again, screened by woven reed and grass matting. Will had a resident black camp servant recruited locally, who did some cooking, kept the camp clean and tidy, and guarded it during the day when the group was out walking in the bush. He ate with the young men in the evenings, and would accept a beer from Will, but he would fairly soon take himself off to sit outside his tent.

In their tent, Alexander and Ralph had a paraffin lamp. They doused it as soon as they were ready to lie down, which was never any later than ten-thirty that night, after the tough day they had spent out walking and learning. Each kept a torch by the side of his camp bed. Their conversation, as they quickly got ready for the night, consisted of little more than a few laconic, but amiable, asides to each other. Sometimes, as they got ready to bed down, they might hear a hunting lion's crescendo of deep grunting roars somewhere in the distance, which the ear felt as a subtle vibration of the air, as much as a noise. Both men would glance at each other then, although neither ever commented on the sometimes disturbingly close proximity of the roars, which once or twice were certainly less than half a kilometer from the camp, for neither man was much worried for his safety in the bushveld. How likely was it, Alexander asked himself, that a lion would come wondering into a camp where there were so many concentrated man-scents? Judging from his breathing, Ralph fell asleep almost immediately every night, and Alexander in those days was sleeping well again, rarely waking for eight hours unless he had to pee, which he would do about six feet from the tent during the night, being careful however to slip his sandals onto his feet against crawling creatures that bit or stung in the dark. He had a particular horror of scorpions, and sitting around the camp fire in the evening, they often saw these horrible creatures, attracted perhaps by the warmth and light from the fire. Alexander feared them more than he did snakes, which he knew would usually get out of your way if you were not walking too fast. One night, as he and Ralph got undressed, he realised that he was more than content: he was happy. Happiness was uncommon enough for him that its presence could still take him by surprise.

Alexander turned the wick of the lantern down, dousing the flame, and lay down on his camp bed. 'G'night Ralph,' he said.

'Night Sandy,' the younger man replied.

Alexander fell quickly asleep to the sounds of the bushveld at night.

When the week was up, after an early lunch on Sunday 17th January, the youngsters went home for two weeks. In Ralph's case, this was to Namibia, where he worked for a boutique bush tours and eco-resort outfit based in Windhoek, called *Bwana Mkubwa*. Will had set them a great deal of reading to do, covering wildlife and natural history, ecology, environmentalism and conservation, geology, climate, firearms protocols, and vehicles maintenance. Some of this was already familiar to Alexander. They also had to prepare a talk to the others, covering any aspect of any of these subjects. Alexander, with his interest in history, researched the history of the Kruger National Park, and prepared a talk on this subject. The young men were to meet again at the camp on Monday the 1st of February, for another week in the bush. The next day they would write an exam based on the subjects they had studied at home. On that same afternoon, each was to deliver his talk to the rest of the group. Will would grade them on their exam results and their talks, and, at the end of that week, he would also grade them on their manner and general attitude during their time spent in the bush. If they scored an acceptable outcome for these grades, each could apply to SATOUR for official recognition as a field guide. SATOUR was the South African parastatal tourism authority. They would thereafter be authorised by SATOUR to conduct not only bush tours anywhere in South Africa, but all and any other tours for which they felt competent.

On the night of Saturday 16th January, Alexander turned to Ralph and said, 'How will you get to Jan Smuts for your return flight to Windhoek, Ralph? I can give you a lift to the airport if you want.'

Chapter Twenty

'Will says he'll give me a lift to Nelspruit Airport, Sandy. I can get a connection for Jan Smuts there.'

'I'll be passing by Jan Smuts tomorrow, Ralph. Are you sure you don't want a lift?'

Ralph grinned. 'OK. That would save me a lot of hassle. Thanks.'

The next morning, having said their temporary goodbyes to the others, Alexander and Ralph got into the car together. Alexander felt it had been far longer than a week since he had last sat behind the wheel. He had only shaved twice during that period, and showered only three times. He was already looking forward to returning on the 1st of February.

At Jan Smuts Airport, Alexander dropped Ralph off. 'Be seeing you in a couple of weeks, Ralph,' Alexander said.

'Yah. Stay cool, Sandy.'

Chapter Twenty-One

The Kwando River

It was an ebullient group of young men who gathered from noon onwards at the camp in the bushveld on the 1st of February. Only two of the original group were missing. Nobody asked Will why this was so, and Will did not elucidate. Alexander greeted Ralph warmly, and Ralph clapped him on the shoulder as he shook his hand. 'Hullo, old man, so you made it!'

'Old man?' Alexander wondered. Well, yes: he would be thirty-eight years old in another three weeks' time. To a twenty year old, a thirty-eight year old must indeed have seemed an old man. Alexander did not look anywhere near thirty-eight years old: he could easily have passed for ten years younger. Nor did he feel thirty-eight years old. He felt young. But most of his class mates at school would have teenage children by now, and lucrative careers, and big houses.

As before, they ate a cold lunch when everyone had gathered, then went for a walk, returning by sundown. They got downwind of, then followed, a small family group of elephants browsing their way through the bush, pausing to push down young trees to get at the tender leaves near the top, and tearing down branches from bigger trees.

Chapter Twenty-One

Once, Will halted and said 'Stand still. Be quiet. Listen' The men could hear the rumblings of the herd at the very lowest periphery of their hearing as the elephants communicated with one another. Will reminded them that they were not hearing the elephants' digestive rumblings: the animals were talking to each other as they moved slowly through the *mopaniveld*. They came across a dozen white rhinos also. Will walked his group slowly through the herd, and the rhinos grazed on as placidly as cattle in a field. 'I would n't try that anywhere near black rhinos,' he said afterwards.

Alexander reveled in walking so close to these big, and potentially very dangerous, animals. So certain was he that Fate had a very different end planned for him, that he felt not the least anxiety. Instead, he felt an almost mad joyfulness, akin to (but far more intense than) the way he had felt when sailing Synchronicity on False Bay, or when riding at a gallop with Mike on Long Beach.

Alexander learned more about his English chum, Ralph, that evening as they sat round the fire. Ralph's father was a London financier, well able to afford having sent his son to Eton. Ralph was an only child. He did not talk about a mother at all. Alexander did not pry. Ralph shared a house in Windhoek with a number of young men who worked for *Bwana Mkubwa*. He had a girlfriend. Alexander was to meet her later that year: a very lovely local girl of German settler descent who worked in the tour company's offices in Windhoek. Ralph intended starting his own eco-tour operation one day. 'And you will, too,' Alexander thought. 'You are one of life's golden boys. You will always have whatever you want.'

Alexander felt no jealousy, just a touch of envy, and he wondered what it felt like to be blessed by Fortune. He did not know that to many observers, he too appeared to be blessed by Fortune.

Those days in the bushveld would have been a time of unalloyed delight for Alexander, had he not suffered occasional bittersweet memories of visits to the bush with Una. Sunday 7th February arrived, it seemed to Alexander, far too soon. After a cold lunch, the young men said goodbye to each other, and to Will. Will would be posting their certificates to those who had passed the course. Alexander had no fears on that count. As he dropped Ralph off again at Jan Smuts Airport, on the way back to Johannesburg, Ralph said, 'I think we'll be seeing each other again before long, you know.'

'That would be good,' Alexander replied.

On the way to Johannesburg, as they left Dullstroom behind them, with its dams stocked with trout, Alexander had felt the onset of *tristesse*. The Highveld plateau, with its corn fields, coal mines and power stations, seemed dull and drear by comparison with the colour and life and warmth of the bushveld. In his pocket Alexander carried a talisman: one of the big rounds from Will's Brno 458 rifle. He felt a mildly superstitious conviction that this heavy slug of lead in its brass cartridge case would call him back to the bushveld. He was very tanned, and he felt fit and healthy. He had not touched alcohol since October the year before, in Malta.

Will posted him his certificate. Alexander wrote to SATOUR, requesting his official accreditation as a field guide, and asking for his badge and ID card. He also wrote to *Bwana Mkubwa*, the tour operator based in Windhoek that Ralph worked for. He was to learn later that it had been Ralph's recommendation that had ensured that within three weeks of his writing to *Bwana Mkubwa*, the company had offered him a job as resident naturalist and guide at their lodge on the Kwando River in the East Caprivi. Alexander's badge and ID card had not yet arrived from SATOUR when he received this job offer. He hoped they would reach him before he had to set off for Namibia.

Bwana Mkubwa operated a private game lodge situated on the banks of the Kwando River, in a vast game concession in the eastern Caprivi. Alexander left Johannesburg by road in the early

Chapter Twenty-One

hours of Sunday 21st March 1993, driving all day, and arriving in Windhoek in the early evening. He spent the night as a houseguest of *Bwana Mkubwa's* operations manager, Graham, a big, friendly white Namibian in his thirties. The two men drank whiskeys together while Graham's girlfriend prepared dinner. Alexander thought he could chance a couple of whiskeys after such a long period of abstinence. In this assumption he was of course to be proven incorrect over time: he still failed to understand the nature and mechanics of alcoholism.

The next morning, Alexander met *Bwana Mkubwa's* managing director, John, a short, rather plain, slightly built man in his thirties. Alexander did not take to the man – or rather, he felt that John was not much impressed by him. Graham, leading the way in a Land Rover Defender, then showed Alexander where he would be living on those occasions when he might find himself in Windhoek: it was an old suburban house in a rather parched garden, which a number of *Bwana Mkubwa* tour guides shared when they were not away on tour. Here, Alexander was delighted to find Ralph, who was staying in Windhoek between tours.

'Sandy! Welcome to the Lost City!' Ralph declared. 'I was right: we meet again.' Alexander grinned with pleasure and shook Ralph's hand warmly. 'I see you're driving the Ford,' Ralph continued. 'Has anyone warned you about Sammy's cavalcade?'

'No – what's that?'

'Uncle Sam likes to drive around Windhoek in a stretched Merc limo, with a couple of troop carriers in front and behind, and Police outriders on big bikes in front. You know he's coming when you see their flashing lights in your rear view mirror, and you get off the road immediately. Get two wheels up onto the pavement. If you don't, you're in deep shit.' Ralph laughed. 'You're not in Kansas now.'

That evening, Ralph took Alexander to Joe's Beerhouse in Eros, a well known restaurant-bar with a bush shack ambience.

Alexander ate a well done springbok steak for supper. They sat with other guests at one of a number of tables beneath a reed thatched canopy fringing an open-air *lapa*, with a wood fire burning in a huge metal brazier in the centre. Alexander nursed a Windhoek lager, and then another one. The bush ambience, the warm night air, the beers, the aroma of roasting meats, and Ralph's company, all combined to induce in Alexander a warm sense of wellbeing. They took their time over supper, but round about nine o' clock, they climbed into Ralph's Land Rover Defender (a *Bwana Mkubwa* company car he seemed to have unlimited use of), and returned to the house in the suburbs, where Alexander had a bedroom to himself.

The next morning, Tuesday 23rd March, Alexander said goodbye to Ralph and set off in his car for the game lodge in the East Caprivi. From Windhoek he headed north along the B1, through Otjiwarongo, and at Otavi he took the B8, stopping at a petrol station at Grootfontein for a Coke and a pee. Leaving Grootfontein behind him, he continued driving north-east, making for Rundu on the Kunene River border with Angola. He recalled that his friend Terrance had crossed the Kunene into Angola with the SADF during the Angolan campaign. After Dlvundu he continued to follow the B8 until, crossing the Kwando River, he left the West Caprivi behind, and entered the East Caprivi. Just beyond the river, at Kongola, he turned right onto the dirt C49, heading south, with the Kwando on his right. It was only mid afternoon. Alexander knew he had fallen through a hole in Time when he overtook a black tribesman with a pair of oxen yoked to a large forked branch, the forked ends trailing in the dirt, across which was a wooden frame, piled high with sacks of meal: this was how the man transported his goods, not yet having moved up to the wheel. At about four o'clock Alexander saw the signboard for Kwando River Lodge and turned down the narrow, sandy track.

Chapter Twenty-One

The terrain – river, swamp and pale sandy soil – sheltered a wide variety of plants and trees. Many of the former, and almost all of the latter, Alexander could recognise, and he knew their Latin names, from his studies and training during his field guide course. Alexander was to see *phoenix reclinata*, or wild date palms, growing in profusion along the banks of the river, with their bunches of date fruits dangling from the crown of the tree; there were large stands of fever trees, *acacia xanthophloea*, with a greenish-yellow tinge to their bark, growing on low lying terrain at seasonal swampy areas (and wherever they grew, fever – that is, malaria – was endemic, thus their name); and there were many deep rooted camel thorns, *acacia erioloba*, the darkest of all the acacias, with their very noticeable seed pods. The umbrella thorn, *acacia tortilis*, that most noble and iconic of the acacias, was ubiquitous, as was the baobab tree, *adansonia digitata*, with its upside-down appearance, and its multiplicity of uses – including (at Katima Mulilo, the nearest shopping town, close to seventy-five miles away, which Alexander was to visit periodically on shopping trips) a lavatory outhouse carved out of the living tree during the Second World War. Jackalberry trees, the *diospyros mespiliformis*, a noble, generously sized tree, which had an excellent, very hard wood (they were sometimes known as the African ebony tree), were scattered across the landscape, and Alexander was to see stands of several jackalberry trees growing atop the giant termite mounds that dotted the terrain. Leadwood, the *combretum imberbe*, another hardwood tree, was also common. This tree provided a sought-after firewood, and a campfire that is meant to burn all night should be made up of leadwood timber, for the wood burns very slowly, with an intense heat. Mopane, *colophospermum mopane*, favouring light, sandy soil, formed a major part of the woodland, along with combretum, in which was found russet bushwillow, or *combretum hereroense*, with its beautiful, autumnal tinted leaves. Mopane and combretum were the most common ground covers in the terrain. Egyptian papyrus grew densely along the banks of the river. Each of these many plant species had its uses to man and beast both. Almost all the acacia species bore highly nutritious seed pods of varying sizes and shapes.

The region's bird life was superb. There were paradise flycatchers with their long pennant-like tails, always a joyful sighting. A variety of kingfisher species could be seen along the river – the lovely little malachite kingfisher, the impressive giant kingfisher, the black and white pied kingfisher, and the delightful dwarf kingfisher. Pygmy geese, so cute and comical, were also found on the water. There were white fronted bee eaters and carmine bee eaters nesting in communities of small holes in the earthen cliff faces at the bends of the river. These brightly decorated birds were a spectacular sight when you drew up quietly in one of the boats, then clapped your hands loudly, or revved the engine, and they flew *en masse* from their nesting holes, a palette of colour in motion. There were herons of every description, including the Goliath heron; there were African jacanas, such dainty lily-trotters, on their extraordinarily long toed feet; there were hornbills, both grey hornbills and yellow billed hornbills, who made such a drama of coming in to a landing in the trees; there were splendid lilac breasted rollers, with their acrobatic flight. The grey louries – the "go away bird" – made a call like a baby crying in the bush. There were Burchell's coucals, their plumage predominantly a rich brown and pure white, which, although members of the cuckoo family, the *cuculidae*, and not the *corvidae*, reminded Alexander nonetheless of crows, for they were quick and clever, and could be tamed up to a point. The list of avian species ran into scores upon scores, each with its distinctive call.

But if there was just one avian cry which embodied the very spirit of the bushveld for Alexander, it was the cry of the fish eagle. These large raptors, with their brown and white plumage, were commonplace in the region, but Alexander never tired of gazing

Chapter Twenty-One

at them, as they perched on the topmost branches of a waterside tree, ready in a moment to dive for their prey. Alexander wished he had a camera – Ralph took wonderful wildlife photographs – but at this stage in his life, Alexander did not own a camera, and so he was to create no visual record of his time in the bushveld.

Of the animal life, the huge herds of elephants were the most spectacular. Alexander, out walking in the bush one day, sat at the foot of a stand of jackalberry trees, his knees drawn up, alone but for the animals and birds around him, and he watched a column of elephants passing by, and he lost count of their number after three hundred animals. There were great herds of buffalo also, and Alexander could walk past them, not so very far away, and they would raise their heavy-bossed heads and stare incuriously at him, just like cattle. He knew to avoid the lone buffalo bulls, or the small groups of two or three bulls together. There were leopards at night. He sometimes heard their sawing roar nearby before dawn, as he was waking up in his *rondavel*, knowing that he would shortly have to walk through the mopani and bushwillow in the grey-black of pre-dawn, to the main lodge building, to light the stove and prepare tea and coffee and rusks for his guests before setting off on a dawn game drive. Alexander only once heard the crashing waves of sound of a lion's roar this side of the river at night. For the most part, lions stayed on the Botswana side of the river. The river was home to many hippos, who came ashore at night to graze, and whom Alexander had to evade before dawn every day, when he left his *rondavel*.

Alexander drove old Land Rovers. The Series III was his favourite, although sometimes he drove a forward control, ex-army Land Rover. (The engine was situated between the two forward seats). The nearest town – Katima Mulilo, on the Zambezi River – was over seventy-five miles away, along a road that was dirt for part of the way, and the nearest commercial airstrip was located at Katima Mulilo. The lodge had its own small grass runway, where light aircraft landed, bringing in guests. Alexander was to get to know some of the bush pilots, and once one of them allowed him to sit in the co-pilot's seat and take the plane up from the dirt strip, and head west along the Caprivi strip for fifteen minutes, before circling and returning for a landing, which the pilot himself then made.

The guests at the lodge were usually wealthy middle aged couples from England, Europe, and North America. Alexander took those who wished to accompany him on a dawn drive every morning, the lodge manager's old army service Lee-Enfield .303 rifle in its rubber-padded brackets across the top of the Land Rover's dashboard. The dawn was announced by a splendid, technicoloured sky which seemed to be catching fire by stages. In the afternoon, round about four o'clock, Alexander took his guests on a river cruise in one of the boats, arriving back at the lodge two hours later as the sun was falling to the horizon, the sky turning scarlet and gold. Well into the tropics as they were, the sun fell almost vertically towards the horizon, and it fell so fast: one moment it was still daylight; the next, it was night. There was no dusk at all. As the sun was tumbling towards the rim of the earth, flooding the sky with bands of changing colour – crimson, cerise and salmon pink, gold and lemon yellow – there would be a frantic shrieking and gobbling, cawing, hooting, and calling, from birds and animals, and then a brief stillness before the night sounds began.

When Alexander was out with guests on an afternoon river cruise in the small boat, and he saw a hippo pod ahead, he would adjust the gear lever until they were holding stationary against the current, and then wait for seven to eight minutes, by which time each hippo in the pod had surfaced at least once, to breathe. Once Alexander had fixed an image of their disposition in his mind's eye, he would warn his guests to have their camcorders and cameras ready, and then he would proceed fairly fast through the pod. Then Alexander would spin the boat round beyond the pod, and the hippos would be roaring in his wake, their great gapes wide, their huge peg-like tusks visible. Alexander called this "hippo slalom."

Sometimes the propeller (or propellers, on the big twin-engined double decker pontoon barge he sometimes took out if there were a great many guests on the cruise) would be fouled by river weed, and Alexander would have to remove his shirt and go over the side, and use the saw toothed edge of his bush knife to hack away the weeds, ducking his head underwater. There were crocodiles in these reaches of the Kwando, but Alexander had seen only a few. Not many miles downstream, however, at another lodge, a young ranger, celebrating his twenty-first birthday, went for a night swim in the Kwando, and disappeared. His remains were found some days later, lodged between the roots of a tree on the river bank, just beneath the water: he had been seized and partially eaten by a crocodile.

Alexander looked after an English guest once, Jim Carter, a man in his late fifties, who was visiting in company with a much younger wife. He and Alexander walked out into the bush one morning after breakfast. Alexander was armed only with his bush knife and a short, broad bladed *asegaai* or stabbing spear he favoured when he was out walking alone. He had found it in one of the outhouses at the lodge, and he had put a new edge to the blade using a file. The Englishman wanted to get up close to buffalo, and Alexander was fairly certain that he knew where he could find an old bull, an *mzee*, and his two *askaris*, the younger bulls who kept him company. He found their spoor after a couple of miles' walking, and the two men followed the spoor, and after a while, having come across some very fresh dung, Alexander tested the air: there was the hint of a wind, and he left the spoor, to get well downwind of the buffalos, and the two men swung out in a wide arc.

Alexander found his guest his buffalos; three of them. Alexander saw a massive termite mound some distance ahead, and he guessed that the animals were close by the other side of it, and – still downwind of the animals' presumed location – he and his guest crept closer, and leopard crawled up to the crest of the termite mound. The three animals were there, only yards away from the men, below the termite mound. There was a massive old bull, with a heavy boss and a spread of double curved horns that spanned three and a half feet in breadth, standing so near that Alexander could see the fat plum coloured ticks gathered in the folds of skin at his throat and behind his ears. Ranged watchfully alongside him were his two younger companions. Alexander and the Englishman lay silently, flat on their bellies just below the crest of the termite mound, peering over the top, and gazed with wonder at those magnificent beasts. Alexander had not allowed his guest to bring his camera – the click of the shutter would have spooked the buffalos, and possibly put the two men into a danger they could not have escaped. So Alexander and the older man simply gazed at the three buffalos, admiring, hardly breathing.

On their way back to the lodge, Jim Carter, whom the experience had filled with wonder, said, 'I've been out deer stalking before, but this was a great deal more exciting. No one I know would believe we did n't have a rifle with us.'

'I was excited too, Jim,' Alexander responded. 'It's something very few people will have experienced – being that close to a solitary group of three buffalo bulls, unarmed, and coming away unscathed.'

During Alexander's time at the lodge, two young men arrived independently of one another, on extended visits. They were not the usual sort of guests. They were spending time at Kwando River Lodge as part of their gap years, having finished school the year before. Their parents had some sort of pull with the directors back

Chapter Twenty-One

in Windhoek; they were there just for fun. The first of the young men to arrive was a Frenchman, Jean.

'*Bienvenue, Jean,*' Alexander greeted him, as the boy clambered from the small aircraft on the lodge's grass strip. '*Je m'appelle Sandy. Je suis le naturaliste et le guide ici.*' They shook hands.

The boy slept in the spare bed in Alexander's own *rondavel*. He was a pleasant youth in every way, inoffensive, keen to participate in Alexander's working day. He followed Alexander around, and Alexander tried to teach him some of what he knew, so that he had something to take away with him when he left.

'*Le plus important chose se souvenir dans le bois de l'Afrique, Jean, c'est à bien courir – oui?*'

Jean laughed. Alexander enjoyed his company, but the young Frenchman stayed for only four or five weeks, leaving again in another small aircraft.

The second youthful visitor was a charming, rather well bred young Englishman, who reminded Alexander very much of Ralph. Miles was a tall, sturdy, good looking boy, and, aged only eighteen, he exerted that particular charm special to boys who know that they are popular and well liked, but who seem just a little embarrassed at the knowledge. Miles' connections must have been of another rank to the young French lad's, for he was given his own *rondavel*. He could not get out of bed early, and he missed almost all Alexander's dawn game drives. He was far less assiduous than the French boy had been in his attention to trying to learn from Alexander, but his charm was such that Alexander found it difficult to be irritated by him.

When he first arrived, Miles had an English pallor, but with his brown hair and brown eyes, he tanned quickly during his first two weeks at the lodge. At first he got horribly bitten by mosquitoes, but in due course he learned to do as Alexander did: to shower and change soon after sundown, getting dressed afterwards in a long sleeved shirt, and slacks, with shoes and socks. Alexander undertook this ritual every evening, and then for good measure he rubbed citronella oil onto the back of his neck, on his wrists, and on his ankles. He was never bitten by mosquitoes. At night, everyone slept under mosquito nets. The black staff however were always going down with malarial attacks, and they were very ill each time, laid up in bed, and sad as sick dogs. Alexander was fortunate: despite taking nothing against malaria (he was afraid that long term anti malarial medication was harmful), either there in the Caprivi, or in the Transvaal Lowveld, he never went down with malaria.

Miles enjoyed joining Alexander on the river cruises in the afternoon. Then he was in his element, lazing elegantly in the sunshine in the boat's stern, and entertaining the guests with witty asides. On one occasion they were attacked by a hippo. Miles was lounging aft; there were perhaps three or four guests in the boat also. Alexander had taken the boat close to the reeds by the river bank, to watch a dainty lily-trotter, and suddenly there was a great bellowing and a thrashing of water, and a hippo broke from the reeds and began to surge through the water towards them, keeping up her bellowing, her jaws agape. Alexander guessed they had accidentally come too close to a cow whose calves were hidden amidst the reeds. With each porpoise-like surge through the water, she covered about four feet, half her full length. Alexander was thrilled; he felt a spirit of wicked mischief seize hold of him (but there was some calculation also; he knew that it was for experiences such as this that their guests visited the game lodge); he held the boat stationary, watching, and at the last possible moment, by which time two of his guests were yelling, he rammed the gear lever into reverse and spun the wheel; the boat turned sharply aside from the hippo cow, almost on its axis, then Alexander engaged forward gear and opened the throttle, and they sped away from the animal. Miles' face had gone white beneath his tan. Later he told Alexander, 'I've never been so scared in all my life.'

Chapter Twenty-One

One day there were no guests staying at the lodge, so Alexander took Miles out walking in the bush. Alexander had no rifle with him; the lodge manager would not permit him to carry it except on duty. Some miles from the lodge, the two men began to come across recent signs of buffalo: the imprints of many hooves, and fresh dung also. The terrain, in which grew the occasional acacia, was sparsely covered by combretum, and by large, dense growths of *wag-n-bietjie* thorn.

'Miles – give the bushes and thorns a wide berth as we pass them: there could be a buff or two behind any one of them,' Alexander advised his companion.

Miles grinned. 'Stop trying to scare me,' he responded.

They were approaching one of these large thorn bushes, and the two men split up, one walking either side of the bush, and there was a sudden, shocking commotion and a snorting beast with a grey-brown hide covered in sparse bristles, with ivories either side of its head, burst forth from behind the bush. Miles and Alexander both yelled and they took off fast in opposite directions, before coming to their senses: the creature was not after all a buffalo, but only a startled warthog. The two men spent the next few minutes laughing uncontrollably at one another.

'You should have seen yourself!' Miles exclaimed, when he could talk again.

'You should have seen *yourself!*' Alexander responded, still laughing.

Over time, Alexander began to drink much more heavily. Up to that time, he had drunk a glass of wine with his meal at dinner time, and perhaps a couple of lagers afterwards in the lounge, marking them against his staff tab. He had not thus far wished to drink in order to get drunk. That changed now. He began to drink every evening in order to get drunk, and short of stealing the liquor, which Alexander would not contemplate, he could not hide the amount he had begun to drink, for he entered his drinks on his tab, to be deducted from his monthly salary. Gary Vorster, the lodge manager, knew exactly how much Alexander was drinking, and this was to give him a stick with which to beat Alexander.

Had he not enjoyed his work so much, Alexander might quickly have descended into highly destructive drinking. It was his work which saved him from this: he took a great pleasure in it. And of course, Alexander spent much of his day in Miles' company, and Miles was a light hearted, cheerful, uncomplicated young man, singing snatches of pop songs and whistling happily. However, in July the youngster returned to England. He would be entering Sandhurst, the British military academy, in September. As Miles was about to climb into the tiny single engined aircraft in which he was to return to Windhoek, he said to Alexander, 'You gave me a good time, Sandy. Even if you scared the hell out of me sometimes!'

'You take care!' Alexander said, shaking his hand.

'Yah – and you take it easy.'

Watching the aircraft as it climbed and circled in the sky and set a course for the west, Alexander felt very alone. But there would be guests whose company he would enjoy during the remaining months he was to spend at Kwando River Lodge. He continued to keep his drinking just barely in check. By the end of the day he was too weary to stay up late, drinking. For the same reason, he read little. There was a collection of popular novels in a bookcase in the lounge for the guests to borrow, along with volumes on natural history. It was one of these that Alexander preferred to have by his bed in his *rondavel*. He was usually too tired to read more than a few pages in the evening.

One day, with no guests booked in at the lodge, Alexander set off on a solitary walk, unarmed but for his bush knife and his *asegaai*, or stabbing spear. By the time he sat down beneath a camel thorn acacia to eat the sandwiches Marge had prepared for him, he was between four and five miles from the lodge. He had seen

Chapter Twenty-One

several family groups of elephants, and a large buffalo herd not far away, along with large herds of zebra and impala. Walking in this terrain was not difficult. Although there were only occasional four wheel drive tracks through the bush, the bush itself was not heavily overgrown. Alexander could set a course and follow it without major deviations. After his snack, Alexander began to head back to the lodge. It was then that he saw what looked like the spoor of many big dogs in the sandy soil. It did not seem to Alexander to be hyena spoor. He began to track the spoor, which was not difficult, and after only ten or fifteen minutes he came to an open clearing, in which a drinking hole, a big pool of muddy water with a pair of knob-billed ducks swimming in it, was still to be found in this dry season. On the far side of the clearing he saw a pack of wild dogs.

Alexander was thrilled. He stood still – he knew he would have been spotted, but the dogs were one hundred yards or more away, with the water between them and him, and they would not be feeling threatened. Alexander had not seen any wild dogs in the region before. He knew from something that Gary Vorster had said at dinner one evening that there were thought to be no wild dogs left in the region. These Cape Hunting Dogs, *Lycaon Pictus*, were smaller than hyenas, fleet of foot, not unlike long-legged, heavy muzzled domestic dogs from afar, except that they had huge, rounded ears. Their coats were individually dappled, blotched, spotted and brindled with tan, dark brown, and patches of white. They were indeed "painted wolves," as their Latin name indicated. Alexander stood and gazed at them for fifteen minutes or more. The pack was resting. He counted their numbers. Several of the dogs were lying down in the shade of an umbrella thorn acacia. There were pups with them, playing and gamboling and mock fighting with each other. Alexander heard a constant chorus of squeaks, whines, and squeals from the little creatures. Watching the pack, Alexander felt supremely happy.

When Alexander mentioned his sighting to Gary over dinner, the normally taciturn man became almost enthused. He told Alexander that wild dogs were thought to be completely absent from the East Caprivi, shot out during the civil war.

'You must describe what you saw in the book of significant game sightings I keep in my office. You counted the dogs, I hope?'

'Yes, and the pups – as best I could.'

'That's good. When I call Windhoek tomorrow on the radio telephone, I'll ask them to report the sighting to the conservation department at the ministry of the environment. It's the sort of report that will please them.' The big, unfriendly man regarded Alexander thoughtfully for a moment. 'I would like to have been there.'

Once in a while, when he had a free day, instead of heading out for a day's walking in the bush, Alexander drove his Ford Granada to Katima Mulilo, because a car standing idle too long becomes a sick car. Amidst his shopping for small items for the lodge (he would check with the kitchen and with housekeeping whether there was anything they needed urgently), and for individual members of staff, he seized the opportunity then to buy a dozen bottles of cheap scotch whiskey, which he would store in the car's locked boot. From this store he would ensure that he always had a bottle of whiskey hidden in his *rondavel*. He knew enough about black domestic staff to realise that his stash was probably no secret from the staff who cleaned his room every day, but he hoped that they saw no reason to talk about it to Gary Vorster or to his common law wife, especially as he tipped the cleaning staff quite generously every month. By September, Alexander was beginning his day with a hefty slug of whiskey before he brushed his teeth, and sometimes, after lunch, he would go to his *rondavel* and take another slug.

It was during the evenings, before and after his glass of wine at dinner, that Alexander drank openly. He would often have a lager before dinner, overtaken by a languorous sense of relaxation, the

Chapter Twenty-One

day's work done. He would talk about the day's events with guests at the bar at one end of the big lounge, beneath its high thatched roof, and tell a few stories about Africa, then after dinner he would drink a couple more lagers, before moving on to a double scotch. He became expansive and loquacious the more he drank. He was aware that he was allowing his tongue to run away with itself, but he was drunk on the sound of his own voice, unable to help himself. Some of the people at the bar were regular visitors who lived locally, such as the young Dutchman who was carrying out a game survey for the WWF. Alexander became inebriated very quickly, because he was tired and ready to go to bed by nine o'clock, and it would soon become obvious to many that he had drunk too much. During the next day, Alexander would know that he could not hope to hide a drinking habit in such a small community, and he would vow to exercise moderation that evening, but his good intentions were soon dissolved in liquor.

One morning in December, just after breakfast, Gary Vorster caught Alexander alone. 'You are drinking too much,' he told him. 'Your behavior is erratic. You're giving the lodge a bad name.'

Alexander feared that he had been particularly full of himself the evening before at the bar. He suspected that he had held forth at length to a variety of local visitors and guests from abroad. He knew that he had had several whiskeys. But he could not remember what he had been talking about. He felt his face grow hot with shame and embarrassment. He did not know how to answer Gary Vorster, so he turned aside and walked away. He understood that his drinking had now become a serious problem. Later that morning, having been busy with Zack, his young black assistant, refueling the Land Rovers and the two boats and topping up their engine oil, Alexander found Gary Vorster in his office. It was extremely warm, and humid, and Alexander looked forward to a shower and a change of clothes before lunch. But he had to get this over with first.

'I want to talk to Graham at head office,' he said. 'I've worked here long enough. I must leave. I need to use the radio telephone.'

'Tell me what you want to say to them. I'll pass on your message.'

'No. I must talk with Graham myself.'

So Gary Vorster permitted Alexander to talk to Windhoek on the radio telephone link. Alexander knew that Gary would be standing listening just beyond the door to the office. There was nothing he could do about that. Graham, the *Bwana Mkubwa* operations manager in Windhoek, at whose home Alexander had spent his first night in Namibia, asked him why he wanted to leave the lodge.

'I've got a problem which I cannot fix if I stay on here. I need to leave the lodge now,' Alexander told him. He was fairly sure that Gary Vorster would already have told Graham that he had a drinking problem.

'Very well. We'll find you something to do here. When do you plan to leave the lodge?'

'Tomorrow morning, Graham. I should reach Windhoek by nightfall.'

Other than young Zack, there was no one at the lodge whom Alexander felt obliged to say goodbye to. He had never grown close to Marge, nor to Gary Vorster and his common law wife. But just before dinner, Alexander visited the black staff lines and sought out Zack, and gave him twenty Rand to keep, in addition to eighty Rand to distribute among the rest of the staff. The money was worth a lot more out here than it would have been in Windhoek. The next morning, at seven o'clock, Zack was the only person waiting outside Alexander's *rondavel* to see him leave. Alexander drove between the gateposts of Kwando River Lodge for the last time.

Chapter Twenty-Two

Running Away Again

Windhoek was a small, schizophrenic city. Depending on your race, your business, and whom you mixed with socially, it was either an entirely white city (excepting only the servants in your home), or almost entirely black. The President, that ex-freedom fighter (or for many, that ex-terrorist), Sam Nujoma, lived in Windhoek, when he was not relaxing at his seaside home, built as a summer residence for the colonial-era German governor, in Swakopmund. For the next few days, Alexander's Windhoek was a white man's city. He socialised with Ralph and one of the other young guides, both of whom were in town at the time, and in the evenings they went out eating and drinking together. Ralph took pains to include Alexander in his social life over the next few days.

Both Ralph and the other guide left Windhoek on the 21st December, on Christmas tours. Alone in the house, no work yet assigned to him, it began to dawn on Alexander that his Namibian interlude was fast approaching its end. He drove to Joe's Beerhouse later that afternoon, and spent the afternoon drinking there, ate a well done beefsteak for supper, and then spent much of the evening there also. By the time he got back to the house he was ready to pass out from drink. It was very warm, but not nearly as humid as the East Caprivi had been. He lay back on the bed in his bush shirt and shorts, kicked his sandals off his feet, and passed out.

Early on the morning of the 22nd of December, Alexander came to. He smelled rank, and he needed a drink. In the kitchen he found someone's tin of instant coffee and some sugar. He stirred some of his whiskey into a cup of coffee. He drank two glasses of water also, brushed his teeth, stripped, stood under the shower for a while, then managed to find some clean underwear. All this was achieved by eight o' clock. He quickly packed his gym bag and his suitcase, checked that he still had cash in his wallet, and took his bags out to his car, which was parked in the front garden. He had had nothing to eat. He closed and locked the front door behind him, and he left the keys in the plant pot nearby, hidden under some cacti. He had quit. He was running away again.

He stopped at a petrol station on the way out of town, topped up the engine oil and the radiator, checked the tyre pressure, and filled the tank. By nine-fifteen that morning he was leaving Windhoek behind him, the road south and sanctuary beckoning. He had a new bottle of scotch, bought two stores along from the petrol station, lying on the passenger seat alongside him, but just for now, he was relatively sober. He had closed his mind to the full implications of what he was doing. It was better not to think at all.

Alexander did not plan on driving back to Johannesburg. He felt ashamed; beaten and broken by drink. He knew he could not stop drinking, so he had run away. He kept driving south, headed for Cape Town and the farm. It was the one place left in the world that he associated with nothing but happiness. Alexander drove all through the day, stopping only thrice. At Keetmanshoop he stopped for some coffee and something to eat, and he needed to use the lavatory; at Springbok, he stopped again, to refuel his car and to drink some more coffee and use the lavatory again. It was dark when he stopped a third time, at Piketberg, for another coffee. Then he drove on, into the night.

He took the Simon Van Der Stel Freeway to the south of Cape Town, and then the Ou Kaapse Weg over the top of Silvermine. The only lights visible were those glimpsed far below. The dark sky was strewn with stars. He reached the Fish Hoek – Kommetjie road around midnight, and was momentarily confused by the changed appearance of the approaches to the farm, for he had entirely forgotten that what had once been his grandfather's land was now a residential suburb, built over with houses, except for a few empty plots here and there (two or three of which had belonged to his father, and presumably belonged now to his mother). He pulled up at last in a wide graveled turning space between the old farmhouse and the new double story house where his aunt and uncle now lived. It was about fifteen minutes past midnight.

Dogs were barking, and Alexander sat in his car, ready to go straight to sleep, but his aunt appeared after a little while, and he wound down the window.

'Sandy! What are you doing here? Never mind – you can tell me in the morning.'

'Can I sleep on the couch in the sitting room until morning, Margaret?' Alexander asked his aunt.

'Yes. Come in.'

Alexander followed his aunt inside via the kitchen. 'Help yourself to coffee if you want. I'll get you a pillow and a blanket for the sofa. Oh, Sandy, you don't look well at all.'

Alexander's aunt disappeared, to reappear within a few minutes with a pillow and a blanket. Alexander bent to kiss her cheek.

'Thank you Margaret. Good night. I'm sorry I got you up.'

'I'll see you in the morning,' his aunt replied, and left Alexander with the two dogs.

Alexander stretched out on the sofa, which was broad and long. He was profoundly disturbed by the conjunction of a sense of home coming, with an interior setting that was new to him, for this house had still been in a state of incompletion when he and his family had visited for his father's funeral. But he fell asleep within minutes of laying his head on the pillow.

Alexander's aunt could not get a clear account from him the next morning. Alexander felt too ashamed to confess that he had drunk himself into a corner, and then run away. However, she was not unfamiliar with alcoholism, and she recognised immediately that Alexander was, or had been, drinking very heavily.

'You can stay here for as long as you like – on one condition, Sandy: you do not bring liquor into my home.'

Alexander agreed, but he knew he would break his word.

And break it he did. There was not much left in the bottle of whiskey he had had with him on the drive south from Windhoek, and later that day he walked to the new Sun Valley shopping complex that had sprung up since he had last lived on the farm, and went inside a bottle store there, and he bought two half-jacks of scotch. He bought half-jacks because they were easier to hide on his person than a single full-sized bottle. He left one of the half-jacks in his car, and the other he sneaked into the bedroom his aunt had given him upstairs, which was not difficult, because Margaret was not in when he returned from his walk to the Sun Valley liquor store, and his uncle was sitting dozing in front of the TV with the sound on.

But Alexander was not entirely lost to consideration for others. On his second morning at the farm, he drove to Fish Hoek. He entered the Standard Bank branch there, and transferred the reasonably healthy credit balance in his Windhoek account, into which his salary had been paid while he had been working for *Bwana Mkubwa*, to the Fish Hoek branch, from which he then withdrew some cash. He bought his aunt a large, lavishly illustrated coffee table book on traditional Cape domestic interiors; for his uncle he bought a carton of Peter Stuyvesant cigarettes; and for his

Chapter Twenty-Two

two cousins (both of whom still lived on the farm: Jennifer with her husband and two small children, in what had been the original farm house; the younger, Mary, in one of the large wooden chalets, with Mike) he bought a bottle of decent Cape white wine each. It was the day before Christmas.

A sense of catastrophic failure haunted Alexander, a failure he seemed to be doomed to repeat over and over, no matter the circumstances in which he found himself. As a consequence, he sought to anesthetize his feelings, and the best way he knew to do this was through drink. And so he continued drinking. Between Christmas and New Year, this became very clear to his aunt. His behaviour became noticeably erratic: his mania was returning.

'You've broken your promise to me,' his aunt said to him shortly before New Year. 'You're drinking every day. I will not tolerate this in my house.'

Alexander, who had a disconcerting trick of maintaining very intent direct eye contact with his interlocutor when he had reason to feel guilt or shame, stared hard at his aunt. This seemed to make her angry.

'Do you even have any plans?' she asked. 'What are you going to do next?'

'I don't know,' Alexander replied.

'If you promise me again not to bring liquor into the house – will you keep your promise?'

'Oh yes,' Alexander said, holding his aunt's gaze. 'I'm sorry.' And even as he spoke, he knew he was lying to her. What he did not yet understand – and was not to understand until some way into recovery from alcoholism, an occasion which lay some years ahead – was that a steady intake of large quantities of alcohol over an extended period was the trigger for the madness that all alcoholics are born with. Alexander, who had always in any case had a gift for living in the moment, refused, when inebriated, to acknowledge that there might be a long term future he should be planning for. In truth, he did not now believe he had a future. He was intelligent enough to know that at the rate of abuse to which he was subjecting his body and soul, he would likely die sooner than later. And this thought hardly distressed him.

Some of these moments he was now living were, however, very pleasant. The high summer weather of the Cape Peninsula was excellent; the days were full of sunshine, warm and dry, and the prevailing south-easterly kept it from growing too warm. Often, Alexander drove to Fish Hoek beach, wearing just shorts, a tee-shirt and sandals, and, having removed his tee-shirt, he sat in the sunshine on a bench on the catwalk (that narrow pathway which wound its way along the edge of the rocky shore to one side of the bay), with the waves breaking against the rocks just below him. He worked on his tan, staring out across the blue, sparkling waters of Fish Hoek Bay. There were public lavatories to hand when he needed them, and he could get coffee at the beach café. He would pass most mornings in this fashion. Back at what he still thought of as the farm (and to be sure, there were still chickens and geese on the property, cats and dogs, and a large paddock remained, with adjoining stables, where his aunt and his married cousin Jennifer still kept a horse each), his family largely shunned him. His two cousins were distant and polite when they saw him. His aunt had nothing anymore to say to him. It was only in memory of his father, the brother she had loved, that she had not yet told Alexander to leave. Only Mike, who had been Alexander's friend in previous years, was still friendly and open towards him. Alexander knew very well that his presence was resented now by the family. However, the prospect of facing up to the reality of his situation scared him, and he took pains via drink to ensure that he did not face up to it.

Fish Hoek had always, by local statute, been a dry town, but in the spirit of the new commercialism that was now engulfing South Africa, that ordinance had been swept aside, and one night in early January of 1994, Alexander had gone drinking

Chapter Twenty-Two

until late at the new O' Halloran's pub in Fish Hoek. By the time he got back to the farm it was after midnight. His aunt and uncle were long asleep in bed. Alexander was extremely drunk, yet (as always) he was physically capable, and he was able to drive back safely to the farm. He had a companion with him: a young man with neat, regular features, short brown hair, and a skinny physique.

'We must keep our voices down,' Alexander told him as they went upstairs. 'My aunt and uncle live here.'

'But wont they want to know who I am, what I'm doing here?' the young man asked Alexander. One of the dogs had followed them upstairs. Margaret and her husband had their bedroom downstairs.

'No – they wont wake up,' Alexander replied. The two sat down on his bed and began to chat quietly. But after a while there came a knock on the bedroom door.

'Sandy. Who's there with you?' asked Margaret from the other side of the closed door.

'No one,' Alexander responded.

'I know there's someone with you. I'm opening the door.'

Alexander's aunt opened the door and looked inside the room, where she could make out the shadowed forms of Alexander and another man. For a moment there was silence, then Margaret said in a very level tone, 'Alexander. Get this person out of my house,' and turned and left them.

'I'm sorry,' Alexander said to his companion. 'I don't know what I was thinking. I'll take you back to Fish Hoek.'

There was no traffic on the road into Fish Hoek. Neither Alexander nor the young man had anything they wished to say, until, as they reached the town, Alexander asked his passenger where he wanted to be dropped off.

'Outside O' Halloran's will do fine,' the young man replied. 'You've humiliated me. I hope I dont see you again.'

'I don't think you will. I think my stay here is over,' Alexander said quietly.

'I'm glad,' said the young man, and Alexander turned the car around.

In the morning, Margaret said to him, 'I do not want you staying here any longer. Go back to Johannesburg. I cannot cope with your drinking anymore.'

Alexander was full of self loathing, and he felt terribly ashamed. 'I'm so sorry for everything, Margaret. I'm sorry for the mess I'm in. I'm sorry I've abused your kindness.'

'You've abused more than my kindness,' his aunt replied. 'You've abused my love, and your Father's memory. I don't want to see you again for a long time.'

Feeling hung over and frail Alexander packed his suitcase and gym bag. He left without seeing anyone. He left without giving any of the animals a hug. He had enjoyed the cats, one of whom was an especially sweet old darling, who had often slept on his bed with him. He was consumed with misery, shame, remorse, and disgust at himself. He wished his father's revolver was to hand, rather than at his mother's home in Johannesburg. He would have found it easy to blow his brains out right now. He was desperately weary of his drinking, of his failures, and of his loneliness. He was stricken by remorse at what he had done to his aunt. He felt an overwhelming sense of loss. He was also in desperate need of a drink. Just before reaching the Fish Hoek main road, he pulled over and found the half-jack of whiskey he had left in the car, and drank quickly from it. After a short while, the trembling eased, and he felt a little less as if he was about to die. It was half past nine by the time he reached Fish Hoek, where he parked near a café in town and he bought a coffee and a croissant. After drinking two cups of black coffee loaded with sugar, and eating the croissant, he felt a little better.

'I need to check myself into a clinic,' he thought. 'I cannot endure living this way any longer.'

Chapter Twenty-Two

Alexander only got as far as Beaufort West, at the start of the Great Karoo, before he knew he could drive no further that day. He checked in at the Wagon Wheel Motel, which he remembered from childhood, and lay down in his clothes on the bed and slept. It was after dark when he awoke. For a minute he did not know where he was, and when he remembered, it took him another minute to find a light switch. He checked his watch: it was half past nine. All he had had to eat all day was one croissant. The restaurant would be closed now. He foresaw a long night ahead of him, with only the remains of his half-jack of whiskey to keep him going.

The next morning, having driven into Beaufort West to find a bottle store (where he bought a carton of Peter Stuyvesant cigarettes, a bottle of Zippo lighter fluid and some flints, and a bottle of scotch), he returned to the motel and ate a breakfast of sorts in the restaurant. Then he settled his bill and hit the road again. It was late afternoon before he reached Johannesburg. He had driven nearly a thousand miles since leaving the farm. He drove straight to the clinic in Boksburg, where he had stayed a year earlier, and they allowed him to check in immediately.

Alexander knew that he was in for a dreadful time. It was not just that the physical withdrawals were very bad, worse each time, but that they were accompanied by a devastating despair, shame and remorse. The first four or five days were the worst. He sweated profusely and he had the shakes all the time, along with sudden convulsive movements of his limbs and head. Sometimes his chest seemed to seize up, and he had difficulties in drawing a full breath. He suffered from periods of extreme anxiety, accompanied by sudden intense panics. The despair and devastating remorse outlasted the period of his physical withdrawals, but these too decreased in intensity over time. His first three days and nights were spent in the acute treatment ward, where he and two others were watched round the clock, then he was moved into a general ward. Within a week he had formed friendships with two or three other patients, one of whom was a solemn, softly spoken, fragile youngster of about eighteen, with a beautiful face, who was coming off a drugs dependency, and towards whom Alexander felt very protective.

By the end of his two weeks stay, Alexander was suffering no physical cravings at all, but he continued to experience moments of acute anguish, along with intense remorse. He could not cease dwelling on how he had abused his aunt's trust and love and care. Alexander became prayerful once again, saying his prayers on his knees before he went to bed, and again when he got up in the morning. He was determined, simply by staying sober, to try to make up for the hurt he had caused others.

On the morning of Friday 28th January, 1994, Alexander left the clinic, completely sober, but whether he was truly recovered, only time would tell. He drove to Roy's home in Honeydew on the far side of Johannesburg. Roy was away at work, but he was expecting his brother. He had hidden the spare front door key at the base of the woodpile against the kitchen wall. Alexander let himself in and deactivated the electronic alarm system by keying in the code his brother had given him, then he picked up Smokie the Persian cat and hugged her to his breast, rocking her gently in his arms. He could not remember the last time he had cried properly (although he had shed a few quiet tears at his father's funeral), but now at last, holding Smokie's warm, soft, furry body in his arms, Alexander began to cry.

Chapter Twenty-Three

Gunfire

There was still one old friend from Alice's gang whom Alexander thought might even now remember him fondly. Graham had remained single when everyone else had, one way or another, paired off with someone else. Alexander remembered him as a somewhat laconic young man who, when he did speak, could display a dry wit, and who had sometimes shown a somewhat mocking fondness for Alexander. In early February, alone all day but for Smokie the cat, at Roy's house in Honeydew, Alexander telephoned Graham one early evening. Astonishingly, the telephone number Alexander had in his old address book still reached him.

'So you're still in the land of the living, Sandro. That's good,' Graham said at the other end of the telephone. 'What have you been up to?'

'Quite a lot, but nothing right now. What about you?'

'I'm still working at Exclusive Books – at the Hyde Park store,' Graham replied. 'The Hillbrow branch closed last year.'

'That's sad,' Alexander responded. 'I've not been anywhere near Hillbrow since 1990.'

'I'm having a party on Friday night,' Graham continued. 'People from the block of flats, mostly. Alice and some of the others will be there. Would you like to come?'

'I'd like that. Do you still live at the same place?'

'I do,' Graham replied. 'Ground floor, number one.'

'What time should I be there?' Alexander asked.

'Eight will be OK.'

'I'll see you Friday evening then. Cheers.'

It had been more than three years since Alexander had last visited Yeoville. From what he could see beneath the streetlights, and the brightly lighted neon signs outside the clubs and pubs and restaurants in Rocky Street, Yeoville appeared to be unchanged, but then Alexander realised how many black faces he was now seeing on the street; a consequence of the abolition of the notorious Group Areas Act in June 1991. It was nearly four years since Alexander had last seen Alice and the other members of the old gang who were at Graham's party tonight. But there was no warmth in their greetings. Even Alice showed little sign of wishing to talk with him. Only Graham was happy to see him.

'Sandro!' Graham exclaimed. 'A blast from the past! Come and get a drink.'

There was dance music playing in the sitting room, and the carpet had been rolled up, revealing the bare, waxed floorboards. In the hall there was an array of drinks and canapés set out. In response to Alexander's assertion that he did not drink, Graham gave Alexander a cold can of Coke, and asked what he had been doing. It was clear that he was impressed by Alexander's adventures in Malta and Namibia.

'Many of us thought you were finished, the last time we saw you,' Graham said. 'You were pitiful!'

'I seem to be at a loose end right now, and I don't know what I'll be doing next.'

Chapter Twenty-Three

'I expect you'll continue to astonish us – *nê?*'

Alexander, sober, felt not the least wish to dance, so he found a chair in the hallway, and sat and drank his Coca-Cola and smoked a cigarette. He already regretted having come. He was afraid he might see Una again. Una did not in fact appear, but when Terrance, Una's older brother, and once Alexander's friend, entered the hallway for a beer, his greeting to Alexander was perfunctory. Alexander knew he had made a mistake in coming here. You could not rekindle a fire from nothing but cold ash and clinkers. He began thinking of leaving. However, at that moment a black man appeared from the sitting room, a can of beer in his hand, and sat on the chair next to Alexander. 'Good evening,' he said to Alexander, who replied 'Hullo.'

The man, who looked to be in his late forties, and who was wearing a rather baggy suit, remarked, 'It is too noisy for me in there.' He smiled. 'And they are dancing white man's dances.'

Alexander laughed. 'I used to dance. I don't think I do anymore. Do you live nearby?'

'I am one of Graham's neighbours in these flats. My name is Lindisizwe. It means, "Waiting for a country." When I was named, we blacks had no country.'

'I'm Sandy.' The two men shook hands.

When the Apartheid laws had been repealed a little under two years earlier, Alexander had been living in Malta. He had barely been aware of that momentous occasion in South Africa's history. However, he did know that South Africa's first multiracial elections were to be held in April – in just two months' time. It was generally thought that the ANC would win the elections comfortably.

Lindisizwe asked Alexander what work he did.

'Until recently I was working as a game ranger in the Caprivi Strip in Namibia,' Alexander replied. 'Before that, I was teaching English in Malta. What business are you in, Lindisizwe?'

'I own a supermarket in Mayfair,' the man replied. Mayfair was a Johannesburg inner city district. 'I also have business interests in the Eastern Cape – in Transkei.'

Each man sipped from the can he was holding, then Lindisizwe turned to Alexander again, and said 'So you are not doing anything now? As a game ranger, what sort of work did you do?'

'I was based at a luxury game lodge in a big wildlife concession. It was my task to show the guests the regional wildlife and explain the natural history.'

'So you know about looking after residential guests?'

'I would n't say that. But yes, I have some knowledge of how a game lodge is run.'

'I am a shareholder in a businessmen's hotel in the black township outside Kingstown,' Lindisizwe continued. 'It was mismanaged. We are trying to get it back on its feet again. We need a manager. Would you be interested in talking about this?'

So that's it, Alexander thought. I thought there must be a purpose to his questions. 'I'm not sure . . .'

'We can meet again, and talk about it, I think?' the man asked.

'OK. When?'

'Are you free tomorrow, at lunchtime? We can meet at the steak house in Rocky Street. It is just round the corner from here.'

'Yes, I know it. I could do that. What time?'

'Let us meet at one o' clock.'

'Right-O.' Alexander had already had enough of the very loud music from the sitting room, and he felt awkward and unwanted here. 'I have to leave now. I'll see you tomorrow at one.' He stood up. 'Cheerio,' he said, and extended his hand.

Lindisizwe stood, and shook Alexander's hand. 'Tomorrow then. I think what I have to say will interest you, Sandy.'

Alexander smiled, found his jacket on the bed in the bedroom, and, unwilling to brave the sitting room to find

Chapter Twenty-Three

Graham, left the flat directly and walked to his car, which was parked not far down the street, and he began the long drive through Johannesburg's night-time suburbs for his brother's home in Honeydew, on the farthest fringes of the far side of the metropolis.

Lindisizwe's English was clearly his second language. Although he had a good grasp of the idiom, his accent was typically that of a black South African. But Alexander appreciated what an achievement it was for a black man, educated in rural apartheid South Africa, his English teacher another black person to whom English was also a foreign language, to speak comprehensible English at all – yet millions of blacks in South Africa did so, and many spoke Afrikaans also. Lindisizwe wore his rumpled suit with only haphazard care. Unlike so many black South Africans he was not a sharp dresser, and this for Alexander was a point in Lindisizwe's favour. Alexander thought that he was probably honest. He was also punctual, arriving at the steak house in Rocky Street the next day only a few minutes after one o' clock. As always, Alexander was hungry. He ordered a steak, well done, with chips and salad and a couple of bread rolls. So too did Lindisizwe, who added a lager to his order. Alexander stuck to Coke.

As Alexander tackled his steak, Lindisizwe explained that they needed someone who would find a way of reactivating the hotel's lines of credit; who would restock the bar, motivate the staff, and turn the hotel into a profitable enterprise once again.

'Does the hotel have substantial debts?' Alexander asked.

'The liquor wholesaler is owed money. So is Eskom: the electricity has been cut off. If you can get the bar running again, and guests checking in, you can generate enough money to pay the Eskom bill.'

'I don't know whether I would be successful,' Alexander responded. 'But if I try, how much would you be paying me?'

'If you can do these things, and you stay on as manager, the directors will pay you a salary of four thousand Rand a month, and you will be living and eating at the hotel for free.'

'I need to think about this for a few days. Can you give me your phone number, Lindisizwe?'

The man handed Alexander a business card. It read "Lindisizwe Dlamini – Managing Director, Lucky Choice Supermarket, Mayfair." A Mayfair, Johannesburg address followed. There was also a Kingstown, Eastern Cape address. There were three telephone numbers, two of which were Johannesburg numbers, and one of which was, presumably, a Kingstown telephone number.

'Please give me your phone number, Sandy,' Lindisizwe said. Alexander gave him Roy's home number. 'Can I phone you in two days' time?' the man asked Alexander.

'OK. Or I'll call you.'

The two men began to pay more attention to their food, and when they had finished their meal, each ordered a coffee. They chatted about Alexander's experiences overseas. Lindisizwe seemed to regard London as something akin to a promised land. When they had finished their coffees (Lindisizwe paid the bill), Alexander stood, and shaking hands with Lindisizwe, he took his leave of the black man. 'We'll be in touch soon. *Sala kakuhle!*'

'*Hamba kakuhle,*' Lindisizwe replied.

Alexander told Lindisizwe, who telephoned him at his brother's number two days later, that he would give the job a go. Despite all his setbacks, Alexander still believed that he could accomplish almost anything he set his mind to. For a boy who had had very few friends at school, and in whom self confidence had been markedly lacking; a solitary boy who had rarely actively sought the company of others, partly for fear of rejection and partly due to an inclination for his own company, Alexander had found within a few years of leaving school that he had a surprising store of belief in himself. And that store

Chapter Twenty-Three

of belief had not been completely emptied in the intervening years.

Roy serviced his car for him at home. Roy, an engineer, was good with cars. Alexander was still sober. He said goodbye to his mother and her cat, hugged Smokie, his brother's cat, and at eight o' clock that morning he set off across Johannesburg for Lindisizwe's flat in Yeoville. Lindisizwe would be accompanying him on the journey. It was ten o' clock before Alexander continued his journey, the black man in the passenger seat next to him, and within a very short while, using the elevated dual carriageway, he had crossed the city and taken the turning for the N1 south for Bloemfontein. Kingstown lay four hundred and seventy miles ahead. The motorway as far as Bloemfontein was familiar to Alexander, for it was the same route one took for Cape Town. Outside Bloemfontein, the two men stopped for fuel, a visit to the lavatories, and some coffee with something to eat, and then set off on the N6 south for East London. There was not very much traffic on the road. It was an easy drive. The day was warm and sunny. Alexander reached Kingstown in the Eastern Cape at half past six in the evening. This was Lindisizwe's home town. Alexander was to spend the night in Lindisizwe's home, and Lindisizwe would show him the hotel the next morning.

In the lounge, where the only pictures on the walls were framed prints of what looked to Alexander like chocolate box reproductions of Alpine and rural English scenes, the over-stuffed furniture was decorated with much faux gilt. There was a vast TV set at one end of the room, and a hi-fi set with massive speakers in one corner. Lindisizwe offered Alexander a beer. Alexander declined. 'I'd prefer a coffee, please.'

Alexander was bewildered by the number of people at Lindisizwe's house that evening. Alexander was not sure which of the two large women he met was his associate's wife; perhaps both of them. But from Alexander's conversation with Lindisizwe over lunch at the steak house in Yeoville a week earlier, Alexander had gathered there was also a wife of some degree in Lindisizwe's Yeoville flat. There were four or five children, ranging in age from a baby still being breast-fed, to two adolescent girls in their late teens, one of whom was nursing the baby. It was clear to Alexander that he was being shown off, for there appeared to be friends and neighbours present also, but as they spoke almost exclusively in Xhosa, he could not be sure who exactly they were. He suspected that at least two men wearing suits, who appeared about half an hour after his arrival, were business associates of Lindisizwe, perhaps even investors in the hotel.

Alexander felt close to being overwhelmed by the alien environment. He felt infinitely more out of his depth than he had ever felt abroad. And perhaps Alexander's reaction was not unusual for a white man who had grown up in South Africa during the apartheid era. Indeed, what was unusual was that he, a white man of his generation and background, was now a houseguest in a black man's family home.

At about eight o' clock a meal was served. They ate at table in the dining room, with the people for whom there was no space at the table being served their food on trays in the sitting room. The two large women served lamb chops with vegetables, and what Alexander knew as *"styve pap"* – a stiff, stodgy maize meal preparation. Alexander, at that stage of his life, could still eat almost anything. He was hungry, and he did the meal justice. He noticed that the others at table made liberal use of the spicy condiment, *Aromat*, sprinkled heavily on their lamb chops. He could not remember using *Aromat* before; it was not something he had grown up with, but he was to use it with eagerness at every meal at the hotel during the three weeks to come.

Feeling increasingly tired, Alexander sat through a gabble of talk in Xhosa in the lounge for an hour after the meal was finished (although Lindisizwe occasionally directed a few words

Chapter Twenty-Three

in English his way). It was half past ten before one of Lindisizwe's (two?) wives showed Alexander to a bedroom with two beds in it, where a bed with fresh linen had been made up. From the two beds and the things on a dressing table, he gathered this room belonged to two of the girls. As he brushed his teeth in the bathroom down the corridor, he wondered what he was doing here, so far from everything familiar. He wished at that moment that he had never agreed to this scheme. He wished he was at home with Roy and Smokie. Alexander felt desperately alone and isolated. He wondered too how much longer he was going to remain sober, because he felt a nagging desire for a very strong drink. Before he got into bed, he did something he had not done since leaving the clinic in Boksburg: he knelt and said his prayers. He woke only once during the quiet night, to use the lavatory down the corridor, and he was asleep again very soon thereafter.

The hotel was a modern, single story brick building situated in the black township outside Kingstown. The township had a population of about twenty thousand people. The hotel had been built to cater to local black travellers and businessmen. There was a small staff remaining, to whom Alexander was introduced by Lindisizwe. Then Lindisizwe left Alexander at the hotel, the only white man in the entire township. Alexander explained to the staff as best he could, in a mix mostly of English, with some *Fanagalo* and Zulu he had picked up over the years (Zulu, which Alexander had been trying to learn at the mission in Natal, was similar in many respects to Xhosa), that they would continue to be paid only a half wage until the hotel was profitable again, but that they could continue to live and eat there for free. During the course of the next two weeks Alexander, using the telephone (which was still connected), and driving into Kingstown several times, managed to resupply the hotel's bar with a basic stock of Coca-Cola, a few bottles of scotch, and several crates of Lion and Castle lagers. His greatest coup was in obtaining credit from Eskom, the state monopoly electricity supplier, who turned the power back on. Water could now be heated other than on top of the gas range; electric heaters could be used during the sometimes surprisingly cool evenings. There were drinkers again in the bar. A scattering of guests began to return to the hotel.

Then, in very early March, Alexander had a visitor, a young black man, who, he was to learn later, had spent the last few years at an ANC bush-camp in Zambia, and had just recently returned to South Africa with some of his *cadres*, in anticipation of the almost certain ANC victory in the forthcoming general election.

'We do not want you here, white man,' the young man spat at him, his face ugly with hate. 'This is our place. You leave now.'

Alexander had never before seen such naked malice in a black man's eyes. There had been no malice in the eyes of the black men who had held him up at knifepoint in Joubert Park four years previously, only mercilessness and cold intent.

Alexander took no action, other than to telephone Lindisizwe and tell him what had transpired. Lindisizwe, by his long silence, followed by a poor attempt over the telephone at reassuring him, did not make him feel very secure, but Alexander continued with his work at the hotel. He was trying to improve the standard of service at the hotel, which meant training the staff in various functions, and although he had no experience of bookkeeping, he was trying to keep simple books as well.

Rather late one evening, Alexander was sitting with the Xhosa night watchman in the foyer, in front of the oil heater which was turned low against the slight chill. The foyer was lighted by only one low wattage wall light. The night watchman's grizzled hair and seamed and lined features placed him somewhere in his fifties, but he could have been as young as Alexander, or as old as seventy. After a certain point, Alexander thought, black people seem to stop aging. Alexander liked him. He had that gentle, patient

Chapter Twenty-Three

forbearance that Alexander associated with some older black men. He had a little English, and Alexander had been chatting to him about the old fellow's herdboy childhood.

Neither man had spoken for a while, and Alexander's thoughts were far away, when there erupted a shockingly loud burst of noise, it seemed just yards away, and the big glass doors shattered.

'My God!' Alexander exclaimed. They were, unbelievably, being fired upon. Alexander and the night watchman, neither of whom was injured, fled, bent double, for the dark kitchens at the far end of the unlighted corridor, and now Alexander could hear shouting behind him. Using the telephone extension in the kitchens (for there was just enough light coming through the windows for Alexander to see the dial on the handset), he telephoned the Police. The gunmen were now inside the hotel, but none had yet entered the kitchens, where he and the night watchman were keeping low, quiet as mice in the near darkness. The armed Police arrived within less than five minutes. Indeed, they would have heard the gunfire from the Police station, which was located less than a mile away. There had been no overnight guests staying that night, nor were there any customers still drinking at the bar, and the staff in their quarters behind the hotel had wisely remained there while the gunmen had rampaged through the lounge and bar, firing off occasional short bursts of gunfire.

With the arrival of the Police and the flight (through the emergency exit at the rear of the lounge) of all but one gunman (who had blundered into a low table in the dark and tripped and fallen, and whom the Police rapidly disarmed and handcuffed), Alexander, who had now begun to feel a slight physical reaction to his fright, went to the bar and poured himself a whiskey. He downed it in one gulp, then poured another, and sat drinking it more slowly, puffing on a cigarette, while two of the black policemen questioned him about the incident. The gunman had been taken outside. As he passed Alexander, under close restraint by a pair of armed policemen, Alexander recognised him as the young man who had warned him that he was not wanted in the township. Alexander told the Police about the visit he had had from this man a few days earlier. That night, Alexander slept in a different bedroom, and the next morning he telephoned Lindisizwe and told him he was quitting the job with immediate effect.

This was the third time in his life that Alexander had been in very close proximity to gunfire. In 1976, during his visit to Pamplona in northern Spain, a twenty-one year old Alexander had been caught up in an excited crowd of demonstrators in the town plaza, when the *Guardia Civil* had opened fire on the gathering. Within a few minutes the plaza was empty, but for several people lying on the ground. Alexander had ducked sharply into a side alley, but he had then peered around the corner and had watched with something akin to total disbelief as a *Civil* draw his sidearm and shot two of the people lying on the ground in the head. Yet then, as now, Alexander had felt a certain detachment from the scene. He had not felt the sort of shock he imagined was proper on such an occasion. That night, in the crowded campsite outside the city where he and his two companions had pitched their small tent, the sound of gunfire close to hand had drawn Alexander from the tent in its wake, and in the starlit night he could just make out the forms of four or five people running up the rocky hillside on the far side of the river, with half a dozen *Guardia Civil* lined up on the near riverbank, firing at them.

Lindisizwe tried, over the telephone, to persuade Alexander not to leave. But Alexander was adamant: the job was not worth his life. An hour after Alexander's telephone call to Lindisizwe, one of the investors in the hotel, the son of a local tribal potentate, called on Alexander. He was a fine looking man of considerable height and girth, and he advised Alexander that he was arranging

Chapter Twenty-Three

for an armed Police guard at the hotel. Alexander however had had enough. His earnings so far had been zero; he felt he owed Lindisizwe and his associates nothing. He did however telephone Lindisizwe again, to tell him where the books for the hotel were kept, and to remind him that the hotel would have to settle the Eskom bill within a very few days, and make a further arrangement with the liquor supplier.

It took Alexander little time to pack and say goodbye to the staff. He drove away in his car at about eleven o' clock. He had one of the bottles of whiskey from the bar with him in the car. Its purchase had been the last entry he had written up in the bar's sales records. It was just after seven-thirty in the evening by the time he reached his brother's home outside Johannesburg.

Chapter Twenty-Four

On Tour

The abandonment of sexual morality, fuelled by alcoholic excesses, was for Alexander a defining feature of 1994. Still billeted on the tolerant and patient Roy (Alexander could no longer afford to rent a place of his own), Alexander began to suffer from nightmares in which he was the intended victim of extreme violence. At times during the day he would experience an extreme agitation of mind, accompanied by a mounting sense of panic. Alexander grew to dread and fear sudden loud noises. The sound of people shouting, or of running feet, made his pulse race and his breath catch in his throat. He went to see a doctor. The medico, without offering a diagnosis (and at the time Alexander had never heard of post-traumatic stress disorder), had prescribed diazepam. Alexander had quickly become dependent on a dosage of ten milligrams in every twenty-four hours, and although his day time mental agitation diminished, the nightmares, although less frequent, continued. He soon noticed that he felt extremely anxious and disturbed if he forgot to take his five milligram dose of diazepam in the morning, or again in the late evening. In addition to taking the diazepam, Alexander did as so many people suffering from a mental disturbance did: he

Chapter Twenty-Four

self-medicated, using alcohol. If he drank enough during the day and evening, he could sleep without nightmares. Alexander became rapidly re-addicted to alcohol, returning to the same levels he had been sustaining before his stay at the clinic.

Anesthetized by alcohol, Alexander was able to visit Cape Town twice in 1994. He travelled there and back by rail each time, with his first journey being made in mid winter, in late June. He justified these visits to Roy by explaining them as attempts to find work as a tour guide in Cape Town, but Alexander knew that he was drinking far too much to do anything of the sort. He was by now living entirely in the moment: he had become the ultimate existentialist.

Alexander made both journeys on the Trans Karoo Express, travelling in a twin berth *coupé* each time, which he had to himself on both journeys, and which he could still afford to pay for from his own resources. Travelling by train exerted a huge appeal for Alexander. The ponderous solidity of the rolling stock and the clever layout of the compartments brought him much satisfaction. The sound of the wheels clacking across the joins in the rails (for the track was not yet welded) was a lullaby as comforting to Alexander as a mother's loving voice is to a small child. It seemed to Alexander a very civilised way of making the nine hundred and ninety mile journey between Johannesburg and Cape Town. The train had an air conditioned lounge car with a bar, where Alexander spent much of his time during the journey. There was also an air conditioned dining car, where he was served dinner on the first day out, and breakfast the next morning, these meals inclusive in the fare. The cuisine on South African Railways was excellent. Alexander had brought a dark jacket and a couple of ties with him: most men still wore a tie and jacket in the South African Railways dining cars at dinner time.

On the way down they crossed the arid Karoo during the night. In the early morning, before it was fully daylight, the train reached Touws River, a once important railway junction, and having made the journey before, Alexander felt a rising anticipation. Breakfast would be served before long, and he knew that the scenery was going to become ever more striking from this point on. At breakfast the tables were set with clean, starched linen, and the cutlery was of heavy silver plate. The crockery was of china and there was a clean folded napkin at each place setting. The waiters, mostly young Afrikaner lads, were smartly turned out, polite and attentive. During breakfast the train wound its way slowly through the startlingly dramatic Hex River Valley, which sheltered vineyards in the valley bottom, and was bounded by soaring mountain peaks, which in late June were already snow capped, the snow a gleaming white in the early morning sunshine. The rail track wound for many miles between the mountains, before beginning its descent of the mighty escarpment, doubling and redoubling on itself, passing through several tunnels cut in the living rock, until at last it reached the coastal plain, and the train halted at Paarl, the first big town. Between Paarl and Cape Town, the track was level, with long straight stretches, and the train picked up speed again as it crossed the Cape Flats, reaching Cape Town Station later that morning.

During both these visits to Cape Town Alexander stayed at an old residential hotel in Long Street, a street which descended from the lower slopes of Table Mountain, reaching down to the old docks. The street, which had been much frequented by visiting seamen for several hundred years, and had been lined with establishments catering to their needs, still retained a somewhat *louche* character. Long Street still carried remnants of easy-going disrespectability and nocturnal liveliness. Early to mid nineteenth century architecture, much of it in the Cape vernacular style, predominated. The residential hotel Alexander stayed in during each of the visits was a mid nineteenth century building, with tall shuttered windows, and a wide first floor verandah with wrought

Chapter Twenty-Four

iron railings, running along the street frontage. The more sought after bedrooms, of which Alexander had one, opened directly onto the verandah. Alexander could sit out there and listen to the street sounds, or watch the parade of street life below.

During both of these visits to Cape Town, Alexander engaged in a number of transient sexual encounters, on one occasion picking up a girl at the Whistle Stop bar at the top of Long Street. She had a slim build, small breasts and a *gamine* face, and in that moment at least, Alexander felt powerfully attracted to her. These loveless, entirely carnal encounters (in which, at best, there might exist a momentary tenderness on Alexander's part) were to add to the sum of Alexander's self loathing in later years. There was no lasting joy for Alexander in a life bereft of its moral foundations. Alexander could not then hear Him, but God was still calling him.

In November, after Alexander's second visit to Cape Town, the express for Johannesburg and Pretoria had been hauled through the night by a steam locomotive. This was by then fairly unusual. Alexander had woken briefly twice during the night, and each time he had heard the rapid beat of the locomotive's pistons up front – and once, he heard the long double wail of the engine's whistle, a sound both lost and defiant as it reached out far into the dark night across a boundless land. Just such a sound had moved Alexander as a child, on journeys by train between Nairobi and Mombasa, and it moved him now. In that moment at least, Alexander shed the depraved, cracked gloss of his adulthood, and reverted for a short while to the innocence of a childhood that seemed so far away now. There was the potential still for redemption alive in Alexander's spirit.

As Christmas of 1994 approached, Alexander felt an urgent need to reclaim his moral and spiritual integrity. He could not endure the prospect of another stay at the clinic, so he began, each day, to drink a little less than the day before. This meant that for almost two weeks, Alexander felt a constant, sometimes fierce yearning for more alcohol than he was permitting himself. He did however spare himself the horrendous withdrawals that accompanied ceasing to drink overnight. He told his brother and his mother what he was doing.

'Oh, Sandy,' his mother said to him, 'If only you could stop drinking. It's clear to us that you dare not drink. I will be so relieved if you can stop.'

'I think I shall manage, Mum,' Alexander replied. 'This time.'

Within a fortnight – by the end of the first week of January 1995 – Alexander was dry, and he no longer craved alcohol. His brother and his mother were happy and relieved.

'This year,' Alexander told them, 'I'm going to do something with my life. Perhaps I'll begin working as a field guide.' He looked down at the floor. 'And I'm sorry.'

He wanted to say more, but there was too much to say. 'I'm sorry,' he said a second time.

Will's report on Alexander at the conclusion of his training as a field guide had been extremely positive. He possessed the full SATOUR accreditation, and he could work as a guide anywhere in South Africa. Alexander approached a wildlife tours operation based in Johannesburg's northern suburbs, which was advertising for field guides. He made no mention of his time in Namibia, and he hoped that they would not have heard of him before. Perhaps they had not, for they signed him on as a field guide for a variety of wildlife tours, ranging from short two and three nighters in the Lowveld to tours lasting nine or ten days. The tours this outfit offered to its foreign clients were expensive; there were no high volume coach tours on offer. The destinations were usually select private game reserves with luxurious lodges and accommodation and *cordon bleu* cuisine. The number of guests in a party was kept very low. Often, Alexander found himself driving and guiding for just one (usually middle aged) couple from abroad. Sometimes he might be guiding for a small family group. Alexander drove an E-class Mercedes or a

Chapter Twenty-Four

BMW 7 series saloon, and on the rare occasions he was in charge of a group of more than two clients, he would drive a top of the range Volkswagen bus with the powerful five cylinder Audi engine and plush upholstery and air conditioning.

On one level, Alexander found this work easy. It called for the practice of skills which he could exercise with little effort. Which is not to say that the work could not sometimes be demanding: he would be on duty round the clock during a tour, sometimes having to deal with a guest's most trivial needs outside of normal working hours. ('Sandy, I need some batteries for my electric razor,' – this on a Sunday afternoon at a game lodge, more than forty miles from the nearest store). He would be driving long distances between Johannesburg and the tour stops; he would have to consider his guests' lavatory needs and rest stops along the way. On the cheaper tours they would be headed for one or two of the camps in the Kruger National Park, where they would stay in pleasant, thatched *rondavels*, and eat their meals at the excellent camp restaurants; and on the more expensive tours their destinations would be one or more of the internationally renowned private game reserves along the western fringes of the Kruger Park; game reserves such as Londolozi, Mala Mala, Manyeleti and Sabi Sands, which offered superb accommodation, highly attractive *ambiances* and excellent cuisine. On the way to the game reserves, Alexander would tell his guests something about the countryside they were driving through, its history and its economy, and he would talk about the sights he was showing them, which might include natural wonders such as the Blyde River Canyon, or one of the many impressive waterfalls in the region, or particular features of the region's history, such as the charming and beautifully restored Victorian gold mining town, Pilgrims Rest, whose structures of corrugated iron (houses, shops, a functioning hotel where Alexander's guests would have lunch) had been preserved, many of them furnished with antique Victoriana, as if time had stood still.

Alexander did not enjoy the two occasions his employers put him in charge of a French speaking party. His French was not up to it; he struggled terribly, and he found these tours extremely stressful. But the company he worked for had a higher opinion of his spoken French than was merited, and they were glad to avoid paying the high rates a fully bilingual French speaking field guide would have demanded. It was during one such French speaking tour in late 1995 that Alexander had his first drink since January that year. He drank a couple of beers one evening. And again the following evening.

The natural charm that had been such a feature of Alexander's personality during his youthful years was still very much in evidence, and he proved to be popular with his guests. He was knowledgeable about the countryside through which he drove them, and he shared his knowledge with enthusiasm. He knew his wildlife and birdlife, and he knew his flora also, and he was able to share a wealth of detail about the birds and animals they saw, and the trees and shrubs he pointed out to them. During evening meals together, where Alexander could advise on which of the Cape wines to order, he was able to engage his guests in wide ranging conversation. He was well spoken and well read, and he was not dismayed by talking with people for whom English was not a first language. His maturity and his years spent living abroad meant that he was free of the gaucheness and parochialism that afflicted many of the (typically) far younger South African field guides. Alexander collected generous tips (often in hard foreign currency) at the end of almost all his tours, and often his guests would give him their contact details as they were saying goodbye, so that he could look them up should he ever be visiting their home countries.

Chapter Twenty-Five

Violence

In December 1995, high summer in South Africa, Alexander rented a flat in Yeoville. It was a fourth floor flat in a nineteen-sixties apartment block, with jacaranda trees growing in the street below, and only local traffic passing by. There was the usual fairly large entrance hall, with a kitchen in which was a 1960s gas cooker, a great, solid piece of engineering, only marginally more modern than the 1930s gas cooker Alexander had used in his Bellevue flat. Alexander liked cooking on gas: he felt you had much more direct and immediate control of the heat settings. The bathroom with a lavatory was a nice sized room, and the sitting room-dining room was very big, as was the single bedroom. Both of these rooms fronted the flat, and opened onto a full length, deep covered verandah. Alexander parked his car in covered parking below the flats, access to which, both from inside the block and from the street, required keys to the locks. The flat came unfurnished, but Alexander had picked up a second hand lounge suite and other items of furniture at good prices from a used furniture dealer in Braamfontein. The shop had delivered for him. Alexander still had some pieces of furniture dating back to his previous stay in the district in 1989 and 1990, which had been stored all this time at his brother's house in Honeydew, and he brought them with him. One of these was the old metal framed single bed he had used since the age of ten, when his family had first arrived in South Africa from Kenya.

Alexander was by now the only white resident in this block of flats. Yeoville had become a very black suburb since Apartheid's collapse. Alexander did not feel that his white skin was unwelcome in the apartment block. His black neighbours were no more rowdy or ill behaved than his white neighbours in Bellevue had been five years earlier. When Alexander walked the two blocks down to Rocky Street, he would sometimes be the only white face within a hundred yards. This did not bother him if it was daytime, but at night, he would usually take the car if he was visiting the pub.

Alexander still had Alice's telephone number for her flat in Hunter Street, and he telephoned her one evening and arranged to visit her the following evening. He had not seen her since Graham's party in February 1994, and then only to exchange a few words with her. When he knocked on her door, bearing a large bunch of chrysanthemums and carnations, he was nervous of the reception he would get. But Alice offered her cheek to be kissed, and sat him down on the couch alongside her, having moved a cat out of the way. Yet things were not right: Alexander felt a distance between the two of them. He tried hard to rekindle something of the old friendship, but his drunken antics some years earlier had created a gulf between them which it was clear would not now be bridged. He left after only an hour with Alice, and he was unhappy. She had been such a good friend, the focus of Alexander's social life years earlier. As Alexander walked downstairs and got into his car, he thought to himself, 'I have no friends left anymore.' How could this have happened?

Most of the pubs and clubs in Rocky Street that Alexander remembered from the old days were gone. But at the eastern end

Chapter Twenty-Five

of Rocky Street, Caravans, one of the pubs he remembered from years gone by, was still open. Alexander would relax here in the afternoons or evenings between tours. There was a small garden in which were tables and chairs beneath large colourful umbrellas, where he could sit outside in good weather. He soon grew to know most of the regulars, and he enjoyed sitting with some of them, chatting over a drink. Alexander had resumed the pattern of his time in Malta; he drank only lager beers. Because he was neither extremely unhappy, nor facing financial problems at the time, Alexander did not find it difficult to avoid spirits. He knew by now that without any doubt, spirits were the beginning of a slippery slope for him.

Sometimes Alexander would visit Hillbrow, to drink at Brief Encounters, or at the Balkan Football Club. He would park his car beneath Highpoint. When he walked the couple of hundred yards to Brief Encounters, near the far end of Pretoria Street, he would be one of very few white faces in the street. Twice, he picked up a woman at the Balkan Football Club. In each case, he did so by the simple and direct means of suggesting that the woman come home with him. On both occasions, the women were in their thirties, and not unattractive. One was an English speaking South African. The other was European, but from what part of Europe, Alexander did not learn. He experienced what even at the time he knew to be a morally repugnant boost to his ego at the ease with which he was able to persuade these women, both of whom had been drinking, to return home with him for the night. In each case, the sex was – for a casual pickup – adequate. Alexander suppressed the self disgust he felt at the time. It was to surface only some years later, allied with a profound sense of shame: to have taken advantage of a woman in drink was a disgusting and immoral thing.

Had Alexander not frequently been able to escape to the bushveld on tour, where the air was clean and his spirit could shrug off the dirt and degeneracy of his city life, he could not have sustained even a shadow of self regard.

Yet Alexander did retain a certain innocence. In some fashion, his sordid life did not affect his soul. The boy he had once been was buried not very deep beneath the surface. Perhaps this was part of his charm: that his partners were drawn to something they saw in him that had remained pure and unspoiled.

One night in early March, Alexander brought a rather pretty, if somewhat common, young woman from Caravans home with him. At his flat however, Alexander experienced a sudden and inexplicable access of self disgust, and an instant cooling of his own ardour.

'I can't do this,' he told the young woman. 'I just can't do this anymore. But you can stay the night if you want to.'

The young woman was angry. She demanded that Alexander take her home. He drove her to her flat in Bezuidenhout Valley and left her there. Alexander did not yet know it, but he was never to have casual sex again. He appeared at last to have achieved satiety: lust – that ravening wolf that had stalked through his life for so many years – was never again to overcome him. He was forty years old. Had his neglected God decided to intervene in Alexander's life? If so, that God had in mind a chastisement to follow.

One Friday night soon after Easter 1996, having finished a three night Kruger Park tour that late afternoon, Alexander decided, having had a nap, to walk to the bar adjacent to the steak house in Rocky Street, where he was likely to meet people he knew. He had forgotten to take his usual evening dose of five milligrams of diazepam. It was not far to the bar. Alexander was tired of driving. He had been driving, on and off, for almost three days. The street lighting on Cavendish Street, running down to Rocky Street, was not very bright, but Alexander was thoroughly at home in Yeoville, for all that he was sometimes the only white man in sight, so that night he said to himself, 'I'll walk.'

Chapter Twenty-Five

Afterwards, he could not remember how it was that suddenly there were two black men confronting him, and as he backed off, he realised there was at least one other behind him also. One of the two men in front of him had something in his hand. It immediately crossed Alexander's mind to shout loudly, and he opened his mouth to yell, and as he did so, he felt a punch to his abdomen. He staggered and felt his legs give way beneath him, and before he had time to realise what had happened, he was lying on the ground. Quick hands ripped his jacket from him, and felt in his trouser pockets, where they found nothing but the keys to his flat, which they ignored. His wallet, inside his jacket, was stuffed with Rand notes and US dollars (for his American guests had tipped him generously in dollars at the end of the tour). Almost before he could work out what had happened, the men were gone, and he became aware after a while of a young black woman bending over him, talking to him.

Alexander took his hand away from his belly, which was in pain, and he could see a heavy stain on his wet palm, almost black in the dim street lighting. Only now did he realise he had been stabbed. '*Sissie,*' he said, 'they have hurt me. Please call an ambulance.'

A dozen or so blacks had gathered by now. Alexander felt his shoes being removed. He experienced no passage of time, although perhaps fifteen minutes passed, before he had a dim awareness of being stretchered into an ambulance. He remembered nothing more after that.

Later the next day, Alexander became aware by slow degrees (his consciousness creeping back as if reluctant to resume residence), through information vouchsafed him by the black nursing staff, and after a while, by a young Swiss doctor, that he was in the Johannesburg General Hospital: he had been stabbed, the knife blade piercing his large intestine, creating an entry and an exit wound.

'We have had to create a stoma,' the doctor told him, 'which we will reverse after eight weeks, to allow the intestine to heal.'

Alexander was not only in physical pain, but he was feeling agitated and anxious. On leaving his flat the evening before, his antique silver cigarette case, with ten cigarettes inside it, had been inside his jacket pocket – but the muggers had taken that when they had stolen his jacket. Now he desperately craved a smoke.

'Years ago I was robbed by knifemen in Joubert Park, Doctor,' Alexander said. 'But I was n't harmed then. Now they've got me at last.' The young Swiss doctor had pleasant, mobile features. 'Doctor,' Alexander continued, 'I've been taking ten milligrams of diazepam daily for some time – on prescription. I'm going to suffer withdrawals if you don't give me some soon.'

'I'll see about that,' the doctor said. 'Right now, we need to know your name, and your home address, and your next of kin.'

It took only a minute for Alexander to provide this information. Then the doctor looked at his watch. 'I must go now. I'll be back later sometime.'

But for the rest of that long day, Alexander did not see the young Swiss doctor again. The nursing staff (all of whom were black) were somewhat lax in their care, and Alexander found it difficult to engage their attention. By the mid afternoon, when another doctor came to check on him briefly, Alexander's mind was in a state of considerable agitation, for he yearned for tobacco, valium, and liquor. He felt not only ill and in physical pain, but nauseous and terribly anxious.

'Doctor,' he said, 'I'm on prescription for ten milligrams of diazepam a day. I last took five milligrams yesterday morning and I'm beginning to suffer withdrawals.'

But the doctor, who twice glanced at his watch, hardly seemed to pay any attention to what Alexander was saying, and once he had checked the wound in Alexander's abdomen, he left again. A nurse administered morphine for the pain of the wound, and

Chapter Twenty-Five

Alexander fell into a long, nightmare filled doze, only to wake in some distress and not know for some moments where he was.

At least two more nights passed, punctuated by even worse nightmares than those which afflicted Alexander during the day. He lost track of time. At times Alexander suspected that he was beginning to hallucinate. Once he thought he saw a mob of blacks bringing a couple of car tyres towards him, and he heard their shouting and laughter as they prepared to place the tyres around him and douse them with petrol and set them alight. He screamed and thrashed in his bed and lashed out at the two nurses trying to hold him still, but they managed to administer a sedative via hypodermic, to calm him. Then he passed out again. The next time he came to, he could not breathe.

Alexander could not draw any breath at all. He clutched in terror at his throat, and heaved for air, but his air passage was completely blocked. Panic and terror overwhelmed him. He was asphyxiating. His limbs began jerking in spasms. He fell off the bed onto the hard tiled floor, and began to bang the back of his head repeatedly against the tiles. The terror and anguish he felt were greater than anything he had ever known. Then mercifully, he passed out. When he came to, he was breathing again, and he was back in the bed. A nurse was sitting by his bedside. She was young and pretty, of mixed race.

'You are with us again. Good,' she said, smiling. 'You must drink this.' She proffered a small plastic cup with some thick pink liquid in it.

'What is it?'

'It is valium – diazepam.'

'Thank God,' Alexander said. 'I almost died.'

'You were choking on your own tongue, you were fitting,' the pretty nurse told him. 'You are alright now. Drink!'

Alexander gulped down the liquid, and within fifteen to twenty minutes he began, for the first time since his arrival at the hospital, to feel almost calm.

Thereafter, Alexander drank the valium in a liquid solution three times a day. He began to pay rational attention to his surroundings and to his circumstances. Later that first day of his resurrection (his third day in the hospital), a senior staff nurse sat down alongside his bed and asked him how she could contact his family. 'We cannot find a record of your details.'

Alexander had to think for a while, then his mother's telephone number came to him suddenly. Roy would be at work all day, it was better to ring his mother.

Alexander was dozing when his brother and his mother arrived. He awoke to find them standing looking down at him. 'Oh – Mum!' he exclaimed.

'Darling boy! We only learned where you were this afternoon.'

'Hullo Sandy,' Roy said, smiling. 'Looks like you've cheated death again.'

'You cannot imagine how happy I am to see you both,' Alexander declared. 'Tell me – have you brought any cigarettes? It's been days since I last had a smoke.'

Roy reached into his pocket and withdrew a packet of Peter Stuyvesant, the brand Alexander smoked. 'I found these in your flat. I thought you would want them.'

'You've been to my flat? How did you get in?'

'I have a spare key. Don't you remember?'

Alexander's mother interrupted. 'We've got you some things you might need in this bag. Pyjamas, clean underwear, clean clothes, your slippers, a dressing gown – and some *takkies*. The sister who rang me told me you were missing your shoes.'

'That's wonderful, Mum. Roy – I'm going to nip into the loo there and have a cigarette. Do you have a light?'

'*Ja* – I found a Bic lighter in your flat, Sandy.' He gave Alexander the lighter.

The hospital (why, he did not know) had placed Alexander in a private room. There was a lavatory and a shower attached. He hobbled to the little room, bent over like an old man, one hand on his stomach. As he drew deeply on his first cigarette in over three days, his head spun and he felt dizzy, but overriding all was the bliss he felt. He felt his mind untangling as he smoked, and when he had finished the cigarette and flushed it down the lavatory, he felt human for the first time in days. He rejoined his family. As he sat back against the pillows, he began to tell them what he remembered of the mugging. But he could not finish: he began to cry and tremble.

'That's alright, Darling,' his mother said. 'Don't think about it. The important thing is that you're safe now.'

'I can't go back there,' Alexander told Roy. 'I can't live there anymore.'

'I know. You can move in with me again. They say you'll be here another week at least. I'll begin to pack your stuff at the flat and take it to my place in the meantime. A lot of it can go in the attic. By the way – I found your cheque book at your flat. I'll take it to Standard Bank and cancel the cards you had in your wallet. I'll explain that you can't do so yourself, that you are seriously injured in hospital.'

'You're a good brother, Roy. I owe you lots,' Alexander said, smiling through his tears.

Roy made four more visits during the next seven days. Their mother accompanied him on three of those visits. Seven days after their first visit, Roy came to collect Alexander. The two brothers drove back via Alexander's flat; it was a bright, sunny weekday, and the residential street was fairly quiet. Alexander was walking, bent and slow, with the aid of a walking stick the hospital had given him. Under his direction, Roy packed the last few things they were taking with them. Roy had brought some large cardboard boxes in the car, and two suitcases.

'Do you think you can drive your car, Sandy? Otherwise, I don't know how we'll get it home.'

'I think so. Will you walk to my car with me? It's in the garage below; I don't want to be alone here, Roy.'

When at last they drove away, quickly leaving Yeoville behind them as they made their way through Houghton and began to cut across the suburbs for Roy's home to the west of Johannesburg, Alexander had no idea that he was never to see Yeoville – or Hillbrow – again. That phase of his life, defined by its frantic lusts, its degradation and depravity, was over at last.

However, it would be some years yet before Alexander finally won his battle with alcoholism.

Chapter Twenty-Six

The Drakensberg

It was mid June, already winter, before Alexander returned to the hospital for the stoma to be reversed. He had been longing for this event for eight weeks. Never before in his life had he had to live with something as disgusting and troublesome as the colostomy. Having to defecate from one side of his belly revolted him. Having to clean the horror at least twice a day appalled him. He became obsessed with the conviction that he stank of faeces all the time. He could not wear proper trousers; he could only wear his tracksuit pants, loosely knotted at the top. He felt intensely self conscious, and for eight weeks he would not leave Roy's house or garden. Smokie the cat was a comfort to him. She was delighted to have someone at home all day, when Roy went out to work.

Alexander did see quite a lot of his mother, who drove across to spend several hours with him three or four mornings a week. Most of their conversation consisted of reminiscences of the distant past, reaching back to Alexander's earliest memories in Kenya.

Alexander developed a revulsion for food. He had already lost a great deal of weight, and he was to lose more. From his usual seventy-seven kilograms he was, within just a few weeks, down to sixty-eight kilograms. Always very lean, he had no reserves of fat to absorb such a loss; he became noticeably emaciated. His skin was pallid, despite the hour or two each day he sat in the winter sunshine in Roy's garden; his hair lost its healthy shine.

Alexander began reading voraciously, something he had not engaged in properly for a long time. In Roy's house he found many of the novels he remembered as an adolescent. His parents had been avid collectors of good fiction in Kenya. Alexander rediscovered writers such as Graham Green, A.J. Cronin, Ernest Hemingway, Daphne du Maurier, Jack Kerouac, Nevil Shute, John Steinbeck and Evelyn Waugh, most of which he had read at home during his adolescent years, but which he was happy to reread so many years later. He also paged his way through a vast collection of American National Geographic magazines from the 1960s, which he remembered enjoying as a child, and had not looked at since. There were also a large number of issues of the monthly magazine publication, *Practical Boat Owner*, from the United Kingdom. Alexander could not remember having given them to Roy, but he supposed he must have done so.

And Alexander began to say his prayers again. He was profoundly convinced that a Divine Providence had saved him from death, and he felt humbled, contrite and grateful. However, he would not go to Mass.

Even after the stoma had been reversed, it was with reluctance that Alexander ventured into the world. His sleep at night was often broken by violent nightmares. In some of these, he relived various versions of the stabbing; sometimes it was he who held the knife, and he who stabbed his attacker. Some of these nightmares saw him a witness to gunfire and killings. In yet others, he was trying desperately to escape – unable to run fast enough – from those who wished to do him terrible harm. He would wake from these nightmares drenched in perspiration, afraid to fall asleep again. Then he would go through to the kitchen and make himself an instant coffee, and smoke a cigarette. It would be some time before he fell asleep again. He was, as a consequence, always tired. At odd moments during the day he would experience a sudden, intense recollection of the punch to his belly that had been the knife blow, and he would begin to tremble, and weep silently. At other times, sensations of horror and fear would overwhelm him. He could not articulate these sensations, but they made him feel nauseous, and he would grow short of breath. He rarely ventured more than a few feet into the garden. He needed to be near Roy's front door, and safety, especially when he sat outside in the sun while Roy was away at work. When his mother wished to see him, she had to come and visit him at Roy's home.

After his release from hospital, Alexander renounced alcohol. He had been through very nasty withdrawals during his hospital stay; he could stay clean now. Roy drank a couple of lagers in the evening when he came home from work, but Alexander would not join him. Alexander knew however that there was no guarantee he would, or could, remain so abstemious indefinitely.

In mid June Alexander spent a week as an in-patient again at the Johannesburg General Hospital, for the stoma to be reversed. Some time later, he kept an appointment – a short outpatient's visit – for the metal clips holding the lips of the wound together to be removed. Once that had been done, he was shown how to clean the wound, which grew smaller every day, by using a large syringe to wash it with sterile saline water, before applying a clean dressing. With the stoma gone, he began to eat again. But it was to take him several months before he regained the weight he had lost.

Alexander made no attempt to return to work for the remainder of 1996. He understood that he needed to heal mentally just as much as physically. But in January 1997 (by now dreaming fewer horrible nightmares, and less prone to distressing daytime flashbacks) he began reading the employment pages in the *Star*, the Johannesburg daily, and in the *Sunday Times*. He came across an advertisement for a business writer with a company in Sandton. He attended two interviews; one with the managing director, and one with a woman in her later middle age, who, as business news editor, would be Alexander's immediate boss. He was offered the position. The pay would more than match what he had been earning as a field guide, and it came with a pension and corporate health insurance, as well as injuries and life insurance.

Alexander was not permitted to smoke at his desk, but he could run downstairs every once in a while for a smoke outside. No one was micro-managing him, or driving him to increase his output. His job was creative and analytical, very similar to the work he had done for Reiters in London. As long as he covered the business, economic and financial news of the day adequately (culled from reports in the business and financial sections of a dozen newspapers and magazines), and uploaded his abstracts and commentaries onto the infant Internet, he could set his own hours. He soon developed a routine of being at his desk by seven in the morning, taking only a twenty minutes' break for lunch, and leaving for Roy's home at half past three – thus avoiding the rush hours both to and from work. Alexander had no computer at home. He did not truly understand what the Internet was. He did understand however that subscribers around the world could read the abstracts and commentaries he downloaded each day.

In late 1997 Alexander rented a garden cottage in Ferndale, not far from the Randburg Waterfront, that complex of shops, restaurants and bars built around a man-made lake. He had little contact with his landlady, who ran a business from the main house on the property, and lived elsewhere. The property comprised an acre in extent, and his cottage was located some distance from the main house. Alexander soon found that spending every evening in his cottage was a lonely business, so he would visit his brother in Honeydew several evenings a week, and on weekends also.

Chapter Twenty-Six

Alexander began attending Mass on Sunday mornings at St. Bonifatius, a Catholic church in Sundowner, Randburg. He formed no friendships here, and he found himself feeling nostalgic sometimes for the traditional Anglican Church, and its friendly, welcoming environment. However, the contemporary Anglican Church had become too liberal for Alexander's taste. In matters of religious belief and practice, Alexander was still deeply conservative. Alexander's attendance at Mass, however, brought him little joy. He knew that he was just going through the motions.

Earlier in 1997, while Alexander had been living with his brother, he and Roy had gone camping in the Drakensberg. It was the Easter weekend, somewhat short of a year after he had been stabbed. Alexander harried Roy relentlessly in the very early morning of Good Friday, which that year fell on the 28th March, urging him to get a move on so they could make an early start. They had a long journey ahead of them. The two of them had taken Smokie to the cattery in the late afternoon of the preceding day.

'Come on Roy!' Alexander nagged. 'Let's get moving!'

'What's the big hurry?' Roy responded.

'I want to arrive before it gets dark.'

They finally set off at about nine that morning. They were making for Injisuthi, a Drakensberg wilderness reserve. Driving past the bare Free State corn fields (the corn had been harvested and only the stubble remained on the ground), where the horizons lay far, far off, and the sun shone from a sky that was infinitely vast, Alexander felt himself succumb to a sense of liberation and peace such as he had not known for a very long time.

The brothers stopped for fuel and something to eat and drink at the Harrismith service stop, with the rough-hewn bulk of Harrismith Mountain overlooking the town. The two brothers spent a few minutes admiring the tiny Shetland ponies and the ostriches, all cohabiting happily together in a large paddock. There were several fast food outlets; they ate hamburgers in one of these. Roy drank a coke. Alexander drank a black coffee with plenty of sugar (he had avoided milk for many years), and half a glass of water.

The two arrived at Injisuthi camp at about three in the afternoon. They set up the small two-man tent, then went walking as far as the contour path. Just before the sun went down, they were grilling one of Alexander's favourite outdoor meals (he had often cooked it during visits to the bushveld with Una): chicken breasts with chopped tomatoes, onions and garlic with tomato paste, wrapped in tinfoil, over a bed of coals. They had wrapped some potatoes in tinfoil also and stuck them in the coals. Roy had a bottle of Castle lager, and Alexander drank coffee brewed at the edge of the fire. They would not be able to barbeque the next two evenings, for lack of fuel.

'I don't remember Dad ever *braaing*,' Alexander said.

'He did once or twice – not often though. He was n't an outdoors person, was he?'

'No, he was n't,' Alexander replied. 'I wonder if that was because of his fear of the sun?'

Alexander senior had been a redhead, with skin which could not take the sun.

'It must have been hard for Dad in the Kenya Regiment, under that equatorial sun,' Alexander mused. 'Perhaps he was put off the outdoors for ever.'

'Maybe... do you miss Dad?'

'Often,' Alexander responded. 'With Dad gone, there's no one we can turn to for advice and help anymore. We have to grow up now.'

'That's the problem. I don't think I can grow up,' Roy responded.

Alexander thought there was a great deal of truth in what Roy said. Neither brother showed any great gift for adult life, but

Chapter Twenty-Six

Roy was the most childlike of the two, and the most innocent. Sometimes, Alexander wondered whether his brother might be mildly autistic. He was a gifted engineer, and he could tackle any sort of practical problem, but he showed little aptitude for the skills of adult life. There was something extraordinarily unworldly about him. He had not, by the age of forty, had a long term relationship with a woman. It was clear however that he was attracted to women.

Alexander loved his brother the more as the two grew older, and Alexander came to understand what a good man Roy was. Alexander, by comparison, was not a good man at all. He had to work hard at being a good man – or so he thought.

'I haven't made a very good job of growing up,' Alexander said. 'At least you have a well paid job, and a house you own, and a cat, to show for it. I'm still living as if I was in my early twenties.'

'You've had some bad luck,' Roy replied. 'But you handle life much better than I do.'

The sun had set behind the mountains. It grew suddenly much colder. The summer was over. The first stars showed in a sky the colour of blued gunmetal. The canopy of the heavens seemed inconceivably vast to Alexander, and he became aware of this infinitude's utter disinterest in him, and that very disinterest was a source of hope, for in it there existed neither malice nor favour. Above the dark silhouette of the mountains, Alexander could see Venus, the evening star. Much of the western sky was hidden behind the mountains. Alexander felt infinitesimally tiny in the face of this uncompromisingly vast universe. He reached for his sleeveless, quilted jacket. The two brothers were silent, leaning back in their folding chairs. The following two evenings they would have only the ground, or such natural features as they could find, to sit on, for they could not take the chairs with them as they hiked in the mountains. Alexander smoked. After a while he commented 'I guess I should have a shower.'

'Is there hot water?'

'There's supposed to be hot water in the ablutions block,' Alexander replied. 'I'll go see.'

He found his sponge bag and a towel, in which he wrapped his tracksuit pants and a pair of *takkies*, and headed for the ablutions block. He was glad to find, when he got there, that there was ample hot water on tap. He wished a middle aged man who was shaving at one of the basins a good evening. *"Naand,"* the man replied. Alexander had a long shower. Tomorrow and the next day, and the morning after that, there would be only icy cold mountain streams to wash in.

The following three mornings the brothers ate eggs, boiled on their tiny gas camping stove, for breakfast, with bread and margarine and a bowl of muesli each. The milk for the muesli was reconstituted from dried milk powder mixed with water from the mountain streams, warmed on the camping stove. On Saturday and Sunday evenings, high above the contour path (with Monk's Cowl emerging at the head of the high valley in which they were camping, its peak towering clear above the mist and cloud, disembodied, ethereal, and with a stream of cold clear water nearby), they cooked a stew of canned beef chunks into which they added chopped fresh onions and garlic, and which they bulked up with canned peeled spring potatoes. They ate the stew on slices of bread with margarine. For dessert they ate some Bournville dark chocolate. Alexander had a large appetite; he ate more than his brother. He felt fit and strong and healthy again.

Alexander felt a tremendous peace settle upon him. He loved the wild places in this world, places where mankind's claim to possession was tenuous. On Saturday morning, as they were walking along the contour path, they had seen a herd of eland; big, golden antelopes with a heavy shoulder hump and mid-sized, slightly curved horns, the lower parts of which were corkscrewed. By the late afternoon on Easter Sunday it was threatening to rain, and in the early evening the rain began. There was no tree cover this high up, only low scrub bush, and they had an uncomfortable, rather miserable evening. They had to cook their supper on the little stove in the entrance of the tent, huddled over it to shield it from the rain. Alexander began yearning for a warm, dry house with a bathroom and a real bed for the night.

'I'm not doing this again,' he told Roy. 'My camping days are over now.'

'You don't really mean that.'

'Oh yes I do. I'm too old for this sort of thing, I've just decided. In future I'm never going away unless there's a proper bed the other end, and a real bathtub.'

Alexander was never to go camping again.

Over the Christmas of 1997 the two brothers went on holiday together to Cape Town. They stayed in one of the University of Cape Town student residences on Main Road in Rondebosch. This was far cheaper than staying in a hotel. It was a good central location too, and close to many useful amenities, one of which was that Rondebosch landmark, the Pig 'n Whistle pub. They had supper here several times.

They visited their aunt Margaret at what remained of the old farm. There were now two acres of land, comprising a paddock and stables for the two horses, and the original farmhouse, in which their oldest cousin, Jenny, and her husband and two tiny children lived; there were two wooden framed cabins, in the largest of which lived Mary, Margaret's youngest daughter, together with Mike (who was pleased to see Alexander again); and there was the new double story house in which their aunt and her husband lived, together with a large collection of dogs and cats. Margaret's manner towards Alexander was cool. She was much more forthcoming with Roy. Alexander added his aunt to the list of people he still loved, people who had once loved him, but whom he appeared to have alienated forever.

Heading up that list of course was Alice, his friend from Hillbrow and Yeoville in the old days.

The visit to their aunt made Alexander sad, not only to find that she had not forgiven him, but to be reminded that his grandfather's farm, a place he had loved so much, was almost all gone. What had he left from childhood and his early manhood? Other than some toys and children's books, there was nothing left from his childhood now. Nor was there anywhere to call "home." The next morning, while Roy went to visit an ex work colleague who had moved to Cape Town, Alexander walked to a liquor store in Main Road and bought himself a bottle of whiskey. 'I will not get hooked on the stuff,' he told himself, but he knew he was lying to himself. He had not touched spirits for three years, not since the end of 1994.

Back at work early the next year, Alexander found himself thinking, 'I'm over forty years old. I should not be sharing an open plan office floor with half day workers, and graduates fresh out of university. At my age I should be in one of the offices down the side. Even the twenty-five year old IT manager has an office of his own.'

Alexander felt stricken by a profound sense of failure and defeat. He became aware that his ship had sailed long ago, leaving him behind on a barren strand, and he began to despise his job, where he was coming to feel that he was undervalued and underpaid. Soon after his forty-third birthday, the family owned company was sold to a national publishing concern. A new managing director was helicoptered in. Alexander approached him in July and asked for a raise. He had to explain first what it was that he did. He realised very soon that what he did was of little interest to the new owners; they had wished to acquire ownership of the titles of some well known business publications the old family run company had been known for. The new owners viewed the rest of their acquisition's business as of little value.

Alexander's request for a raise in salary was refused. He now began drinking more frequently. He felt a dark foreboding for the future. His moods began to fluctuate markedly. At times he felt as if he were aboard a runaway train; at others, he felt that the more appropriate metaphor was a train shunted into a siding, and forgotten.

Yet the year marched on, and Alexander continued to bring to his work the same careful, economical prose and insightful analysis that brought him some small sense of personal validation. He continued to spend several evenings a week with Roy, and he was often at his brother's home over the weekend, or visiting their mother with him. Twice, Alexander (nostalgic for the bushveld) spent a weekend alone at a hutted camp in the Kruger National Park, and in September, Alexander flew via Blantyre to Cape Maclear, to a small resort on the shores of Lake Malawi. Here he taught himself to go snorkeling in the limpid water, where shoals of tiny cichlid fish all the colours of the rainbow made him feel as if he was swimming in a giant aquarium, and he sailed the dinghy. He soon became obsessed with the board game, *Bao*, found across East Africa, which one of the black staff taught him to play. Most afternoons during his ten day stay he sat in the lounge, with its high, thatched roof, and its sides open to the elements, and its view across the lake, a body of water so vast it was like an inland sea, and he drank lagers during the day, and whiskeys in the evening, and played *Bao* with the staff (learning some words of Chichewa, which he mixed with the Swahili he remembered from his childhood). Back home again he began visiting some of the bars at the waterfront development near his cottage, where he found that he was still able to befriend strangers.

But his brother remained his only real friend during this unhappy, lonely, frustrated period of Alexander's life.

Chapter Twenty-Seven

An Amputation

Alexander took two weeks away from work over the holiday season at the end of 1998, planning to return to work early in the new year. With a Christmas bonus in sight, he felt rich, and he spent his money at bars in the waterfront development near his cottage, arriving in the mid or late afternoons, and often staying until after midnight, when the last of the bars finally closed.

His frustrations and unhappiness at work had mounted since the new managing director had refused his request for a rise in salary. During this leave, Alexander began drinking whiskey chasers with his lagers at the bars he frequented. Away from the office, he was now inebriated for most of the time.

When Alexander was intoxicated, neither his speech nor his mobility were at all impaired. It was very difficult for people who did not know him well to realise that he had drunk too much. Barmen saw no warning signs as they served him the drinks he bought. Until, of a sudden, he would do something outrageous, such as leaping up onto a table and dancing to the beat of the music playing over the bar's sound system, or accosting strangers in such an intrusive and eccentric fashion as to cause the barman to ask him to leave. Very soon, Alexander was barred from two of the four bars in the lakeside complex, and from most of the restaurants which also served drinks at a bar. By the time he returned to work on Tuesday 5th January 1999, Alexander was firmly hooked again on spirits. He was topping up throughout the working day, taking frequent breaks from his desk (which were not in themselves a cause of suspicion, for he had often taken almost hourly breaks in the past to go downstairs and out into the garden for a quick smoke), but now he would hurry downstairs to the parking basement, where he kept a bottle of scotch in his car.

He began to be something of a nuisance to his colleagues at work, for when Alexander became very drunk, his loneliness welled up, and he sought out company. By now, his behaviour was noticeably erratic, and some of the half day female workers grew nervous of him. He adopted an exaggerated old world manner towards these women, and regaled them with what often seemed to them, with their limited experience of life, rather improbable stories. On the afternoon of Friday 8th January his manager spoke to him in her office. 'Sandy, I suggest you take some sick leave due you, and return to work when you are feeling well again.'

His manager made no reference to the fact that Alexander was drunk all the time now, but he understood very well what she was saying: if he would not sober up, he would have no job to return to.

Alexander knew that he could not sober up unaided anymore, not now that spirits had gained such a grip on him. He knew therefore that he was going to lose his job, and he would likely lose any further prospects of employment also, for he was forty-three years old, and in South Africa (and in Britain also, as he would learn later), you were unemployable in any meaningful sense if you lost your job after you had turned forty.

Having left the office that Friday afternoon, he did not return to his cottage to change out of his suit, but drove straight to the waterfront development, and began drinking at the one bar left to him, where there was a saturnine, good looking young man with a curl to his lip serving behind the bar counter. This barman permitted Alexander to drink himself into the farther reaches of intoxication. Perhaps he was curious to see how long Alexander could keep going. Alexander no longer realised when he was humiliating himself.

Alexander spent the entire evening in this bar, drinking lagers with whiskey chasers. He had had nothing to eat all day, having had no breakfast before going to work, and he had not bought himself a toasted sandwich or a chicken pie at the little fast food kiosk near the office complex during his lunch break (as he usually did when sober). He was awash with liquor by the time a group of three or four young men entered the bar at about nine-thirty that evening. Within minutes, Alexander had stood them all drinks, and had begun to entertain them with stories of his time in the Caprivi. These stories, although well told and true, sounded highly improbable in his present state of advanced intoxication. The more he drank, the more pronounced his acquired upper class drawl became. Outside of Chelsea and Kensington in London, this exaggerated public school accent, a sign of Alexander's advanced intoxication, did him no favours. In Johannesburg he was often taken to be merely a *moffie* or a fool – or both.

How Alexander did humiliate himself when in the throes of extreme intoxication! And, all judgement lost, all inhibitions abandoned, how blind he was to his foolishness.

Alexander was later to remember very little of that evening. Indeed, his last clear memory was of going to find a cash machine in the lakeside complex, the young men accompanying him, and of drawing some cash. Thereafter his memory became a blank (and indeed, was never to return).

The following morning, Alexander found himself lying on the sofa beneath the window in the lounge of his cottage. He felt

Chapter Twenty-Seven

cold, for his clothes were damp. He had a fleeting impression of waking during the night to find his leg raised above him, his foot stuck in some fashion in the window, and of waking again much later as his foot suddenly came free. But none of these dreamlike recollections made any sort of sense. He sat up, and tried to stand. An intense pain, like a shaft of flame, shot through his left leg and foot as they took his weight, and he collapsed back onto the sofa. What had happened to him?

Alexander's left foot and ankle were horribly swollen, and he was missing both sock and shoe. So too was his jacket missing, together with his wallet, cell phone and car keys, and – he was to find – the keys to the cottage. His clothes were so damp, he began to think that he had been in the lake, and he was shivering. He had a pounding headache, and his face hurt. He desperately needed to visit the lavatory and have a drink. It was with very great difficulty that he crawled to the lavatory on his hands and knees, for even to touch his left foot to anything sent sharp shocks of pain up his left leg. He stood up on one leg at the toilet bowl and managed to urinate. He saw himself in the bathroom mirror: his face was bruised, and he had a black eye, which was half closed. In the sitting room he found a bottle in which about a quarter of scotch remained. He drank some of it, and fought down the urge to vomit it straight up again. He knew he had to keep the liquor inside him, if he was to avoid the shakes. Next, Alexander heaved himself upright at the sink in the kitchenette which adjoined the lounge, and drank copious amounts of tap water.

Alexander needed diazepam also. He was prescribed ten milligrams a day by his compliant young general practitioner. He could find no diazepam in his cottage. He searched again for the keys to the cottage's only exterior door, which he had established was locked. His left foot kept sending hot fiery bursts of pain up his leg. He could not find the keys to the outer door. He did however find a cigarette packet with about ten cigarettes inside it.

He dragged himself back to the sofa on which he had first come to, and lighted a cigarette. It began to grow clear to Alexander that something very bad had happened to him, and that he was in serious difficulties, for he was severely injured, trapped inside his cottage, with little alcohol left, no diazepam, and no telephone. He could not get out via the door, and he could not hope to exit via the windows either, for, as was commonplace in South Africa, the windows (except the window high above the sofa in the lounge) had sturdy metal burglar bars fixed firmly across them. What was more, the main house would, he knew, be unoccupied if today was (as he thought it might be) a Saturday – and it would be empty tomorrow also, for nobody would be there over the weekend. Alexander doubted whether anyone would hear him if he tried to shout out of an open window. The neighbourhood's residential plots were each an acre in extent; the houses were set far apart behind screens of trees. The full extent of his predicament became suddenly very clear to Alexander, and he grew afraid.

Alexander realised that he was very cold indeed, and he was shivering violently. He stripped his wet clothes off him, having dragged himself painfully and slowly to the bedroom, and put on a clean pair of underpants, a pair of shorts, a clean vest and a pullover. He found that his entire left leg below the knee appeared to be terribly bruised, and was hugely swollen as far as the knee. He dragged the duvet from his bed back with him to the sitting room, where he wrapped himself in it and lay back on the sofa.

Time passed very slowly. As the day progressed, Alexander began to crave both alcohol and valium with increasing fervour. For the moment he could have an occasional sip from what remained in the bottle of whiskey. He was pacing himself with the cigarettes. He felt ill, both hot and cold at the same time, and the shivering began again. He began to perspire heavily also. He thought to himself, 'I'm sick, and I've got valium withdrawals; I must drink some sugar water,' so he crawled to the kitchenette

Chapter Twenty-Seven

and heaved himself up on one leg at the sink, and stirred two teaspoons of sugar into a mug of water, and drank it down. Shortly, he needed to urinate again. He could not face crawling to the lavatory, so he relieved himself in his shorts.

Alexander began to pray for help. He prayed to Our Lady; he prayed to Jesus; he prayed to God. It seemed to him that his prayers were bounced straight back to him, as indeed might be expected. Who was he, who had turned aside from God, to expect God's help now?

The second night passed so slowly it felt eternal. Alexander thought about his parents, and how good they had been to him as a child. He thought about his brother, Roy. He remembered the cats he had loved. He did not think about the many casual sexual encounters he had indulged in, nor the few longer term relationships he had known. It was memories of his family and of his childhood that his tormented mind was conjuring up in the dark. He wept at times. Dawn broke for a second time. He had finished the remaining whiskey, and his valium withdrawals were advanced. He smoked his second-last cigarette. As the day progressed, he began to lose his breath every once in a while, and at random intervals he shook and shuddered convulsively. Despite feeling cold, he continued to sweat. The skin on his swollen leg below the knee had begun to darken ominously.

Alexander drank more sugar water, and urinated again where he stood by the side of the kitchen counter, supporting himself with one hand while directing the jet of urine onto the floor with the other. He lay down again, wrapped in the duvet, and began to pray again. Sometime during the early afternoon, that Sunday of the 10th January 1999, Alexander thought he heard movement outside. He began to shout for help as loudly as he could.

'*Baas?*' he heard from the little courtyard in front of the cottage. The voice was that of a black man, the language Afrikaans. '*Wat's verkeerd baas?*'

Alexander had to think hard. His mind was not working properly. *'Ek is siek!'* he shouted. *'Ek's baaie siek, en ek het die sleutel vir die deur verlos. Ek kan nie uit kom nie. Ek's binne gesluit. Ek het nie n foon in die huis nie. Asseblief, bel vir my n ambulans!'*

'Ja baas,' the man replied. Then there was silence.

'God help me,' Alexander prayed. 'God please help me, and I will change my life.' He wondered whether the man would telephone for an ambulance. Amazingly, he did so.

After some shouting back and forth through the closed door, the ambulance crew called the Police, who forced the lock on the front door, and gained entry, and when the paramedics following hard on their heels saw Alexander's condition, they carried him out to the ambulance. Then they asked him whether he had medical insurance.

'Ja, I've got medical aid,' he answered.

'We'll take you to the Sunninghill, then,' they said.

'Can you please phone my brother?' Alexander asked. One of the paramedics wrote down Roy's telephone number.

Roy drove straight to the hospital after receiving the telephone call. The Sunninghill was a private hospital in the northern suburbs. Roy arrived not long after the ambulance did. Alexander had already had a catheter installed, and was being made to drink huge quantities of water to encourage urination. Roy was with his brother when the surgeon, using a needle to prick the skin, found that Alexander had zero skin sensation to his swollen and blackened lower left leg until about three and a half inches below the knee. The surgeon told Alexander that he had gangrene, and that if his life was to be saved, he must have his left leg amputated below the knee.

'OK. Go ahead,' Alexander said. He signed the documents the nurse gave him. Then he was wheeled to the operating theatre, and within a moment, a mask being held to his face, the anesthetic had knocked him out . . .

Chapter Twenty-Seven

... Alexander had been having a terrible nightmare; a leopard was chewing his left leg off, and when he came to, he did not know where he was. But his left leg from the knee down was in great pain. He lay there, suffering, his vision clearing, then blurring again, for an indeterminate time, slowly taking in his surroundings. It became clear to him after a while that he was in a hospital, in a noisy, rather crowded area full of beds with metal side guards raised, a room crammed with complex looking machinery, and in the beds lay other patients. Then Alexander discerned that like them, he too was linked to a number of machines via tubes and monitors that were attached to him. All the nurses were black women. At last, one of them approached him.

'Where am I?' Alexander asked her.

'You are in intensive care,' the nurse answered. 'You have undergone surgery.'

'Surgery? For what?'

The nurse's face, the colour of coffee with but a dash of milk in it, went blank. 'You wait. I will get a doctor,' she replied.

The doctor was a middle aged white man. 'Excellent,' he said. 'You have woken up. How do you feel?'

'Dreadful. And my left leg hurts terribly.'

'Let me look at it,' the doctor said. He raised a sheet which appeared to be arranged over a framework of some sort, for it was arched across Alexander's legs. He bent his head and sniffed at the limb.

'Yah... mmmm... so far so good,' the man said.

'What's happened to me, Doctor?' Alexander asked.

'You don't remember?'

Alexander grimaced as a wave of pain stabbed through his lower leg. He shook his head.

'We had to amputate your left leg just below the knee, Alexander,' the surgeon told him. 'It was gangrenous; it was killing you.'

'It's hurting me badly.'

'I'll give you something for that,' the surgeon said. 'Nurse – increase the morphine to twelve, but monitor the patient closely.'

Alexander shook his head once more, and fell into an uneasy doze.

When next he awoke, Roy was sitting by his bedside, with their mother.

'Oh my darling, what has happened to you?' she asked Alexander.

'Hullo Mum. I don't know. I feel rotten.'

Roy smiled at Alexander. 'I'm not surprised,' he remarked.

'I need a cigarette,' Alexander declared.

'You can't smoke in here, Sandy,' Roy answered him. 'Maybe later on.'

'Do you not remember anything at all, Sandy?' Alexander's mother asked him.

'No, I don't.'

Alexander's family sat with him for a while. He had nothing to say, except to ask again for a cigarette, but smoking was out of the question as long as he was in intensive care. After some time had passed, one of the black nurses, looking as usual extremely smart in her gleaming, spotless, pressed and starched white uniform, and wearing a host of merit badges, awards and decorations (for so they looked to Alexander), appeared at this juncture. 'The patient must sleep now,' she said. 'You can see him again tomorrow morning.'

'Please take care of my son,' Alexander's mother asked the nurse.

'We do that,' replied the nurse.

Alexander did not remember his family leaving.

Alexander was never to forget the horror of the next two or three days and nights. For the rest of his life, although he was often unsure whether there was a Heaven, he knew with absolute certainty that Hell existed: he had been there. He was by now suffering advanced withdrawals from valium and alcohol deprivation, and he longed for a cigarette. He hallucinated often: nightmarish fancies, during one of which he found himself in Hell, and the Devil, with truly wicked cunning, told him that if he renounced Christ, his sufferings would end. The despair Alexander felt in that terrible place, where there was an utter absence of God's grace; a profound, eternal, limitless chasm of horror, was beyond bearing, and he was driven to deny his only hope of deliverance. 'I renounce Jesus Christ.' And then he was back in the private room he had been moved into in the hospital.

Roy visited him every evening, almost always bringing their mother with him, but for much of the time, Alexander was trapped in his nightmare world, and they could get nothing but nonsense from him.

Later, Alexander learned that it was Roy who had brought the doctors' attention to his brother's withdrawals from alcohol and valium, and it was he who had insisted they re-introduce valium to his brother's treatment regime. Within a very short while thereafter, Alexander was lucid once more, his hallucinations gone. From then on Alexander's condition improved rapidly. By the 18th of January he was propelling himself around in a wheelchair, unsupervised, taking the lifts down to the entrance atrium and out through the front doors, where he would wheel himself to one side and smoke a cigarette. Then he would use his wheelchair to reach the café in the atrium, where he would drink a properly made coffee. By the 22nd of January, the remedial therapist had taught Alexander how to use a pair of crutches to get about, and he dispensed with the wheelchair.

Alexander's amputation continued however to cause him a lot of pain. He experienced this pain in that part of his leg which was now missing, particularly in the absent foot. He could not reach the pain. He could not alleviate it. It felt as if he was being electrocuted; as if tremendously powerful electric shocks in very rapid succession were being passed through his non-existent foot, or toes, or heel; hour after hour. Sometimes the pain would persist right through the night, leaving Alexander exhausted in the morning, and he would spend most of the morning dozing on his bed. The doctors told him this phantom limb pain was not uncommon, and they prescribed carbamazepine by mouth. But this did not seem to Alexander to be of much help.

Towards the end of January Alexander was discharged from the Sunninghill, and he moved back in with his brother in Honeydew. Alexander had become tremendously skilled with his pair of crutches; there was little he could not manage. He found that he could still drive his Ford Granada, although at present this knowledge was academic. All he needed, after all, to operate the automatic car's foot controls (there was no clutch pedal) was his right foot. Roy had found the spare ignition keys for the Granada in Alexander's cottage a day or two after he had been admitted to hospital. He had, amazingly, found the car still parked where Alexander had left it in the waterfront car park, undamaged. Roy drove the car back to his own home in Honeydew, leaving his own car at the waterfront. Then he returned with their mother driving her car, and Roy then drove his own car back home, with their mother following behind. Unsure of the position regarding his insurance, and anyway very scared of the world out there, Alexander did not use his own car. His mother drove him to his twice weekly remedial therapy sessions at the hospital.

Sober, eating well again, Alexander soon rebuilt his strength, and he was able to get up off the floor on his right leg alone, with an ease which impressed Roy. Alexander continued to undergo twice weekly therapy sessions at the hospital. He had a routine of exercises, and he was made to stretch his left leg repeatedly until it was fully straightened, to counter the tendency of below knee amputees to clench the remains of their lower limb in beneath the knee, and thus contract the big tendons. He was taught how to

Chapter Twenty-Seven

apply a length of wide elasticated bandaging every day to his stump, to reduce its size and "cone" it, in preparation for a prosthesis to be fitted. He was taught a variety of exercises to undertake at home, designed to keep him supple and fit. His mother visited him at Roy's home and encouraged and coached him in these exercises. Alexander no longer used a wheelchair. He got around on his pair of aluminium crutches. He grew very fit, and his shoulders and upper arms became very strong.

But Alexander's mind was unquiet. The return of his nightmares; of nighttime horrors soaked in blood; of images of blades and gunfire; of malicious plots directed against him, was evidence of this. And during his waking hours, Alexander lived in a state of constant alertness, as if he were some small animal in an environment filled with potential enemies. For the rest of his life, the sound of running feet behind him, or of voices nearby raised in anger, would send his pulse racing. Loud noise distressed him beyond measure.

Alexander had quite forgotten that one of the perks of his employment had been life and injuries insurance. He was astonished when his manager telephoned him at Roy's house to tell him that he was due a substantial payout, and she was couriering him the documentation to complete. When in due course his bank informed him that his account had been credited with sixty-seven thousand Rand, he battled to believe he was not dreaming it.

Alexander found his sobriety (achieved at such cost) to be a blessing. Instead of resorting to liquor, he indulged in a giant bar of Cadbury's dark chocolate every day. His internal economy was so greedy for fuel, he could do so without erupting in the spots on his face such a diet would normally have induced.

And Alexander prayed. He prayed every morning and evening. Despite his amputation, he did so on his knees by the side of his bed. He thanked God for saving his life. He was filled with gratitude for having been granted deliverance from a terrible death. He was certain too that Jesus understood that he had been, literally, out of his mind when he had renounced Him at the Devil's bidding. He knew that Christ had welcomed him back again. Alexander tried hard to maintain a positive outlook, although the loss of his leg – he who had loved walking and hiking in the wild places – was a cause of great distress to him. In addition his self image as a whole, good looking (albeit rather thin) man, was now under severe assault.

In April Alexander was measured for a false limb, and a cast was taken of his stump. When the prosthesis was ready, towards the end of the month, it proved to be so painful to wear, he was unable to use it. He could not see himself ever growing accustomed to it. He felt certain that it should not be so painful. Alexander refused to accept the prosthesis and said, 'Let's start again, and make another one.'

The second prosthesis, ready by early June, was only a little better.

'I'm struggling to believe this,' Alexander told Roy. 'You would think that South African prosthetic technicians, used to dealing with landmine amputees, could make a wearable false leg. I'm going to have to get one made in Britain.'

Alexander understood that as a British citizen who possessed a National Insurance number, he would be able to have a prosthesis made for him free of charge on the National Health Service in Britain. The more he thought about this, the more sensible a move to Britain became. He was finished in South Africa. He had blotted his copy book too many times in South Africa. Furthermore, there was the impact of affirmative action employment legislation in South Africa. Where there was both a black and a white applicant for a job, and both were in theory equally qualified, the black candidate must be offered the position rather than the white candidate.

Chapter Twenty-Seven

The family began to accept that Alexander would be returning to Britain. But Alexander had never before felt quite so much reluctance to leave South Africa and his family. Both were precious to him now to an extent they had never been in the past. Since the violence he had suffered in Yeoville in 1996, he had grown much closer to his family, and with the loss of his leg he had grown particularly close to his mother, who had spent so much time visiting him, and coaching him at home with his exercises.

Alexander knew Britain well enough now to have lost the passionate regard he had felt long ago for that cold, damp, unfriendly island. He reveled in South Africa's hot sun; in its life-giving and healing properties. He understood and related to South Africa's people – black and white both – as he could never understand or relate to those of Britain. Britain had become more than ever a foreign country for him. Yet if he was to hope to walk properly again, he feared he must return to England. Perhaps the sixty-seven thousand Rand – worth about seven thousand Pounds in late June – would make things a bit easier for him over there. He had last seen England almost seven years earlier. So much had happened in his life since then. There had been his stay in Malta, and his time at the Kwando River Lodge. There had been his work as a field guide in South Africa. Since leaving England for Malta in March 1991, Alexander had experienced so much, discovered so many wonderful places, and enjoyed a number of cherished friendships.

Alexander had to decide which of his remaining household effects he would take with him to England. There was very little. Much of the furniture had simply been abandoned in the flat in Yeoville after Alexander had been stabbed. With Alexander's permission, the few pieces of furniture that remained at the cottage in Ferndale had been sold by Roy for a few Rand to a house clearance company, while Alexander had been in hospital. But there was a good bookcase of pale oak which Roy had brought back from Ferndale on the roof of his car, which Alexander wished to take with him to England, along with several metal trunks full of paintings, ornaments, books and childhood memorabilia.

Alexander bought an open return air fare to Heathrow, departing Jan Smuts Airport the evening of the 5th of July. He knew that he would never be living in South Africa again (of this he was certain, as he was certain of few things), but he wished to avoid the formalities of emigration.

Then tragedy struck the Honeydew household. One early evening, shortly before sunset, Roy began to worry because Smokie was not to be found for her suppertime.

'She's always here, Sandy. You've seen – she's never late for her supper,' Roy said.

'I know. Should you look in the *veld* behind the house, Roy?'

Behind the house was an area of about ten acres of scrub and *veld*. Smokie could reach this unkempt ground easily via a hole in the fence behind the house next door. This ground was separated from Roy's garden by a concrete wall six feet high. To reach the *veld*, Roy had to walk down his driveway and continue past three more houses, then he could make his way up into the open ground. The sun was now low in the sky. In Africa, where twilight was brief, there would not be much more daylight left. Roy took a torch with him. He was still away by the time it began to grow properly dark, and Alexander began to feel a growing anxiety. He was by now convinced there was something wrong. Just before it grew fully dark, he heard Roy walking up the driveway. Using his crutches, Alexander went out the front door and into the garden. Roy was carrying Smokie, held in his forearms against his chest. He was sobbing.

'Oh Sandy – Smokie is dead! The dogs... they . . .' his voice choked up and he could not continue.

Alexander felt a horrible sense of shock, then a great compassion for his brother. 'Oh, Roy . . .'

Chapter Twenty-Seven

Roy walked unsteadily towards the sofa, and half fell onto the cushions, the pathetic body of his darling Smokie cat on his lap. Alexander sat alongside him, and put his arm around his brother's shoulders. He felt tears begin to gather in his eyes, the harbingers of pain and anguish. He held his brother's shoulders while Roy cried. He touched Smokie's soft fur, and the two brothers wept together. They had been through just such a tragic scene together in childhood, with the loss of their pet, Simba. Now they remembered again.

Chapter Twenty-Eight

A Return to London

Smokie must have been trapped by a dog, or dogs, against the six foot high concrete fence behind Roy's house. The brothers could not understand how they had heard nothing. The cat had probably died very quickly, her neck broken, but she would have known terror. Neither Alexander nor Roy, in time to come, could bear to think about her end. With the passage of years, they dared not allow themselves to recall Smokie's death – and the violent deaths of other cats they had loved – for to do so would have caused them too much distress.

For now, Alexander persuaded Roy to wrap the cat's body in her favourite sleeping blanket, and although both brothers went to bed later that night, neither slept at all well. In the morning, Alexander followed Roy outside, and watched as Roy dug a deep grave for Smokie's body at the top of the garden. Afterwards, Alexander said, 'I think we should go see Mum now. What do you think?'

'Yeah, OK.'

Alexander telephoned South African Airways and had his departure date changed to the 26th July. This gave him an extra

Chapter Twenty-Eight

three weeks with Roy. He could not leave him alone right now. They were unhappy weeks. They were both grieving for Smokie, but Alexander knew it would be easier for him; he was going to new things. Roy would have to remain behind, alone.

Roy said one evening, 'I don't want to stay here anymore, not with Smokie gone. And anyway, I don't want to stay in the new South Africa, watching the country being progressively barbarized. I'm thinking of joining you in England in a few months' time, after I've sold the house.'

'I'd like that a lot, Roy, but what about Mum?'

'Once we're settled there, I'll fly back and bring her out too. She's getting old now. This is no place for an old white woman alone.'

'Then it makes sense for Pickfords to pack some of your things together with my stuff.'

'*Ja*. It'll be cheaper if we pay for a half container. We can fill a half container with both our things.'

'But it would mean your camping in your house for a while, Roy. Can you do that?'

'I think so.'

So Alexander paid Pickfords, the international removers, for a half container, and when on the 23rd July the men from Pickfords arrived, Roy's bed, along with other items of furniture, and a great many boxes of his own possessions, were hauled away in the van with Alexander's things. By the time they arrived at Pickfords' warehouse in southern England, Alexander planned to have a home for them to be delivered to; a home where Roy could join him.

At heart, Alexander was convinced that all his employment options had run out now; that he was probably unemployable anywhere at all, given his age and circumstances. He felt as if the mainspring that powered him had lost its tension; he would trust to Providence to show him his path. He had one certain aim only in England: to obtain a false leg that he could walk with. He did not yet have in mind a particular town or district in which he would be looking for somewhere to live.

As if he was reading his mind, Roy remarked, 'If Dad was still alive, he would know what to do.'

'Yeah, we're babes in the wood without Dad,' Alexander agreed.

Alexander and Roy went to fetch their mother that Saturday afternoon, then they continued to the botanic gardens up against the ridge in Roodepoort municipality, not far from Roy's home. Alexander could not manage any of the paths alongside the *kloof*, let alone follow the path which climbed the cliff face, but he could stand on the little footbridge that crossed the nascent Crocodile River, and watch the Southern masked weavers, bright yellow birds the size of sparrows, with black masks, as they flitted from their woven nests that hung from the trees above the stream, and he could walk across the lawns to the pond where the waterfall disgorged, and watch for the black winged eagles which nested in the cliff face.

As the day of his departure drew nearer, Alexander felt increasingly unhappy. He did not have a good feeling about this move to England. It seemed to him as if he were hastening some fell doom. Often he considered canceling his air ticket, then he would remember that having posted his formal resignation to his employers, his medical insurance had come to an end, and he would have to pay out of his own pocket for a third attempt at a prosthesis.

So he accepted that he would soon be departing for a country he knew by now could be cold in a manner far more profound than was the consequence merely of its long, cold winters. He had loved England long ago, but then he had had a wealth of family relations who loved him, who welcomed his visits, who made him feel valued. His aunt was growing old now, older than

Chapter Twenty-Eight

his mother, and she was bound up with the lives of her children and grandchildren; his last remaining great aunts and great uncles were in their extreme dotage; his cousins led busy lives of their own, and some of them had long ago left Britain for Australia, or New Zealand, or even the United States. Alexander was under no illusions that Britain would prove to be a welcoming place anymore.

At Jan Smuts Airport in the early evening of Monday 26th July, neither Alexander, nor his brother, nor their mother, expressed much in the way of emotion. Rather than sit for two hours drinking coffee together and finding there was nothing left to be said anymore, Alexander checked his luggage in immediately, then he took his leave of his family.

He said to the two of them, 'I don't think it will be very long before we're all together again. Don't be sad.' But it was his own spirits he was trying to raise.

Alexander, despite having been brought up in a family that rarely hugged, hugged his mother tightly, and when he took his leave of Roy, he shook his hand and squeezed his brother's shoulder. Then he walked through the barrier and entered the international departures hall, possessed by a growing conviction that he was making a terrible mistake.

On that Tuesday morning the 27th of July 1999, as Alexander landed at Heathrow, he was not entirely sober, for he had begun drinking again during the eleven hour flight, afflicted by sleeplessness and a profound sense of loss. Furthermore, his stump was tormenting him, and his injured bowels, crunched up in the tiny economy class seat, were also hurting him.

From Heathrow Airport Alexander took an expensive taxi ride into London to a small hotel in a Regency townhouse in Belgrave Road in Pimlico. With his luggage, and an artificial limb which was causing him much pain, he could not manage the Underground from Heathrow into London. With his luggage stacked on a trolley, Alexander had made his way to the accommodation bureau at Heathrow, where he had chosen this hotel as being fairly central and relatively inexpensive. It was also close to Pimlico Underground station. He did not want to have to walk any great distances.

It was mid morning by the time he had checked into the hotel. He removed his jacket, his prosthesis and his shoe, lay down on the bed, pulled the coverlet over himself, and slept for one and a half hours. When he awoke, the sun was streaming into his south facing room, which overlooked Belgrave Road. It took him two or three minutes to remember where he was. He needed to get out in this fine summer weather. He brushed his teeth and washed his face, then put on a light linen jacket, and a Panama hat he had bought in London many years earlier. He walked down Belgrave Road, swinging between his crutches, and along Lupus Street and crossed Vauxhall Road, where he found a pub, the White Swan, where he bought a Kronenbourg Pilsner which was brought to him, along with a large slice of fish pie, at one of the small iron tables on the pavement in front of the pub. Soon the other three pavement tables were occupied by couples, two of whom were foreign. His table had the only remaining seat available. Despite his current circumstances, something of the old excitement Alexander had always experienced when in London during the summertime began to energize him. The fine weather helped. He could remember again what it had felt like, to be young and optimistic, during his early days in London.

A man who looked to be in his mid thirties came out of the pub with a glass and a bottle in his hands. He approached Alexander. 'Would you mind if I joined you? I hope to sit outside in this wonderful weather.'

The man was tall, almost as tall as Alexander. He was bare headed, with light brown hair which shone in the sun. He had a slight tan. He had pleasant, rather boyish features. He smiled. A dimple formed either side of his mouth. He spoke with a public school accent.

'By all means,' Alexander replied, smiling in return.

Having sat down, this attractive person introduced himself. 'I'm Piers Hawkins,' he remarked, sticking his hand out.

'Sandy Maclean. How d'you do.' They shook hands. Alexander knew of an absolute certainty that this was one of those meetings that was fated. All of a sudden he felt less of an exile abroad.

Piers poured his beer into his glass. He told Alexander that he had been visiting an elderly cousin who lived in Lupus Street. 'Are you a regular here?' he asked Alexander.

Alexander laughed. 'Far from it! Yesterday I was still in South Africa. I landed at Heathrow early this morning. I'm spending a few days at a hotel in Belgrave Road.'

'You don't sound at all South African,' Piers remarked. 'I would have taken you for English.'

'Well, I am British. I'm certainly not English though, not with a surname like mine. I have n't lived in Britain for more than eight years. I'm back now. I must find somewhere to live.'

'Here in London?'

'I'm not sure. It might be nice to live somewhere in the country,' Alexander replied. 'I suppose you live in London, Piers?'

'Yes I do. I have a flat in Soho.'

The two men chatted while they drank their beers, then Piers said, 'I must go now. I wonder – may I give you my phone number?'

'I'd like that.'

'Right-O!' Piers Hawkins reached inside his blazer and took out a small notebook, from which he tore a piece of paper. He took a pen from another inside pocket. He wrote on the piece of paper.

'Here's my mobile number.'

'That's kind of you, Piers. I'll let you have my number as soon as I get hold of a cell phone.'

'Look, I must be going now, Sandy. Why dont we meet again soon?'

'OK. Can it be during the daytime?'

'My late mornings are fairly flexible,' Piers told Alexander.

'Then what about meeting somewhere for a drink one morning?'

'Let's say this Thursday – eleven-thirty at the Queen's Head in Tryon Street? Do you know it?'

'No.'

'Tryon Street is off the Kings Road. The nearest Tube is Sloane Square. But what about your walking?'

'I can find it,' Alexander said. 'I can get a taxi from Sloane Square.'

'Super. The Queen's Head is an old fashioned, low key gay pub. That's not a problem, Sandy?'

'No, that's not a problem.'

'By the way – your crutches: do you have to use them all the time?'

'I do right now. But I foresee a time in the near future when I'll be able to get by without them again.'

'Were you in an accident?'

Alexander gave an abrupt laugh. 'You could say that.'

His newfound friend stood, drained his glass, shook Alexander's hand, and saying, 'See you Thursday at eleven-thirty, then,' he strode off in the direction of the River.

Alexander spent Wednesday reacquainting himself with the West End, visiting again some of his favourite locations. He was limited by how far he could comfortably walk using a pair of crutches, but this was in fact a surprising distance. He was fit and strong now, and his resumption of drinking had not yet made any impact on his health. The weather was superb. It reminded him of his first summer in England in 1976. Alexander had a huge capacity for sitting at pavement tables outside pubs and coffee shops, watching the Human parade. He was a born *flâneur*.

Chapter Twenty-Eight

Alexander was early for his rendezvous with Piers at the Queen's Head in Chelsea. He was always early for appointments. In this he differed radically from his brother, Roy, who was never on time for anything. Alexander smiled at the young barman and asked for a Kronenbourg. 'Would you mind bringing my beer to a table outside?'

'OK sir.'

When Piers arrived, a few minutes late, he was wearing a cotton navy blue shirt with the sleeves rolled up over his brown forearms, a pair of brogues, fawn chinos, and a pair of sun glasses. His hair shone in the sun. Alexander too was wearing chinos, brogues, a cream cotton shirt, a cream linen jacket and sun glasses. He had his Panama hat with him again. Piers grinned at him, looking younger than his years.

'Sandy! I hope I find you well?'

'Indeed you do. I'm enjoying the sun. How are you?'

'Not bad at all. I'll go get a drink. Would you like another?'

'I'm OK for now, thanks.'

Piers reappeared after some minutes, a glass and an opened bottle of lager in his hands. 'Do tell me, Sandy; what brings you to England?'

Alexander told Piers he had lost his leg in a traffic accident in Johannesburg in January. He now needed a prosthesis he could wear comfortably. He made it clear however that he had hopped hemispheres many times in the past. Alexander told Piers no lies, but he withheld a great deal of the truth. He did not, after all, know Piers very well yet.

'My God, what a horrible thing to have happened, Sandy.'

'Things happen… and you, are you a native Londoner, Piers?'

'No. My people live in Hertfordshire, near a small town called Berkhamsted.'

'I knew Berkhamsted. I lived not far from Berkhamsted in the late eighties, up on the hill above Kings Langley.'

'Who would credit it?' Piers exclaimed. 'We'd never met before; you're from the far side of the world – and we're both familiar with that little corner of England. I would be indulging in a cliché if I said that it's a small world.' He laughed.

During the next hour or so, each learned more about the other. Alexander learned, for example, that Piers worked at an advertising agency in the Kings Road, not at all far from the pub. Alexander had drunk two bottles of Pilsner by then. His new friend had matched his intake. A genuine *rapport* had developed between the two men.

If, as Piers had told Alexander it was, the Queen's Head was a gay pub, it barely registered on the gay radar. Alexander had gone inside to use the gents, and he saw no one who struck him as overtly camp. Other than the fact that of the dozen or so customers inside the pub, only two were women, Alexander would not have guessed the pub was a gay rendezvous. Any more than he would have guessed that Piers was gay. If that was what, indeed, he was. Alexander knew that in London it was sometimes not uncommon for straight men to drink at gay venues. Even in Johannesburg, he had sometimes found that he was not the only predominantly heterosexual customer drinking at Brief Encounters in Hillbrow.

Piers and Alexander met twice more during the next six days. The weather remained idyllic. But Alexander's intake of spirits rose by the day, until he was keeping a bottle of whiskey in his hotel room to supplement his public drinking at pubs. Within just under a week of his landing at Heathrow, Alexander was drinking almost half a bottle of scotch a day – in addition to the several beers he drank when he was out and about. He took to keeping a tube of toothpaste in his pocket, with which he would periodically attempt to disguise the smell of spirits on his breath.

Despite the friendship that was developing between himself and Piers, Alexander was deeply unhappy. He had made no sustained effort yet to find somewhere to live, and as his drinking

Chapter Twenty-Eight

increased, his will to do so grew less. The despair he had felt after his leg was amputated was as strong as ever. Wearing the false leg put him in mind of the story by Hans Christian Andersen: the little mermaid who, in exchange for a pair of legs, felt always as if she was walking on knife blades.

The shadows were drawing in on Alexander's life.

Alexander had ascertained that in France he did not need a firearms licence to buy a shotgun and ammunition. He did not think he wanted to live like this. He made up his mind to visit Paris.

Chapter Twenty-Nine

Cannes and Beyond

On Tuesday 3rd August Alexander checked out of the hotel and took a taxi to Waterloo Station, where he bought a ticket for Eurostar, the fast train that crossed beneath the Channel from London to Paris. The journey would take something over three hours. Having recently managed to cope with eleven hours in the air without a smoke, he had no struggle in going without a cigarette on this comparatively short journey. The last time Alexander had made the Channel crossing had been in October 1988, when he had been visiting his friend in Paris by car. Then he had crossed by ferry. This was the first time he had set off for Paris by train.

Technically, Alexander was never sober anymore, but a stranger would have been hard pressed to recognise the fact. Alexander himself was not good at recognising when he was approaching his capacious limit. One moment he would be in control of his functions; his speech would not be slurred, and it would appear that he had his wits about him; the next, he was embarked upon some wild action – or simply comatose. During these periods of extended heavy drinking, Alexander seemed overtaken by an almost demonic energy; he was possessed of an

Chapter Twenty-Nine

inexplicable fund of stamina, for he ate very little, and that only infrequently.

But Alexander's reason had become unseated. Caught firmly in the grip of an alcoholic manic depressive state, he intended ending his life on the Continent. To this end, the day after he arrived at the *Gare du Nord* in Paris (having spent the night at a hotel near the *Parc de Montholon*, a small park situated on *rue Lafayette* about half way between the *Gare du Nord* and *l'Opéra*, in which mature plane trees provided shade for the colourfully dressed Senegalese nannies as they tended their employers' infant children on the lawns, and gossiped together), he bought a twelve gauge side-by-side shotgun and a box of boar shot ammunition from an *armurerie* in central Paris. He used his credit card. Perhaps, had he not, the purchase would not have been so easily transacted. He had read that he required no licence to buy a shotgun in France, but he was surprised that he was not even asked for proof of his identity, let alone for proof of domicile. He sat in the park near the hotel that afternoon, reading Evelyn Waugh's *Brideshead Revisited*, which he had brought with him, and ate a simple but well prepared supper in the small *brasserie* opposite the hotel. The next morning he arrived three quarters of an hour early at the *Gare de Lyon* for the TGV to Cannes, and he tipped the taxi driver fifty francs (about five Pounds) to go find a porter for him.

Alexander drank throughout the long journey to the Mediterranean coast. He was therefore only partially aware of the increasingly attractive scenery through which he travelled as the train sped south. He had no idea where he would stay in Cannes, but, as he had done upon arrival in Paris, he would ask the taxi driver to take him to a good four or five star hotel. At Cannes he requested a hotel *"à la promenade."* The taxi driver drove him to the Radisson Blu 1835 Hotel, at the start of the *Boulevard du Midi*, and adjacent to *le Vieux Port*, which was crammed with yachts and luxury cruisers. Alexander obtained a seafront room with a balcony, and commenced to live as if he was a rich man. He was no longer concerned with running out of funds. He did not intend living long enough for this to be a problem.

This luxurious, modern hotel was situated on the *Golfe de la Napoule*, and from his balcony, Alexander could see a heavily wooded island offshore, about one and a half or two miles long; *l'Île Sainte Marguerite*. He could make out what appeared to be medieval fortifications on the island. Alexander ate dinner every night at the hotel's rooftop restaurant, and although drunk, he appreciated that the cuisine was excellent. He drank champagne (which he would order from the wine list in his bedroom) on his balcony in the afternoons, the sleeves of his shirt rolled up in the sun, his tie loosened.

Alexander rarely got a full night's sleep anymore. He passed out on the bed for a few hours at a time, most often in the late afternoon, and slept a few more hours at night, waking in the early hours and sitting drinking, recharging his alcohol levels. He continued to have distressing nightmares, although far fewer than when he had been sober, but sometimes he dreamed that he was running, fleet of foot and light of body, with Patrick on the mountain slopes below Kirstenbosch, or climbing in the mountains, a whole person again, fit and strong.

Most mornings, wearing his false leg (which did not pain him as long as he had anesthetised himself with sufficient alcohol), and using only a walking stick as an aid, he would go gaze at the yachts and cruisers moored in the harbour, or walk in *le Suquet*, Cannes' original medieval quarter. This was a picturesque district, and Alexander gained much pleasure from the ancient architecture and the narrow, winding lanes and alleys. He sat at *cafés*, always outdoors, and drank coffee from tiny cups, with a glass of water to chase the strong coffee down. Alexander, wearing his linen jacket (one of the two jackets he had brought with him), and a white or cream or pink or pale blue cotton shirt, laundered and pressed by the hotel laundry, and a tie, together with well pressed chinos

Chapter Twenty-Nine

and a pair of well polished shoes on his feet, his head protected from the sun by a Panama, would gaze from behind his sun glasses at the people passing by, many of whose numbers projected an aura of wealth, good looks and ease which Alexander gave every impression of sharing. He had not lost his South African tan.

The warm days were filled with sunshine. The light, which possessed much the same quality of glowing intensity that the light in Cape Town held, gave the colours a liveliness that Alexander rarely saw in Britain. Alexander luxuriated in the warmth. Walking slowly, topping up his alcohol levels frequently, he could manage to get about on the prosthesis which had been so painful when he had still been sober.

Alexander was far from feeling the complete emptiness of spirit and the utter despair which are surely preconditions of suicide. During rare moments of honesty with himself, he knew that he would not after all be blowing his head off. Yet he lacked the volition to end his idyll and return to Britain, and – while he still had some money left – make plans to find somewhere to settle. Alexander stayed on at the Radisson Blu 1835 for more than a week, before he screwed his will to the sticking point, and set off on Monday the 16th on his return journey to England.

He spent one more night in the hotel near the *Parc de Montholon*, and at the British Customs desk at the *Gare du Nord* the next morning, he handed over his shotgun and cartridges, providing his Aunt's Wiltshire address as his own residential address. He had three months to obtain a British shotgun licence and reclaim the weapon, but he thought it unlikely he would be doing so. Alexander arrived back in London in the early evening of Tuesday the 17th August 1999. He checked into the hotel in Belgrave Road once again. He had two thousand Pounds left. The following morning, as he was walking with the aid of his crutches to Pimlico Tube station, on his way to meet Piers, he collapsed on the pavement and passed out.

Roy arrived in London on Monday the 4th October. Alexander had remained at the Middlesex hospital in London for about five weeks. As soon as he was able, he had telephoned Piers and asked him to fetch him his things from the hotel, along with the hotel's bill for his stay. Piers returned to the hotel a day or two later with some cash Alexander had given him to settle his hotel bill. Piers visited Alexander several times during his stay at the hospital. He kept him supplied with cigarettes.

Alexander wondered what it was that Piers saw in him. 'Why do you do so much for me?' he asked Piers during one of his visits.

Piers' laugh was somewhat uncertain. 'There's something… you have a certain quality about you.' Then he laughed more naturally. 'I think you're worth the investment, Sandy.'

'Thanks. Anyway.'

The hospital organised a visit from a social worker, who arranged for Alexander to register for unemployment benefit, and who ensured too that there was somewhere for him to go when the hospital discharged him.

Once he was over the inevitable nightmare of alcoholic withdrawals (this time the doctors had believed Alexander when he had told them about his valium habit, and they had prescribed him an ongoing supply of the drug), Alexander enjoyed his stay at the Middlesex. The ward sister had taken a liking to him. 'You look just like a young Peter O' Toole,' she told him.

The Middlesex was not a new hospital. Some of the buildings were at least one hundred years old, and Alexander grew to love the walled garden where he could sit and smoke in the sun. There was a very beautiful late nineteenth century chapel also, which put Alexander in mind of a jewel box. Its walls were sheathed in gleaming, patterned polychromatic marble, and its sanctuary and altar front comprised intricate mosaic work which scintillated in the light from the beaten copper lanterns. Alexander guessed the chapel had been decorated at about the same time as the splendid interior of the Catholic Cathedral at Westminster, and probably by the same craftsmen. Alexander spent much time here in prayer, directing his devotions particularly to Our Lady, who comforted him. He wrote almost twenty pages of what amounted to an apologia, outlining the circumstances that had brought him to this pass, and begging understanding and forgiveness. He meant for his mother to read it, but she was never to see it, for after Alexander had left hospital, he destroyed it.

By the time Roy arrived in London in early October, Alexander had been staying at a residential hotel near King's Cross and St. Pancras for about a week, the bill being picked up by the Camden local authority. He had not been unhappy here. He had a room of his own, which was situated along such a warren of narrow, dog legging corridors and small flights of stairs going up, and then down again, that he was happily isolated, he felt, from the other residents and their noises. His room overlooked an interior court. The hotel provided a proper breakfast. Alexander ate lunch at a pub nearby. He was of course no longer drinking alcohol. He felt a profound sense of deliverance at being sober, and at having landed up in a safe place, where he need make no decisions that he did not wish to have to make. Yet Alexander, sober, was prone to sadness. Sobriety was welcomed with relief, but along with sobriety there returned a melancholy which Alexander had known in varying degrees since his adolescence. At its root was a sense of alienation.

The hospital had made an appointment for Alexander at the Royal National Orthopaedic Hospital at Stanmore. A taxi had been sent for him within a couple of days of his moving into the residential hotel near Kings' Cross, and he had spent a morning having a cast of his stump made, and measurements taken for a new prosthesis to be built for him.

Landing at Heathrow, Roy hired a car and bravely drove into London, where he managed to locate the residential hotel near

King's Cross where Alexander was staying. This was for Roy, who had no sense of direction at all, an admirable achievement. The two brothers shook hands, then, moved by an access of affection, Alexander embraced his brother, a gesture Roy then returned.

'I am so glad to see you, Roy.'

'I'm glad I managed to find you.'

'You did very well!'

Alexander checked out of the residential hotel immediately, and the two set off in the hired car for the Thames Valley, for they had decided to look for somewhere to live near – but not in – Maidenhead, Reading or Slough, where jobs in engineering were (they hoped) likely to be found. Heading out of London up the A40, the two brothers had lunch at Gerrards Cross, having already decided – from their viewing of properties to rent in estate agents' windows in the High Street – that they could not afford the rents being demanded here. So they proceeded further along the A40, driving past urban ribbon development which alternated with tracts of rural country. What they could see of it was pretty countryside, well wooded, with fields and pastures bounded by old established hedgerows. Alexander and his brother repeated their examination of estate agents' windows at Beaconsfield.

'I think we're still out of our league, Roy,' Alexander remarked, frowning at the rental prices.

'What's the next town called?'

'High Wycombe.'

'OK. Let's head there.'

It was after four o' clock when they reached High Wycombe, which appeared suddenly amidst countryside which was beginning to consist of gently rolling hills, the foothills of the Chilterns, a range of high hills and chalk ridges which ran in a line to the west of London from the south-west to the north-east, through Buckinghamshire and into Hertfordshire. Sheep grazed in wide pasture land, and

Chapter Twenty-Nine

there were broad empty fields in which the bare soil looked dark and rich. Of course, Alexander thought, the wheat would long since have been harvested. They took a chance (for they could find no suitable parking) and parked the hire car in a loading zone behind the Octagon shopping centre, for they needed somewhere to spend the night, and Alexander had spotted a tourist information office adjacent to the shopping centre. After some searching, with the help of the woman behind the counter, they two decided on a bed and breakfast in Marlow Bottom, near Marlow, a town that Alexander was to visit many times over the coming years, for it was located on the Thames, and water – rivers, streams, lakes, the sea – always drew him. After buying a coffee each in a café on the first floor of the Octagon centre, looking down on the main shopping thoroughfare below, they walked along the High Street, but soon realised that the estate agencies must be located in some other part of the town.

'We'll return tomorrow, and have a proper look,' Alexander said. Alexander, sober, could not endure wearing the prosthesis he had from South Africa. Instead, he had his left trouser leg rolled up, and he was swinging along one-legged between a pair of aluminium crutches.

With Alexander navigating with the aid of a map provided by the tourist information centre, Roy drove up the steep A404 out of High Wycombe, crossing over the M40 motorway at the crest of the hill, then continuing along the A404 dual carriageway which descended, a long, gentle slope through farmland, all the way to the Marlow off-ramp. No sooner were they heading into Marlow than they had to turn right for Marlow Bottom, a small community which was almost entirely surrounded by farmland. The evening was beginning to draw in. Alexander especially was weary, for getting about one-legged on crutches was tiring. Both men were glad to check in at the bed and breakfast.

'Let me rest for half an hour, Roy, then we'll head for a pub and supper.'

Roy as usual was restless, and found it difficult to stay still, but Alexander fell back in a comfortable armchair and closed his eyes.

'Don't let me fall asleep, Roy.'

'I wont.'

Chapter Thirty

Life Unravels

The High Wycombe flat that Alexander and Roy signed the six months' lease for (six months was all the initial security of tenure that private tenants usually had in Britain) was located on Priory Road, just beyond the archway carrying the Chiltern Railways permanent way. The town centre was a mere two hundred yards down the hill from the converted red brick Edwardian house. Opposite the house was a primary school, and the shrill shrieks from the children at play during break time combined to create a crescendo of sound. The two brothers' furnished flat, on the far side of the house, was however very quiet. It looked across a neighbouring garden, and the property's own rather wild back garden, and consisted of a bedroom (which Alexander took), a long narrow sitting room and dining area (in which Roy slept), a fairly large and well appointed kitchen, a bathroom, and a laundry room doubling as a storage room. The flat was on the first floor, and Alexander had by now become so skilled with his single leg and pair of crutches, that he could get up and down the stairs unaided.

They had to make the best of it in the flat for three or four days, having left the bed and breakfast in Marlow Bottom on Friday morning the 8th October, before Pickfords delivered their few items of furniture (which included Alexander's desk, Roy's extra-long bed, and a large bookcase) and their boxes of household effects, amongst which were several boxes of books. Both brothers experienced great pleasure in the arrival of these familiar items – they were a breath of home – and they had much fun in arranging them in the flat. However, Roy learned that finding an engineering job nearby (he was searching primarily in and around Maidenhead, Reading and Slough) was going to be far more difficult than either of them had anticipated. October slipped into a grey, wet November, and the temperature fell, and Roy in particular (for he had never lived in Britain before) yearned for South Africa's benign, sunny climate. He felt terribly homesick, and he fretted far more than Alexander over their mother, left behind alone in Johannesburg.

Their Christmas was a sad affair, just the two of them, although they telephoned their mother on Christmas Day and tried to put a positive spin on things.

'Mum, we'll be together again, you must believe that,' Alexander told her over the telephone.

Then the cold, drear, dark month of January was upon them. As indeed was the year 2000. The century had turned. It snowed, which Alexander found pleasing (he enjoyed the clean purity and beauty of a snowy landscape), but his brother did not. Roy's optimism was fading. His mood was turning sour. He was beset by concern for their mother, and by regret at having left South Africa for this cold, unfriendly land. Alexander too felt homesick and unhappy. What were they doing here?

The two brothers began to bicker and quarrel. When two grown men live together for a long time in a confined space, they will eventually end up wanting to fight each other. This includes two brothers. Alexander found Roy's carelessness in the kitchen more and more irritating. 'For God's sake!' he exclaimed, 'Cant you clean up after yourself?'

Chapter Thirty

'Why are you so uptight?' Roy responded. 'What's a little mess in the kitchen matter? You can be so horrible sometimes.'

Alexander persisted with his own job searching. However, neither he nor Roy was able to gain even a single job interview, and both of them were beginning to despair of finding employment. Alexander remembered something he had said when his manager from work had visited him in hospital one evening after his leg had been amputated: 'I will never work again.'

There was one piece of good news for Alexander that month. The Royal National Orthopaedic Hospital at Stanmore in London sent a car for him. It seemed that his prosthesis had been ready since late November, but the hospital had lost track of him. It was only when, in mid January, Alexander had thought to telephone the hospital, that he had learned his prosthesis was ready. He spent the whole day away, and he was thrilled with the false leg. The fit was excellent, and best of all, it was almost entirely pain free, although if Alexander wore the prosthesis for a long time, the toes of his non-existent left foot began to feel painfully pinched, as if he was wearing a tight shoe a size too small on his ghost foot. But Alexander could walk with little pain with just the aid of a walking stick. He had become mobile again, almost exactly a year after his leg had been amputated.

Why then did Alexander begin drinking again around this time?

Alexander was no nearer finding deliverance from the heavy burden of guilt he bore for his sins – real and imagined – than he had been aged twelve, when he had been sure that his grandfather's death was a punishment sent him for his failings. He drank to seek release from the loneliness, shame and self loathing he so often felt.

By mid February, Alexander was buying a bottle of Scotch every second day. He drank in his bedroom, and it was impossible to disguise this fact, for Roy was well versed in recognising the symptoms. Even had he not been, Alexander stank of liquor. Alexander's desperate drinking added to Roy's unhappiness, and the brothers' quarrelling became more frequent, and harsh words were sometimes exchanged between them. In late February, shortly before Alexander's forty-fifth birthday, Roy told him that he would be returning to South Africa within the week, for he had found a well paid engineering job online in the Transvaal. Within just a few more days (abandoning into Alexander's keeping most of the things he had brought from South Africa), Roy had left Alexander alone in High Wycombe. Alexander felt no resentment towards his brother for having done so, only shame and guilt at having driven him away. What was more, he was almost certain that with Roy, who was a co-signatory on the lease, gone, he would not have the lease rolled over in early April. On the 8th March, just over a week after Roy had flown out of Heathrow, Alexander's notice to vacate the flat by the morning of the 9th April, was placed in his letter box.

Alexander felt utterly defeated by his circumstances. Consequently, his drinking increased markedly. He made his way every night from one town centre pub to the next, drinking prodigious volumes, yet remaining upright and coherent. Desperately lonely, he sought out company, relying on his well bred, educated accent to sustain the image of eccentric toff somewhat down on his luck, rather than one-legged town drunk, and up to a point, his strategy worked. Alexander struck up several acquaintances with younger men, and sometimes he would take one of these men back to his flat, where he regaled them with more liquor, along with stories so tall it was hard to believe that many of them were essentially true, and he played Pink Floyd, or The Doors, very loudly and very late at night, on the tape and CD player that Roy had left behind. Alexander had no desire to strike up any form of sexual relationship with any of these people, who may have been almost as lonely as he was.

Chapter Thirty

When, some time during the morning that would follow, Alexander regained consciousness, he was always alone, and he could remember almost nothing from the night before. However, he suspected he would have told many exaggerations, and made many false claims, and he feared being found out or called out for words he could no longer remember. Until he had managed to overcome his terrors once again, as the alcohol he consumed as rapidly as possible during the rest of the morning took effect, he lived in fear. He was terrified of the possibility of violence in town – or worse, of violence in the flat, not being sure how many, and what sort of people knew that he lived there, alone, crippled and incapable.

Alexander never found out who had alerted the social services – perhaps one of his neighbours; perhaps one of these night-time visitors – but one day a woman social worker, accompanied by a Policeman, knocked on his door. Alexander by now was in a dreadful way. The flat was a tip, for he had given up trying to keep it clean. There were the remains of half-eaten meals in the sitting room, and empty whiskey bottles littered the room. Alexander had not shaved for four or five days. He thought he had probably peed in his trousers, for he stank of urine, along with sweat and drink.

'Alexander, I'm from social services, and I'm here to help you,' the rather young woman said.

Alexander felt overwhelmed by an intense relief. His eyes filled with tears, and he responded, 'I need help. Please help me.'

The woman waved a hand at the Policeman, who stepped outside. 'May I help you pack some things for a stay at a clinic? We could leave immediately.'

'Yes,' Alexander replied. 'Yes. I'ld like that.'

Chapter Thirty-One

Harrow and Oxford

The private clinic was a luxurious retreat in Harrow on the Hill, in north-west London, set in its own large garden near the élite Harrow school, and Alexander wondered how the National Health Service could afford to send him (and the other very ordinary, generally very poor patients with whom he shared a large wing of the establishment) to such a select institution. He knew he was very fortunate, and he determined to get his act cleaned up fast.

'In layman's terms, Alexander, it appears you have been suffering from periods of mania,' the psychiatrist told him, after he had spent the night mildly medicated in a stark, bare room with just a single bed, a lavatory, a basin, and a large mirror on one wall – which Alexander correctly surmised was a one-way viewing window.

'Once I'm sober, Doctor, you'll find a rational, sane, stable man underneath the mess I'm in right now,' Alexander replied. 'The difference will amaze you. It's getting sober that's the thing; I could no longer manage that alone, not without help.'

After less than one and a half weeks, a new, neatly turned out, very presentable Alexander, his red-blonde hair shining, his skin clear, his eyes sparkling, his manner quiet, rational and restrained,

Chapter Thirty-One

was granted permission (alone among the patients in the lockdown wing, all of whom were suffering from one or another psychotic condition) to eat in the luxurious dining room that served the fee-paying private patients, and to venture unaccompanied into the grounds. It was mid April. The swallows were returning from Africa, the sun shone, the trees were clothed in vivid, fresh new foliage, and the lawns were bordered by beds of yellow and red tulips. Beneath the trees bordering the lawns grew bluebells, wood anemones, violets and hyacinths. Clumps of butter yellow primroses grew along the edge of the lawns. Alexander's spirit absorbed the garden's tranquility thirstily, and he spent several hours every day seated on a bench in the sunshine, with a novel from the clinic's library lying unopened alongside him. He also wrote a very long, loving and remorseful letter to his mother, and another shorter, apologetic one to his brother, which he placed inside his mother's letter, and one of the staff posted them.

Alexander, whom most of the other National Health patients liked for his quiet, calm manner, which they found reassuring, became even better liked among the other patients, for after two weeks at the clinic he was given permission to leave the grounds unaccompanied, and every morning he would take orders for cigarettes, crisps, sweets, and the occasional newspaper or magazine, and note the sums of money each of his fellows had given him, against their orders. Then he would set off up the High Street with his walking stick, a large gym bag slung from one shoulder, headed for the corner shop which was a few hundred yards down the street.

Alexander had become thoroughly and happily institutionalised when, in mid May, he was discharged.

'I must confess I am amazed at how well you are, Alexander,' the psychiatrist told him.

'I remember telling you that if the alcohol was removed, you would find a sane man underneath,' Alexander replied.

'It seems you were correct.'

How little, Alexander thought, the medical profession seems to know about alcoholism.

The social services in High Wycombe had packed up and removed Alexander's possessions from the flat, including (they told Alexander) the sound system, the TV, his desk, his brother's extra-long bed, the paintings that he and Roy had hung on the walls, and the ornaments, books and bookcase, and were now storing them. The same social worker who had first visited him at the flat had packed Alexander's clothing into two of his large suitcases, and she brought them to him at the clinic. She told him that social services would store the rest of his possessions until they had found him a permanent home in the Wycombe district. She also brought him some additional toiletries.

A National Health Service minibus transferred Alexander to Oxford. He spent the next seven weeks living in solitude in a house set one street back from the Cowley Road. The rent for his room was paid by Wycombe District Council, although Oxford was a long way outside the District Council's authority. There was at the time no one else staying in the house; Alexander was entirely alone. He was glad of his solitude, glad of the peace it brought him. There was a kitchen, in which he boiled eggs and made toast for his breakfast, and where he boiled the kettle for instant coffee, but he ate his main meal of the day at the City Arms pub nearby, where he drank Coca-Cola or coffee with his meal. The weather continued fine. Indeed, it was a warm May. Alexander often went out wearing a pair of wide shorts, his sandals, and a bush shirt, eager to get a tan again if he could. He did not allow his false leg to make him feel self conscious.

The house next door was occupied by a Pakistani family. The little boy asked across the low garden fence one Saturday morning, 'What happened to your leg?'

'I had an accident.'

Chapter Thirty-One

'Where are you from?'

'I'm from Africa.'

'Have you seen a lion?'

'Oh yes, I saw a whole pride of lions when I was out walking one day.'

'Gosh! Did one of them eat your leg?'

Alexander laughed. 'No! The lions were n't hungry, and it was midday. They were feeling too sleepy to eat me.'

Thereafter, on a Saturday or Sunday morning, when the little boy was not at school but was playing in his front garden, he would always greet Alexander as he left the house.

Alexander could walk a fair distance, perhaps half a mile, with his new prosthesis, before it became uncomfortable. But he caught a bus into Oxford (which was not far at all; he would have walked the distance easily before his amputation), and alighted at Magdalen Bridge, then he strolled around the Botanic Gardens, or sat by the banks of the River Cherwell and read a newspaper. Sometimes he walked down Rose Lane and then down the path that ran along the edge of Christ Church Meadow, where he followed the course of the River Cherwell. The horse chestnuts were in magnificent bloom, their pink and white blossoms like fanciful candles, and Alexander often walked as far as the Cherwell's confluence with the Thames (which of course was called the Isis here in Oxford), where he sat on a bench and watched the cruisers and narrow boats going by. There were youngsters out on the Cherwell along the way, some of them foreign visitors, punting or rowing.

Alexander visited the boathouse below Magdalen Bridge one morning and hired a fast rowing skiff. He was a good rower, having learned to row on Zoo Lake in Johannesburg. Being on the water delighted him. He smiled happily at the swans, mallards and coots, many of them with their cute, fluffy young in tow, and once or twice he saw a water vole. He would row as far as the Isis, then turn around and make his way back upstream to

Magdalen Bridge. He could row this distance comfortably in an hour, and the hire of the boat for an hour, although fairly costly, was not prohibitively so. Alexander enjoyed the sunshine; he enjoyed watching the attractive, long-legged young people out on the river, and he relished the exercise that rowing gave him, which he could pursue without regard for his false leg. Because he had eaten well for four weeks at the clinic in Harrow on the Hill, he was fit and strong.

One morning a late middle aged man asked, 'Do you mind if I sit here?' and joined Alexander on the bench by the water's edge. The two began chatting after a while. It transpired that the man ran an agency recruiting English language teachers for the Far East.

'That could interest me,' Alexander said.

'I imagine you have at least an undergraduate degree, yes?'

'I do.'

'I'm not sure about your false leg, though. They're difficult about physical issues of that nature in the Far East.'

'Perhaps now would n't have been the best time . . .' Alexander remarked. But he was to recall that conversation before long.

After a while, this pleasant but aimless life in Oxford (during which, having sought advice from a general practitioner with whose practice he had registered, Alexander reduced his use of diazepam by gradual degrees to zero) began to make Alexander feel bored and restless. He had not heard from Wycombe District Council. He had no idea how long this arrangement might continue. He presumed it would last until the Council found him somewhere permanent to live. But when might that be?

Alexander was homesick. He longed to see his mother and brother again. He also wished to talk to them about buying a cottage in the Wycombe district (because he knew, when he was honest with himself, that he had no future in South Africa anymore). Registered in his mother's name, the cottage would

Chapter Thirty-One

be somewhere he could make a permanent home for himself. It would serve as a base for the family when the time came for Roy and their mother to leave South Africa for good. Alexander was convinced that day would come. On Monday morning the 26th June, after brooding about it through the course of the weekend, Alexander found a travel agency in the Clarendon shopping centre in central Oxford. They confirmed that his return air ticket to Johannesburg was still valid.

Alexander should have telephoned his mother, and told her he was planning to fly back to Johannesburg. He should have telephoned social services, and made a plan for the ongoing storage of his goods. He should above all have ditched completely the idea of returning to South Africa. But he did none of these things. Within less than two years, during true recovery, he would understand that mere sobriety alone does not of itself rid the alcoholic entirely of his often crazed mindset. For now, he possessed boundless energy, both mental and physical energy, and this energy would be moderated neither by reason nor caution. Instead, Alexander was within three weeks to find himself living and working in the Republic of China, better known as Taiwan.

Chapter Thirty-Two

The Far Side of the World

On the morning of the last day of June, Alexander took a taxi to the coach station in Oxford. He had with him his pair of aluminium crutches, two large suitcases, a gym bag and a small shoulder bag. He flew from Heathrow that evening, flying through the night, arriving at Jan Smuts Airport in Johannesburg early on Saturday morning the 1st July 2000. He had been away just over eleven months. It was winter in the southern hemisphere, and the Highveld landscape was drear and dry, but even so, Alexander felt a joyful lifting of his spirits at being back in Africa. He rang his mother from the airport, and told her he would be arriving at her home within the next couple of hours. 'I must try to find a taxi I can trust not to hijack me.'

'Oh, Sandy. You never fail to surprise me,' his mother said.

Alexander's mother lived in a walled and gated community with a security guard always stationed at the gate. The Northgate Mall was not far away. Roy, who was living and working in Sekunda, a small Highveld town a couple of hours' drive from Johannesburg, happened to be staying at their mother's home that weekend. After a slight hesitation, the two brothers embraced.

Chapter Thirty-Two

'I wish I could stay,' Alexander told Roy. 'I miss South Africa so much.'

'I can understand that.'

Sooty, the tiny black cat Alexander had obtained for his mother from a friend from his Hillbrow days, soon after the old Siamese cat, Lulu, had died, had herself died of pancreatic cancer not long before Alexander had left for England, but another cat had turned up very soon after and moved in, in the way that cats do. Alexander's brother had named him Tyson, but his nature was in fact amiable and affectionate. Alexander had not realised how much he had missed having a cat to love, and he made much of Tyson, a big gray neutered tom with white socks and a white bib. Alexander sat on the veranda in the Highveld winter sun during the day, with Tyson nearby, and he checked the situations vacant columns in the high circulation Johannesburg daily, the *Star*, every afternoon, and in the *Sunday Times* at the weekend. It very soon became clear to Alexander that the possibility of finding a worthwhile job in South Africa at his age (he was forty-five years old now) was slim, and with only one leg, he could not return to field guiding. Then Alexander saw a small advertisement for a business English language teacher in Taiwan. He knew immediately that he could get this job if he applied for it. Working in Taiwan would, he felt, be a happier option than unemployment in post-Thatcherite Britain. And it would be an adventure.

The man who interviewed him was an English immigrant who introduced himself as Gavin. He lived on a smallholding not very far from Roy's old house in Honeydew. He acted as a recruiter of English language teachers for Taiwan and other Far Eastern countries. Once Alexander had mentioned his experience as a business English language teacher in Malta, he was immediately offered the job.

'Will my false leg be a problem?' Alexander asked.

'I don't think so.'

Alexander agreed to a year's contract in Kaohsiung, Taiwan's second city, a port city of more than two million people in the south of the island. He would be provided with a furnished flat and paid the equivalent of two thousand five hundred Rand a month locally in Taiwan Dollars. Gavin told him he would buy Alexander an open return air ticket, valid for a year, with Singapore Airlines, flying from Johannesburg to Kaohsiung via Changi Airport in Singapore.

Later that afternoon, back at his mother's home, Alexander searched through various documents in his bag. He found a telephone number for social services in High Wycombe. He remembered the social worker's name. Astonishingly, she was in the office when he telephoned, and he was able to talk to her.

'Gillian, I'm phoning from Johannesburg. Yes – Johannesburg, South Africa. There's been a family crisis. I'm going to have to stay here for quite a while. But I'm worried about my stuff you're storing for me. What will become of it until I can return?'

'How long will you be away?'

'I don't know.'

'I expect social services can store it for you for a while. But if you're not back within three months, we'll have to levy quite a steep storage charge. I need your contact address while you're abroad, too.'

Alexander gave the woman his mother's address, although he wished he had not had to do so. But he could see no real harm in it. He thanked her for her help, and said he would stay in touch. 'Goodbye for now, Gillian.'

Roy had taken Wednesday the 19th July, and the next two days, off work, and he was staying with their mother. He drove Alexander and their mother to the airport on the morning of Thursday the 20th July. Alexander had said goodbye to his mother so many times before, and flown so very far from home so often before, that it almost felt as if this was just another such goodbye. But Alexander had no idea when next he would see his family.

Chapter Thirty-Two

Alexander found the flight burdensome in the extreme. Sixteen hours trapped in an aluminium cigar tube, and forbidden to smoke, left his mind increasingly agitated and his nerves jumpy. At Changi Airport – the biggest airport terminal Alexander had ever seen – he managed after a considerable search to find a glass enclosed smokers' pod, where he joined an entirely ethnic Chinese and entirely male throng, some of whom were smoking so much so fast that they had turned a curious green in the face. Then, after two cigarettes in succession (oh, the bliss of those first drags, the sublime joy of the hit, the sweet soothing of his jangled nerves), Alexander made his way along what he felt was at least a mile of corridors, and found his connecting flight for Kaohsiung. He had been travelling now for almost nineteen hours – not counting the two and a half hours he had spent in the Johannesburg airport terminal before departure – by the time the plane began its descent for Kaohsiung. There was a lot of turbulence; the aircraft bounced and juddered as it descended, and Alexander thought, 'I don't like this . . .' then suddenly the noise of the jet engines rose to an angry scream as they began to climb again. Kaohsiung was being touched by the fringes of a typhoon, and the runway had become blocked by an aircraft that had smashed its undercarriage in attempting a landing just minutes earlier.

Alexander spent the night, courtesy of Singapore Airlines, in a very luxuriously appointed hotel in Taipei, Taiwan's capital city, located at the northern end of the island, a stay which included a good dinner in one of the hotel's restaurants that evening. Alexander had gone for a walk in the city that late afternoon, and he was impressed at the evidence of a thriving economy and a well-ordered society. After a very early breakfast the next morning, a Saturday, an airport shuttle bus took him and some others to the airport, and he landed at Kaohsiung International Airport at about nine in the morning, considerably more alert and rested than would have been the case had he arrived at Kaohsiung the day before. A small Chinese man, who introduced himself as Steve Huang (Alexander knew that most Chinese had a European name which they used when they wished to interact with westerners), and who was the owner of the language school Alexander would be working at, arrived at the airport an hour later, after Alexander (who of course spoke no Mandarin, and could read no Chinese ideograms) managed to find someone who could telephone him.

'I not know when you come,' Steve told him. 'Airport closed yesterday.'

'I'm very glad to see you now, Steve. Thanks for meeting me.'

'We go my office now. I take you to flat later. OK?'

'That sounds fine.'

Alexander's first impression of Kaohsiung, from the front passenger seat of the Mercedes car Steve was driving, was of an entirely modern city, a high-rise city sweltering in humid tropical heat, with an extraordinary amount of traffic on the roads, traffic which included a high proportion of scooters buzzing in and out of the traffic lanes. Nobody wore jackets, nor long sleeved shirts. After some time, they entered a district lined with two, three and four story buildings, and pulled up outside one of these. This district appeared to comprise small retail outlets, tiny factories and nondescript offices and apartment blocks.

At the back of Steve's office a spirit stove stood on a small table, and Steve lighted the stove and prepared a pot of green tea. Alexander was given some tea in a small round cup without a handle. Never much of a tea drinker, he thought it tasted mostly of pulped blotting paper, but he sipped at it because it was hot and wet. Steve's English was poor, but Alexander had always possessed a flair for understanding, and being understood by, foreigners whose languages he did not speak, and the two men were able to communicate at a very basic level. Alexander showed Steve the contract he had signed with Gavin in Johannesburg, and he took care to communicate that it was for a year's duration; that he was

Chapter Thirty-Two

to be paid locally the equivalent of two thousand five hundred Rand monthly, and that a flat was to be provided. Steve agreed that these terms were all in order.

'Where will I be teaching?' Alexander asked.

'Ah – here upstairs; some other place – you see. Why you use this?' Steve pointed at Alexander's walking stick.

Alexander pulled up his left trouser leg. 'An accident,' he remarked. He could not read Steve's features as the little man stared at the short length of metal alloy shaft that was revealed beneath the turn-up of Alexander's trouser leg.

Steve looked up from Alexander's prosthesis. 'We go flat now, OK?'

Back in the car, they re-entered the high-rise district. They pulled up outside a block of flats of about ten stories in height, amidst many other tall blocks of flats. Alexander wondered why Steve had taken him to the office first. Was he expected to find his way there and back now? Steve grabbed both Alexander's large, heavy suitcases. Alexander followed behind him, with his gym bag and shoulder bag over his shoulders, and his pair of crutches under one arm. They entered a shabby, rather dingy and ill-lit lobby only a couple of steps up from street level, and ascended the lift to the unlucky fourth floor. In China the number four is considered an unlucky number, being nearly homophonous to the word "death," (*si*). In many apartment blocks, the floor numbering passes straight from the third floor to the fifth floor. Here, as they passed down a corridor on the fourth floor, Alexander saw through an open door that the apartment was being used not to live in, but as a box room and store room.

The flat comprised a large furnished living room, with a kitchenette, in which a kettle was evident, and which also contained some basic crockery along with some cooking implements. There was a bedroom, with a bed made up, and a properly appointed western bathroom with a lavatory with a ceramic bowl and a tip-up plastic seat. The floor throughout the flat was of large white tiles. There were air-conditioning units in the windows of both rooms. A TV set stood against one wall in the living area.

'You like?' Steve asked.

'It's very nice.'

'I come back Monday morning, eight o' clock, pick you up.' Steve pressed a wad of Taiwan dollars into Alexander's hand. 'This from your salary. You rest now.'

'I'll see you on Monday morning, then, Steve. Goodbye.'

It was coming up for two o' clock. What Alexander really wanted more than anything, was a coffee, but he had noticed not one coffee shop as they had driven through the city. He counted the Taiwan dollars: there seemed to be a great many of them. He locked the flat behind him, wearing the same cotton shirt (but having removed his tie) and the light linen jacket he had traveled in, and descended to street level in the lift. 'This is an adventure,' he thought to himself.

The heat and humidity struck Alexander as if he had walked into a sauna. It was worse than Durban in the summer. He was the only man on the street wearing a jacket. Alexander walked around the corner into the main street fronting the block of flats, because he had seen a 7-Eleven supermarket not far away. Inside the shop he found a jar of instant coffee and a bag of sugar, and at the check-out counter he greeted the man at the till, *'Wei ni hao.'*

'Ni hao.' The man then continued speaking in Mandarin. Alexander understood not a word he was saying.

'How much?' Alexander asked.

'Thirty dollar.'

Alexander counted out the unfamiliar notes.

After Alexander had left the supermarket, he turned down a narrow side street, and then down another, and he found himself in a world somewhat removed from that of the main thoroughfare he had first set out on. The narrow street was lined with tiny shops and

Chapter Thirty-Two

minute manufactories, with flats on the one or two floors above, and there were many small restaurants, places with just two, three or sometimes four little tables, where customers were hunched over their bowls, shoveling the contents into their mouths. Alexander, who was hungry, not having eaten since breakfast in Taipei, went inside one of these. Large numbered photographs of the dishes were mounted on the wall behind the counter, and when the short tempered woman serving behind the counter at last acknowledged him, Alexander pointed at a photograph of a bowl of noodles with what looked like slivers of beef in it, and at a can of iced coffee behind the glass fronted counter. (Iced coffee! You live and you learn, he thought). The woman yelled through an open door behind her, beyond which was the kitchen, in which a man was busy at a range (Alexander could feel the heat from where he stood). Alexander managed with some small difficulty to pay for his meal, and was given a token numbered with an Arabic numeral.

There was some confusion and much shouting when Alexander's number was called, for the Mandarin meant nothing to him, but it was sorted out. The miniature restaurant was busy with customers, most of whom were standing eating at a counter alongside one wall. He took his bowl of beef noodles and his can of iced coffee to one of the small tables, where just one other customer sat eating. He greeted the man, *'Ni hao,'* pointed at the chair and raised his eyebrows. The man nodded, then returned to his meal. Alexander ate his meal using chopsticks, watching the street life. He was familiar with chopsticks. He used them the way the Chinese used them: to shovel with, the bowl of food brought as close to the mouth as possible. The narrow street was very busy with pedestrians and scooters. The people yelled at each other. Although it sounded as if they were all quarrelling with each other, Alexander doubted this was so. The humidity bore down on him. He quickly removed his jacket and hung it behind him on the back of the chair, first transferring his wallet to his trouser pocket.

After the meal, Alexander set off to explore these back streets, which brought to mind a grittier, rougher, far less sanitised and prettified version of Soho's Chinatown in London. He felt as if he had been transported to some completely alien, off-world society. He lacked any cultural or linguistic reference points in common, anything he could grasp and find familiar. He had only as much command of the language as he was trying to learn from his "Teach Yourself Mandarin" guide, and what his quick ear for languages gave him as he listened to the people around him talking, and he lacked even the least comprehension of the ideographic script. Yet he felt for now no particular distress (although he did wonder whether exposure for long to the heat and humidity, and the constant noise and the crush of an alien humanity, might not trigger an episode of panic and terror). Eventually he found his way back to the main thoroughfare his block of flats fronted onto.

'I'm going to have to get a tourist's guide and map of Kaohsiung,' he thought, looking down the wide road which seemed to be lined with high-rises as far as the eye could see. 'There must be more to Kaohsiung than high-rises and spatchcocked glazed ducks hanging up in restaurant windows.'

Alexander felt tired. The cumulative effects of the oppressive climate and of this very alien culture were getting to him. He made his way back to his air-conditioned flat through the sweltering afternoon air, put his jar of instant coffee and his bag of sugar on the kitchen counter, filled the kettle, and made himself a long anticipated hot coffee. He only drank half of it, before removing his shoe and his prosthesis, unbuttoning his shirt, and lying down on top of the bed cover. Before long he was asleep.

When Alexander awoke, the night had fallen. For a minute or two he was extremely disoriented, but his sense of place and time returned in an instant of sudden awareness. It was not much darker; neon lights up the street flashed and flickered, their colours garish and shocking, and street lighting shone bright through the

Chapter Thirty-Two

wide bedroom windows with their undrawn curtains. The streets sounded just as busy as they had earlier that day. Alexander made some coffee and played with the TV remote while he drank it and smoked a cigarette. He found only Chinese language channels. He felt hungry, so he washed his face, combed his hair, put on his shoes and grabbed his jacket and went downstairs, headed for one of the tiny eateries he had found in the streets behind the apartment block.

Alexander had touched no alcohol for three months.

Chapter Thirty-Three

Johnny Chen

The next morning, a Sunday, Alexander realised he had nothing to eat in the flat. Perhaps travel weariness and his off-world surroundings had affected him more than he had realised the day before. He should have stocked up on basic groceries at the 7-Eleven yesterday afternoon. He drank a coffee, smoked a cigarette, then shaved and dressed, and went downstairs without his jacket, his shirt sleeves rolled up to the elbows, his wallet stuffed in one of the back pockets of his trousers. At the 7-Eleven supermarket he bought dry and canned goods, along with a loaf of bread, some margarine, a dozen eggs, and some powdered milk, and he bought a can opener also. It would be a while before he needed to buy cigarettes, for he had bought two cartons of Peter Stuyvesant duty frees at Jan Smuts Airport. He found a map of Kaohsiung annotated in both English and Chinese, which he added to his purchases. Steve had given Alexander a card with the address of his flat written on it in Chinese script. Alexander showed it to the man at check out, and asked him to indicate this address on the map. The man pointed with his pen at a spot just off Wufu 2nd Road in the Xinxing district.

Chapter Thirty-Three

Back at the flat Alexander ate two slices of toast which he made under the grill on the cooker, two boiled eggs, and some cereal with milk made up from the milk powder. Peering at the map Alexander began to feel a little less disoriented. At least he now knew what direction his flat faced – west for his bedroom, north for the lounge – and where it was in relation to other features of the city. Further down Wufu 2nd Road, on the right hand side of the road, was a large park; Central Park. Less than half a mile further on was located the Holy Rosary Cathedral, and the mouth of the Heart of Love River, as it disgorged into Kaohsiung harbour. About two miles to the north – a distance Alexander thought he could walk, even with his false leg – was the Heart of Love River Park, and reading a small block of bad English on the back of the map, he learned that it contained attractive walkways and paths, as well as cafés and restaurants. He decided to head there after another coffee.

With the card on which his address was written safe in his wallet, Alexander felt happier about exploring on his own. He knew he could always take a taxi back to the flat now. It took him forty-five minutes to reach the park along the banks of the Heart of Love River. He was perspiring freely, and he removed his panama hat again and again to wipe his brow and face. 'I need to sit somewhere in the shade and drink something cold,' he thought.

The riverside park had pathways meandering between Chinese plum, pagoda trees and ginkgo biloba. The one species with which Alexander was familiar, planted near the water, was the weeping willow. On the bright green lawns, families were setting out blankets and folding chairs, their kids running around like puppies. There was a section of broad paved walkway along the river bank itself which was lined with cafés and restaurants and fast food eateries. Alexander, who felt weary, hot and thirsty after the two mile walk to the park, chose a café whose front was open to the river walkway. The clientele seemed younger than usual:

young men with their girlfriends. After buying a can of iced coffee, accompanied by a glass of cold water, and a sort of pork and pickles hamburger, with the filling closed inside a soft white steamed bun, Alexander looked around for somewhere to sit. The tables were all taken. He saw a table at which a young man was seated, and he greeted him in Mandarin and smiled. 'May I sit here?' he asked in English.

'You are welcome,' the young man replied in slightly American-accented English. 'Are you American?'

'No, British.'

'What are you doing here in Kaohsiung?' The young man pronounced the "K" of Kaohsiung with something between a glottal and an explosive sound.

'I've only just arrived. I'm here to teach business English.'

The young man, whose shining black hair flopped across one side of his forehead, had the fine, narrow headed features seen among some of the northern Chinese, with lively dark eyes, and a high arched nose. He extended his hand. 'My name is Johnny Chen. I am pleased to meet you.'

'I'm Sandy Maclean. Well, Alexander actually, but Sandy for short. I'm pleased to meet you too.' Alexander shook Johnny's hand. 'Your English is very good. Were you taught English at school?'

'Yes, we study English at high school. I would like to speak English better. I like your English accent. We mostly hear American English.'

Alexander popped the ring tab on his can of iced coffee and poured it into the glass provided. He liked this young Chinaman. 'This is only my first full day in Kaohsiung. The city seems vast – it is daunting, in fact. I am hoping I'll learn my way around.'

'What is *"fast"*? And that other word, *"dhorting,"* what do they mean, please?"

Alexander drank deeply from his glass of iced coffee – ahh! – the bliss of that ice-cold liquid! He put the glass down. 'Vast,' he

Chapter Thirty-Three

said, emphasizing the "V" sound. 'It means "big." And "daunting" means frightening, scary, too much to handle.'

While Alexander drank his iced coffee, along with an occasional sip of water, and began to eat the pork and pickles bunburger, the two men continued to chat. Johnny told Alexander he was a student at the National Sun Yat-sen University, studying business management. 'I hope my company will send me to work in America, or England.'

'Perhaps you would n't find it as challenging as I find moving to Taiwan. There are so many American movies, are n't there? But in Britain we get little on TV about Taiwan or China.'

Johnny laughed. 'We *are* in China! The Republic of China!'

Alexander smiled. 'Of course. I'm sorry. I do in fact think of Taiwan as legitimist China, and the mainland as revolutionary China.' He offered the young Chinaman a cigarette, which was declined, and lighted one himself.

'Tell me, not all Taiwanese are descended from people who were living here already. What percentage of Taiwanese citizens descends from mainland Chinese immigrants?'

'Most of us, I think. My own family were merchants on the mainland, but they fleed – fleed?'

'Fled'

'Thank you. My own grandparents fled mainland China in 1949, in fear of their lives under the communist dictatorship.'

'That's interesting. I too descend from immigrants. My grandfather was Scottish, but he settled in Kenya with his family when it was a brand new British colony.'

'But you were not born in England?'

'No, I was n't. I was born in Kenya, and I grew up in Kenya and South Africa. But I have a British passport, and I have lived many years in England.'

Johnny laughed again. 'So your family is what the Communists call imperialists.'

Alexander grinned. 'Yes, I'm proud of my imperialist roots.'

'Would you like to walk with me? We can talk more.'

'Right-O.'

The two got up and set off along the riverside walkway. Johnny was full of questions. Alexander, who was now forty-five years old (although he looked ten years younger), enjoyed his companion's youthful enthusiasm. He missed the days of his own youth, and he missed having young people around him. At about three o' clock in the afternoon, as they sat on a bench and looked across the river, Johnny said, 'I must go now. I would like to see you again. Can we meet again – not next Saturday; the Saturday after that? I can show you some of the city of Kaohsiung.'

'I would enjoy that tremendously.'

'Where do you live?'

Alexander found the card on which his address was printed. 'Xinxing district. This is the only card I have, but this is my address.'

'I have a pen.' The young man took a pen from his shirt pocket, along with a cash receipt. 'Give me the card, Sandy, and I will copy your address. Do you have a cell?'

'No, not yet. I must get a cell phone.'

'No trouble. I will write my cell number on your card.' He did so. 'It is OK if I come for you at ten a.m?'

'That'll be fine. It's a date.'

Johnny smiled. 'It's a date! Yes, it's a date. I will like to learn from you.'

'And I shall enjoy learning from you.'

'*Zàijiàn!*'

Alexander repeated Johnny's goodbye. '*Zàijiàn*, Johnny.' The two men shook hands, and the young man walked away, a head taller than most of his compatriots. Alexander took his little notebook from his shirt pocket and wrote what he had just heard, transcribing the word phonetically, thus: "goodbye – *zheh-*

jiyan." Alexander wondered, as he often had in the past, at the way destiny worked. He felt less alone now. He hoped very much that Johnny would indeed come fetch him the Saturday after next.

Alexander found a taxi rank, and showing the driver the card with his address, he took a taxi back to the flat and lay down for a nap.

During the week that followed, Alexander did not have to work very hard. Steve fetched him each morning at eight, riding his scooter. Despite his false leg, and the necessity of carrying his walking stick with him, Alexander was able to ride pillion behind his employer, as they wove their way through the traffic and across town to Steve's office and the classroom upstairs. There were in fact two classrooms, but Alexander was at present the only teacher on the premises. There was also a small library of TEFL primers and texts. Alexander took three two-hour classes a day – two in the morning and one in the afternoon. His students were adult Chinese, one hundred percent male, ranging in age from their twenties to their forties (although in judging the age of a Chinese person, Alexander was at something of a loss). Alexander presumed most of the men had been sent there by their employers, companies which traded with, or hoped to trade with, the west.

There was a small park nearby, and after a modest lunch at one of the tiny local restaurants, Alexander would sit in the park under a shade tree before returning to the office for his afternoon class. During his first week in Kaohsiung, Alexander saw not one other westerner. He was totally immersed within an entirely Chinese environment.

Steve usually returned Alexander to his flat around five in the afternoon, although once, he told Alexander that he would have to get a taxi back to his flat. Early during his second week at work Alexander said to Steve, 'I would like to buy a scooter. How can I do that, Steve?'

'I get for you, no problem.'

Alexander was not sure whether Steve meant that he would find a scooter for Alexander to buy – or whether he would buy a scooter for him. He frequently gathered only the broad gist of what Steve was telling him. But on Friday afternoon, after his class had finished, Steve showed him a well-used scooter parked on the pavement in front of the office, alongside the one Steve himself rode. A helmet hung from one handlebar. 'This for you,' Steve told Alexander. 'You use – I keep.'

Alexander understood that he was to have not the ownership, but the use, of this scooter. He grinned with pleasure and bent to examine it. It was a pretty little scooter, although far from new; very simple to operate, with an automatic gearbox. There were only three controls: the throttle, the hand-operated front brake on the right handlebar, and a footbrake which operated on the rear wheel.

'What fuel does it use, Steve?'

'Hah?'

Alexander pointed at the cap on the tiny fuel tank. 'What gas does it take? Please write it for me in Chinese.'

'This for regular gas, this . . .' Steve pointed at a small filler cap on a tiny tank below the petrol tank '. . . this for oil. Come my office please.'

In Steve's office, which was scented with the tea he brewed on the spirit burner, he searched through a couple of drawers in his desk, before finding a user's manual for the scooter – written in English and Chinese. Paging through it, Alexander saw that the diagrams were clear enough. Steve took it back from him, and wrote something on the inside back page.

'Here is name of gas and oil you use.'

Alexander pointed at the first of these two groups of ideograms. 'Is this the gas?'

"Yes, that the gas. And this . . .' Steve pointed at the second group of ideograms. 'This the oil.'

Chapter Thirty-Three

Steve was struggling to communicate something further. Then he abandoned his struggle and said, 'You come with me,' and he disappeared through a door at the back of the office. Alexander followed him into a small courtyard, off which a number of doors led. Steve opened one of these. It gave access to a small storeroom. In one corner stood a jerrycan. Steve pointed to it.

'Gas.' Steve indicated a funnel with a built-in filter lying on a shelf. Then he pointed to a small can standing on a shelf, and said, 'This is oil. You use these for scooter. I not mind.'

'*Xièxiè* Steve.'

Then Steve said, 'Friend come fetch you flat at seven, we go restaurant. OK?'

'OK,' Alexander replied. Then he said, 'Steve, I need to see a map of Kaohsiung, so I can find my way back to my flat.'

'I show you on map. Come back to office.'

The route between the school and the apartment block was not complicated. The distance was about two or three miles, as best Alexander could judge. He hoped he would not get lost, but if he did, he would have to keep showing people his written address card, until he was back on track again. As Alexander climbed onto the scooter, Steve handed him a mobile phone and a small piece of paper with a row of numerals written on it. 'This old cell I not use. And cell number. You need.'

'*Xièxiè* Steve. *Zàijiàn!*'

Alexander found the best way of dealing with his walking stick was to rest the stick's rubber-tipped ferrule against the upcurve of the left hand running-board, the stick then being held between his left thigh and the saddle. He had not driven on the right hand side of the road since visiting Paris in 1988. He made it back to the flat without mishap, his nerves jangling. The traffic, especially the myriad other scooters, was a nightmare. Perhaps he would find it became easier over time. Removing the helmet, Alexander mopped perspiration from his face as he stood next to the scooter outside the block of flats. Now that he was not moving, it felt even hotter, even more humid than usual. Alexander hoped it meant that a storm was brewing. Then he bumped the scooter up the shallow pavement kerb, and up against the wall alongside a number of other scooters, where he fastened the chain-lock Steve had given him round the front wheel and the suspension strut.

Upstairs, Alexander made himself a coffee and lighted a cigarette, and sitting down in one of the comfortable armchairs in the lounge, he played with the mobile phone until he had found the "English language" option. He wondered whether he should telephone or text Johnny. 'I'll just send a text,' he decided. He felt strung out, taut-stretched. He needed to go somewhere where there were no high-rises leaning in against him. He texted Johnny: "Hi Johnny. I'm looking forward to our date tomorrow morning. Cheers – Sandy."

After a few minutes had passed Alexander's mobile phone beeped. It was a text from Johnny. "Hi Sandy. Me too. See you at 10 tomorrow. Johnny."

Alexander smiled happily. He turned the TV on. He had found an English – or rather, American – language channel. He watched TV while he waited for his lift to the restaurant to arrive. Shortly after seven o' clock there was a knock at the door.

A large Chinese man in his forties, with pleasant, friendly features, stood in the corridor. 'Hi,' he said, 'My name is Phil Zhou. I'm a friend of Steve's. Would you like to join us for a meal out?' His English was fluent American.

'Sandy Maclean. How do you do.' They shook hands.

Phil was driving the same Mercedes car in which Steve had collected Alexander from the airport. 'How's the teaching going?' Phil asked as he drove.

'It's good, thanks. My students are keen to learn, and quick on the uptake.'

Chapter Thirty-Three

'I picked up my English in America as a teenager. My father was in the diplomatic service in Washington.'

The restaurant was located on top of a high-rise in the city. Waiting there at the roof terrace bar were Steve and another man, who appeared to have no English at his command. The four men sat at a table under the night sky, high above the city. Two big six hundred and forty milliliter bottles of Tiger Beer were brought to the table. Alexander attempted to explain, without making more of an issue of it than he had to, that for health reasons, he would not be able to have a glass of the pale lager.

'I'll get you something else, Sandy,' said Phil. 'What would you like?'

'A sparkling mineral water would be nice, thanks Phil.'

The meal, served on a huge revolving platter divided into small compartments in which a variety of dishes were arranged, was excellent. For the most part, the three Chinese men chatted among themselves in Mandarin, but both Steve and Phil made an effort to include Alexander in the conversation at times, although their attempts consisted mostly of questions directed at him about his education and travels. By ten o' clock the three Chinese men were fairly merry. Alexander presumed they were married, but looking around the roof terrace, he saw very few women at any of the tables, and the few who were present did not look like wives. Alexander felt tired, and he longed for a coffee, but at the end of the meal, only tea was served.

It was just after eleven when Phil, with Steve as a passenger, dropped Alexander off at the flat. Upstairs he made an instant coffee and began to unwind. It had been an interesting and in part, enjoyable, evening, but it had been a strain also.

Chapter Thirty-Four

A Kaohsiung Tour

At five minutes past ten the next morning Alexander's mobile phone beeped. He put down the English language *Taiwan News* he was reading. He read the text from Johnny. "I'm downstairs. Are you ready? Johnny."

Alexander texted in reply: "On my way – Sandy." He put on his linen jacket and grabbed his wallet, cigarettes, lighter and walking stick.

Johnny was standing by a scooter downstairs. He looked very young and clean-cut, his neatly barbered jet-black hair shining with vitality, his freshly ironed white short sleeved shirt gleaming in the sunshine. He wore fawn chinos and slim loafers. His smooth bare arms and face had a dark golden tan. 'Hi Sandy,' he said, his teeth very white in his broad smile. He shook Alexander's hand. 'How are you doing?'

'Well thanks, Johnny. How are you?'

'I'm good. Are you ready for some sightseeing?'

'Sounds good.'

'Let's go then. You can carry this… this… what do you say?'

'Daypack.'

Chapter Thirty-Four

'That's right. This daypack.'

Alexander shrugged the small pack onto his back.

Johnny said, 'I will not tell you where we are going. It must be a surprise.'

Johnny wore no helmet and he had none to offer Alexander. It was cooler riding bare-headed. Until a short while ago, Alexander had never rode pillion on a motorcycle, but he had taken to it naturally. He placed his hands either side of Johnny's slim waist (his stick resting against the running board, and held by his forearm against his body), not so much to hold on, as to steady himself, and he leant into the turns with Johnny. They zipped west down the major thoroughfare which fronted Alexander's block of flats – Wufu 2nd Road – and just beyond what Alexander knew as Central Park, at a large traffic island, Johnny sped round the island and took the exit into another very busy street, heading south. That evening, back in his flat, Alexander retraced the route on his map of Kaohsiung. He knew that they had followed this street – Zhonghua 5th Road – for about a quarter of a mile, and then turned off it to the right for a hundred yards or so, and at a narrow harbour-side dock near the Kaohsiung Exhibition Centre, Johnny had come to a halt.

'You OK, Sandy?'

Alexander grinned happily. 'I'm fine, thanks!'

'Here we catch a ferry boat. We will take the scooter with us. I will buy the tickets, please.'

'Sure, Johnny.'

Johnny declined a cigarette, but Alexander lighted one for himself. While they were waiting for the ferry, Johnny asked him questions about life in the West. He had a voracious curiosity. Alexander could not answer all Johnny's questions. After ten or fifteen minutes Alexander saw a short, tubby three deck ferry boat approaching the dock. Ramps along the side, and a big ramp at one end, were let down once it was tied on, and two or three cars drove down the main ramp. A trickle of people, most with bicycles or scooters, came ashore via the side ramps. Johnny had bought their tickets at a booth at the dockside. Once they had parked the scooter on the lower deck, the two men mounted a companionway to the deck above, where they leant over the railings. The ferry pulled away and rumbled unhurriedly across the harbour, which seemed to Alexander to enclose a vast expanse of water, and Johnny pointed out the mouth of the Heart of Love River to starboard. Alexander could see many ocean-going vessels and a wide variety of smaller boats tied up alongside the quays they passed to port. The crossing took about ten minutes. Alexander, to whom boats and ships were of infinite fascination, enjoyed it.

'This is Qijin Island,' Johnny said as the ferry docked on the far side of the harbour. 'The town is old.'

Riding pillion once again, Alexander could see that most of the two, three and four story buildings that lined the broad thoroughfare they were following probably dated no further back than the fifties, but there were some structures among them that clearly dated from the turn of the century, to a period when Taiwan, then known as Formosa, was a Japanese colony. Narrow streets took off on either side from the road they were following, the buildings lining them crammed against one another, but suddenly they were through the town and Johnny followed the road in a broad sweep to the left into a wide avenue which ran parallel with a deep stretch of parkland on the right, with palm trees growing on it, and somewhat sparse lawns beneath them.

'This is Qijin 3rd Road,' Johnny shouted over his shoulder. 'It is the beachside road.'

Beyond the strip of parkland were the calm blue waters of the sea. The opposite side of the street was lined with apartment blocks, many of which were no taller than four stories. There were shops and restaurants also. Johnny pulled over. 'Let's walk on the beach,' he said.

Chapter Thirty-Four

They walked beneath the trees across the patchy lawn, then Johnny sat on a bench and rolled his chinos up his calves, following which he removed his loafers and socks. It was very warm. He turned to Alexander and smiled as they crossed the expanse of very dark, almost black, beach sand. 'It is surprising, huh?' he remarked. 'It is volcanic sand.'

As they walked along the beach, Johnny paddled in the water lapping at the shore. The beach was at least half a mile long, perhaps longer. Alexander walked in the dark sand, unwilling to get his false leg wet, but he too was happy. He had known that he was missing the open spaces, but he had not realised by how much, until Johnny had brought him to this unexpected place with the sparkling sea and big sky and far horizon.

'What do you think?' asked Johnny.

'It's wonderful! In the city I forget Kaohsiung is a seaport.'

'Our university is near the sea. There is a beach below the university. Maybe I'll take you there after lunch.'

The two men, the one dark, the other blonde, but both of them tall, slim and straight, walked the full length of the beach. It was a fair distance for Alexander, with his limp, walking in the sand. Towards the end of the beach they found a bench beneath a palm tree, and drank hot green tea from a thermos flask Johnny had packed inside the daypack. Johnny had brought an extra mug for Alexander. 'Unless you want some Coca-Cola, Sandy? I have some cans of Coke in the bag.'

'No – the tea will be nice, thanks. You know, all my life I've been a coffee drinker, not a tea drinker. But the tea you are so fond of in Taiwan is beginning to grow on me. It can be quite refreshing.'

'The tea "grows" on you? What does that mean?'

'Oh – it means you become accustomed to it, and after a while you start to enjoy it.'

Alexander smoked a cigarette as he sipped at the very hot tea. They sat and looked out across the sea, beyond which – although unseen – lay mainland China. After having rested a while, the two men began the walk back along the beach, Johnny still barefoot.

Back at their starting point, Johnny sat down on a bench and wiped his feet with a handkerchief, which he then shook out, before putting his shoes and socks back on again, saying 'Time for lunch. But we will not ride – we'll walk. It is not far.'

They crossed the wide strip of scraggly green lawn beneath its palm trees, and then crossed the road. As they walked they passed several restaurants. Outside one of these, Johnny stopped. 'Here we are.' He stood back for Alexander, who pushed the door open and went inside ahead of him.

Alexander was not yet used to the Chinese approach to mealtimes, which consisted not – as in the West – of a large main course and perhaps an entrée and a dessert course, but of many smaller dishes. He ordered only two of these: cuttlefish *geng*, (*youyu geng*), a clear, thick soup with cuttlefish prepared with fish paste (it had never occurred to Alexander that people could eat any part of the cuttlefish), and at Johnny's insistence, pan fried milkfish, whose flaky flesh had a sweetish taste to it. Craving a caffeine hit, Alexander drank an iced coffee with the meal.

'When I'm eating at one of the tiny restaurants behind my block of flats, what should I ask for, Johnny?' Alexander extracted his little notebook and a pen. 'All I've had so far is beef or pork with noodles.' He smiled. 'Luckily, I like noodles.'

Johnny smiled and laughed. 'It must be difficult for you – I understand our food is very different to what you are used to in the West. If you have not already been to one of the night markets – there's one nearby where you live, the Liuhe night market – you must try oysters with egg. It is called *ezijian*.'

Alexander wrote down the name as it sounded to him. 'Real oysters, with egg?'

Chapter Thirty-Four

'Yes. Egg with oysters. Uhh... oyster omelette, I think you would call it. It is chewy. And it is made also with sweet potatoes. It is a very popular snack in the city at night.' Johnny thought for a moment. 'And you must try pork and rice – it is called *lu rou fan*. It is pieces of pork; not stewed or fried, but cooked to... to seal the pork, in soy sauce, served with rice.'

'*Lu rou fan?*'

'Yes, that's right. But our most popular snack is like a hamburger. It is called *gua bao*. It is a steamed bun with pork and pickled vegetables inside it. Very filling.'

Alexander wrote the name down. 'I was eating that the day I first met you, at the Heart of Love River Park.'

'That was a good day,' Johnny said. 'I was expecting to meet my girlfriend there, then she phoned me to say she could not make it. I thought the day was a washout – that is correct, yes? Washout?'

'Yes, that's right.'

'Then I met you.'

Alexander contemplated how lonely he would be feeling had he not met Johnny; how much less tolerable his experience of Kaohsiung would be. While Johnny drank a very dark, almost black tea after the meal, Alexander ordered another iced coffee.

'I will show you a very beautiful natural district,' said Johnny. 'There are monkeys, and much open ground for walking.'

'Do you ever go hiking, Johnny?'

'Oh yes – I like to hike. We go hiking in the mountains you can sometimes see from the city. They are unspoiled.'

'I was a keen hiker,' Alexander responded. 'I have n't done much hiking for some years, but even as a teenager at school, I needed to go for long walks in open country. My soul feels smothered if I don't get out in the open sometimes.'

'I understand what you are saying. What sort of country do you like to hike in, Sandy?'

'We used to spend two or three days high in the mountains, at... uh... almost four thousand metres. Or we would head for some hills an hour's drive from Johannesburg, just for the day. There are monkeys and antelope there – you would know them as "deer," I think – and there have been sightings of leopards reported. But my most amazing hikes have been day walks in the bush, in the wilderness, in "big five" country, where you see elephants, buffalo, many antelope species, giraffes, zebras, and sometimes lions.'

Johnny was staring at Alexander. 'That is wonderful! I can understand why you must feel trapped in urban districts.'

'Sometimes I do. I worry that I wont be able to keep my sanity if I spend a whole year in Kaohsiung.'

'Perhaps I can take you hiking in the mountains with some of my friends some day, Sandy.'

'I cannot hike at all far anymore, not with a false leg, but I still need to get out into the open. It has done me good, just walking along the beach here, and seeing the ocean.'

'You have a false leg? You mean, you have only one leg? I did not know.' Johnny frowned momentarily, then his face cleared. 'But no one would know. You walk very naturally.' He smiled at Alexander. 'I would never know. Was it an accident?'

'Yes, it was. One and a half years ago.'

'You are brave, I think. Come! Let's go to Monkey Mountain! There is plenty of open space there, and some nice walking trails, which perhaps you can manage.' Johnny laughed. 'There are no big dangerous animals, but there are many big greedy monkeys.'

After a wait of ten minutes, where Qi Jin Old Street ran up against the quayside, the two crossed the narrow harbour mouth by ferry. The terrain on the far side of the harbor mouth was hilly and steep. With the daypack on his back, Alexander held Johnny's waist as they sped north. At the Kaohsiung Martyrs' Shrine at the foot of the hill, Johnny swung onto a narrow road which climbed up the hillside, and then began to zig-zag its way up the increasingly steep slope. At the top, Johnny turned into a parking area, and killed the engine. The view was spectacular. Alexander could see far out across the sea, although the Chinese mainland lay too far away to be glimpsed. The coastline as it ran north up the length of the island appeared to be fairly densely built up. Turning around, he could see much of Kaohsiung city laid out beneath him, and to the east, far beyond the city, the mountains loomed clear against the blue sky. From here they seemed so close, but Alexander suspected they were too far away to tackle on his tiny scooter. To the south lay the vast natural harbour, protected by Qijin Island. As the two men stood there, they were joined by a troop of rather large monkeys with grayish-brown coats and pink faces, which Alexander correctly guessed were some sort of macaques.

'This is fantastic, Johnny! What an incredible view. As for these monkeys, I guess they hope we'll feed them.'

'Yes, they're greedy for food. People feed them. I will not. It makes them too tame.'

'We have the same problem in Cape Town with our monkeys, the baboons. Tourists feed them. They lose their respect for humans, and sometimes become dangerous.'

'I have heard that word "baboon," but I did not know what it meant. So it means a type of monkey? Like these?'

'Similar, but their muzzles are more dog-like.'

'Do you want to walk for a while, Sandy?'

'Yes – I'd like that.'

The trail they followed, paved in tough wooden planking and incorporating wood planked stairways with sturdy wooden railings, wound its way along the side of the steep hill and through stands of dense tropical forest. Sometimes the two men were walking beneath an arboreal canopy of interlaced branches. Some of the smooth barked trees were very large. In the open, there was a light wind and the air did not feel as humid as it did down below in the city. Alexander relished walking amidst such riotous greenery. They frequently saw monkeys. The impression of elevation and space made Alexander's spirits rise. But it was a pity, he thought, that they came across quite a few other walkers. This was a far cry from the wilderness which Alexander had loved so much in Africa, but it also felt far removed from the city of Kaohsiung. After half an hour's fairly strenuous walking – for the path was rarely level, but ascended and descended constantly – Johnny said, 'We turn around now. I will show you a café by the edge of the sea.'

They had been walking an hour by the time they got back to Johnny's scooter. Alexander felt as if, for a while, he had been freed of a heavy weight. 'I must come here again Johnny,' he said. 'It is a wonderful place.'

'I am pleased you like it. Sometimes I walk here with my girlfriend after classes at university. The university is at the bottom of this mountain.'

They descended a narrow, very steep road via a series of tight hairpin bends. The shoreline, far below, grew rapidly closer. The location of the Ocean Corner Café, squeezed between cliff-side and shoreline, built several metres above the sea, could not have been bettered. It was an open, unpretentious place, with little attention paid to the décor or furnishings. They sat on the deck outside, on plastic chairs, and whilst Johnny drank more tea, and munched on something that looked to Alexander's eye overly gooey and sweet, Alexander had another iced coffee. He did not think the caffeine strength in the cans of iced coffee was very high.

'What do you think of this café, Sandy?' asked Johnny.

'I like it, Johnny. I've enjoyed everything you've shown me today. It has been wonderful to escape from the city. It is hard to believe the city is so close.'

'I enjoy showing you. Showing off? Showing it off to you.' Johnny grinned. 'We in Kaohsiung are more than just high-rises and shops and factories and traffic.'

Chapter Thirty-Five

The Chiltern Hills

Johnny met up with Alexander twice in August, and again twice in September. Johnny enjoyed listening to the stories Alexander told him, and to descriptions both of Africa and of Britain.

'You know,' he said to Alexander one Saturday, 'We are both exiles. Our families originally came from somewhere else.'

Alexander smiled and nodded. 'Yah. I sometimes feel quite lost, as if I had nowhere to call home. My heart belongs to Africa, but my culture is broadly British and my ancestry is British. The empire into which I was born does not exist anymore. The Africa I love is fast disappearing. I sometimes feel a profound sadness.'

Johnny stared solemnly at Alexander. 'It is the same for those of us whose families escaped from the Communists on the mainland. Our ancestors' graves are far away. Our history is far away. We dream of returning some day, but we cannot.'

'People like your family have built a great country here in Taiwan, though,' Alexander responded. 'You have made the best of your exile. But I understand how it must be for you.'

Johnny smiled. 'My generation does not worry about it so much. It is my grandparents who dream of their homeland across the straits.'

Alexander's three months temporary work and residence visa would expire on the 21st October. In early October he communicated his concerns to Steve.

'Government doctors at hospital will test you on Monday, nine day October,' Steve told him. 'I have made appointment for you. You must be in good health to extend your visa.'

Alexander had not considered that a health check would be necessary. He worried about his amputation, which he feared might be a cause of concern to the health officials. It was with trepidation that he attended the appointment at the Kaohsiung Municipal Da-Tung Hospital. For the examination, he had to strip to his underwear. When it became apparent that he had a false leg, there was considerable conversation between the examining doctor and another doctor who then joined him. Alexander did not like the sense he got of an overly critical interest in his amputation and in the prosthesis.

On Tuesday 17th October, Alexander arrived at Steve's school as usual at eight-thirty on his scooter. After his morning class, Steve said to him, 'Sandy, you come my office please.'

Inside Steve's rather shabby office, Alexander knew that his employer had something unpleasant to tell him. Steve would not meet his eye.

'You cannot stay in Taiwan,' Steve said. 'Government not – not give visa. You must leave at end of the week. You not pass health examination.'

Alexander was not as surprised at his reaction as he might have been: it was in fact one of relief. Only at this moment did he realise that he had been living under an increasing strain, beset by a crush of humanity, constantly made aware of his foreignness, and homesick for another European to talk to. Now he had no choice but to return to a familiar world, a world where he did not always feel as if he had landed on an alien planet. Relief flooded him. But he put on a sad face for Steve.

Chapter Thirty-Five

'You work until Friday. You leave next day.'

'That is sad, Steve. I must telephone Singapore Airlines,' he said, 'if you will let me use your phone here.'

'You a good teacher. I sorry to see you go.'

Alexander returned to his flat during his lunch break and found his air ticket. Later that afternoon, his air ticket in front of him on the desk, he telephoned Singapore Airlines from Steve's office. He would be flying on Saturday evening – but headed for Heathrow, not for Jan Smuts at Johannesburg.

Alexander knew he could not realistically return to South Africa. There was nothing for him there now. He would have to return to England. His mind began racing. Would he have enough money to find somewhere to live in the short term? His mother had agreed in principle, during his brief stay in South Africa, to put up the cash to buy a small house – a bungalow – in England. Did it in fact have to be in England? Why could he not live in Argyll, on Scotland's west coast, where he had been happy way back in 1976? He did not particularly wish to return to High Wycombe, where his history of drunkenness and failure troubled his memory. But were his chances of ever working again in Britain really over? If not, then south-east England made far more sense than western Scotland.

'I will miss Johnny,' Alexander thought.

Johnny came by Alexander's flat on Thursday evening, to say goodbye, and he gave Alexander his parents' postal address. Alexander in turn gave Johnny his aunt's address in Wiltshire as a contact point.

'I will visit you when I am in England someday,' Johnny said.

But Alexander knew that their friendship had been a thing located in a particular place and time: it would not survive beyond those limitations.

'I would like that very much indeed. Perhaps I can repay your kindness here, by showing you around London one day.'

'It was not kindness, Sandy. Listening to the way you speak, to your clear English, and hearing your accent, has helped me speak a better English, I think.'

They said goodbye outside Alexander's apartment block, shaking hands and wishing each other well. Alexander stood watching as Johnny zipped up the street on his scooter and turned into Wufu 2nd Road.

'Oh, gosh . . .' Alexander said out loud; another parting, another goodbye. Then he began thinking of the flights that lay ahead of him, and of his uncertain plans once he arrived in Britain. 'I wish it was all behind me.'

Steve and Phil drove Alexander to Kaohsiung International Airport in the early evening on Saturday. It was not a long drive; the airport lay on the very edge of the city. Alexander had time to visit one of the smoking pods at Changi Airport. His flight for London left at half past eleven that night. Alexander flew west through the night. When the flight arrived at Heathrow, it was – because of the time difference – only just before six on Sunday morning in England. Alexander found a luggage trolley and piled his few pieces of luggage onto it. He sat and drank a couple of coffees and ate two croissants at one of the airport cafés, then he bought a newspaper and sat reading it, killing time. At about eight in the morning he made for a bank of telephones, and telephoned his London friend, Piers Hawkins, at his flat in Soho.

'Piers? Yes – it's Sandy. I hope I have n't woken you. How are you?... Oh, I'm well. Look, I'm at Heathrow. I've just returned from Taiwan... yes, Taiwan. I was teaching business English out there, but my three month work visa was n't renewed, so I couldn't stay, and I was wondering: could you put me up just for a night or two?'

Piers told Alexander he was welcome to stay with him for a while. Unable to manage his luggage on the train from Heathrow to Paddington station, he took a very expensive taxi from the

Chapter Thirty-Five

airport to Pier's flat in Frith Street. Piers lived on the first and second floors of a Georgian townhouse. His high ceilinged sitting room was paneled in oak painted a dark, glossy, bottle green. The fireplace was of carved, gleaming white marble, with a number of antique porcelain vases and ornaments on the mantelpiece, and a heavy Georgian silver candle holder at either end. Above the fireplace was fixed a large mirror in an ornate gilt frame. The floorboards, where they could be seen between Persian rugs, were of old, dark, polished oak. It was a long room, taking up two thirds of the entire length of the building's street façade. Alongside it was a smaller room, used as a dining room, paneled in polished oak that had a deep, ancient patina. Both the rooms had a great many framed, original oils and watercolours hanging on the walls, some of which, Alexander knew, had come down to Piers from his family and were very old. Piers, like Alexander, valued old things.

There was a display of antique swords mounted on one wall, and on the opposite wall, between two windows, there was arranged a collection of flintlock and percussion cap pistols, with a Brown Bess Tower musket and an Enfield percussion cap .577 musket-rifle in the centre of the display. The windows had interior folding shutters, those in the sitting room painted the same bottle green as the walls, and those in the dining room painted a soft salmon pink. Either side of the fireplace in the sitting room (there was another fireplace in the dining room) were bookcases, crammed with books ranging from contemporary non-fiction paperbacks to antique volumes bound in leather. Two long sofas covered in plum coloured velvet were arranged in front of the fireplace, and there were two armchairs in matching velvet. There were several reproduction Sheraton chairs arranged around the room. There was a low coffee table between the two sofas, on which were two or three brass ashtrays, a cut glass vase, several books, and a number of glossy magazines.

'Sandy! From the far side of the world! Welcome home!'

The two men embraced, Piers warmly, Alexander a trifle awkwardly, as he did not feel entirely easy with such displays of affection.

'It's good to be back – I guess. Thank you for putting me up, Piers.'

'Think nothing of it. Would you like a sherry – or something stronger?'

'What I would really like is a coffee, if you could. It was n't easy finding coffee in Kaohsiung.' Alexander reached into his shoulder bag, and found the bottle of scotch he had bought in the duty free shop at Kaohsiung Airport. 'Here's a small gift for you, Piers – a thank you, you know.'

The two friends chatted over their drinks. Piers had poured himself a sherry. Alexander had a good, strong, sweet black coffee, which went down very well.

'What are your plans now?' Piers asked, after Alexander had told him something about his stay in Taiwan.

'I think I'm going to look for a bungalow near High Wycombe. My mother will buy it for the family, of which I am the sole representative at present here in England.'

'Why High Wycombe in particular?'

'I'm familiar with the district. The countryside in the Chilterns is very lovely. It's hilly and well wooded. I need hills if I'm to be happy. But it's within easy reach of London.'

'Good. So I shall still see something of you, Sandy.'

"Yah – I'm not that easy to get rid of!' Both men laughed.

Alexander stayed at Piers' home for four nights, leaving on Thursday morning the 26th October. The days and nights were cool; the intense, humid warmth of summer time in London had long passed. It was dry, generally overcast, and the evening of Alexander's arrival the two men went out to a pub nearby, where they had some supper. Alexander refused alcohol. 'I'm not drinking at the moment,' he told Piers.

Chapter Thirty-Five

'Good for you. You don't mind if I do?'

'Of course not. Go ahead, please.'

On Tuesday night Piers entertained two friends to supper at home. One was a musician with the London Philharmonic, the other a mid-ranking civil servant. They reminded Alexander of the men he used to know at the Salisbury. He found their conversation stimulating, and they appeared to find him agreeable company. Piers and Alexander walked to a pub for supper again on Wednesday night. Alexander enjoyed Soho, which, although no longer the sink of iniquity it had been during his first stay in London, was still full of character. The two friends got along easily, and both were fundamentally chaste – or at least, Piers appeared to be that way to Alexander, whose own chastity, whilst hardly of any great historical standing, was genuine now.

On Thursday morning Alexander took a taxi to Marylebone Station, the terminus of the Chiltern Railways line, and caught a train for High Wycombe. On arrival in High Wycombe he moved into a small residential hotel in Priory Avenue, not far from the flat he and Roy had shared together. Alexander bought himself a cheap, simple, prepaid mobile phone. He telephoned his mother, using a service the salesman at the mobile phone shop had told him about, that provided him with very cheap call rates to South Africa. Alexander's mother gave him the go ahead to look for a small house.

Alexander had already viewed half a dozen properties (using one of High Wycombe's taxi services for his travelling), before, in late November, he decided on a bungalow located in a cul-de-sac leading off the High Street in Chinnor, a village a few miles from High Wycombe, just over the county border into Oxfordshire. Chinnor village crouched beneath the heavily wooded chalk scarp that marked the edge of the Chiltern Hills. The bungalow had two generously sized bedrooms (one of which was upstairs in a loft conversion, with a small WC attached), and a third, rather smaller bedroom. The lounge was south facing, with a small dining room alongside it through a wide archway. There was a kitchen with a utility room. There was a bathroom with a lavatory on the ground floor, and a small entrance hall. A driveway down the side of the house led to an extra wide single garage. The house was located on about a fifth of an acre. A trio of decorative fir trees grew to one side of the front garden, and in the somewhat larger back garden stood a mature beech tree, leafless and stark at this time of year.

Alexander's stay at the residential hotel in High Wycombe had to be extended into December, for there were complications with the transfer of funds from South Africa to his own bank account, but on Friday 15th December, a miserable, cold, grey, damp day, Alexander, acting for his mother, exchanged contracts at the solicitor's office in High Wycombe's High Street. Alexander then telephoned Social Services and spoke to Gillian, his contact there.

'My family has bought a bungalow in Chinnor,' he told her. 'I'm moving in this week – as soon as I can get hold of the things you're storing for me.'

'I'm glad to hear it, Sandy,' she responded. 'I will have to send you an invoice for the last couple of months' storage of your goods, you realise. Would you give me your new address?'

Alexander did so. He next telephoned a car hire agency with an office in West Wycombe Road, and arranged to hire a small car for a few days. As soon as he had settled into his new home, he would see about buying a second hand car. But right now he had to buy some furniture. Alexander felt tired when he contemplated how much he had to do, and without anyone to help him. He could not remember what he had in the way of household goods, kitchenware *et cetera*, in the boxes that had been stored for him all this time. The day his things were delivered from Social Services was set to be extremely busy and very exhausting.

It was. On Wednesday, five days before Christmas, the goods that Social Services had been storing for Alexander were delivered

Chapter Thirty-Five

to the bungalow. The two beds – a double and a single – that Alexander had bought from a discount furniture outlet on the London Road, had been delivered on Monday morning. From a second hand furniture shop in High Wycombe, Alexander bought a very fine 1950s sideboard with a glass fronted display cabinet, to show off his Lady Carlyle tea set, which he had bought second hand from a shop in Yeoville. The unit was beautifully veneered and of top quality construction, and it cost him only five Pounds. From the same shop he also bought a second hand lounge suite with a coffee table, along with a dining table with four chairs. For the kitchen he had bought a reconditioned second hand electric cooker, very much like the one he remembered from his childhood, together with a washing machine and a refrigerator. These had all been delivered on Tuesday morning, and on Wednesday morning Alexander at last checked out of the hotel in Priory Avenue, and drove in his hire car to Chinnor, to wait at the bungalow for the delivery from Social Services to be made.

By New Year's Eve, with snow lying three inches deep on the ground (for there had been a snowfall across much of Britain on the 29th December), and Christmas having passed almost unnoticed, Alexander had arranged things in the house the way he wanted them. The oil paintings were hanging on the walls in the sitting room and dining room. There were photographs hanging on the walls in his bedroom upstairs. There was a framed print or two on the wall in each of the remaining two bedrooms. He now knew what he possessed in the way of kitchenware, crockery and cutlery. His double bed was made up with bedding which had traveled from South Africa. The single bed in the small bedroom downstairs he left unmade with a dust sheet over it. Roy would use the larger of the two bedrooms downstairs when he came to visit (in which was Roy's custom made extra long single bed). The large empty packing boxes were stored alongside one wall in the wide garage. Alexander had stocked the kitchen cupboards and the refrigerator with groceries and foodstuffs. There were things still to buy; gardening tools for one, and although the bungalow was carpeted wall to wall, Alexander wanted to find some large colourful rugs for the sitting room and the bedrooms. And he needed some colourful plump cushions in the sitting room. But these could wait.

Early in the new year of 2001, Alexander submitted an application for the non means-tested Disability Living Allowance that he (and anyone with a qualifying disability or medical condition) was entitled to. He had calculated that with this allowance, and living frugally, he could afford to run a small car. In late February he began hunting for a second hand car. His mother would help him with the cost of the car's purchase. Having returned the hire car shortly before the end of the year, he had resorted to catching the bus into High Wycombe or Thame (which, only four and a half miles away, was the nearest sizable Oxfordshire town to Chinnor).

Alexander found a 1994 Citroën Xantia in Marlow for only six hundred Pounds, the last of the Citroëns made with the classic pneumatic suspension of the marque. The car had a fairly high mileage, but it was in very good condition, with a complete service history from new. The car had an automatic gearbox, a necessity for Alexander, with no fully functioning left leg with which to operate a clutch. Alexander was to drive this car for the next sixteen and a half years. No one in his family, least of all his father, had ever kept a car for anything like that long.

In March, with bright daffodils and narcissi bringing cheer to every garden in the village, including Alexander's own, in which there were also primroses, butter yellow, blooming, he began to think about finding himself a cat to love and care for. He spoke to some of the people he had come to know at Saint Andrew's church in the village. Saint Andrew's was a Church of England parish. There was a Catholic church in Thame, but Alexander

Chapter Thirty-Five

had grown aware that he no longer loved the Catholic Church. It was, Alexander had come to feel, a priest-ridden church, and that priesthood, closed to all except those who had a calling to celibacy, represented an unnatural body of men. It was too (so Alexander now believed) a church of peasant superstitions and empty ritual devoid of spirituality. Perhaps if he had felt a greater sense that the Catholic Church loved him, he would not have taken so adamantly against it, but he had never felt the sort of love within the Catholic Church that he remembered experiencing within the Anglican Church as a young man.

Alexander enjoyed walking to the top of High Street and into Church Road on Sunday mornings. He reverted easily to the Anglican rite. It was, after all (although the language had become more contemporary), the rite of his youth. One of Alexander's acquaintances in the congregation, in response to his enquiry about cats, asked, 'Do you know of the cat sanctuary in Beaconsfield? I can give you their phone number if you like.'

'Thanks. Yes, please do.'

The privately owned cat sanctuary in Beaconsfield in Buckinghamshire was run by a husband and wife team. When Alexander visited it, he wished the cats had larger enclosures, but they were clearly loved, and the enclosures and surroundings were clean. As he walked slowly past them, he wanted to adopt all the pathetic, homeless, unwanted moggies. His heart filled with painful compassion.

'Which cat is most in need of being adopted?' Alexander asked Joan, who ran the sanctuary. She pointed at an old tabby cat.

'She's been with us since early December last year. She's very old, possibly twenty or twenty-one already. She's a darling, but people don't want to adopt very old cats. They're afraid of the expense when they fall ill.'

Joan opened the wide mesh covered door to Ortie's enclosure (for Ortie was the cat's unusual name). Alexander stepped inside slowly so as not to startle the cat, but she miaowed at him, looking up at him, and he bent down and stroked her.

'I'll give her a loving home and take care of her as long as she lives,' he said.

Alexander had brought a cat's traveling basket with him. He gave the cat sanctuary a donation of fifteen Pounds, and all the way back to Chinnor, a fairly long drive, Ortie miaowed in her old, husky voice.

'It's alright darling,' Alexander told her. 'We'll soon be home.'

Ortie reminded Alexander so much of Lulu during her old age. She was gentle, affectionate, and happy to stay inside the house, preferably in a patch of sunshine. Alexander poured out all the love that had become choked inside him for want of a recipient. He was lonely and often homesick, and still tormented by occasional nightmares filled with violence, or with the threat of violence, and less frequently, by occasional racking flashbacks during the day, but with Ortie he was able to ground himself again. She needed him, and he needed to be needed. She was loveable, and he needed to love.

It was a lovely summer that year. Often, Alexander went walking in the country, following pathways along the top of the great chalk scarp above the village. In general his crippled leg and his tendency to tire quickly would limit him to little more than half an hour's walking each way, but every now and then he surprised himself by walking further, once walking for more than two hours. During the week he met few other walkers.

Alexander began to take an interest in butterflies. He had never given them much conscious attention before, although taking pleasure in their presence, but as he walked now, he became aware of how many butterfly species there were, in such a variety of wonderful designs and colours, so he bought himself a butterfly

Chapter Thirty-Five

guide and he began to learn their names and characteristics. He quickly learned to recognise the small tortoiseshell, that classic British butterfly, and the smaller and larger whites, together with the meadow browns, fritillaries, brimstones and small blues. He was delighted with his first sighting of the orange and dark brown comma, with its ragged edged wings. He was particularly pleased whenever he saw a red admiral, that splendid large butterfly that had once been a European summer migrant only, but was now beginning to overwinter in southern England. The peacock butterfly brought him more delight than any of the other species, for its exotic, lush beauty. He kept a butterfly diary, in which he wrote down his "take" that day: the names of the species, their locations, and the dominant plant species near each. The happiness he felt as he watched one of his favourite butterflies was as pure and joyful as that which he had experienced in the bushveld when he spotted a noteworthy bird – such as the paradise flycatcher, for example, or one of the raptors. This interest in butterflies gave Alexander's walks a purpose, if indeed any purpose was required.

The ridge (in fact, much of the Chilterns) was heavily wooded, covered in a canopy of ancient beech trees amidst which were also found oak, ash and hazel. There were also occasional plantations of firs, conifers or spruce. Walking these pathways, Alexander would sometimes come across a break in the trees, then the vista would open up as he passed by a wide meadow, in which he might see a herd of cows, dappled black and white, placid and content as they munched the thick juicy green grass, or a couple of horses standing dreaming beneath the sun, and the outlook would suddenly extend for many miles across the wide vale that reached below the ridge to the south. There were no towns to be seen, but only scattered farmsteads and the occasional hint of tiny hamlets sheltering in the combs.

Once, Alexander came across a fox – its coat a rich, shining red – sunning itself on the pathway, and because Alexander (even with a false leg) still walked with a very light tread, the fox, for several minutes, did not know that it was being observed. Alexander gazed at it with happiness in his heart. Sometimes Alexander would hear a blood curdling, shrieking barking in the woods, and the first time he heard this dreadful sound, he felt a prickling on the nape of his neck. But the next time he heard this terrible noise, he was able to identify its source: it was a tiny muntjac deer, a male with a pair of miniature horns, standing in the trees and yelling at the woods around him. As Alexander walked through the woods, the tree canopy above and all around him was alive with birdsong, but it was only rarely that he was able to identify any particular species, for he could not see the birds clearly through the dense leafy cover of summer.

Alexander had obtained a Blue Badge card, which, placed face up on top of his car's dashboard, allowed him, as a disabled person, to park his car for free in pay parking zones, and to park it against the kerbside on white lines. He joined the public library in Thame, and he also bought second hand books, fiction and non-fiction, from the charity shops in High Wycombe. He began to read voraciously once again. He discovered the only recently deceased writer, Patrick O'Brian, who had authored several dozen superbly researched and beautifully written stories set in the Royal Navy during the Napoleonic wars. As he read about the adventures of Captain Jack Aubrey, and his "particular friend," Dr. Steven Maturin, Alexander realised he had found the most mature, most rewarding historical fiction he had ever read.

Alexander did not watch much television, although he took to watching *Neighbours* every week day. What was it about this popular Australian soap that he enjoyed so much? It was not the muscle bound young male characters in it, who were uniformly dumb as oxen (and whose overblown physiques repelled Alexander); it was, he realised, that the setting reminded him so much of suburban South Africa back in the seventies and eighties.

Chapter Thirty-Five

In November, Ortie's health commenced a rapid decline. She was being sick after almost every meal, and she was losing weight fast. Alexander took her to the vet in Princes Risborough.

'She's dying of old age, Mr. Maclean,' the vet told Alexander after examining Ortie. 'There's not a great deal we could do for her. It would be a kindness to have her put to sleep.'

The diagnosis did not shock Alexander. It was as he had feared. But the pain he felt was intense.

'I'll take her home, and think it over,' he said.

Alexander had tears in his eyes as he drove home with the old cat. He put her on his lap when he got home, and caressed her and spoke to her. Later, after eating very little for supper, and that only because he stroked her tummy, she was sick again. That night he sat up with her until she was fast asleep. The next morning he rang the vet and asked him to make a home visit. 'It will be kinder if we put her to sleep at home,' he explained.

The morning passed slowly, as in a horrible nightmare, but Alexander struggled, for the cat's sake, not to allow his distress to show. He held Ortie on his lap, and then she lay in the sun on the carpet. When the vet arrived in the early afternoon, Alexander insisted that Ortie be put to sleep in his arms, and so she died in Alexander's embrace, his unashamed tears falling on her fur coat.

How truly alone Alexander felt he now was! There was no one in England with whom he felt really close; no one with whom he could share his grief. He buried the old cat's body, wrapped in her favourite sleeping blanket, in a corner of the back garden, and as he did so he was remembering other much loved cats who had died, including Simba, who had been killed when Alexander was twelve years old. After a few days had passed, Alexander found a large piece of slate on which he painted Ortie's name, and the date she had died, and he placed it at the head of the grave.

Two unhappy weeks followed, then on the 3rd December Alexander bought a bottle of scotch and poured himself a double when he got back home. He followed it immediately with another large measure. He was telling himself his favourite lie: that he could control his drinking, even of spirits; that he would have only two drinks, then he would put the bottle away until tomorrow. Oh, what a liar Alexander was! Two days later he had to buy another bottle of scotch. To do so, he drove into High Wycombe, where there were many liquor stores. Within just a few days, he was drinking as heavily again as when he had entered the clinic in Harrow in April 2000. (Following his final recovery, early in 2002, Alexander was to understand at last that when a dry alcoholic picks up the bottle again, he very quickly returns to the levels he had last left off).

Alexander had managed to remain sober for seventeen months. This time, his bout with alcohol would almost kill him.

Chapter Thirty-Six

Deliverance

Alexander refrained from behaving as outrageously as he had done in High Wycombe, but he became known as something of an eccentric – and some would say, as a bit of a lush – at the Red Lion, the pub not far from his home, at the bottom of the High Street in Chinnor, where he did all his public drinking. His eccentricities of character became hugely exaggerated under the influence of prodigious quantities of alcohol, only a fraction of which was taken in public. He would arrive at the Red Lion in the evening having been drinking on and off all through the day, and because he made an enormous effort to keep himself looking presentable, clean and freshly shaved (his experiences in High Wycombe having given him a consciousness, even when very drunk indeed, of the importance of avoiding becoming a byword in Chinnor, which was to be his home for the foreseeable future), no one, not even the landlord, realised just how drunk he was.

That Alexander, who routinely drove into High Wycombe or Princes Risborough to buy his liquor, managed to avoid having an accident with the car, was nothing less than miraculous. But by the beginning of February the following year, he was struggling even to drive anymore. Alexander was consuming a bottle of scotch a day (together with several pints of beer, along with whiskey chasers, at the Red Lion), and although his craving for liquor remained unabated, his tolerance was diminishing rapidly. He was struggling now to reach that point where he felt he had drunk enough not to feel the anxiety associated with an unsatisfied craving for alcohol. No matter how much he drank, he still felt agitated and distressed. But drinking less was not an option. His mind and body still craved the same large quantities of alcohol as previously, or the symptoms of withdrawal would quickly set in.

By midway through February 2002, Alexander had ceased visiting the Red Lion. He was no longer fit to be seen in public. He seemed to be suffering from near permanent withdrawals, and no amount of drink would calm them. He was no longer able to keep up the struggle to maintain his personal hygiene, and he could no longer organise himself sufficiently to tackle his laundry. By the 24th February he was trapped in his home, his larder bare, his clothes filthy, and he was soiling himself, losing control of his bowels and bladder. Alexander, with about a quarter of a bottle of scotch left in the house, and aware that he was now incapable of obtaining another bottle, telephoned Alcoholics Anonymous in the early morning of the 24th. He had in effect already had his final drink shortly before making the telephone call, for he could not now keep alcohol down without vomiting, although his craving for liquor continued unabated.

Alexander suffered the pangs of what was known as "cold turkey." He felt an extreme anxiety and mental agitation; he shook and trembled; he sweated profusely; seizures would grip and shake him like a rat in a terrier dog's jaws; he would be unable to catch his breath; agonizing cramps would rack his limbs. He took a telephone call on the 26th, expecting that someone from Alcoholics Anonymous was checking up on him, but the call was from his mother; it was his forty-seventh birthday. He told his mother he had the flu, that he was being looked after, and that he loved her, and would telephone her when he felt better.

Alexander was sustained by daily visits from representatives of Alcoholics Anonymous. 'You poor sorry bastard,' one of the men, Nick, said to him. 'The Hell is necessary: without reaching rock bottom, there can be no lasting recovery. But you're getting there, Sandy. And we're here for you, mate.'

Nick was to become Alexander's sponsor within the brotherhood, and guide him through the Twelve Steps recovery programme.

These men, when they visited Alexander, spoke not one word of judgment against him. They neither lectured nor browbeat him, but kept him supplied with cigarettes, sugar, tea and coffee, and at his own request, with jars of Bovril (with which Alexander made strong meaty hot drinks rich in vitamin B). After three or four days had passed, Alexander began drinking mugs of instant soup, accompanied by a couple of slices of toast. Alexander lived from visit to visit, suffering the horrors of medically unsupervised withdrawals with a grim, desperate fortitude. When, on the second night, the demon of alcoholism being driven out of him called up a host of its fellows to torment him (and these nightmarish creatures were as visually real to Alexander as were the familiar objects in his house), he said these words, 'Jesus help me!' over and over.

By the fifth day, the worst was over. If, as Alexander later came to believe, alcoholism was a form of possession, then he had been exorcised. Filthy, stinking, trembling with weakness and fatigue, Alexander found that he was able to think straight again; that he was suffering no more seizures, and that he could sleep again. After a full week had passed since Alexander had vomited up his final drink, Nick (having first removed enough of Alexander's soiled clothing to make a clean change of clothes for him, once he had taken the ghastly bundle back home with him and stuck it in the laundry) drove Alexander to his first AA meeting. It was a Sunday afternoon. The meeting, held in a beautiful high ceilinged room in what had once been the private chapel of a large house in the country, was well attended, and perhaps a quarter of those present were women. Alexander's welcome was genuine. He felt safe. He felt that he could be himself – the wreck of a Human being that he was – and no one would judge him.

Alexander was to attend at least four meetings of Alcoholics Anonymous a week for the next four years. He made many friends. His social life blossomed. He was invited to barbeques and garden parties throughout that first summer, and the summers that followed. He experienced a sense of community and belonging that had thus far evaded him throughout his life. And he remained sober. Within a very short while, it was no longer an effort to remain sober, and it would never again be difficult for Alexander to remain sober. A genuine miracle had occurred; the compulsion to drink had been lifted from him.

Within three to four months, Alexander had become aware that he had been delivered from far more than merely a compulsion to drink: he had been delivered from the alcoholic's manic-depressive mindset; from that pattern of insane alcoholic thinking that had blighted his life for so long. An equally unexpected and welcome consequence of true sobriety was that his libido was much dampened down. He could view the young people whose grace and beauty would once have filled him with a painful yearning, with something close to equanimity.

Alexander ascribed such a complete and total deliverance from alcoholism, and from its many hurtful and damaging symptoms, to his renewed Christian faith. But the God in whom Alexander found himself believing so passionately again was a demanding deity. In return for gifting Alexander with a profound and wide reaching sobriety, and a greatly renewed faith (along with the comforts and strengths that this faith

Chapter Thirty-Six

brought him), God desired that Alexander take ownership of his own fallen nature.

Alexander began to learn how to live honestly; to face up to the worst within his nature – and to recognise and acknowledge what was best in his nature, also. During those nightmarish four or five days of extreme withdrawals from alcohol addiction (a period which had seemed at the time to last an eternity), Alexander had felt as if he was being crucified, and the nails being hammered into his wrists and feet were forged of every wickedness he had ever committed; of every selfish act he had ever perpetrated. For the rest of his life, Alexander was periodically to suffer agonies of remorse for the many callous, self-centred and sometimes depraved acts of which he now knew he had been guilty.

Alexander's anguish at the way he had lived much of his life was acute. It was not (he knew) that he had consciously sought to be wicked; rather, he had felt little active regard for others' welfare. He feared he had exploited the vulnerability and need and helplessness of every drunken woman he had ever taken home, upon whom he had sought temporary satiation of his lust. And he was stricken with remorse and regret at the self imposed emotional distance he had maintained for much of his adult life with his father. Alexander had done with weeping for his sins during the worst of those withdrawals, but the remorse he still experienced was heartfelt.

However, Alexander knew now that God had never, after all, loosed His hold on him. It seemed that God still required Alexander's active and willing participation in the fulfillment of His plan for him. Sometimes Alexander rode the wings of his gratitude, soaring blissfully close to an enraptured sense of union with the divine.

His deliverance from alcoholism was to mark for Alexander a watershed greater than any other in his life, and when remorse and regret threatened to overwhelm him, he need only consider this deliverance to know that God had surely forgiven him; that he was no longer under condemnation.

Sometimes Alexander attended both the Communion services at Saint Andrew's on a Sunday, and he would attend Communion at least once during the week also. In addition he usually went to Evensong once or twice during the week, sometimes also on a Sunday. He found that the sense of belonging he experienced in Alcoholics Anonymous was replicated to a lesser extent at Church.

In May, Piers Hawkins came down from London by train one Saturday to spend the day with Alexander. Alexander met him at High Wycombe Station, off a fast train non-stop from Marylebone.

'Sandy! How good you're looking! Living in the country suits you,' Piers greeted Alexander with a smile. 'Lucky you – away from the crowds and noise and petrol fumes of London.'

The two friends shook hands and Piers clasped Alexander's shoulder.

'You're looking good too, Piers,' Alexander responded. 'Indeed, we're both a sight for sore eyes, eh?'

Piers grinned.

Once through High Wycombe, the bucolic atmosphere became intensified as Alexander drove Piers past fields of new wheat, and pastures in which sheep (with lambs already big and chubby) or cows were grazing. The hedgerows were white with mayflower. As they left the valley floor below them and climbed into the hills, they drove past the occasional tiny hamlet, each just a scattering of houses, with dense green woodland between each settlement. The traffic was light. The weather was glorious, a bright, clear day, and the blue sky had fluffy white cumulus clouds drifting by high above. There was a slight breeze and the air had a clarity which emphasized the fresh colours in every scene.

Chapter Thirty-Six

Alexander took Piers for lunch to the Pink and Whistle near Princes Risborough, a pub famed for its food. Piers drank wine with his meal, Alexander stuck to sparkling mineral water. They found they were able to chat without the least sense of restraint, and by the time Alexander drove Piers back to the railway station at High Wycombe in the early evening, he judged the day to have been a success.

'I look forward to my next visit, my country friend,' said Piers.

It was in June that year of 2002 that Alexander began to experience frequent extremely painful bowel cramps, which effectively crippled him for as long as they lasted. He rapidly grew to dread them. He felt intuitively that they were associated with his knife injury. His doctor arranged for a consultant at Wycombe General Hospital to examine him. A barium meal examination and other tests persuaded the specialist that Alexander needed bowel surgery to relieve him of the intestinal lesions the clinician said he was suffering from.

'They almost certainly arise from the trauma surgery you describe undergoing following the stabbing incident in 1996,' the man told Alexander.

The bowel surgery, performed at the hospital in High Wycombe, was very unpleasant indeed. Alexander suffered a great deal of post operative pain. He remained in hospital for two weeks; a fortnight that was only made tolerable by the constant stream of visitors from among his Alcoholics Anonymous friends and acquaintances. The most diligent of these visitors was undoubtedly a middle aged woman named Sarah, and Alexander was surprised at her dedication, for up until then, she had been only one of many acquaintances he had made through the Tuesday evenings Alcoholics Anonymous meetings in Beaconsfield.

'I am so grateful for your visits, Sarah,' Alexander told her. They were sitting smoking together, along with several other patients and some hospital staff, in the tiny garden courtyard in the hospital, Alexander in a dressing gown. He was in a wheelchair, which Sarah had taken charge of.

'I know how miserable it can be, lying in a hospital bed, Sandy. And perhaps one day you will do the same for someone else.'

Alexander was touched by the kindness of these friends and acquaintances, and often his eyes would fill with tears of gratitude and he would have to knuckle his eyes and blow his nose. But the surgery was pronounced a success, and Alexander was not to suffer episodes of bowel pain nearly as often in the future. However, those episodes he did suffer were very bad indeed, and were quite likely to land him in Accident and Emergency at Wycombe General Hospital. It would always be something he had eaten, some foodstuff he had thought was harmless, which had brought on an intestinal pseudo-obstruction, and then the pain was severe, several times causing him to phone for an ambulance. Alexander would invariably spend the night in hospital, until (with the aid of an intramuscular morphine injection) the bowel restriction had cleared.

Alexander began to learn, by trial and error, that there were certain foods it was better to avoid. Anything with high volume roughage, such as peas, sweet corn, raisins and sultanas, had to be avoided completely. He learned also that fried foods, in particular, fried eggs, disagreed with him. In this painful experience of trial and error, Alexander was given no guidance by the National Health Service. His visit to the dietician to whom his doctor referred him was worse than useless, he felt: the foolish young woman (who appeared to be of only moderate intelligence) seemed unable to grasp the nutritional challenges Alexander faced, and the question of which foods to be avoided in his situation was beyond her.

Chapter Thirty-Seven

Vicky

In September 2002 Alexander visited Paris for three nights with an Australian friend he had made via Alcoholics Anonymous. Tim, a bachelor, was a passionate collector of antique *bric à brac* and antique furniture. Alexander shared Tim's interest in antique furniture, although he was not as knowledgeable on the subject as Tim was. Tim lived in a rather large old farmhouse built of brick and flints near Princes Risborough. Although only in his early fifties, he had already retired and seemed to have plenty of money. Alexander had no idea how he had earned his money.

One day in late summer Tim expressed an interest in the French language and culture, and when Alexander suggested they visit Paris together, he agreed eagerly. At the public library in Thame, Alexander researched some of the famous Paris *brasseries* and restaurants. On their first evening in Paris they had supper at *Le Train Bleu*, with its opulent, *fin de siècle*, heavily gilded interior, in the *Gare de Lyon*. The two friends ordered *boeuf bourguignon* for their main course, and for dessert, they both ordered the establishment's famous *Paris-Brest*, made from *choux* pastry and hazelnut cream. On their second night in Paris they ate at *Au Rendezvous des Chauffeurs*, in *rue des Portes Blanches*.

'The French cook with wine a great deal of the time, Tim,' Alexander told his friend. 'If we're to exclude dishes cooked with wine, we're going to exclude most of the well known dishes. I pay it no heed – alcohol evaporates during cooking, so I'm not bothered. But I thought I ought to warn you.'

Tim looked thoughtful. Then he said, 'I had n't really thought about it, but I guess you're right.'

Alexander ordered *lapin à la cocotte* – rabbit stew; Tim ordered *bavettes de boeuf*. And on their third night, Tim and Alexander had supper at *Terminus Nord*, opposite the *Gare du Nord*. Another very well known *brasserie* dating from the grand era of rail travel, it was known for its seafood. Declining a traditional main course, Alexander ordered wine poached salmon with black truffle sauce. Tim ordered a seafood *bouillabaisse*, followed by lobster *thermidor*.

During their first morning in Paris they spent about four hours in the Louvre, where both men stared for some time at Leonardo da Vinci's *Mona Lisa*.

'I had n't realised how large it was,' Alexander commented.

'Yeah… her gaze does seem to follow you, does n't it?'

They visited Montmartre and the basilica of *Sacré-Coeur*, admiring the panoramic view across Paris from the terrace. They visited the cathedral of *Notre-Dame de Paris* and also *L'Église du Dôme*, which housed Napoleon's tomb, carved from a massive block of blood-red porphyry. Alexander was fascinated by Napoleon, whom he saw as the embodiment of utterly amoral, unfettered ego and masculine genius.

In March 2003, Alexander spent ten days holidaying in Malta. Since leaving the island in September 1992, he had stayed in touch with his Maltese friend, Filippu Dingli. Filippu, looking somewhat older now, met him at Malta's neat little airport.

Chapter Thirty-Seven

'Sandy!' he exclaimed, shaking hands with Alexander, 'How nice to see you again, it's been at least ten years, has n't it?'

'I think so Filippu. *Kif int?*'

'Bearing up – as you used to say. And what about you?'

'*Jien tajjeb, grazzi.*'

Filippu smiled again. 'You remember some Maltese. That's pretty good. Do you want to carry on straight to the Preluna Hotel, or shall we look in at the Bolthole?'

'The hotel, I think, Filippu. I no longer drink. A good Maltese coffee is what I would enjoy right now.'

At the Preluna, which was located on *Triq It-Torri*, not far from Alexander's old flat, the two men sat in the open air at street level in front of the hotel café. Across the street was the wide promenade that Alexander remembered so well, and beyond that was the Mediterranean. Filippu drank a *Kinnie*, while Alexander sipped at his black coffee. They chatted, catching up with each other's lives. Filippu had retired, and when he was not researching a book he was writing (a few years earlier he had had a well received history of Malta's Jewish community published), he spent his days at cafés and bars, or sailing a friend's restored *luzzu*. Listening to Filippu talking, basking in the warmth and sunshine after the raw March weather of England, Alexander experienced an emotion still infrequent enough to come to his notice: it was happiness. 'This is where I belong,' he thought. 'Not in England.'

During his visit, Alexander made no attempt to contact Marija Caruana. He knew better than to revisit that particular past. He hired a car for some of the while, driving all round the main island, and crossing over to Gozo also. He met up with Filippu on three occasions, once visiting the Bolthole, where he contented himself with a couple of *Kinnies* while Fillipu drank lagers. Alexander had happy memories of the Bolthole, and of Robbie, his Scottish friend and lover. He had long ago lost touch with Robbie, having found over time that they no longer had anything to say to each other, for all the closeness of their friendship in Malta. He sent Piers, his friend in London, a postcard. He also sent postcards to Roy, and to his mother.

'I'm treading in Grandpa's footsteps,' he had written on the postcard to his mother. In his memoirs, published in Kenya, Alexander's maternal grandfather had written with much fondness of his time based in Valletta as a young lieutenant in the Royal Navy before the Great War.

By the time of Alexander's return to England, he had decided that if he could, someday he would live permanently in Malta. It was not only that the magnificent Baroque architecture of Valletta and Mdina, and the honey coloured limestone that you saw everywhere used as a building material in Malta, appealed to his sense of aesthetics: he was drawn to the African feel of the island's somewhat stark, rock-girt landscapes. And there was the sea, which was never far away. After England's often vile weather, the steady, benign Maltese climate was of great attraction also. But this wish was to go unfulfilled. Alexander was to spend the latter part of his life living somewhere far removed in spirit from Malta.

During the spring of 2003, following Alexander's return from his Maltese break, he began to take closer notice of an attractive woman he had seen at many of the Alcoholics Anonymous meetings. Her name was Victoria, and she looked to Alexander to be about ten years younger than himself. (He was to learn later that she was only four years his junior). He listened to her addressing some of the meetings. She was modest and self-possessed, with an appealing, self deprecating sense of humour. Her pale, flawless complexion, her fair hair gathered up from the neck in a chignon, and her blue eyes, short, straight nose, small, shapely mouth and the touch of colour on each cheek, made Alexander think of a porcelain doll from the nineteenth century.

Alexander approached Victoria after one meeting. 'I admire the way you tell your story, Victoria,' he said.

Chapter Thirty-Seven

Victoria smiled at Alexander. 'Some of us are going for coffee at the *Café Rouge*,' she said. 'Would you like to join us?'

Thereafter, Alexander often joined Victoria and her friends for coffee after meetings. He found that not only could Victoria make him laugh at life's comedy, but he was able to make her laugh also. This shared sense of the absurd drew them together after meetings during the course of that summer. One mild August evening, after an Alcoholics Anonymous meeting they had both attended in the district, Alexander learned that Victoria lived in Monks Risborough, not far from Chinnor.

'Would you like to stop off at my house in Chinnor for a coffee on your way home, Victoria?' he asked her.

'That would be nice, Sandy.'

On Wednesday evenings there was an Alcoholics Anonymous meeting at Princes Risborough, which Victoria always attended. In time, Alexander fell into the habit of having a coffee at Victoria's tiny cottage in Monks Risborough after this meeting. She had a plump, friendly cat which Alexander enjoyed petting. 'I must get myself another cat,' he told himself.

Alexander found that where he was fundamentally a conservative on social and cultural issues, Victoria inclined to the liberal-left, but neither of them wished to preach to the other. They only rarely talked about their drinking days, and each afforded the other the courtesy of assuming that sobriety was no longer an issue. This was not always the case with members of Alcoholics Anonymous. Alexander felt not the least temptation to drink, and nor did Victoria. In fact, she sometimes referred to herself as a "recovered alcoholic," a term that was anathema to many Alcoholics Anonymous members, but which Alexander related to.

By the winter of 2003, the friendship between the two had deepened. They shared an interest in classical music, art, and even architecture, and each enjoyed playing the other sound tracks from their favourite musical recordings. Although much of their conversation was fairly deep (they had both read Philosophy at university, although Alexander had majored in History, and Victoria in Sociology), there was a lot of shared laughter in their friendship.

Theirs was initially a platonic friendship, but Alexander had, from the start, found Victoria physically compelling. Excepting only Catherine, his English girlfriend in Cape Town, all the women with whom Alexander had so far had relationships, had been dark haired. Marija of course had been a classic olive skinned Mediterranean beauty. Victoria could not have been more different, with her English complexion and her gentle spirit. One evening, after an Alcoholics Anonymous meeting in midsummer of 2004, Alexander and Victoria had continued on to his bungalow, where, after Alexander had made them both some coffee, they sat together on the sofa. Although after nine, it was still light outside.

'We used to spend our summer holidays in Wales, on the coast, round about this time every year,' Victoria remarked. 'Mum and Dad, my brother and I.' She smiled. 'Where did that memory surface from?'

'Right through my teenage years, we lived in Johannesburg,' Alexander responded. 'The nearest sea was almost six hundred miles away, at Durban. My Dad had a Jaguar. We would cover that distance in eight hours. I remember the old, narrow, highway which would pass through every dusty, sleepy *dorp*; the thrill of the descent of the escarpment, with an even older road appearing below us at intervals, and the occasional wreck far below of a car that had gone over the edge.' Alexander's face had taken on a faraway look. 'Durban was so exciting! It was hot and humid, and there was a funfair on the Promenade, with little motor boats we kids could drive. There were Indians everywhere – you would call them Asians – and the smell of curry was in the air. Staying in the fancy hotel was such an adventure.'

Chapter Thirty-Seven

Victoria was gazing at Alexander, her face rapt. 'Sandy,' she said, 'you look so young right now! It's as if you've cast off twenty years.' Then she leant across and kissed him on the mouth. It was much more than merely a kiss between friends; it was a passionate, lingering kiss, and as if a fire, banked so low that Alexander had barely been aware of it, had suddenly flared up, Alexander felt a powerful response. He took Victoria's face between his hands and returned her kiss at length. Victoria drew him down above her as she lay back on the sofa cushions.

After a while Alexander sat up and took Victoria's hand and the two stood, and he led her upstairs to his bedroom.

They were to make love together often during the next two years, although they only occasionally spent the entire night together. It quickly became apparent to fellow members of Alcoholics Anonymous that the two were now a couple.

Chapter Thirty-Eight

Intimacy

In September 2004 one of Alexander's friends from Alcoholics Anonymous, David, a wealthy businessman, advised him on buying a personal computer. Alexander went online for the first time. Early the following year, David said, 'Sandy, you have done quite a lot of business research, have n't you? You mentioned that you had worked for Reiters once.'

'That's true,' Alexander replied.

'I have a friend looking to invest in sub-Saharan Africa. I mentioned that I knew someone from South Africa who had some experience as a business researcher. He wondered whether you would be able to provide him with a report on investment opportunities in the region; fields likely to show the most growth in the coming years? And some background on the political and economic situations of the various countries in the region?'

'I think I could do that,' Alexander replied.

'He is willing to pay up to five hundred Pounds for a detailed report,' David continued. 'It's possible that he could bring more work your way if you were interested.'

Chapter Thirty-Eight

'You can tell him I'm willing in principle to tackle a job like this. Can he write or email me, David? You've got my email address.'

'Good. I'll ask him to do that.'

Alexander found that business research had become in some respects very much easier since the introduction of the Internet, but he quickly learned always to question the data he was offered online. It was not always accurate, and it was wise to refer to multiple sources before making an assertion as fact. Alexander familiarised himself with Microsoft Office, and with Word. He learned how to draw up graphs online, and to tabulate figures. His very first client was extremely pleased with the report he received from Alexander, and over time he directed a number of business acquaintances of his to him. By late 2005, Alexander had completed several commissions, always focusing on sub-Saharan Africa. Using a free template, he created a simple website of his own.

During the next few years, Alexander was to supplement his income by up to two thousand Pounds a year, providing business clients with commercial reports and investment analyses for sub-Saharan African regions. The work, at first, appealed to him. With each commission, his skills improved. His reports became very polished. He provided hard copies, printed and bound by a commercial printer in High Wycombe, to back up the Word files he sent his customers.

Alexander deposited most of his earnings in a savings account. He did not buy a new car with his money. He was happy with his Citroën, which he could afford to maintain in top mechanical condition.

Although Alexander's political thinking in late 2004 was somewhat naive and simplistic, it was to mature over the next ten years to such a degree that by 2014 he had discarded many of his earlier political beliefs – including, in fact, the fierce British patriotism that had been part of his life since his adolescent years.

But in 2004 Alexander was still an old fashioned British patriot and unionist, proud of his imperial roots, and (as a product himself of that empire) nostalgic for the lost Empire. After a while he began submitting articles which were published in several right wing online magazines and forums. These essays, while conventional enough in nationalistic terms, were maverick where economics were concerned: they promoted an extremely conservative social culture, yet espoused socialist, redistributive economics. Alexander argued consistently against what he soon took to calling "corporatism," and against high capitalism and the cult of consumerism, and he favoured a form of national socialism that had nothing at all to do with fascism.

Alexander loathed anti-Semitism; he would savagely criticise the anti-Semitic comments that sometimes appeared in these online outlets. He also pursued a growing interest in environmental and conservation issues, and he began to write about the dangers to the natural environment and to its fauna and flora posed by growing consumerism.

'If anyone had told me a few years ago that I would have a friend with political views like yours, I would have laughed in disbelief,' Victoria told Alexander. 'But I know you're a decent man, Sandy, and I know you're not a racist, and you're no cheerleader for capitalism, so I have to accept your political stance, even if I don't agree with it.'

Alexander thought that was fair enough.

Towards the end of October in 2004, Alexander began to fall prey to a growing physical exhaustion. He lost weight. He found himself falling asleep suddenly, without warning, and several times he came very close to setting his bed on fire at night when he was sitting up in bed with a cigarette in his fingers, reading a book. Frequently he fell asleep unawares in his armchair also, a lighted cigarette tumbling from his nerveless fingers onto the carpeted floor, burning a hole in the carpet. His doctor referred

Chapter Thirty-Eight

him to a consultant in London, who, after carrying out a variety of tests, diagnosed Alexander as suffering from enteric neuropathy, a chronic, progressive, and incurable debilitating disease. Alexander was, quite literally, slowly starving to death.

Alexander's ability to derive adequate nourishment from solids had been severely compromised by the damage done to his bowels as a consequence of the injuries he had sustained when he had been stabbed in Johannesburg in 1996. It was likely that a regime of powerful codeine based analgesics prescribed him for more than two years by his doctor to control his bowel pains, had worsened his condition.

The London specialist prescribed a clinically formulated liquid food supplement, and within a very short while after commencing this regime, Alexander's weight loss had ceased, and he had recovered something of his energy. He only rarely fell asleep now without warning, and he ceased burning holes in his bedding and in the carpet with his cigarettes. Alexander was to rely on this food supplement to keep him alive for the rest of his life, and as the years went by, he was able to tolerate less and less solid food.

In mid January 2005, carrying a large supply in powder form of his nutritional supplement, Alexander flew out to South Africa, landing at Jan Smuts Airport, where Roy met him in the early morning. The summer grasses were green, the air warm, the sun so bright and hot after the universal sombreness of an English winter that Alexander was glad of the sun glasses he was wearing.

'Oh gosh, it feels good to be home again!' he exclaimed, as Roy drove to his home in Sekunda, an hour and a half away, to collect his cat, load her into a traveling basket, and continue their journey through the maize fields of the Orange Free State. Once they had descended the escarpment at Harrismith, the northern Drakensberg range was visible on the western horizon, a pale grey-blue, jagged line against the deeper blue of the sky.

Continuing down the N2 they took the off-ramp for the sprawling Natal Midlands village of Hilton, where their mother now lived in a walled and gated retirement complex. She owned a three bedroom house in a row of other identikit houses, and the complex contained a community centre, with a dining room which served passable meals, a bar and a lounge with a big open fireplace, a frail care wing, and kitchens (which not only serviced the dining room, but from which residents could order meals to be delivered to their homes). Alexander was to make another four visits to his mother's home in Hilton, with his final visit being made in 2013, for in early 2014 Roy and their mother left South Africa for good, moving to England.

Alexander loved his mother's home, which was full of old familiar things dating back to his childhood, and he walked every day in the extensive grounds with their wide lawns and the big dam which attracted a wealth of water fowl. There were black and white pied kingfishers, grey herons, Egyptian geese, and coots, to be seen, with bright chrome yellow masked weaver birds in the willows that overhung the water, and black and crimson red bishop weavers busy in the dense reed beds at one end of the dam. Once, as Alexander stood by the banks of the dam, a *hammerkop* bird stood companionably nearby, quite unafraid of him, also gazing at the water.

After only a few days back in South Africa, Alexander felt a profound lightening of his spirit. He hired a car during part of his stay, so that he could drive his mother around the pretty, scenic Natal Midlands countryside, stopping for lunch at a number of well known restaurants in the region. Yellowwood restaurant at Howick, with its view of the splendid Howick Falls, and the old, beautifully restored house furnished with period antiques, was one of their favourite destinations.

Roy, who had returned to Sekunda after their first weekend together, drove down again towards the end of Alexander's stay,

Chapter Thirty-Eight

and the two brothers (plus Roy's cat) made the three and a half hour journey to Jan Smuts Airport on the Monday following, where Alexander boarded the evening departure for Heathrow, eleven and a half hours away.

In March 2005 Alexander and Victoria holidayed together in Malta. Alexander had turned fifty the month before. He did not yet look his age. He stood very straight, and he was still very slim, although he had a small paunch, a consequence of the enteric neuropathy he suffered from, but this he hid beneath his generously cut shirts, and his trousers with a high, thirty-three inch waistband, held up by suspenders. His hair, although thinning a little, was still golden (even if some of the shine was beginning to fade). His face was comparatively unlined. He knew that he and Victoria made an attractive couple. It was a tremendously happy holiday. The two of them found that they had no serious disagreements of any sort while away together.

'Sandy,' Victoria remarked one morning as they were sitting drinking coffee in the warm spring sunshine in Valletta, with Alexander outlining his plans for the rest of the day, 'you know on principle I do not defer to men, but when I'm with you, it's easier just to go along with your plans, because you always know exactly what you're doing.'

This was delivered with a wry smile, and Alexander laughed.

'I've always been very good at deciding how the people around me must live their lives!'

Alexander remembered having read somewhere that taking a holiday together was an excellent test of a friendship. Alexander felt that their friendship had passed that test with a high score. Victoria was as fascinated and delighted by Malta as Alexander was. It pleased Alexander that at the hotel the staff and the other guests they spoke with took them for a married couple. Alexander noted also that people were far friendlier towards a couple than they had generally been towards him when he was holidaying alone. He supposed they felt less threatened by a couple than by a single man.

'Do you ever think you might marry again?' Alexander asked Victoria, as they sat on the terrace at lunch one day at the Cockney Bar. Alexander was eating linguine with mussels. Victoria had been married briefly when she had been much younger. The marriage had ended in an amicable divorce.

Victoria thought a while. 'Sometimes,' she replied. 'It might be nice – to make that commitment again, with someone I loved.'

'What if I were to ask you to marry me some day? I think we suit one another amazingly well.'

Victoria smiled. 'Are you proposing to me, Sandy?'

Alexander grinned. 'I think I am.'

'If I ever married anyone again,' Victoria said, 'it would be you.'

'So that's a maybe?'

Victoria laughed. 'Yes. Maybe I'll marry you – one day!'

Alexander, who had surprised himself at the direction his unplanned words had taken, felt both happiness – and relief. It would be right to marry Vicky – but after all, not yet.

Alexander enjoyed introducing Victoria to Filippu. Alexander knew that Victoria was a lovely woman; bright, attractive and personable, and he was proud of her. Victoria took to Filippu, who was very charming towards her.

Despite the business research he had begun to undertake earlier that year, Alexander was looking for a further interest; something in the way of a hobby which might earn him some money also. Soon after his return from the holiday in Malta with Victoria, he went to an auction of general household goods in the district. Here he admired some of the English bone china services on auction. He had always been drawn to the delicacy, strength and beauty of fine bone china. He came away from his first auction with a Spode tea set, which he sold via eBay to a buyer in the States. His

Chapter Thirty-Eight

markup on this first occasion did no more than cover the packing and postage costs, from which Alexander learned that he must take care in future to detail delivery costs, both locally and abroad, alongside his advertised sales price.

By August that year Alexander had developed a reliable feel for what he thought the bone china pieces he was after that day would fetch in the wider market, and how much, therefore, he was prepared to bid for them. He began making regular markups, after packing and postage costs, of between twenty-five to fifty percent on the bone china tea sets, dinner services, tea pots and other pieces he was selling. Most of his customers lived abroad: he sold to buyers in the USA, Canada, Australia and South Africa. He had bought a cheap compact digital camera with which he photographed the china, arranged on a large piece of black velvet, uploading these photographs onto his eBay site. He packed the china himself at home, buying the packaging materials he needed online. Alexander's eBay vendor's site scored a consistently high customer satisfaction rating.

Alexander was still trading in bone china on eBay after three years had passed, but by mid 2008 he was beginning to find that this hobby-venture was becoming increasingly physically exhausting: transporting the china from the auction house to his home, and from his home, once packed, to the post office for despatch, was a mounting challenge. Alexander's stamina was declining. Alexander ceased trading, and by the end of that year the only evidence that he had ever been a successful trader in a small way in English bone china were a few pieces of Wedgwood he had kept back for himself, and which he displayed (together with his Royal Albert Lady Carlyle tea set) behind the glass front of his 1950s sideboard.

In July 2005 Roy flew from South Africa to stay with his brother for two weeks. Roy, who had fairly large reserves of energy, none the less sometimes battled to match Alexander's enthusiasm for getting out and about during his visit. Despite his lowered energy levels, Alexander was still possessed of a great hunger for living, and he could drive himself to a point just short of collapse. Together, the two brothers took the train into London twice, and Alexander enjoyed showing Roy some of his favourite sights. It was the Catholic cathedral in Westminster, with its magnificent towering campanile and its splendid glittering Lady Chapel and side chapels, which seemed to impress Roy most. Bach's Toccata and Fugue in D Minor was being played on the cathedral's huge organ when they visited, the sound filling the vast building, making the air vibrate, and Roy was astonished and impressed at the profundity of the organ's bass notes, which, as he commented, you felt through the soles of your shoes, rather than heard. They took a pleasure cruise down the River to Greenwich, passing beneath London Bridge and Tower Bridge, and having visited the great tea clipper, the "Cutty Sark," in her dry dock, they admired the displays in the National Maritime Museum. At the Royal Observatory they stood astride the prime meridian, a foot in either hemisphere. On their second visit to London they went aboard a full scale, sailing replica of Sir Francis Drake's "Golden Hind," where both tall brothers had to take constant care not to bang their heads on the low deck beams, and they visited the Tower, where the Royal Armouries, with their magnificent collection of armour and weapons, particularly fascinated Alexander.

'Some of these suits of armour seem made for a fourteen year old boy,' Roy commented. 'Our ancestors really were small men, were n't they?'

They visited Oxford also, half an hour's drive from Chinnor, and Alexander hired one of the clinker-built, lightly framed, wooden skiffs from the boathouse below Magdalen Bridge, and he and Roy rowed down the Cherwell as far as the Thames, and back again. The footpath alongside the river teemed with tourists and idlers dressed for summer; the waterfowl on the river quacked

Chapter Thirty-Eight

contentedly in the sunshine; the Cherwell itself was busy with young visitors from abroad, most trying, very ineptly, to punt. Alexander knew how to punt, but he did not wish to tackle punting anymore, not with a false leg. They walked in the Botanic Gardens alongside the Cherwell, where they spent some time exploring the hothouses. At Alexander's insistence, they also visited the world famous Ashmolean Museum, which, with its magnificent collections of English silver and Minoan and Egyptian artefacts and art, was admittedly of greater interest to Alexander than to Roy.

'I guess these are the sort of things an educated person ought to be interested in, Sandy,' Roy remarked.

'I think a cultured man needs to know of the existence of such things, yes – but we cannot all be passionately interested in this sort of stuff. The Minoan and Egyptian art fascinates me. I remember studying Egyptian and Minoan art at university, and it is wonderful to see many of the actual items I had only known of through photographs back then.'

Chapter Thirty-Nine

Tragedy

In September, Alexander and Victoria spent two nights in Paris. Victoria had not visited Paris since her final year at school. They travelled to Paris by Eurostar, the cross-Channel train. During their meal together on their first evening in Paris, a meal Alexander had negotiated in passable French, at a tiny restaurant they had chosen pretty much at random on *l'Île de la Cité*, Victoria said, 'You've brought adventure into my life, Sandy. Nothing scares you. I feel safe when I'm with you.'

Alexander was moved by her words. He reached across the table and took her hand. 'You have brought happiness into my life, Vicky,' he responded. 'I'm happier than I ever thought I would be again.'

They smiled at each other. In that moment, it was a loving tenderness, *agape*, rather than passion, which Alexander felt above all for Victoria.

The summer drew suddenly to a close, with the coming of grey skies and days of relentless rain from late September onwards. Alexander's outdoor excursions ceased. He spent long comfortable evenings with Victoria, either at her cottage in Monks

Chapter Thirty-Nine

Risborough, or at his own home, sitting in front of a wood fire. He spent Christmas day with Sarah, the friend whose visits to him in hospital had done so much to raise his spirits. But he spent Christmas Eve with Victoria at her home, and they had exchanged small but thoughtful gifts.

Alexander kissed Victoria on the mouth. 'Happy Christmas, my love.'

'Happy Christmas, darling Sandy,' Victoria answered.

If Alexander ever remembered his mad, unhappy passion for Una, it was with an inward shudder. He felt loved and valued now, as he had never felt with Una.

In March 2006, Alexander and Victoria once again holidayed together in Malta. As before, there was not a single moment of tension or disagreement between them. Alexander had hired a car, and crossing to Gozo by ferry, they had spent a magical day exploring the island, with lunch on the hotel terrace at the water's edge in Xlendi Bay.

Roy had booked his annual three weeks' vacation and was planning a trip to England again in July to stay with his brother. But this visit was not to take place. In June, Victoria and a girlfriend flew to Turkey for a ten day holiday on the Black Sea shore. During the afternoon of Sunday 25th June, Alexander received a telephone call from Victoria's younger brother, Edward, who lived with his parents in Holmer Green, near High Wycombe.

'Sandy – it's Edward. I'm afraid I have dreadful news.'

Alexander knew in an instant – it was the quality of raw pain in Edward's voice – what he was about to hear. He felt the blood drain from his face, and his breath caught in his throat.

'Vicky died in a car accident this morning.'

Edward continued speaking for a while, but Alexander did not hear him. After some minutes, he said, 'Edward, I'm so terribly sorry. I need – May I phone you later?' and he put the telephone down.

After the telephone call, Alexander went for a walk along the ridge, and far above him he could hear the red winged kites calling in the summer sky, their whistling cries high, thin, and lonely. The wild roses were in bloom in the hedgerows, and the verges of the path were rank with nettles and heavy with tall foxgloves and Queen Anne's lace and cow parsley. There were scores of butterflies, most of them brimstones, large whites and meadow browns. The heads of golden wheat in the big field he was passing would be harvested before long. The beech woods below and to one side of the wheat field were heavy and dark with leaf. Everywhere Alexander saw lush, verdant growth. He came to a gate giving access to the wheat field. He leant his arms on the top bar of the gate and looked across woodland in the distance as the gentle slope fell away into the far valley, and although he closed his eyes, the tears kept coming.

Chapter Forty

The Family Reunited

The next day, Alexander telephoned his brother in the Transvaal. Roy was due to spend two weeks with him in July. Alexander cancelled that visit. 'I need time alone to grieve, Roy.'

A week later Alexander telephoned the cat sanctuary in Beaconsfield and spoke to Joan, who had founded the sanctuary and who ran it with her husband.

'We have a cat, twelve or thirteen years old, whom no one wants to adopt, because she's deaf,' Joan told him. 'She's a darling though, a pure white cat called Bridie.'

'May I come by later today?'

'You're more than welcome, Sandy.'

Bridie proved to be an affectionate, playful cat with a pure white coat and green eyes. Alexander loved her from the start. Responding to her need for loving attention, and via the daily routine of caring for her, Alexander was able to prevent his grief for Victoria from overwhelming him. Bridie was with Alexander for the next four years, before, in late 2010, he had to have her put to sleep, for by then she had become very frail and emaciated, and was obviously suffering.

One morning in December 2006, as Alexander stood shaving in the bathroom, he became conscious for the first time that his hair now showed more grey than faded gold in the mirror above the basin. Alexander was already aware that if he were to grow a moustache, it would come out grey also. He decided anyway to grow a moustache.

'I feel old now,' he thought to himself. 'I have a right to my grey hair.'

Alexander did not go abroad for almost five years. He did not want to place Bridie in a cattery. During these years, his relationship with Sarah grew closer.

Sarah, attractive and vivacious, was a few years older than Alexander. Childless, she had been widowed in her thirties and left comfortably provided for, and she was not searching for a romantic attachment. Their easy-going friendship suited both of them. Sarah went abroad several times a year. Sometimes Alexander would drive her to Heathrow, and meet her again on her return. In the summer they often went out together for lunch at country pubs, and several times Alexander drove the two of them to Oxford, where, using his disabled badge, he was able to park his car just off the High Street, not far from Magdalen Bridge, and they would take a small picnic hamper with them and hire a rowing boat on the Cherwell for two hours. One summer they visited Waddesdon Manor, the splendid nineteenth century Rothschild mansion near Aylesbury, built in the style of a grand French chateau. This fabulous country house, with its opulent interiors and magnificent landscaped grounds, was already known to Alexander from a visit he had made with his mother in May 1976. He had been living in London then, and when his mother had visited England to see family, Alexander had hired a car for the day to drive her to the Rothschild house in the lovely Buckinghamshire countryside.

Alexander made two visits to Walters, the old fashioned gentlemen's outfitters in The Turl, in Oxford, to buy four more pairs

Chapter Forty

of trousers, tailored for button-on suspenders. He ordered two pairs of sturdy corduroy trousers and two pairs of summer chinos, all four trousers to be altered to his exact measurements. These trousers were cut in a pattern very close to that which had prevailed in England during the War; they had high waists which incorporated a particularly high "fish-tail" cut at the back, and pleats, and the trouser legs had broad turn ups. They had buttoned flies, which Alexander had not had to contend with since he was a boy at primary school. Walters also sold Alexander three more cravats. Alexander was to gain many years of wear out of these trousers.

For several years, hardly a day went by that Alexander did not remember Victoria. How different his life might have been had she lived! Alexander feared that Victoria had been his last chance at a truly close and intimate friendship. Following Victoria's death, Alexander's social life almost ceased to exist. He had less and less to do with people. For the most part, he lived a self contained life. There were times when he felt lonely, but those times were few. With fragile, quickly exhausted energy, he could no longer engage in protracted physical activity. With uncertain bowels and bladder, he had to bear in mind speedy and timely access, often with only minimal warning, to a lavatory whenever he went out. Alexander no longer attended Alcoholics Anonymous meetings. Friends he knew from Alcoholics Anonymous ceased over time to telephone him, for he was not very forthcoming when they did, and he always declined invitations to social gatherings.

Alexander gave up smoking and turned to "vaping." He switched from what he thought of as "hot" tobacco cigarettes to electronic or e-cigarettes without any difficulty. Within a week or two his wind was returning, along with his sense of smell and his sense of taste. Alexander never smoked another cigarette again. He put away his Zippo lighters – old friends they were! – for he would have no more need of their service.

During this period, a time when he was becoming otherwise increasingly solitary in his habits, Sarah remained Alexander's only true friend. Although a close friendship (they saw a lot of each other), it was a friendship of no great emotional depth. Alexander did not understand that he was now afraid of emotional investment in any human relationship.

Alexander read extensively, almost entirely works of non-fiction, and his own library of non-fiction grew year by year. He leant his life a sense of purpose through his writing. He continued writing for online publications. Once in a while he had an essay accepted by a print journal. These articles were increasingly politically left wing, although Alexander retained a broadly conservative social and cultural outlook.

For almost two years following Victoria's death, Alexander ceased attending church services. It was only during the Easter of 2008 that he rediscovered his faith, and he began to attend communion services once again at Saint Andrew's in the village.

Roy visited for ten days in October 2006, and again each year for several years thereafter, usually in July or August. It was only once Bridie had died that Alexander was able to travel again. He made three more visits to South Africa, one each in 2011, 2012 and 2013, where Roy would meet him at the airport, and they would drive down together to Hilton, to their mother's home. Alexander cherished these visits. He found that he was now much closer to his mother than he had been during his thirties and forties. But he never imagined living in South Africa again. He did not like the direction the South African social culture had taken since 1994, and the manner in which the most corrupt and toxic version possible of corporatist high capitalism now flourished in that country, appalled and disgusted him. It was the South Africa of his young manhood that Alexander missed so much, not the South Africa of this present day.

By 2011 then, although far from a total recluse, Alexander seemed marked by an abiding loneliness of spirit. The only deep

Chapter Forty

love he felt for another human being, he reserved now for his mother. Nor did he acquire another cat following Bridie's death in November 2010. He wished to be able to go abroad two or three times a year, and he knew that once he had another cat, he would be unable to bring himself to do so.

Yet the years passed, and in March 2014 Roy's cat died of a kidney disease. Roy lost heart, as he had after Smokie's death. Despite his previous experience of living in England, Roy and their mother quit South Africa for good, traveling to England together. Alexander met them at Heathrow Airport in the morning. His mother was in a wheelchair.

'Hullo Mum,' he said, bending to kiss her.

'Where am I now?' she asked him. Alexander was nonplussed. What did his mother mean? Roy, looking thoroughly stressed, rolled his eyes.

'We're going home to our house in Chinnor, Mum – where I live,' Alexander responded.

As Roy was helping Alexander load the car's boot, he said in a low voice, 'I don't know what's happened to her. She's lost her mind.'

'Perhaps she'll improve once she's settled,' Alexander said.

Their mother did not, however, improve once Alexander had shown her to her room downstairs, and then made her a coffee. She was both confused and agitated, and for the rest of the day she was forever unpacking and repacking the contents of her airline bag. During the next few days it became very clear to Alexander that their mother was suffering from what he thought must be a form of dementia. She appeared to be incapable of comprehending that she was now in Alexander's home, in England. 'When are we going home?' she kept on asking Roy.

'How long has Mum been like this?' Alexander asked Roy. 'Why didn't I pick it up from my phone calls?'

'I think it was the move that did this,' Roy replied. 'That, and the flights.'

'But Mum must have been working up to this for a long time,' Alexander responded. 'Did n't you notice?'

'She was n't anything like as bad as this back home – after all, you did n't pick up anything from your phone calls to her – and anyway, I put it down to the stress of packing up and getting rid of the furniture and stuff.'

'Perhaps Mum will settle down.'

In some respects their mother did improve during the next few weeks. Alexander however found it exhausting looking after her. There were times when she no longer appeared to know what her colostomy bag was, and both brothers were called on at different times to undertake changing it for their mother. This was a vile task, something at once very intimate and also extremely repellent: demeaning and humiliating for all parties. But far worse in some respects was their mother's failing memory, both short term and long term. Alexander found that when narratives could no longer be sustained, conversation at any meaningful level became very difficult to achieve. And worse than both the horror of dealing with the stoma, and the increasing infantilisation of their conversations with their mother, was the sometimes very pronounced sense for Alexander that the mother he remembered loving so much, was now absent.

'Mum can't stay here indefinitely,' Alexander told Roy. 'She needs constant attention. I'll become ill trying to look after her like this. And she's going to get worse, you do realise?'

Alexander, with two guests staying with him, one of whom had lost much of her mind, was indeed worn to exhaustion after a couple of weeks. Worse than the physical strain was the mental strain. He began looking at care homes in the district, and of the three or four he visited in person (Roy could not accompany him, as it would clearly be unsafe to leave their mother alone),

Chapter Forty

it was a home in Princes Risborough which impressed him the most. The location, opposite the old parish church (which was built of flints strengthened with bands of pink brick, in whose churchyard grew large, well established trees), charmed Alexander. The home's residents appeared to be middle class, well spoken; he could imagine their mother being able to relate to them. The staff seemed to him to be both friendly and professional. And there were two *en suite* rooms coming vacant within days. One of these was at the back of the house, overlooking the walled garden, in which grew an apple tree which would soon be covered in blossom. Roy was very reluctant to move their mother into the care home, but Alexander prevailed upon him by sheer force of will. On Friday 21st March, the two brothers moved their mother into the home.

'How could we have done this to her?' Roy asked, as they drove back to the bungalow in Chinnor in the early evening, having stayed with their mother all afternoon, during which time they walked with her in the churchyard, and sat on a bench in the garden. 'I must get a car soon, so I can visit Mum often,' Roy said.

'We'll both visit her often, and if you want to make independent visits too, you can borrow my car for now, Roy. We were very lucky, finding a good care home so close by. We're doing the right thing. If Mum was living with us, you'd never find the time to look for a job, and I think I would become ill.'

But Alexander was grieving for the mother he had loved so much: the creative, capable, intelligent, loving mother he had known. He knew he was never going to get her back. This, from what he had been reading online of dementia, was the beginning of a long road leading only through ever darker, ever more unhappy terrain.

Chapter Forty-One

Changes

During the next few years, Roy struggled to believe just how bad their mother's mental condition was becoming. At times he grew very frustrated with her. Alexander however had foreseen this ongoing decline. Illness, pain and loss had taught Alexander that you faced up to uncomfortable truths and dealt with them. Alexander convinced his brother of the need to obtain power of attorney for their mother's health and wellbeing, and for her financial affairs also. The two brothers took their mother to a solicitors' office in High Wycombe. A new will was drawn up. In due course, power of attorney was granted to the brothers.

Within a short while Roy was able to escape the ravaging of their mother's mind, for soon after buying a car of his own, he began working for an engineering company in Portsmouth, coming home only on the weekends. Alexander however felt obliged to visit his mother at least three times a week, and he found that she still enjoyed being taken for drives. His mother took pleasure in the rolling, wooded hills, the fertile combs and picturesque old farm houses of the Chiltern Hills, with sudden distant vistas of scenes so pretty they might have been found on the cover of a glossy guide for tourists to England. Alexander's mother had by now accepted that she was living in England, for her memories of South Africa were fading fast.

When in late October Roy's six month contract ended, and he returned to Alexander's home in Chinnor, Alexander soon found that he yearned to have his home to himself. He longed for the opportunities to rest his mind and soothe his spirit that only solitude could bring him. He missed very much no longer being able to sit and read, undisturbed. He regretted that he could no longer take a nap in his armchair whenever he pleased. Living alone for such a long time, he had become set in his bachelor's ways. He began searching for a flat for Roy. Alexander found a flat advertised in the property section of the local weekly newspaper, and after he and Roy had looked at it together, Alexander persuaded Roy to sign the lease.

'You need a place of your own. It's unnatural to live together permanently at our age,' he told Roy. 'And I need time to be alone.'

Alexander hardened his heart to Roy's obvious unhappiness.

The flat was in a short *cul-de-sac* leading off the West Wycombe road, shortly before the road reached the village of West Wycombe. The countryside was on Roy's doorstep; he could hear sheep bleating from his flat and he could go running up a narrow farm road round the corner from the block of flats, and so into the countryside and the hills above the town.

With Roy at a loose end until he managed to find another engineering contract, Alexander could reduce the frequency of his visits to their mother. Roy was only too happy to take up the slack. Indeed, he visited their mother almost every day. Alexander did not understand how his brother could bear to spend so much time with this less than accurately rendered facsimile of the mother he had once loved so much. But even so, Alexander brought their mother home every Sunday after he had been to the ten o'clock communion service in the village, and he prepared a meal for the three of them. Alexander enjoyed cooking for other people. He became more adventurous after a while, although his culinary tastes remained fundamentally conservative. Chicken à la King, which Alexander prepared with real ginger beer and whole cream, remained a family favourite, as did Alexander's twenty-four hour chicken curry (which he began preparing twenty-four hours ahead of the eating).

During the week Alexander sometimes drove to High Wycombe, which was only a few miles away, and sat drinking coffee at the Costa coffee shop on Church Square, looking onto the rear of the eighteenth century octagonal Cornmarket building, rebuilt in 1761 to a design by Robert Adam. He had often met Victoria at the coffee shop, and he had come to know two or three of the regulars after her death. With the arrival of his family, Alexander had become less reclusive. His friends from Saint Andrew's in Chinnor invited him into their homes for a meal sometimes. Alexander reciprocated on two or three occasions. At heart, however, Alexander remained a solitary creature. His life had, it seemed, come full circle; he had rediscovered his enjoyment of solitude.

In the south of England the summers were growing much warmer; the sultry summer heat waves that Alexander loathed so much and which made him feel ill, were becoming more commonplace. The winters were growing shorter; the snowfalls scarcer and less deep. The country lanes carried so much more traffic than Alexander remembered from his earlier years in the district. Driving through the hills and woods and combs was no longer as pleasant as it had once been. There were more people out walking now, when Alexander took one of his favourite ridgeway walks in the countryside. The south of England, Alexander felt, was buckling under excessive and growing human population numbers.

In the summer of 2016, during Alexander's sixty-second year, he experienced several rather frightening episodes of extreme chest pain and breathlessness. The first time this happened to him he thought he should probably telephone for an ambulance, but he dreaded the idea of a hospital stay, and he made the decision to sit it out.

During these episodes (which almost always occurred at night) Alexander would lean back against his pillows, close his eyes, say a prayer, and concentrate on mastering his breathing, and after what seemed a long while, the pain would diminish, and his breathing would return to normal. But afterwards, Alexander would feel ill and very frail for many hours. When Alexander mentioned these episodes to his doctor, he was referred to the cardiology unit at Stokenchurch Hospital near Aylesbury for tests, and these tests, which were conducted over a period of two months, were exhaustive. Alexander was diagnosed with angina. He was prescribed a glyceryl trinitrate spray, to spray beneath his tongue when the pains began, and it proved to be effective. However, following a particularly savage and unexpected attack one night in September 2017, and further tests (this time at Raigmore Hospital in Inverness, for Alexander, as we shall see, was by then living in the Scottish Highlands), he had begun taking statins and beta blockers every day. These medications were extremely effective, although Alexander found that he had to be careful not to over exert himself physically, nor become badly stressed, for if he did so, he would feel his upper left chest begin to ache, and he would become short of breath.

Alexander accepted this latest affliction as he had accepted the ones that had gone before: calmly, without rancour. Over the years he had arrived at a stoic's acceptance of pain and debilitation, for it seemed to him that his sufferings were deserved. The burden of guilt and remorse that he bore required that he suffer his afflictions in silence, without complaint. Alexander hoped that this illness might spare him from growing too old; that he might thus evade the slow, pain-filled anguish of gradually starving to death that otherwise awaited him because of the progressive nature of the enteric neuropathy he suffered from.

On a more profound level of consciousness, Alexander believed that his suffering was cleansing his corrupt spirit. He hoped that when he died, his spirit might find its way straight to some blessed realm. Alexander did not truly believe in a Heaven anymore. If it existed at all, it was not, he thought, a cosy, cuddly place where you lived happily ever after with all your loved ones, but a spiritual state, in which it was more than probable that your consciousness of your unique earthly identity would have faded away altogether. Heaven, Alexander believed, was a condition of union with the eternal Creator. Alexander's idea of Heaven had become as rarified and stripped down as his hopes in the here and now.

Alexander drew up a will, which was translated into legal form by a firm of solicitors. He always had a large sum of cash in his current account, and a substantial savings account, and he owned several good oil paintings that had been in the family for some generations. He had more than a dozen Kruger Rands secreted away. He owned a valuable collection of half a dozen antique swords, along with a couple of black powder percussion cap antique firearms in working order, which were each about one hundred and sixty years old. If his mother predeceased him, then Alexander would inherit a half share of her estate. Aside from a bequest to the charity Cats Protection, he made his brother, Roy, his only beneficiary. Roy was also named as his primary executor, with his friend, Sarah, as an additional executor.

By late 2016 Roy had not yet found another engineering contract. Alexander believed that if Roy continued to devote so much of his time to their mother – he made almost daily, lengthy visits to see her – he would never find another job.

Chapter Forty-Two

The West Highlands

In late 2016 Alexander told Roy, 'I want to move to Scotland's West Highlands. You know how much I've grown to dislike the overcrowded south-east of England.'

'But how will you manage a move like that?'

'By making it happen! If you want something in life, you have to make it happen.'

'What about me?'

'I think you should stay down here. There's the bungalow – it would be yours to move into if you found an engineering job locally. You wont find the work you're after in the West Highlands. And I think Mum should join me up there, after I'm settled. I'll find a care home near where I land up. It would leave you free to conduct a thorough job search – and to take up employment when you did find it. If your job meant moving elsewhere in England, as it might well do, you would be free to do so, if Mum was living near me.'

Roy was looking stricken. Alexander continued, 'You wont find another job at this rate, not with so much of your time spent visiting Mum. You must know that.'

Alexander had learned to be hard on himself, and he saw no reason to be soft on his brother. But perhaps, had he realised how distressed Roy was at his plans, he would have relented; perhaps, at the very least, he would have sought to include Roy in his plans to move to the West Highlands.

The two brothers talked the idea through for the next two months. It was only in December that year that Roy finally agreed it made sense to leave him behind in southern England. 'Molly should go with you, I think,' he said.

'Yes, she needs a garden; after all, she was a bold street cat when you found her. She misses the outdoors.'

Molly was a young female tabby cat whom Roy in particular had got to know on his visits to the care home in Princes Risborough. She was almost always to be found near the care home, and the cat had made it clear that she was looking for a home. Roy had a very tender heart indeed. As a little boy he had frequently come home with a strange cat in his arms, and their mother had had to find out where he had found it, and take the cat back there. It had become clear over time to both Roy and Alexander, during their visits to their mother, that this friendly, pretty tabby was homeless, living on the streets, and in March 2016 Roy had adopted her and taken her back to his flat to live with him. But both brothers knew that she missed the outdoor life, and that she needed a home with a garden. To be sure, the bungalow at Chinnor had a garden, but would Roy's work permit him to live there?

Roy looked thoughtful. 'I would be able to come stay with you and see Molly as often as I wished, would n't I?'

'Of course. You would be welcome.'

'What's five hundred miles, after all?'

In January 2017 Alexander began searching online for a house to rent in Lochaber in the West Highlands. He longed to escape the overcrowded and polyglot south-east of England. Scotland's West Highland coast beckoned him in his memory. There was

Chapter Forty-Two

something akin to wilderness there in the dramatic mountainous landscapes; there were great stretches of dark forest; there were lonely, uninhabited glens; and Alexander remembered the long sea lochs, like Norwegian fjords, thrusting many miles inland between the high hills and mountains.

Alexander saw an advertisement in the *Gumtree* online site, "To rent – long stay tenant preferred," for a house situated in a high, sparsely inhabited glen above Fort William. In March 2017 Roy drove Alexander to Luton Airport, where he caught a flight for Glasgow. Alexander had a hire car waiting for him at Glasgow Airport, with which he followed the M8 motorway across Glasgow, and after crossing the high Erskine Bridge which spanned the Clyde (and as he did so, he thought of the mighty ship building industry that had once flourished on the Clyde, all gone now), he drove north up the A82, very soon finding himself north of the Highland Line (a boundary both geographical and conceptual), following the western shore of Loch Lomond, that island studded and immensely picturesque inland loch more than twenty-four miles long. He stopped for a coffee and a visit to the lavatory at the village of Crianlarich, before continuing across the bleak, austere uplands of Rannoch Moor, where, for many miles, there was not a trace of human habitation, not a tree to be seen.

This upland was a watery landscape of lochans, bogs and marshes, broken by rocky outcrops, with low groundcover growing: bog myrtle and rushes, grasses and mosses. It was a land of no practical use to Man at all. The far mountains which bounded the moor were capped in snow. Alexander had left the rain behind somewhere north of Glasgow, and the sky was now a perfect, cloudless, deep blue. As he began his descent into Glencoe on the far side of the moor, the exterior temperature reading on the car's dashboard rose to an unusually high 11 Centigrade. Alexander was to ascend Glencoe pass by car many times during the coming years, never tiring of the dramatic, sublime beauty of the landscape, but that first time he gazed down Glencoe as he descended from Rannoch Moor, he thought he had never seen any landscape quite so awe inspiring, nor so beautiful. On the far horizon range after range of snow capped mountains disappeared into infinity. Steep sided crags tumbled to the road's edge. At the Glencoe Visitors' Centre at the foot of the pass Alexander parked the car and used the lavatory, then drank a coffee in the cafeteria. It was a Friday afternoon, the 10th March.

Alexander checked in at the Alexandra Hotel in Fort William, a commercially important but aesthetically neglected town squeezed between the lower slopes of Ben Nevis and the shores of Loch Linnhe. He had an appointment to view the house and to meet the owner at eleven the next morning. On Saturday morning he ascended the hill behind Fort William. Driving slowly up Lundavra Road, and crossing a sheep grid, he left the town behind, following the single track Old Military Road (part of the road system built by General Wade in the eighteenth century to keep the Highlands down) through very beautiful, sparsely inhabited upland countryside. Away to the east, over his left shoulder, Alexander could see Ben Nevis' vast bulk rising high above the rest of the skyline. Britain's highest mountain was crowned with snow which showed a brilliant white against the blue sky. There were sheep everywhere, some wandering along the verges of the track. The road wound and dipped and climbed for several miles, passing the occasional isolated house or steading. After some time Alexander crossed another sheep grid, and he realised he had driven too far. With some care he managed to turn the car around on the narrow road, and after a couple of miles of retracing his route he saw the house he had at first passed without noticing it, for a belt of pines had hidden it from his view coming the other way. The house sat in just over an acre of land, bounded by a sheep fence strung on wooden posts, except on the property's northern boundary, where a small burn flowed over rounded and worn rocks and pebbles. The house was surrounded by open, treeless country in which sheep grazed and in which heather and broom grew, the latter now in bright acid yellow bloom. Its nearest neighbor was about half a mile distant. Alexander turned into the driveway.

The small west facing double story house, built of grey cut stone with a steeply pitched slate roof, was located well back from the road, situated on a gently rising slope. It had a pair of windows projecting under small stone gables from the roof, and there was a separate brick built garage, along with some much older outbuildings built of stone. The driveway was of packed gravel and stones. There was a rough, bumpy lawn in front of the house, with a large, wintry oak tree standing in the middle of the lawn, with cheerful yellow daffodils and some clusters of late, tiny white snowdrops in bloom beneath it. Alexander was to learn that daffodils are one of the few flowers that deer will never eat. There was a Land Rover Defender parked in front of the garage.

'Molly would love it here,' Alexander thought.

Alexander met the middle aged couple who owned the house. Upstairs, the house had two fairly big bedrooms, and a lavatory, with a big lounge-dining room downstairs, a bathroom with another lavatory, a kitchen of average size, and a back door opening off a pantry with a lean-to roof, in which was a washing machine and a tumble dryer. There was a solid fuel iron stove in the lounge hearth place, whose flue disappeared up the chimney. Alexander, always decisive, signed the lease before he left. It was agreed that Alexander would begin paying the rent in a month's time, on the 11th April. It would be springtime in the Highlands by then. It was the very best time of year to make a new start.

Alexander spent a second night at the hotel in Fort William, and on Sunday, after a breakfast of kippers and toast, he drove back to Glasgow Airport, returned the hire car, and caught a flight for Luton. Roy was waiting for him at the airport. Alexander spent a month packing up slowly. He arranged for the hire of a small removals van owned by a young man who, with his mate, would drive it, and searching online, he found a pet-friendly hotel in Carlisle, where the two brothers would break their journey on their way up to the West Highlands by road. With Roy following behind with Molly, they set off from Chinnor on Monday morning 10th April. They spent the night at Carlisle, just south of the border with Scotland, at what proved to be a very pleasant, family run hotel, where Molly (reassured by the presence of her two humans with her in the bedroom all night) was quite content. The two brothers reached the outskirts of Fort William, the dark, cold waters of the loch on their left, shortly after three the next afternoon. The sky was low and leaden and there were flurries of wind-borne rain from the west. It was much colder than it had been during Alexander's visit in mid March.

The two brothers turned into the driveway of the little double story house in its high lonely glen. The removals van was only half an hour behind them, with the BT telephone technician whom Alexander had arranged beforehand, arriving only five minutes after that, to reconnect the telephone line. Before they went to sleep that night, Alexander, in the grip of an astonishing, sustained bout of energy, had found their bedding, and unpacked the coffee, milk and sugar, along with Molly's supper and the makings of their own microwave suppers. He had also set up his PC and was back online.

Roy stayed a week. 'I've never known anywhere so quiet,' he said.

'It's exactly what I need,' Alexander replied. 'It's taken me a lifetime to find.'

Alexander spent every day during Roy's stay unpacking, and setting the house in order, and Roy supervised acclimatizing Molly to her new home, a home the cat took to within three days, and which she gave every sign of finding much to her taste. Alexander was amazed and gratified at the energy he was able to draw on:

Chapter Forty-Two

what was its source? Would it last? He was careful however not to push himself; he did not wish to trigger an episode of chest pains and breathlessness. Much to Roy's disgust it rained most of the time, although when the rain slackened, Molly would go outside. Whenever the rain cleared momentarily, snow-capped hilltops were visible. Alexander kept the wood stove burning in the lounge's fireplace. Most of the time Molly lay stretched out in front of the stove on the hearth rug, and in the evenings, both brothers gazed into the flames, chatting quietly. Alexander thanked God at night, before he went to bed, for His blessings: for the strength and energy he was enjoying, and for Roy's help and company; and he prayed for their mother, whom he would be seeing within a few months, if all went as planned, for there was a care home about an hour's drive from the house in Ballachulish, on the far side of the narrows of Loch Leven (which, like Loch Linnhe, was a long sea loch reaching far into the mountains).

In July Roy hitched a trailer to his car, and piled the few bulky personal possessions their mother had with her in the care home at Princes Risborough, onto the trailer, and drove up to Fort William with her. She stayed with Alexander and Roy in the little house for two nights (two days and nights which Alexander found stressful and distressing, for their mother was on vacation from what remained of her mind), then the two brothers drove her and her modest possessions to the care home at Ballachulish, and settled her there. Alexander was to visit her two or three times a week. There were moments when he could still recognise in her the mother he had loved so much all his life. Her simple pleasure in drives in the dramatic countryside was to persist into 2018. Alexander took his camera with him during these outings, and he took some of his best photographs of the region while his mother sat contentedly in the car.

But when Roy returned alone to Chinnor, he felt bereft three times over: he had lost his mother, his cat, and his brother. Roy was not as well equipped as his brother was to live a completely solitary life; he had not suffered the same harsh lessons, nor had he had to learn the same inner fortitude. A time would come when Alexander would realise this, and suffer pangs of conscience.

By the end of May Alexander had met his nearest neighbours, who lived on a croft half a mile further along the Old Military Road. He heard a car coming up his driveway one mid morning, and looking out the window he saw a rather battered Land Rover Discovery come to a halt. The middle aged couple who got out of the car introduced themselves to him as his nearest neighbours, the Mackenzies.

'Come in,' Alexander invited them. 'Would you like some coffee?'

Alexander found a packet of chocolate biscuits in his larder and made coffee in his cafetière. 'It's very kind of you to call on me,' he said as he served them their coffee.

'Ye'll find we're a community up the glen,' said Colin Mackenzie, who looked to be in his late fifties and had short grey hair, heavy black eyebrows, and craggy, high coloured features. 'Which is not to say we stick our noses in others' affairs.'

'But we wanted you to feel you could call on us for anything you needed,' Colin's wife, Kirstie, continued. Her age was harder to tell. Her black hair was untouched by grey, and her complexion was pale, seemingly unaffected by the elements, with that quality of denseness and glowing depth and purity Alexander had first admired in a girlfriend of his in Oban, way back in 1976. Alexander supposed that the black hair and very pale, clear complexions he admired in the West Highlands were a remnant of the pure Celto-Gaelic line predating the later Nordic invasions that had colonised the islands and the west coast of the Highlands. As the couple drank their coffees, Molly, who enjoyed company, came and rubbed herself against Kirstie's ankles.

'Hullo puss,' she said. 'You're a bra' wee cat, are n't ye?' Kirstie

Chapter Forty-Two

bent and petted Molly, and Alexander smiled, inclined to like anyone who liked Molly.

The Mackenzies told Alexander a little about some of the families living in the high glen, and there were not many of them; perhaps two dozen, including the owners of the sizable farm at the end of the vehicular road. Alexander was grateful to Colin and Kirstie. He had no great wish to socialise anymore, but he felt less isolated after their visit.

Despite the frequent wet weather, the springtime and summer of 2017 was an extended honeymoon period of magical discovery and exploration. It was a time of near happiness for Alexander. He was very conscious of his good fortune in being able to live in this magnificent West Highlands region of Scotland. He had yet to face his first winter . . .

Chapter Forty-Three

Solitude

As the winter of 2017-2018 set in, Alexander's health began to decline again. By the beginning of Advent, in a winter already well advanced, he had ceased attending Sunday morning communion services in Fort William. He abandoned the struggle to try to ready himself early enough to get to church on time for the service – in a daytime hardly begun, and often in the face of appalling weather and bitter cold. The narrow single track Old Military Road, his only access to the town, would become impassable for his saloon car after a heavy snowfall, until the gritting lorry, with its bulldozer blade mounted in front, had cleared the drifts from the road later in the day. Alexander maintained a huge woodpile of sawn logs in one of the outbuildings, for the stove in the lounge. He kept up stocks of light bulbs, of candles, of torch batteries, and he had a small gas camping stove with spare gas cylinders, to boil water in the event of power cuts. He kept his larder well stocked with tea, coffee, sugar, milk for Molly, marmalade, margarine, packets of crisps and tins of fruit salad, with three or four loaves of bread always to be found in the freezer. He always ensured that he had a reserve stock of his nutritional food supplement drinks in store,

Chapter Forty-Three

along with several bags of Molly's dry and wet cat foods and a couple of spare bags of Molly's cat litter. He made sure that he never ran out of medicines. He kept a first aid kit in the house. He tried to ensure that in the event of being snowed in, or of feeling unwell, he and Molly could cope comfortably for quite a while alone in the house.

Molly loved the house, with its upstairs-downstairs, and its large garden barely distinguishable from the surrounding heather, broom and bracken of the rough sheep pasture. She spent a great deal of time outside during the long summer days (although Alexander always brought her inside for the night). Her thick fur coat was impervious to light drizzle. She enjoyed climbing the big oak tree in front of the house. With the onset however of very cold weather in November 2017, Molly began staying indoors for longer and longer. Alexander had provided her with a litter tray in the pantry where the washing machine was kept.

Molly spent the winter evenings on his lap, or stretched out in front of the wood burner. Alexander was concerned that Molly be taken care of should he become long term hospitalized, or – at the worst – die suddenly. With his heart condition, these were always possibilities. Quite a number of the boys he had been to school with, men his own age, had since died. So Alexander made arrangements with a national charity for cats for Molly to be cared for by them, should his brother Roy, for whatever reason, be unable to care for Molly himself. The two brothers agreed that if Roy did not hear from Alexander for more than twenty-four hours, either by text, telephone call or email, and if he could then elicit no response from Alexander when he tried to contact him, Roy was to telephone the MacKays, an elderly couple Alexander knew from church, who lived a few miles away; they would then come to check on him and Molly. The MacKays were aware of the spare key to the back door that Alexander kept hidden in one of the outhouses.

Alexander watched some TV, but for the most part he relaxed by reading and writing, or by listening to music CDs. Alexander's musical tastes were catholic: they ranged from female vocalists such as Savina Yannatou (whose songs in Greek were hauntingly beautiful), through a selection of traditional Scots Gaelic and Scottish Highlands and Islands recordings, and across the entire body of classical music, including of course, grand opera. Alexander's musical interests included some more arcane *genres*, such as that represented by the two recordings he had of instrumental duets performed by a pair of musicians from Mali, Ali Farka Touré (who played guitar) and Toumani Diabaté (who played the *kora*).

Sometimes Alexander simply sat in silence and allowed his thoughts to wander. He found himself remembering incidents, places and people dating from his childhood, or from his early manhood. He was sometimes moved to spontaneous penitential prayer, generally on his knees, but these prayers were shot through not just with sorrow for his failings, but with joy and gratitude for his deliverance. At such moments he experienced an intense awareness of God's presence: he was transported near to bliss. Then he gave thanks that, against the odds, he had lived long enough to have attained a penitent's heart, and to have known forgiveness. He was grateful, after all the anxiety he had caused his parents during his years of drinking, that he now had the opportunity to help care for his mother. The flame of Alexander's Christian faith, although sometimes it might still grow dim and flicker for brief periods (particularly when he had to suffer prolonged pain and ill health), burned without cease. Alexander rationalized his physical sufferings as a penance he must welcome paying. Through his sufferings, he reasoned, he was being made spiritually whole again. God had indeed won Alexander at last: wholly, utterly, without the least conditionality on Alexander's part.

Sitting outside in the summer, Alexander could hear only the sound of birdsong in the ancient oak tree and in the belt of Scots

Chapter Forty-Three

pines that fronted the property alongside the road, or the bleating of sheep, or the wind blowing. At night the peace was profound, although from October through to March the Atlantic gales would sometimes roar across the hills from the west with such an intensity that the air was filled with howling and shrieking. Alexander, who was not in general very fond of his own species anymore, felt deeply grateful that he had no neighbor living nearer than half a mile away.

Alexander had become a solitary, and sometimes lonely, man. He was sure now that he was never to meet anyone again who threatened his solitude – but he was wrong. He would meet someone in the spring of 2019 who breached the walls he had built around himself. The God in whom Alexander believed again, did not wish him after all to suffer loneliness for the rest of his life.

In 2004 the specialist in London had told Alexander that his condition was chronic, progressive, and incurable. He found during that winter of 2017-2018 that he had far less stamina than previously; he could not imagine holidaying abroad anymore. He often felt exhausted and frail. He was frequently in some degree of bowel pain, sometimes fairly severe pain sustained over several hours. His doctor had earlier prescribed opiates; tramadol hydrochloride 50mg capsules. Within a short while Alexander was regularly taking the maximum dose he was permitted; six tablets over a period of twenty-four hours. His appetite began to diminish at the same time as his physical capacity for food continued to decline. During the winter of 2017-2018 Alexander gave up eating meat, fish and fowl, as he was finding these foods increasingly difficult to digest. He was glad to have to do so: he had been experiencing growing moral qualms with eating meat for many years. By the time the first snowdrops of late winter appeared in early 2018, the nutritional liquid supplements prescribed him were his main source of nourishment.

'I'm glad I no longer eat meat,' he told Roy, during one of the visits his brother made every three to four months. 'I've wished to become a vegetarian for a long time, and now I'm able to do so.'

There were rare mornings during the spring or summertime, particularly when the sun was shining, when Alexander felt stronger and more energetic than usual, and he would take a proper walk along the Old Military Road, or he would set out along the West Highland Way, parking his car and beginning his walk at the point where, for a short distance, the trail met with the Old Military Road, and he would follow the trail south through the forest. Once or twice he walked far enough to see a glimpse of Loch Leven in the distance, and he could just make out the mountains through which the A82 to Glasgow ascended Glencoe Pass. There were however many days when fatigue or bowel pains kept Alexander at home in his armchair. Alexander found that the seasons of the year had a far more profound effect on his health and wellbeing than he had experienced in the south.

Alexander experienced the winter as a physical and mental assault. There were periods when gale force winds howled, sometimes rising to a banshee wail, for two or three days, with driving rain and sleet borne in from the Atlantic. A good snowfall was a blessing, because after the snowfall the sky was often clear, the air still, and the weak winter sun would invariably shine for two, or even three, days. Then Alexander would take his camera, and (as long as the Old Military Road had been cleared of snow drifts) he would go for long drives, capturing the fairytale beauty of the snowy landscape. He posted the best of his photographs on Flickr, where, after he had requested Facebook to delete and close his account in April 2018, the few online friends abroad who had kept in touch with him, could continue to view them.

Since moving to the West Highlands, Alexander had developed an interest in Scots Gaelic, which was only spoken now as a first language in some of the Western Isles, but was actively promoted

Chapter Forty-Three

across Scotland by the Scottish administration. He bought a primer in the language, and began paying attention to place names in Gaelic on road signs, and to the Gaelic written on notice boards. He strove to make sense of the structure of the Gaelic in light of the English translations which followed. In this way, for example, he realised early on that the name of the village where his mother's care home was located, Ballachulish, was an Anglicised contraction of the Gaelic *"Baile a' Chaolais,"* or "Village on the Narrows" (for Ballachulish was located at the very narrow mouth of Loch Leven).

In February 2018, as a birthday present from himself, Alexander threw away his cheap, poor CD recordings of Verdi's *La Traviata* and Puccini's *La Bohème* (which would always be the two operas he loved the most), replacing them with two excellent and expensive Decca recordings. Sometimes Alexander would play just the final scene from Act Four of *La Bohème*, and the pathos of the duet between Rodolfo and the dying Mimi, and Rodolfo's anguished cry, "Mimi! Mimi!" (when he realises Mimi has died), would so move Alexander that he would have to sniff, and wipe away tears from his eyes.

A production of *La Bohème* in 1974 had been the first live opera performance Alexander had ever attended. The Nico Malan Theatre in Cape Town was a splendid, dramatic venue, and Alexander was just nineteen years old. He bought a season ticket for the following year also, and by the end of the 1975 season he had heard most of the best loved grand operas performed live.

Shortly after his sixty-third birthday, Alexander undertook an exhaustive online search for his friend, Patrick, from so long ago in Cape Town. He remembered that Patrick had intended teaching when he left university, and so it was that he eventually found a reference to him as the headmaster of a private school in Cape Town. Alexander emailed the school's secretary, asking her to forward a message to Patrick, and she did so. Two days later, Alexander received a rather charming and very friendly email from the friend whom he had remembered faithfully for so many decades. The resumption, after more than four decades, of this friendship, even if only online, at first brought Alexander much joy.

Alexander and Patrick exchanged many emails over the next two or three years. But the closeness that had existed between the two as young men was no longer there, and over time, the gaps between their emails grew longer. This was a Patrick who had grown up and grown away, and Alexander knew that this was only natural, for his friend had a family of his own – children and grandchildren. One day, Alexander realised that he was free; the intense love for his friend that he had nurtured for decades had faded away, like the last faint wisps of smoke from a fire that had gone out.

With the coming of spring in April 2018, there came a general improvement in Alexander's health. He began to feel glad to be alive again. In late April he discovered a wonderful forest walk at Glen Righ, which he reached via a narrow, winding road off the A82 between the Corran Ferry and Onich, about twelve miles from Fort William. The trail led him through a forest of Scots pine and larch, the latter in bright green new leaf. The ground between the tall trees was densely covered in a lush, deep growth of verdant moss more luxurious than the most expensive deep pile carpeting. The well made trail climbed by degrees, the slope gradual and easy except towards the top, where it grew steeper for a while. But even here, the path was well constructed, and Alexander could tackle the gradient with the aid of his walking stick. As he walked, he came across not one other member of his own fallen species, and he heard no sound of Man's blighting presence. He heard bird song high in the tree canopy above him, and he made out the call of a very early cuckoo nearby. He could hear the wind soughing in the tree tops, and when he stopped to ease his breathing, he could feel the beating of his own heart.

Chapter Forty-Three

Rising from a deeply cut, narrow watercourse to the left of the trail, Alexander could hear the music of an aquatic symphony, whose profound echoing bass notes underscored a musical range of far higher octaves; a symphony performed by a mountain burn flowing urgently across the boulders and stones as it descended through the forest. Alexander's gradual ascent took him about one hour and twenty minutes to complete, and gained him sufficient elevation to reach an open, sun-lit tableland above the forest, where the dead brown bracken of the past winter had just begun to send up new green shoots, and heather and broom grew, the dense blossom of the broom a bright mustard yellow, and Alexander saw dozens of early peacock butterflies, brought to life by the sunshine, their bright colours like the dabs of a brush on a pointillist canvas. The warm sun on the dusty trail of broken schist and sandstone and gleaming white quartzite rock put Alexander in mind of countless hikes in the mountains around Cape Town when he was a young man, and his spirit felt glad. Beyond the open tableland, the trees continued again, dark forest seemingly reaching as far as the distant Nevis Range, with Ben Nevis just breaking the farthest horizon, pale and indistinct under its mantle of snow.

'I love this land,' Alexander thought.

Alexander sat for a while on a flat topped boulder in the sunshine, taking a drink of cool water from the water bottle he had in his satchel, and sipping at a bottle of his nutritional supplement to recharge his energy levels. As he made his way back down the hillside again, a robin hopped onto a branch only just above Alexander's sight line and regarded him from a cheery, curious, shining eye, as if to say "I see you!" Alexander felt as if, via these hours spent in the open air, a blessing had been vouchsafed him.

That spring of 2018, Alexander began work on a novel with a strong autobiographical element. Writing it quickly became an act of spiritual catharsis; a penitential exercise. He had completed the first draft by mid April 2019. The work stretched to more than four hundred pages. By early 2020 he had revised and edited this novel, which he then put to one side, as he began work on its prequel, another loosely autobiographical work, about a 1960s Cape Town childhood. This brought him a great deal more joy to write than his far longer earlier work had done. In August 2021, after more than a dozen fruitless approaches, he at last found an agent for this prequel, who managed to place it with a publishing house in London. Working with the publishers, Alexander commenced preparing it for a publication date of late January 2022.

Alexander intended that his far longer earlier novel (which followed on chronologically from where the story, set for the most part in 1960s Cape Town, left off) would be published towards the end of 2022.

'I have left no children to remember me,' he thought, 'but I shall leave these two novels to be remembered by.'

Alexander began going to church again in early April 2018. His outlook on life became more positive, but how he craved the sunshine; he could not get enough sun. The West Highlands were notoriously damp. But the first half of the summer of 2018 was glorious, with almost daily sunshine for ten weeks, from early May through to late July, and Alexander sat out in the garden every day with Molly until mid June, when the midges drove him indoors, and his face and the backs of his hands and forearms became tanned. But with the coming of August, the rains set in again, and thereafter they alternated only with sleet or snow until mid April in 2019.

'You don't come here for love of the weather,' an acquaintance at church joked. But of course Alexander, with his loathing for the breathless, sweaty, humid heat waves of a southern English summer, could be said to have done just that.

Chapter Forty-Four

Winter

Alexander had completed his final research commission in 2010. He had begun to lose interest in the work, and with no pressing need for extra income (for he lived very modestly, and he no longer travelled abroad), and with several thousand Pounds sitting in a savings account, he allowed this endeavour to wither. He deleted his LinkedIn account. However, within three months of moving to the West Highlands (encouraged by an old school friend with whom he was in communication, who had enjoyed some of the short essays he had once posted on Facebook), Alexander had set up an online blog page of his own. In it he posted essays of between seven hundred and two and a half thousand words, in which he expressed his views on Britain's social culture. He also wrote about economics, and political theory. He commented on current affairs around the world. He sometimes wrote poetry, or reminiscences, or short historical pieces. He explored spiritual and moral themes. He developed a growing hatred of high capitalism. In a series of articles for his blog, Alexander explored his ideas for replacing capitalism with some less rapacious, less environmentally damaging economic system. When the "Green new deal" of the

US Democrats began to gain traction and supporters around the world, Alexander seized eagerly upon its ideas. During the latter half of 2018 Alexander underwent an almost Damascene conversion. He had previously denied the part played by Man in the phenomenon of global warming; now he came to believe unreservedly in man-made global warming. From that time on he began to research and write increasingly frequently about global warming, and its impact on environmental and conservation issues.

Alexander's blog pieces became more polished: he spent much more time in researching them online (although in certain fields he referred to books in his own library of non-fiction). Alexander took to drawing up a list of online citations after each blog piece, referenced and numbered within the text. Alexander publicized his blog in the early days via mention in comments he posted in the Guardian's online readers' forum. The Guardian was a British national daily with a liberal-left editorial slant, whose online readership far exceeded in numbers its print readership.

The views Alexander expressed on Britain's social culture were often contentious and unfashionable. In a blog piece titled *"The Unhappy Homosexual,"* he wrote: *A great many homosexual men and women are not "Gay." Quite a few are in fact celibate, a state much recommended by Saint Paul, as a condition superior to that of marriage – which is reserved for those unable to control their (heterosexual) sexual urges: "It is better to marry than to burn." (1st Corinthians 7:9)*

Being "Gay" (as opposed to homosexual) is to embrace a sub-culture, a lifestyle choice, which – because the gay "scene" is the embodiment of a brittle, superficial, bitchy, fragile, promiscuous, lascivious and shallow culture – is rejected outright by many homosexual men and women.

By late 2018, so his blog statistics informed him, Alexander had perhaps three score fairly regular readers from around the world, including Russia, China, South Korea, Canada, the USA, Ireland, a number of European countries, and the United Kingdom itself, with less frequent visitors from South Africa, Saudi Arabia, Israel, Japan, India and Pakistan. Over time, a few readers began to post in the comments section below the individual articles. Some of these comments were highly critical; a very few were downright nasty; but the majority were honest and generally supportive responses to the articles.

Researching and writing articles for his blog brought Alexander much satisfaction. He was no longer physically fit enough to consider political and environmental activism in the field, but via his blog, he felt that he was doing all he could on behalf of a world which he hoped might one day be liberated from the socially and environmentally destructive embrace of high capitalism and the excesses of consumerism.

'I am surprised at how radical your writing is,' the minister of Saint Andrew's, the beautiful stone built Scottish Episcopal church near the Parade in Fort William, said to him one day, having read some of the entries in his blog.

'This is an age when a radical response to global issues is called for,' Alexander responded.

The autumn of 2018 was a season of great splendour, the hardwoods decked in chrome yellow, ochre, scarlet and gold, and the sun shone frequently, but Alexander felt acutely the melancholy of the drawing in of the days and the winding down of the cycle of life. Following another dreadful winter, during which Alexander sometimes saw no sunshine for more than three weeks at a time, he felt hugely grateful for the coming of spring in 2019. He had suffered frequent bouts of low spirits during the long dark wintertime. Lacking the spiritual renewal and rejuvenation he experienced when he attended Holy Communion (for Alexander had not been to church since Christmas, unable to overcome his abhorrence of the horrible, dark, cold winter mornings), and often sick and hurting, his view of God's works had become somewhat embittered; it sometimes appeared to him that suffering, pain and death were in fact the foundation stones of all Creation. With Donald Trump's demented Twitter Presidency much in the news, and the election of the anti-environmentalist and climate change denier, Jair Bolsonaro, as President of Brazil, Alexander's views of his own species became noticeably jaundiced. He recognised the dangers of succumbing to such a wholly negative outlook, and he sought to counter this near despairing view of the world, and of Man's part in it, through assiduous prayer. But the winter days were short, dark and wet, and the sturdy little stone house was often caught in the grip of shrieking gale force westerlies racing in from across the Atlantic and the Outer Isles, and Alexander found it a struggle to keep up his spirits.

As far as possible that winter, Alexander rarely left the house. However, as often as his health permitted him, he kept up his duty visits to his mother at Ballachulish, a journey of about forty minutes each way. Alexander's mother struggled to find and form her words, and this made conversing with her even more difficult. She had become in some respects a toddler again. Alexander would observe the struggle her nurses had with dosing her with medicines, for she would not swallow the tablets given her without resistance, and she would sometimes swear at the nurse. Olivia Maclean could no longer recall either the distant past (she was unable to access once cherished memories of her childhood in Kenya, and of her life in South Africa), nor the words that Alexander had spoken to her only a minute earlier. She lived an eternal and uncomprehending present tense. Yet she knew who Alexander was, despite his grey hair and moustache, and she would smile with pleasure when he visited, and (as she had only rarely done while her mind had still functioned) she would offer him the most affectionate embraces.

Sometimes one of the nurses would ask Alexander to obtain some item of clothing for his mother, and he would visit the only women's outfitters in Fort William, where the staff – mostly middle aged women – came to know him, and were helpful and kind to him.

Alexander found his mother's increasingly rapid mental deterioration heartbreaking. It cast a pall over his days. But he never showed her anything but patience and love: she too was part of the penance he must pay as recompense for his sins (as were his physical afflictions, and the physical pain he often experienced).

Alexander's work on his first novel during the course of that winter continued to serve him as a vehicle for catharsis. By means of it, he shed much of the legacy of hurt and shame which still afflicted him, and by late February of 2019, with the snowdrops appearing beneath the oak tree in his garden (although the tiny flowers were often covered by fresh snowfalls), Alexander's spirits were beginning to look up again, although he was obsessed by the dearth of sunshine. Almost always after a heavy snowfall, however, there would arrive a rare crisp, cold, clear, still day or two, and the sun, low above the hills, would shine bravely, the snow lying heavy on the ground, its surface alternating between blue shadows and dazzling sun-lit white, and the cloudless sky, shading through azure to an intense, deep blue directly overhead, was pristine and pure. Then Alexander would experience an intense joyfulness, along with a sense of deep gratitude, and he would know a rejuvenation of the love he felt for this wild region.

Two weeks into April (having completed the first draft of his novel), Alexander was able to sit out in the garden without having to wear a woolen beanie, a scarf, or a coat. Molly always joined him then. She was a companionable, affectionate cat, always happy in his company. Alexander resumed his church going that year in mid April, on Palm Sunday. During the past two years he had come to know a dozen members of the congregation of Saint Andrew's in Fort William, but he was closest to a couple in their early seventies, the MacKays (with whom, at sixty-four years old,

Alexander now felt as if he was a contemporary). Thomas MacKay was a church warden. The MacKays lived in a bungalow on Lundavra Road, the street climbing the hill above Fort William, from which the Old Military Road continued. Thomas was almost as tall and lean as Alexander, with a shock of thick white hair and dark bushy eyebrows. He and Mairi MacKay, who was short and plump, with grey hair cut rather short and features of exceptional sweetness, had called on Alexander two or three times during the long winter months. With the coming of spring the MacKays twice invited Alexander over for coffee during the late morning, and he was expected to stay for lunch, but because his diet was so restricted, he would accept only a bowl of soup and a bread roll. Alexander recognised these two Highlanders to be truly good and decent people. He felt privileged to call them friends.

Over tea, cakes and coffee in the church hall after Holy Communion on Easter Sunday (which fell on the 21st April that year), a woman – perhaps in her mid forties – approached Alexander, her white teeth flashing in a lovely smile. Alexander would not have forgotten her had he once seen her before. She stood out like a goldfinch amidst this gathering of somber Highland crows. She wore a very full black frock which reached well below her knees and was richly embroidered along the hem in heavy gold, green and scarlet thread in a stylized floral design. Above this she wore a tailored green jacket with a narrow waist, left unbuttoned, showing a butter yellow silk blouse beneath it. Across her bosom was a necklace of several strands of large amber beads. Her dark hair was bound in an iridescent green silk headscarf, and she wore calf length black leather boots. She had an olive complexion, with eyes of such a dark brown they appeared to be almost black. She was small and slightly built, and altogether very attractive indeed. Alexander thought there must surely be Mediterranean or Middle Eastern ancestry in her background.

Chapter Forty-Four

'I saw you standing by yourself,' she said. 'I'm Maryam.' Her English was accented but idiomatic.

'I'm Sandy Maclean,' Alexander responded. He put down his mug of coffee and shook her hand, which seemed tiny in his own hand.

'Are you visiting the district?' she asked him.

Alexander was smiling back at her. 'No, I live here,' he replied.

'Why have n't I seen you before?' Maryam asked.

'I don't come to church during the winter,' Alexander replied. 'How long have you been coming here?'

'I live in North Ballachulish. There's only one minister for half a dozen local parishes, including St. Bride's. So I've been visiting here quite often recently.'

Alexander felt an astonishingly powerful empathy with this woman. He was reminded of those occasions so common when he was a young man, but grown increasingly rare, when a meeting with a stranger had quickly developed into a close friendship. Alexander felt excitement and happy anticipation well up inside him. Maryam sat down alongside him, and talking to her, Alexander almost forgot that there were people nearby all around him.

'May I ask, where do you come from?' he enquired.

Again that wonderful smile. 'My family were Palestinian Christians. We belonged to the Orthodox faith. My husband and I left Israel in 2005. Prospects are not good for Palestinian Christians in Israel.'

'You speak such excellent English!'

'I studied English at secondary school, and at university.'

'And you are married, then?'

'I was. My husband has passed away.'

'I'm sorry,' he said. He was silent for a moment, then he continued, 'I know it's not the same, but I lost someone to illness whom I loved very much, in 2006.'

Maryam rested her hand on Alexander's for a moment. 'I have learned that one can survive heartache and loss. I think happiness can take us by surprise at any stage during our lives.'

Alexander wrote in his diary that evening, "I met a lovely woman, Maryam, a Palestinian Christian (!) at church today. I feel a strong empathetic connection with her. I hope and think we shall become friends."

The two met again the following Sunday, the 28th April, and after the communion service, with the sun shining, they went for a stroll together along the High Street. The street was busy with people, many of them the season's first visitors, come out to enjoy the sun. Halfway along the High Street was a café, the old Mac Gillivray's grocery, with a couple of tables and chairs on the pavement.

'Would you like a coffee, Maryam?' Alexander asked. 'Maybe something to eat also?'

'I would enjoy a coffee, thanks Sandy.'

'You take this table, and I'll get the coffees.'

As they drank their coffees, Alexander asked Maryam to tell him about Palestinian Christians.

'We are one of the world's oldest Christian communities. Our ancestors were Christians when Byzantium ruled the Holy Land. But there are comparatively few of us left now in Israel. Most of us have emigrated, seeking lands where we need not feel like an unwanted minority.'

Their coffees were mere cold dregs in the bottom of their cups before they finally left the table and walked slowly back towards Saint Andrew's, near which both of them had parked their cars. They had talked with extraordinary animation on a wide range of topics. It struck Alexander that Vicky was the last person he had spoken to with such a sense of intense personal engagement.

At Maryam's car, Alexander said, 'Perhaps we could have supper together soon at the Spice Tandoori restaurant. They're

Chapter Forty-Four

here in the High Street, and I was told that they do excellent vegetarian dishes.'

'Are you a vegetarian, Sandy?' Maryam asked.

'Yes, but not a vegan.'

'I admire you. Yes, let's do that soon. I'll give you my number.'

Maryam had confounded Alexander's preconceptions about women from a Middle Eastern culture. Unless she was a singularly unique representative of such a culture? He suspected that this was very likely the case.

Maryam tore a page from a small notebook she took from an embroidered handbag she was carrying. She produced a pen, and they exchanged telephone numbers. When Alexander drove back to the high glen and his peaceful home, he felt a wonderful lightness of heart.

Alexander went up to bed shortly after ten-thirty that night. Molly was already fast asleep; she was curled up in her snug little covered cat bed on a table near the radiator. Alexander said good night to her and stroked the top of her head, then he got into bed and leant back against the pillows. He heard the short, harsh screech of a barn owl; otherwise, the night was silent. He had a book with him. He had finally gotten round to reading Harper Lee's *To Kill a Mockingbird*. He was enjoying it tremendously. It was one of the few novels that his parents had bought in Kenya during the late fifties and early sixties that Alexander had not already read as a teenager. He wondered why he had spurned it, when he had read so much else during those years?

Alexander turned his bedside light off at half past eleven. His extraordinary lightness of heart persisted. He dreamed no troubling dreams that night.

Chapter Forty-Five

Loss and Renewal

Just before eight o' clock on the morning of Friday 3rd of May, 2019, Alexander was skimming the headlines in the online edition of the Guardian, when his mobile phone rang. The call was, he saw, from his mother's care home. Alexander knew that there was something wrong; the care home never telephoned him that early in the day. He answered the call.

'Sandy, its Megan, the night nurse.'

Alexander knew immediately, from the nurse's tone, that the news was bad. He thought perhaps his mother had had a bad fall.

'What is it, Megan? Is my mother OK?'

'You must brace yourself: it's the worst news, I'm afraid.'

'Oh no...'

'Yes, I'm afraid so. Your mother died in her sleep this morning.'

Alexander felt tears start to his eyes. But he felt no great shock or surprise.

'What happened? I mean, how did she die?'

'I checked on her at five-thirty, and she was sound asleep. I looked in on her again just after seven, and I knew straight away that she had passed away. I cannot tell you what the cause of death was. Once the doctor has been round we'll know more.'

'Was her death a peaceful one, do you think?'

'Yes, I think so. Her face was very peaceful; she was lying on her back, with her arms crossed on her chest; her eyes were closed.'

Alexander got to his knees after the call and said a prayer for his mother's soul. Then he telephoned his brother. He was surprised at how well Roy took the news. Perhaps there would be a reaction later. Thereafter he telephoned one of the two funeral directors in Fort William. The body would have to be collected after the doctor had issued a death certificate. In addition, he telephoned the Registrar of Births, Deaths and Marriages in Fort William; the funeral directors had told him that they would need documentation from the Registrar as soon as possible.

Alexander knew that his mother had wished to be cremated. Although Inverness Crematorium was nearest to Fort William, the route there and back was – as Alexander knew from experience, having had to follow it several times to keep hospital appointments in Inverness – a nightmare one, and instead, the funeral directors advised him to choose Cardross Crematorium, some miles this side of Glasgow. On the 15th May, Alexander and his brother (with Alexander driving, as he had a far better sense of direction than Roy), accompanied by Maryam in the back seat, followed the A82 south from Fort William. The scenery was splendid, the trees decked in bright new leaf. The sun was shining for much of the way, and even Rannoch Moor looked far less bleak than Alexander had ever seen it before. They hugged the western shore of Loch Lomond, that beautiful, island studded body of water more than twenty miles long, and some distance before they reached Glasgow, they left the A82 and made for Helensburgh. Cardross Crematorium lay in open countryside between Helensburgh and the village of Cardross, on the shores of the Clyde.

There were only five mourners at the funeral service, which was conducted by the minister of Saint Andrew's, the church Alexander attended. In the minds of both brothers was the thought, 'Is this all that Mum's life amounted to in the end? Just five people present at her funeral.'

Olivia Maclean had outlived both her brother and her sister, and she had spent her final years far from home, far from surviving friends, and Alexander was very grateful to the care home manager, and to the nurse who had been closest to his mother, who had made the long drive to be at his mother's funeral. He was also deeply touched that Maryam had asked to be there.

Alexander's eyes were dry throughout the service, until the second of the two hymns he had chosen was played on the sound system. Then his eyes were suddenly awash. The hymn he had chosen with which to close the service was, *The Day Thou Gavest, Lord, is Ended.* This hymn had been popular across the British Empire, and Olivia Maclean had been so very much a product of Empire. Alexander thought that if her spirit was observing the service, his mother would have approved his choice of closing hymn. During the long drive back, neither brother said very much. Each was dwelling on his own thoughts. Maryam had the delicacy not to chat from the back seat. But at a quarter to five, as Alexander was turning off the narrow road into his driveway, Roy said suddenly, 'Mum deserved better than that. She had known so many people in her lifetime, and had had so many friends, many of them since schooldays – and at the end there were just five people at her funeral.'

'I agree. That's just what I've been thinking,' Alexander responded. 'But it was a good service nonetheless. The minister had gone to some trouble to ask me about Mum's life, and to make sure that the people who were there knew how special she was.'

Inside the house, where Alexander had lighted the wood stove, for it was cold now, the three of them drank their coffees, Molly on

Alexander's lap. Alexander had put a plate of Scottish shortbread on the coffee table between them, which Roy was piling into as if he was starving. As indeed he probably was; they had had nothing to eat since breakfast, and unlike Alexander, Roy was not accustomed to extended fasting.

Alexander smiled at Maryam. 'It was so kind of you to come all that way. You never knew our mother, but you cared anyway. We're grateful to you, Maryam.'

'She was such a gifted person, Maryam,' Roy told her. 'And she was gentle and self sacrificing.'

'Your mother does sound a really special person, from what the minister told us at the service. You and Sandy were fortunate to have had a mother like her,' Maryam responded.

'I am grateful our Mum died in her sleep,' Alexander commented, 'and that she was spared the horrors of hospitalization. So many oldies die miserably in hospital. Mum was very old; she was not herself anymore; perhaps it was time she was called to God.'

Maryam, who was sitting alongside Alexander on the sofa, took his hand for a moment. Alexander turned his head and smiled at her. 'On occasions like this we should be drinking sherries with our shortbread,' he remarked. 'But neither you nor I drink, and Roy drinks only rarely. I do have a bottle of wine in the kitchen. Would you like some, Roy?'

'No thanks. The coffee hit the spot.'

In early spring of 2020, Alexander completed editing and revising his semi-autobiographical novel, and putting it to one side, he began writing its prequel, which he planned to have published first. This story – again, very loosely autobiographical – chronicled the 1960s and 1970s Cape Town and Johannesburg childhood of the hero of his first novel.

Confirmation, as it was termed in Scotland, of Olivia Maclean's will was not granted by the Inverness Sheriff Clerk's

Office until mid March 2020 (shortly before the commencement of the first Covid 19 lockdown in the United Kingdom). The process took so long because the brothers' mother had possessed assets in South Africa as well as in the United Kingdom. (There had been a monthly private pension that had continued to be paid into a South African bank account after their mother had left South Africa, and Olivia Maclean had still owned the three plots of land on the old farm near Fish Hoek; Roy had arranged the sale of her home in Hilton shortly before they had quit South Africa). In Britain there was of course the bungalow in Chinnor, in which Roy was living, and a large capital sum in their mother's bank account. There were only two beneficiaries; the two brothers themselves. Alexander and Roy were also the executors of their mother's estate. They agreed to sell the vacant plots on the old farm, and they asked their cousin, James, who was based in Cape Town, to handle the sale for them (and to take a commission for his trouble). It was November of 2020 before the plots of land were sold, and the money transferred to Britain.

In February 2021 Alexander used his inheritance to buy the stone house which he had been renting. His landlords were happy to sell. He was almost sixty-six years old, and this was the first house he had ever owned.

Roy used part of his inheritance to buy his brother's half share in the bungalow in Chinnor. Both brothers at last owned their own homes in Britain.

Throughout this period, Alexander and Maryam had continued to spend time together. During lockdown they had formed what the Scottish government called a Covid support bubble, for both lived alone, and neither had formed a support bubble with anyone else. Essentially, a Covid support bubble allowed members of two households to meet and mix socially, and to overnight in each other's homes, disregarding the obligations of social distancing. Even so, Alexander did not visit Maryam, for he felt that her

There was by now a depth to Alexander's relationship with Maryam which was, in some respects, almost the equal of that that had existed between Alexander and Victoria. However, their friendship, although very close, remained a platonic one. Maryam seemed to want nothing more from him. How long such a relationship could last, remained to be seen. There was already a model in Alexander's life for a long standing platonic friendship with a woman: this was his friendship with Sarah, which was now nineteen years old. For now, Alexander felt that he was being given a second chance at love and companionship; an opportunity he had thought would never again come his way following Victoria's death. When he was with Maryam, Alexander felt completely free of the burden of guilt and remorse for his past that even now, after so many years, had continued at times to weigh on him heavily. The knowledge that someone found him loveable convinced him, as nothing else could, that his past had been forgiven him.

Chapter Forty-Five

home in North Ballachulish was too much in the pu[blic eye?] and he did not wish to give rise to possible scandal on [the part?] of neighbours who themselves were observing the full r[igour of?] lockdown, but she visited him quite often, for there wa[s no one?] near Alexander's home to see her come and go. Each tr[usted the?] other to behave sensibly in the world outside, a world w[hich was?] now much restricted.

According to the letter of the law, Roy should have bee[n unable?] to visit his brother during periods of lockdown, for the [two of?] them could not now form a support bubble of their own. [Roy?] raged against the restrictions imposed by the English and [Scottish?] governments, and he seemed to believe that they were a[imed at?] him personally. Despite the Covid restrictions in force, Al[exander?] could not prevent Roy from visiting in September 202[0 and?] once again in May 2021. Alexander, with his history of chi[ldhood?] asthma, was especially at risk of Covid 19, but Providence [smiled?] upon him and Roy did not bring sickness from the crowded [south?] into his home. By May 2021, Alexander was no longer as w[orried?] for his safety, for he had received his first Covid vaccination [in?] February that year, and his second in early April. In Nov[ember?] he was given his third, or "booster" vaccination. He was n[ow as?] safe as it was possible to be. So when Roy paid him a visi[t at?] Christmas that year, Alexander did not fret for his health.

Then, in early 2022, Roy adopted a cat of his own, fro[m a?] cat sanctuary in Beaconsfield, and he was content at last to re[turn?] home. Alexander was delighted for him. In some measure, he [also?] felt an easing of his own troubled conscience for Roy.

By high summer of 2021, Alexander had at last found a lit[erary?] agent, who managed to place his story of a sixties and seve[nties?] South African childhood with a publishing house in London [He?] spent much time during the remainder of that year working [with?] the publishers, readying the novel for its scheduled publicatio[n in?] January 2022.

A Note to the Reader

Hemispheres is not an autobiography, although some of the events in the story parallel broadly similar events in my own life. When I write a work of fiction, I am not writing in a vacuum. I necessarily draw on experiences from my own life, and I gain inspiration from places and people I have known. However, none of the characters in this story are exact renditions of, or even necessarily the same gender as, any real characters, living or dead, and where I write of real locations, you would seek there in vain for any recollection of the events I describe ever having taken place.

Robert Dewar, Lochaber, May 2022.

This book is printed on paper from sustainable sources managed under the Forest Stewardship Council (FSC) scheme.

It has been printed in the UK to reduce transportation miles and their impact upon the environment.

For every new title that Matador publishes, we plant a tree to offset CO_2, partnering with the More Trees scheme.

For more about how Matador offsets its environmental impact, see www.troubador.co.uk/about/